# Other Books By Luke Smitherd:

## **<u>Full-Length Novels:</u>**

*The Physics Of The Dead*

*The Stone Man*

*A Head Full Of Knives*

*Weird. Dark.*

*How To Be A Vigilante: A Diary*

*Kill Someone*

*The Empty Men: The Stone Man, Book Two*

*Coming Soon: You See The Monster*

## **<u>Novellas</u>**

*The Man On Table Ten*

*Hold On Until Your Fingers Break*

*My Name Is Mister Grief*

*He Waits*

*Do Anything*

*The Man with All the Answers*

For an up-to-date list of Luke Smitherd's other books, YouTube clips, his podcast, and to sign up for the Spam-Free Book Release Mailing List, visit www.lukesmitherd.com

# For Everyone Who Took a Chance on THE STONE MAN

Reviewer Acknowledgements:

At the time of writing, the following people wrote a nice Amazon or Audible) review of *THE MAN WITH ALL THE ANSWERS.* Thank you so, so much. I'm a little bit higher up the novelist totem pole these days, but those reviews still mean *everything.* I'm only using the names you put on your reviews, as these will be ones you're happy to have associated with my work (I hope). In alphabetical order they are:

Simon211175, Kelly G, Suzzane S, Jason Goldsmid, Mike, Elliot Brown, NelMel, Ged Byrne, Hatty B-R, Eluned, Cat Payton, Adrian Trickett, Janice Clark, R. Mark Say, LouiseTheFox, Mr. Christopher A. Wells, Rachel Jane, Amazon Customer, Jinny, David Plank, James Farler, Happy Shopper, Neil, Gilaine, Tino1440, Kerry Heron, The Fro, Mrs Kindle, Crows, Steve Blencowe, Shadowfire5371, C. Murphy, Hillary, L. J, Angie Hackett (Stormageddon), MrCymru, JMM52, Martin Hansen-lennox, Danielle Gregg, Jonny Barr, Carly May, Rebekah Jones, Lauren McCartney, Karenr, Doug Ridley, Caroline W, Pandachris, Consumer, Rickard, Sharon McLachlan, Melanie, BoneyD, J. D. Cobbett, Juliem, AJ777, Abigail, Richard C, Jamie Greenwood, Close, Oneofmany, Dave T, Book Thief, Scrooby1, Dale, Andrew, Jools, M. G. Gilbert, Hendo, 3minutemaths, Bradley, Esme Kennedy, Sarah H, Philip M A, Nathan, Paul B, Mossycloud, Victoria, Barbara Irwin, Derek Cooper, Jason, P W R Wilcox, Simon, Damo, Steven Stewart, Geary, Hopkinson, Fox, Zidanny, Niki, Becky, K Adams, R, Ian Rendall, Linbot, Cherrie Tom S. MacMaster, TerryF, Lee Swain, Catherine, Robert Wyburn Anderson, Kathryn Booker, Durnio, Danny, Grangier, Annie Mains, Wesser, Rob Pomroy, Andy Holden, Jon Perry, Wendy Crisp, AK 1111, Silversmith, Amabel Thornton, Mutter, Matthew Tee, Worm, Marilyn Stanbrook, Megan Davies, DMH, Tina, Osseous, Simone, Froggy, Adrian, Kamran, LindaK, Kindle Sally Crisford, Abigaildemunnik, Debra Piller, Lesleyr, Vacman, Bimmy, Dom JacobDeZoet, Fogharty, Bsm, Julie Blaskie, Henry, Drac1968, JoanneG, Bnbboy, Ladybug567Green, In Honor Of Books, Don, MetalHead, Michelle Jo Cranford, Fancyflyer, Jobes, Blanchepadgett, Tracey, Daniel Smith, Jayg324, Bailey Humphries, Gaylor, Katrina, Hebol, KC, Bluemoon1972, Jamaeson Skaife, Caregiver, Colorado Smithereen, McConnell, Stephanie Simmons, RobW, Tirza de Forest Zwaanswijk, Chris Eire, Gray, Lockie, Walker, John Buckingham, Sailorgirl, Avon P, Carnes, Wwriter87, Joan Burke, Once Burned, Tejadab, Melissa Quimby, JC, Sushi, Suzanne Bigwood, WR Anne J.C.Fairbrother, Dowell, KeldallRN, Barbra, Gabby, Cooke, Joni, Mr Ken Anonymous User, Kyle Vilic, MBNA, Samuel, Bernie Kelly, TD, Ledsom, Fowler, Anthony, UnionJack, Bad Monkey, Maveric78, Mick, Lmiller, Paul, Hazel, Peart, Felix Reviews, Marc, MR, Susana Silvestre, Craig, Julja, Armitage, Elentari This Mum Works, ScottP, Stephen, Laura, and TerryF. Thanks a million, all of you.

If you asked for a Smithereen title, check out the list after the afterword to see yours!

# THE EMPTY MEN

By Luke Smitherd

# Prologue

The difference was only around half an hour. Yet the children were still aware that this was an earlier pickup time than normal.

"Coat, Simon. *Yes,* I'll deal with that in a minute, but I need everyone to get their coats on and sit on the red rug. Okay? *Coats.*"

Tiny bodies topped with wide-eyed faces—some excited, some scared, most a mixture of the two—headed to the waist-height coat hooks by the classroom door, buzzing at an unusually low volume that perfectly summed up the quiet chaos of the moment. Maria was doing her best to keep the tension out of her voice, but she was failing.

Something very, very bad had happened.

Even before the phone call, even before the news alert on her phone, hell, even before the *day had started*, hadn't something just felt... *off*? For the last few days, in fact? Her husband Marcus hadn't helped; he'd kept subtly-yet-not-that-subtly asking if she was on her period. Whenever she'd snapped that she *wasn't,* his *whatever-you-say-but-you-just-proved-me-right* nod of the head had only made her feel more on edge.

And *then* today. The phone call. To the classroom landline of course, because suddenly her phone didn't seem to have any signal, and even when it did, she wasn't able to dial out. Even the landline was extremely scratchy; something was really screwing with all of the networks, it seemed.

The police were on the phone.

When she'd agreed to sub Kerry's school-holiday kids' club—teaching yoga only paid so much, and she and Marcus still had credit card debt from their honeymoon—she hadn't expected to hear from the boys in blue. What they'd said was terrifying because of what they'd left out.

A bus was coming to collect the kids. Not their parents, but a *bus.* They were being taken to a 'holding centre'. *What's happened?* she'd managed to ask. *We don't know yet,* they'd said, *and we're not at liberty to discuss it. Please have the children ready, and an officer will attend. We are informing the parents.* Shocked and scared, the question—the selfish one that stung the second it left her lips—had come straight out.

*But what do I do?*

*We advise taking that bus to the holding centre too or making your own way there as quickly as possible. Here's the address; do you have a pen?*

She did, of course—she was in a classroom after all—and she'd written it down, simultaneously realizing that the holding centre was outside of the city and marvelling at her own emotional detachment from the situation. She'd tried to call Kerry, but her number was going straight to voicemail, exactly the way Kerry had promised it wouldn't.

*It's a terrorist attack,* she thought. *There's been a terrorist attack. It's close enough that they're trying to get everyone to safety, to get the children out of the city.*

Then...

*Wait. There's been a terrorist attack in* Coventry? *Why the hell are they attacking* Cov?

Chloe, the other childminder, looked as scared as the kids as she repeatedly tried to dial her boyfriend—she was almost a child herself at only twenty-one—and while Maria liked Chloe, she began to worry that the painfully hip-looking youngster might need looking after too. Maria was getting a headache. That in itself was strange. She rarely got them.

"Chloe," Maria said kindly, "I've got this here. Why don't you go outside? The signal might be better." She knew it wasn't true. She'd tried earlier herself.

"Yeah. Yeah, okay." Chloe left. That was better.

Eleven children were now seated on the red rug, chattering away to themselves, while Maria paced anxiously. The twelfth child was standing by the coat rack, one arm inside a coat sleeve and the other holding her phone, worry etched all over her face. It was Cecily, she of the huge eyes and beautiful dark curly hair.

"Cecily," said Maria, softly. "Get your coat on and sit on the red rug, please."

"My phone," said Cecily, in a trembling voice that broke Maria's heart. "It's not working at all. Something's wrong."

Maria didn't know how to respond. The kid was absolutely right, after all. "It just means that something's wrong with the signal," she said, trying to sound convincing. "They're going to fix it soon. I promise."

"Can you try? Can you call my parents?"

"If you come and sit on the rug, yes. I'll try on the landline phone. Okay? Give me the number."

Cecily glumly obeyed—finding *Mummy* in her phone's contact list and handing it to Maria—and tromped over to join her peers as if her shoes were made of lead. Keeping a watchful eye on the cluster of small people in front of her, Maria dialled out on the landline. It went to voicemail. *Daddy* too. She handed Cecily her phone back. The worried look in the girl's eyes deepened and made something inside Maria ache.

"I got their voicemail too," Maria said gently, "but I think the network is just having problems. It's okay, there's nothing to worry about."

*Story,* Maria thought. *Tell them a story until the police arrive. It'll take all of our minds off it.*

That was only half right. *Her* mind would not be taken off it, going absolutely haywire as it was. It didn't even make sense to be this unsettled. Terrorist attacks were of course worrying, but this felt like something... *personal.* The thought was stupid, but it was the best way to put it. She forced a smile and was warmed slightly as it was returned by the twelve seated, staring and expectant pairs of eyes in front of her. If those guys were handling their nerves, she could damn well do the same.

"Ready?"

She began.

Soon after she did, Chloe came back in to say that the bus was there. It had arrived so quickly that some of the kids even complained that they didn't hear the end of the chapter. To her surprise, a police car was accompanying the bus. The children's mood perked up at the sight—this was more exciting than just a *bus!*—but Maria's nerves hit a new level, her headache worsening with it.

*Something's wrong,* she thought. *I can feel it.*

She stiffened, breathing in sharply as she reminded herself to focus on doing her job. She led the kids outside.

"Okay, everybody, nice and slow," she said, herself and Chloe leading the children across the car park. The bus door hissed as it opened. "No pushing. No running either, Stephanie. I'm watching you," she said, pulling a joke scowl-face that made Stephanie smile slightly; it was replaced almost immediately by a look of intense worry.

Normally, she'd have spoken to the police first to find out what was happening. She would waste *no* time today. She had to get the kids on the bus and out of there and ask questions later. She instinctively knew this with every fibre of her being. *How* she knew this could be figured out later.

*Something terrible is happening,* she thought. *Something terrible is coming this way.*

That was her chimp-brain whispering, panicking as usual, and familiar like an old boyfriend, the kind that shows up when you're vulnerable and lonely and just wants to *talk*. Marcus had helped stop her panic attacks a long time ago. Even so, the voice in her head kept whispering. *You have to get the kids away. You have to be away. You have to be hidden in a hole somewhere—*

*What is this feeling?*

*Tension.*

*Where in my body is it manifesting?*

*Same as always. Chest. Stomach. Neck.*

*Okay. The thought I am having is* tension.

The police officer, a youngish white guy not much older than Maria, had stepped out of his car and was standing by the bus entrance, trying to smile warmly at the kids as they got on board. The bus was empty; Maria had wondered if there would be people already on it.

*I accept that I am feeling tension. I am not the thought. It is simply currently here.*

That was all it usually took. With practice it had become enough to give her screaming chimp-brain a banana and send it to sleep.

"Is that everybody, miss?" the smiling police officer asked Maria after the last kid was on the bus. She noticed the tension in his eyes, the pallor of his skin; he was forcing the calm expression. He was terrified.

"Head count of twelve says yes," Maria replied, and then paused on the steps. "Listen," she whispered, "what's *happening,* man?" She didn't expect an answer but hoped using the word *man* would trigger an I'm-an-Average-Joanne, you're-an-Average-Joe interaction, despite her usual discomfort around uniformed or official people.

It didn't work.

"I don't know, miss." The smile vanished. "I wish I did. I've been instructed to only tell you that we're going to a holding centre in Bell Green, but what I *have* been told doesn't make any sense either way. You don't have to stay there but the kids do so they can meet their parents later. We can't reach them all, and the roads in the town centre are locking up. You don't *have* to come, but we'd really like to have you on the bus so the kids feel safe. You'll be safer there too; they have a doctor—"

"But why can't you tell me what you've—"

"Miss, I'm genuinely sorry. I mean, I *really* am, and I can't imagine how frustrating all this is, but I've literally told you everything I can. I just want to get this done so I can try to get home to my wife, so could you..." His jaw clenched and Maria could see the frustration he was holding back. The man was having a rough day. "Please?" he finished, his eyes closing.

"Uh... yes. Yes, sorry," Maria said, her headache now pounding in her brain with a dull, heavy throb.

"No, it's... don't worry," the police officer soothed, composing himself and stepping back as Maria climbed up onto the bus. She turned in the doorway to face Chloe. "Chloe," she said, to the now deathly pale young woman. "You don't have to come. I know it's against the rules, but I think... well, it's an emergency so..."

"You're sure? I can—"

"It's okay."

Chloe shuffled awkwardly on the spot for a moment and then darted in to hug Maria.

"Thank you."

She ran—actually *ran*—over to her beat-up old Micra, waving at the kids on the bus as she went. They waved back, albeit unenthusiastically. Maria watched her enviously. *She* wanted to get home to her partner, Marcus, too—*needed* it... but she wouldn't leave the kids. She got on the bus and the police officer gave the driver the thumbs up before getting into his car to escort them.

Maria looked down the aisle; the kids' heads didn't reach past halfway up the back of the threadbare seats. While it was an old piece of crap, it was still a full-sized bus... surely, they must be picking up more people?

"Can you turn on the local radio?" she asked the driver. There would be news.

"I've been told not to, miss," the elderly driver replied, a man who looked like he was born decades before even the ancient bus was built. "It don't really work well anyway."

The doors closed and the bus pulled away.

The kids were more excited than scared now, and the chatter became a loud buzz as the bus got onto the main road and the children began to shout and laugh with each other. The headache was now worse than any she'd ever had in her life—she attributed her growing dizziness to it—but she wouldn't ask the children to be quiet. If they were laughing, they weren't scared. Maria closed her eyes and breathed slowly as she scanned the streets through the window, looking for information. A helicopter passed overhead, flying low.

*I accept that I am feeling tension,* Maria told herself. *I feel it in my head. It really fucking hurts though.*

Five minutes later, they hit two-way traffic and stopped moving.

Five minutes after *that*, their escorting police car's lights and siren exploded into life, and Maria thought that it would be clearing a path for them. It abandoned them instead, executing a three-point turn as the cars around it awkwardly made room. What the hell did that mean? The police car oozed its way away down a line of traffic that reluctantly rippled apart and snapped aggressively back into place the second the cops passed.

She checked her phone. Still no signal. The traffic jam was in a residential area Maria didn't recognize. Terraced houses flanked the main road. A corner shop. A few people stood outside their houses, talking with their arms pulled tight around their chests. Maria looked through the front windscreen; the cars were completely stationary. Minutes passed. They didn't move.

Maria noticed her nose was bleeding and fumbled with her purse for a tissue. Her hands were shaking. She watched the people in the street talking and *by God she wanted answers.*

"I'm getting off for a second," Maria said to the driver. Before he could respond she stood up and turned to the kids. "Okay, quiet for a second, *quiet for a second, please.* It looks like we're going to be sitting here for a little while, so I'm going to go and see if there's any food or drink in that shop there. Maybe get you all something to drink and some crisps as a treat for behaving." The triumphant group-hiss of *yesssss* passed among the kids. Normally, she would never give them any unapproved snacks. "However! Listen… *listen.* Thank you. The driver's going to tell me if anybody misbehaves, and anyone who does *won't get any crisps.* Okay?" Vigorous nods all round. "Okay. Back in a second." She turned and looked at the driver expectantly. The driver glared at her with an expression that said, *Lady, I'm just trying to do my job,* but then he sighed and hit the button to open the door.

Maria walked briskly from the bus and across the street, but immediately, she could smell it: smoke. She looked above the line of houses and saw it. Yes, it *was* smoke, and several more lines of it further beyond, trailing into the sky in the near distance. This was big. This was *bad.* Several drivers had now stepped out of their cars and were looking at the smoke too. Maria forced herself to ignore the sights and smells and headed straight for her target: a young-ish couple standing outside their house, talking to their elderly female neighbour. She couldn't help but notice the Porsche parked in their driveway, a flashy motor incongruous with the wealth level of the area.

"Excuse me," she said, hearing the shake in her voice. The trio turned politely to her. They didn't seem worried, to Maria's surprise, more excited than anything. "Do you know what's going on? I have a bus full of kids, they're taking us to a holding centre."

"*Nobody knows,*" the young blonde said eagerly, seeming to relish the mystery. Her boyfriend and the old woman nodded their eager confirmation of this. "There's pictures online and some people are saying it's all CGI, but I reckon—"

There was a sudden *BANG* from some distance away... but not *that* far away. Everybody flinched, and the old woman put her hand to her chest. Maria and the other two reached out a hand but the old woman shooed them away.

"I'm fine, I'm *fine,*" the old woman said, and then there was another *BANG*, louder, closer. The old woman gasped. "Oh... that was close," she said. "That was really close. What do you think we...?"

The young man shrugged and turned lazily to the line of cars in the street. Maria realized that he was drunk.

"Where we gonna *go?*" he asked rhetorically, shrugging.

"But what did the news *say?*" Maria snapped, trying to hide the frustration in her voice. "CGI you said, what did—"

Sirens filled the air. A police motorbike pulled up, and the rider started shouting at the people in the street, so wound up that he didn't even think to use the bike's speakers.

"You need to *move!* You need to move *out of here*, all of you, you need to—" He remembered the bike's built-in megaphone after all and snatched up the mouthpiece. "ALL OF YOU NEED TO LEAVE THIS AREA IMMEDIATELY. YOU ARE IN DANGER. LEAVE YOUR CARS AND YOUR HOMES. YOU HAVE TO MOVE *NOW*. MAKE YOUR WAY ON FOOT TO THE END OF THE STREET AND HEAD WEST *NOW*, ALL OF YOU—" He suddenly rode his bike a hundred feet further down the road, making the same announcement as he went, and the drivers standing in the street surged forwards to ask questions. "NO QUESTIONS, PLEASE DISPERSE IMMEDIATELY. IF YOU ARE IN A VEHICLE YOU NEED TO ABANDON IT NOW AND RETURN ONCE THE AREA IS SAFE. YOU NEED TO EVACUATE THE AREA *IMMEDIATELY*—" The motorbike moved further down the line as Maria's limbs felt light and hollow. Some of the neighbours in the street got the message and began to walk quickly down the road. Others followed a little more uncertainly, not wanting to leave.

"Should... should we go?" the blonde asked her boyfriend, and then another *BANG* filled the air, followed by the clear sound of many falling bricks. Was the ground shaking a little?

"Oh my God," the old woman said, and without another word, turned and walked as briskly as she could down the road. Other people started running. Maria spun back to face the bus, saw that the driver had left his seat and was standing outside the vehicle. He was staring at the motorbike as it continued down the line. Maria looked up to see the twelve tiny pairs of eyes staring at something above the houses behind her. She followed their gaze. The sky was now turning grey from all the spreading dust and smoke pluming into it, and fresh trails of smoke were rising from much closer by. Was that from the next street over?

*The food, the shop,* she managed to think. *I said I'd get them snacks.*

Dazed, Maria actually took ten steps towards the shop, before the spell was broken by the sight of the shopkeeper running out of the building.

*Screw the snacks,* her chimp-brain screeched, the strongest part, elbowing its way to the front. It knew all about survival. *Get the kids off that bus! NOW!*

Maria ran back to the bus as another *BANG* sounded behind her, her hands flying to her ears this time. That one was deafening; something was coming this way and it was almost here.

*You knew it!* the Chimp screeched. *You felt it for days! How did you know that?*

She pushed past the gaping, useless driver and ran up the steps. The shaking, that constant, terrible, *slow* pounding, could now be felt even through the floor of the bus. The chatter and noise she'd left behind had vanished. The kids were terrified. They looked to her for answers.

"We're getting off now," she said, trying to sound calm but failing, "so everybody stand up—"

*BANG.* She had time to see a fresh burst of dust billow into the sky from behind the Porsche-house. The young couple out in front jumped and began to step back. Had the house shaken just then? It looked like it did, but then it couldn't have as it was still standing and—

*BANG.*

The roof toppled *inwards* as the front of the house exploded *outwards*, an eruption of brick and plaster. The building disappeared into a ball of dust and rubble with a deafening roar; a torrent of clattering concrete blocks and wood fell to earth as broken electrical connections popped and arced in the midst of the tumbling wreckage. The young couple yelled in fright and then ran away down the street, out of Maria's sight, not even hesitating. The kids screamed and clutched at each other, and then their cries heightened as they could now see that *something was coming towards them,* something walking straight through the falling building without missing a step.

Something big. Something relentless.

"*Okay, we've got to go,*" Maria yelled. "*We've got to go. Come on come on come on!*"

As the kids surged forwards, the shape of the oncoming *thing* became clearer; was it a gorilla? A gorilla wouldn't be big enough, but it walked like a man and a man couldn't be—

A Range Rover tried to pull around the bus from behind it, startled by the collapse of the house and mounting the kerb on the bus' left flank.

It was a pointless attempt to make an escape in a both-ways-dead line of traffic, a blind-panic move when confronted with an impossible terror. Perhaps the driver thought, in his shock and fear, that he could avoid the packed road and slip along the pavement, making an escape that way. The timing was lousy; a terrified and middle-aged couple had fled their car and were sprinting around the bus' front, racing to use the more open pavement rather than winding along the line of cars.

"No!" Maria cried, seeing it happen in slow motion: the couple passing across the front of the bus from right to left, the Range Rover unknowingly lurching towards them along the bus' left-hand side. The pair emerged into the Range Rover's path, saw it, froze; Maria's fists came up to her face, willing the impact away and helpless to do anything to stop it. The panicked Range Rover driver saw the couple's terrified faces before him and, in a second blind-panic move, yanked the steering wheel sideways to avoid them.

The Range Rover slammed into the side of the bus, which rocked sharply as the car ground along the side of the larger vehicle with an ear-splitting screech of metal. The force of the impact knocked Maria into the driver's seat and the kids fell to the floor, yelling as they went, and the Range Rover stopped moving as it became half-wedged in the front end of the bus.

"Hold on! Hold on!" Maria yelled pointlessly, pulling herself by the bus' steering wheel, the world turning grey before her eyes. The noise of it all, the falling house, the Range Rover, the crash, the screams of the kids, and the *pounding,* was simply mind-bending.

*Those are footsteps,* she thought wildly. *It's coming.*

"*Everybody off the bus!*" she screamed, and started pulling kids to their feet, yanking them towards the front. "*Everybody up, come on, up!*" She looked desperately out of the windows as she moved along the bus, hands flying as she pulled the children up from the rubber floor, the kids who were already on their feet sprinting past her. Her breath caught as she saw what had smashed through the house.

It was an eight-feet-tall man made of stone, its body out of proportion and featureless, and it was walking.

It trailed the dust of the building behind it, unmarked and undamaged by its passage through an entire house. It was walking straight over the Porsche in its path, not rising up and over it like a hill, but like a human stepping on a cardboard box. The Porsche crumpled flat beneath each step as if the car were hollow and made of foil. It wasn't *possible...*

"*Maria! Maria!*" That was Cecily. "*We can't get off the bus!*"

Maria turned, even as the Chimp screamed, *What the fuck is that thing?* and tried to stop her looking away. Dazed and horrified, she looked down the bus. The exit was completely blocked by the Range Rover, wedged in so tightly on the left against the bus door that the frame had buckled. The car's driver was slumped over his own steering wheel, motionless, the airbag deployed. Maria immediately knew that she might be able to squeeze maybe two kids at the most out of the small driver's window on the right-hand side of the bus, but that would be it; there was no *time.* The air outside was full of smoke and screams and running people and—

*BOOM. BOOM. BOOM.* It was stepping over a now-vacated car in the opposite line of traffic—flattening the vehicle just as it had the Porsche—and was crossing the road directly towards them from the right, just *a few steps away.*

It was going to hit the bus.

The footsteps were drums, a death march. Twelve pairs of eyes, wide and filled with tears, looked at her for an answer. There were about four seconds before impact.

At the back! The emergency exit! How had she forgotten it? Would it even work, the bus was so *old—*

"*Everybody back down the bus! Everybody to the back seats! Now! Now now now!*"

Maria leaped out of the driver's seat and hustled the kids forwards like a miniature tide. Outside, the monstrosity drew closer and larger and filled the glass, separated from them by a moment and the thinnest of barriers. She knew that it was too late; that there would not be time to even *open* the emergency exit before it hit them.

*It's like a man,* Maria thought, her mind an electrified shriek, *a man that became a monster. It's not possible—*

"Get down!" she yelled. *"Get down! Cover your eyes, cover your eyes—"*

The last head darted past her hips and Maria jumped forwards as the monster collided with the side of the bus with a sound like a bomb going off. The windows exploded inwards as the entire side of the bus screeched and buckled and *gave way* as the thing just kept coming. Several kids rolled on the floor, knocked completely off their feet, and Maria could hear tiny limbs and heads bumping off unforgiving surfaces as the end of the bus swung to the right; the vehicle was bending in the middle like a glowstick being snapped into life. Still it came. Maria screamed now, clasping her hands to her ears as the roar of bending and rending metal became painful. Empty seats were swept aside as the thing walked through the bus, its legs striding through the solid floor of the vehicle like a man wading through the shallows at low tide.

For a few deafening seconds, she watched it pass as if she were in deep water and a blue whale had suddenly passed close by, the sheer magnitude of it mingling terror and awe and—incredibly—making her feel alive. To see it walk was to change everything you knew about the inherent properties and logistics of the world; you didn't need to know the laws of motion to know that an apple weighed a certain amount, or that a stick will likely travel a certain distance in a certain way if you threw it as hard as you could. You knew all these things as soon as you were old enough to experience physically moving objects around. *This* thing could not be. Yet it was.

Thoughts ricocheted behind her wide and unbelieving eyes.

*Nothing will ever be the same after this, whatever it is.*

*It's going to walk straight through and carry on. It's not here for us. The kids are hurt but I think they're okay.*

*We're going to live.*

And then, admitted against her will, *It is magnificent.*

Then the Stone Man turned its head and looked at her.

Not in her *direction*, not at the kids, but at *her*. She knew it the way she knew her stomach was cramping painfully as the thing's expressionless face gazed into hers. It had felt her. Marked her?

"*Not me...*" Maria whispered, desperately and unconsciously, unaware she'd even spoken, but then the moment was passing as its head turned forwards again, and now its legs had reached the opposite row of seats as sparks continued to fizz up from the floor. For a moment, the world went mad as the entire bus snagged on the creature somehow and began to drag sideways with its forwards motion. It only lasted a second as the metal gave up the battle and submitted to the superior, irresistible force. Distracted by the noise and magical carnage going on right in front of her, Maria realized too late that the opposite glass was about to blow outwards. She opened her mouth to warn the kids, but her words were drowned out by the crashing noise; the force of the impact was so strong that every window on that side exploded. With a final wrench of metal, the monster's legs and torso punched their way out of the other side of the bus. The world became quieter for a few seconds, a sudden and eerie end to the cacophony of shouting metal and fizzing wiring, broken only by the rhythm of the thing's pounding feet.

Maria parted her hands and blinked as the children, emerging from their own shocked silence, began to cry; there was another *BANG* as the Stone Man presumably began its path through the next row of terraced houses, the echoes of collapsing rubble of little interest when compared to Maria's realisation that they were alive. She looked at the twisted gap where the thing had entered the bus, a window into the impossible. She saw the flattened cars, the people starting to mill nearby.

She smelled petrol.

She looked at the sparks.

"Everybody up! Right now, everybody up, come on, it's gone—"

Sniffles became wailing sobs and she pulled little hands upwards once more. She quickly led them to the freshly-smashed hole in the bus; it was far larger than the emergency exit and would be a much quicker doorway. Spectators, hearing the young cries, were already gathering, ostensibly to help the children but also to get a glimpse of the Stone Man's progress beyond the blockade of smashed bus and cars. Maria breathlessly began handing crying children into the arms of complete strangers. "Here, take them to those people over there. Please, help us—" A chain began and that was good, that was something she could work with. The Chimp was beating itself senseless against the bars of its enclosure.

*WHAT THE HELL WAS—*

*Not now,* she told it. With an effort—all that meditation had paid off—she got the Chimp settled down again. She had to get the children off the bus.

Soon all twelve children were clear of the wreckage, a frantic operation carried out under a diminishing audio backdrop of explosions and crumbling buildings as the Stone Man moved away. Next to the crushed Porsche, Maria managed to get a full head count of kids as they huddled on the driveway. The owner himself, returned now with his partner to assess the wreckage, sat sobbing by his most prized possession. After a check of the children for injuries—there were bruises, bumped heads, and a little bleeding but, mercifully, nothing serious—and not knowing what else to do, Maria sent a willing nearby teenager to the shop to get plasters and a selection of ice lollies for the kids. After that, the children all sat semi-contentedly eating their treats and—blessedly—not yet asking where their parents were. Occasionally, word would come down the line about contradicting titbits of information on the news, but nothing was concrete.

*It's the only one*, they said.

*There are loads of them*, they said.

Maria tried to keep the kids' mood upbeat, frantically worrying about Marcus, if he was okay, and checking for a signal on her useless phone. She waited impatiently for assistance to come.

*Then* she would deal with it. Then the Chimp could scream the place down.

The smoke on the horizon was now coming from further and further away.

*There'll be a solution to this somehow,* she thought. *Where do I feel my fear?*

*In my neck. In my chest.*

But her hands still wouldn't stop shaking. She tried to hide it from the kids.

An hour passed. The crushed cars had been moved to the sides of the road, or at least as far over as willing groups of people would risk pushing them. The line of traffic began to move again. The kids had increased the frequency of their complaining and worrying about their parents, and helpful homeowners nearby didn't seem to mind the constant knocks on their doors for bathroom visits. Just as Maria was beginning to wonder if they could walk somewhere to get shelter for twelve kids in one place—she wished she could chance offloading them two at a time into the passing cars to take them to the holding centre, and occasionally felt like she would be happy to—another police car finally arrived. He informed her that another bus would be there in half an hour. The plan was the same, the holding centre was still standing, and the parents were either inside or on their way.

"What's going on? What is it?" she asked, surrounded by an immediate group of shouting people who wanted the same answers. The police officer just got back into his car before the group became a mob.

"Half an hour," he said through his wound-down window before weaving his car away. She told the kids the news and they cheered while helicopters began to buzz back and forth across the air above them, moving with astonishing speed.

An hour and a half passed.

The second bus finally arrived, led by another flashing-lights police escort. By now the traffic was starting to move normally; Maria wondered if the thing's progress away from the centre of the city meant that people felt safer staying at home and watching for more news. The kids were understandably a little reluctant to board the bus, but they did, sitting and talking quietly, the buzz a great deal quieter than before.

"One of us will ride with them to the centre, miss," the police officer told Maria, standing with her outside the bus. He was young, perhaps new to the force. Maria wondered how he could have been even halfway prepared for the likes of what was happening. "You've done enough."

Maria hesitated, tired and torn. She *did* want to go home so very badly, but the kids...

"... Okay."

"Which way is home for you?"

"Earlsdon," Maria replied, glad to be going there but knowing that, now her task was ending, she would have more mental freedom for the strange worry and fear that had been gnawing and gnawing.

"Ah, we're not going that way I'm afraid, miss," the cop said. He sounded tired beyond belief. "We're going past the hospital and can drop you there if you like? Get you checked over? *That's* still standing, but there'll be a wait." He shook his head bitterly—*What has he seen?* Maria wondered—before registering the implication of '*that's* still standing'.

The police officer stiffened, realising that he shouldn't have said anything of the sort. Too late; the Chimp had smelled something and was already beginning to stir.

"How many buildings have been destroyed?" she asked, but the cop heard the deeper concern behind the question.

"I'd best be moving on with the children," he said, far too quickly, beginning to head back to his car. "We've got to get back to the, uh, job. If you don't want to go to the hospital, then good luck and be safe."

"Buildings in town?" she asked, and now her voice cracked.

"Yes, some buildings," he  replied tersely, opening the car's door.

"The... Transport Museum?" she asked, terrified to do so. "In Millennium Place? Did anything happen at the Transport Museum?" The police officer held up a hand to wave goodbye, his head down as he lowered into the car. Maria darted forwards a few steps.

"My husband works at the Transport Museum," she said quietly. The police officer froze halfway into the car. "He does security. Can you just tell me if anything happened there?"

The police officer's head came up, and he stared at her for a moment, blinking in the sun. "Could you hold on a second, please?" he said.

Something inside Maria turned over.

"... Yes."

The young cop then dropped all the way into the car, and Maria now saw that there was a man in the passenger seat. The sun was reflecting too strongly off the windscreen for her to see, but she thought that the passenger was talking into the police radio. After a moment, the young police officer got out, looked briefly at Maria, then walked straight past her with his head down and got onto the bus.

"What happened?" Maria asked the back of his retreating head.

No answer.

"Sir? Sir, what *happened*?"

The police officer said something to the bus driver and the bus doors closed suddenly, leaving Maria looking at her reflection in the glass. She spun to face the other cop, now getting out of the car. She would never forget the way he looked: the sunglasses, the bald head, the security guard's body inside a police officer's uniform. He looked out of place, like a small-town sheriff or middle-of-nowhere state trooper you saw in movies pulling people over.

Something continued to tug at the inside of her mind, whispering to her. She reached blindly for answers, but none came.

Cecily suddenly banged on the inside of the bus' window, trying to get Maria's attention. She looked up and saw the girl's concerned face.

*"Maria,"* came Cecily's muffled voice through the glass. *"Are you okay? What's wrong? Are you coming with us?"*

*Something...* Maria thought, her thoughts dreamlike. *What... am I feeling?*

The answer came to her, and it was awful.

*... something terrible,* came the delayed answer. *Not a feeling. You* know *something terrible.*

"I'm... I'm fine... Cecily..."

Cecily blinked, knowing Maria's words were untrue and not wanting to correct an adult.

"Hello," the police officer said quietly. Maria turned to face him, dazed. He took off his sunglasses, looking weary and reluctant. He didn't hold out his hand. "Hello, I'm PC Watterson. Are you... are you alright?"

Maria didn't respond. The experienced PC Watterson darted forwards to put his arm around her, stopping the growing arc of her back-and-forth swaying.

"Okay. Okay," he grunted, looking over his shoulder, sternly catching his colleague's gaze through the bus window. The young officer onboard understood and ushered the kids away from the windows as they pointed and yelled, concerned for Maria. They liked her. "Let's get you a seat."

Maria pushed away from him, straightening up, moving before he could stop her. She then turned to clutch his sleeve and his shocked eyes held hers for a moment.

"My husband... my husband, *Marcus,*" she gasped. From somewhere, a cool breeze blew up, utterly at odds with the baking heat from the sun. "The Transport Museum, he works there... is it... is it...?"

The police officer's eyes darted downwards.

"Let's... first, let's..."

She knew.

*I feel it in my heart,* Maria thought. *I feel it in my head.*

A terrible, terrible weight began to settle into her, sinking deep into her bones and seeming to infect their very marrow like rot.

*I feel it in my spine. In my brain. In my eyes.*

*In my brain, forever.*

She knew it to be true.

Then, with the worst possible timing, the feeling that had been building all day suddenly *broke.* Her blinding headache *broke,* reached a climax as whatever her twitching, *knowing* brain had been picking up finally arrived all the way with devastating force.

The convulsions hit her.

Something shot down her spine, and her bladder involuntarily emptied all over the inside of her navy blue leggings. The urine soaked through instantly, forming a huge dark spot around Maria's crotch as her mouth worked silently and her fingers trembled as if she were being electrocuted. Then, bizarre and alien to the situation, as her world died around her, the vision came, swimming to the surface of her mind like bubbles released from somewhere far below.

*A man. A thin, scared, blond-haired man.*

She saw him as clearly as if she'd held her own hand in front of her face. She could hear the police officer's cries for an ambulance—"Something's happening here!"—and then she realized that she'd fallen. She could feel the police officer holding her but all she could see was that strange, skinny blond man.

"She's fitting, I need help!" she heard the cop bark to someone.

And then the blond-haired stranger was gone and she saw the street once more, the distraction over—for that was all it was in this moment of insanity and pain as her mind began to scream,

*Marcus, Marcus, Marcus.* She looked up to see Cecily's open-mouthed expression of shock on the other side of the new bus window as Maria curled up into a ball in the police officer's arms and began to scream.

The vision of the blond-haired man would come back, returning to her repeatedly all of that day—in the night, when she lay in a hospital bed, pumped full of drugs—and would continue all of the following day until Patrick Marshall, the blond man of her vision, was finally met and taken by the Stone Man.

For this was the day that the Stone Man arrived, a day that would forever be known as the First Arrival. The people of Coventry were the first losses in *Caementum's* steady march across the country—the first loss in what the media would eventually term *the March of the Stone Men*, from the First Arrival to the Third—but she would never care about the others. She wouldn't care when the journalist and TV personality Andy Pointer would later appear on the news and the world would briefly revolve around him, didn't care that the Stone Man would return twice more with its comrades and wreak havoc on the country she called home. If Andy himself had told her in that moment that one day the entire world would revolve around her and her choices, she would not have cared about that either.

All she had now, gained in an instant, was loss, and the rest of her life to bear it.

*It saw me,* Maria thought. *It's in me. It's in me.*

# Part One:
# Maria and Eric
## Five Years Later

*You will find what you most need where you least want to look.*

**—Alchemist proverb**

# Chapter One:

# Maria and the View from the Beach

*** 

## <u>Maria</u>

Maria walked along the beach promenade, trying to enjoy the 3 p.m.-ish fuzzy wash that British people call late September sunlight. She breathed slowly and tried to be present, fighting to keep thoughts of the too-slowly-ticking clock at bay. It was a battle against a relentless opponent that she knew would continue until her dying day.

*Eight hours until the flight. Eight hours until the flight. Come on. Come on.*

She could be at the airport already. Later, the thought of this would drive her nearly insane. *You could have been* long *gone before all of this started. Why did you even* risk *it?*

Because of the beach. Because of the sea air. Because for once, today of all days, she'd thought that maybe her ridiculous paranoia could take a back seat, and she could get in front of endless nature and let it go to work. There was still more than enough time to get to the airport, even by the standards she'd set for this trip. Maria had already planned to extend the recommended arrive-three-hours-before-international-departure time to five. She didn't take chances. She nearly hadn't come to the beach at all, but Maria felt that doing so was important. She'd barely had a relationship with her mother for most of her adult life—Maria's anxiety combined with her parent's cold and authoritarian ways had never been a good mix—but the beach had been her mother's favourite place. Regardless, the funeral had been a ritual that Maria needed to observe. It was the *done thing,* and Maria had at least respected her mother. That respect had to be shown here. She tried to understand what she was feeling about her mother being gone… and couldn't.

*That's okay,* she thought. *It'll come. Probably when you're back in Barcelona. You can process it then.*

Plus, coming to the beach was a goodbye of another kind. Now both parents were gone, Maria knew that her first trip home in nearly five years would also be the last time she would ever return to the United Kingdom. She could seize this important and cathartic moment and *still* get to the airport with enough time to make missing her flight impossible.

In and out of the country in twenty-four hours. No sweat, even if being here only reminded her of what she'd lost. No matter how many years had passed, she would never allow herself to be caught in the midst of another Arrival again. The old thought popped in for the first time in a while.

*It looked at me, that means something—*

She stared at the waves and breathed in and out. The air was cold and crisp, and the beach was relatively quiet, the late summer season thinning the already-small number of holidaymakers in this tiny part of the Lincolnshire coast. Maria sipped at her coffee, still warm in her hands, and glanced down from the elevated walkway to the sand. An old man with a metal detector was slowly passing along the beach, lost in his movements, and he looked up for a moment to see Maria watching him. He raised a hand in a genial manner, and Maria raised a small salute in return, feeling a tiny bit embarrassed, exposed... but also, to her surprise, *good*. Peaceful. She reminded herself she should start meditating again, but that had been something Marcus had taught her. Marcus, the hippy who had transformed her from economics student to yoga instructor. Sitting there without him always seemed wrong. She settled instead for taking these moments of stillness when she found them—something that had been happening more and more in the last year or so. When she did, she felt truly capable and strong again. She'd been off the antidepressants for a little while as well. That was something.

*But you know,* said the all too familiar voice inside her, *that's just vapour talking. Wait until you feel full of concrete again, wondering where this beach motivation and belief is when you need it, why you can't summon it forth. And you'll realize it's just empty words. Accept things the way they are and don't set yourself up for disappointment—*

The water moved steadily inwards. She *could* truly put the March of the Stone Men behind her, though she scowled slightly as the term popped into her head. She hated the buzz phrase; the media had used it to describe the First to Third Arrivals. It made those *things* sound so gracious and admirable.

*Five years grieving,* the voice told her. *Shouldn't you have sorted your shit out by now? Wouldn't a better,* stronger *person be back on top already?*

She took a deep breath, closed her eyes. The Chimp had learned to disguise itself, to sound like her own voice. *She'd* had to learn to spot the difference, to counter its words with truth. *Cut that shit and give yourself a break,* she thought. *Remember what Doctor Harris said.*

She did. He'd explained it perfectly: she'd experienced a major trauma that had occurred at the same time as—that which the government called—a *Stone Phenomenon.* She had anchored her grief in perhaps the worst way.

*Even so,* the Chimp muttered. *Five years.*

*Well, I'm bloody well here, aren't I?* she barked back. *Like the good doctor said,* Small Steps—*and today was a big one. Now let me look at the wonderment of God's creation and shut your bloody trap.*

She shivered. That was one thing she didn't miss about the UK: the cold. Barcelona's climate suited her just fine, especially these days; she was finally starting to gain a little weight back, a little muscle, but she knew she was still dangerously thin. Once upon a time, she'd have killed to fit into these jeans (she'd changed out of her funeral clothes the moment the thing was complete; she wasn't doing the wake). She missed her old job and the health that came with it—although she couldn't do a King Pigeon pose any more, let alone teach it—but she liked working in the café. She was assistant manager, it was quiet, the people were nice and her Spanish was now excellent—

She looked at the horizon and gasped a little. The view was suddenly *beautiful.* Something inside her ached and suddenly, despite everything, she missed being here. Her home. For the briefest of moments, she even found herself considering risking a permanent return... but no. She had been held by the Stone Man's gaze once and, until there was a guarantee that they would never return, neither would she. She had never told anyone about that moment.

*Call Ruth.*

The thought came out of nowhere, startling her with the force of guilt that came with it. She shouldn't have been surprised; it was the other reason for coming here. She had to make it right with Ruth. She *needed* to.

*Then why haven't I done it?* she thought. *It's more important than some bloody symbolic funeral visit. Ruth's alive, after all. I could just pop in for a cup of tea. She's only a short drive away. I'd still be hours early for the flight.*

She really, really wanted to. They'd been very close, yet Maria had cut her off. She *missed* Ruth. And now she was just too damned ashamed to see her... even though she thought she might regret it for the rest of her life if she didn't.

*You can live with it,* she lied to herself, watching the sunset's incredible colours of yellows and golds—

Maria looked at her watch. Sunset? It wasn't even four o'clock yet. What the hell?

She looked at Mr Metal Detector to see if he was getting this and *yes*, he was stopping too, taking off his hat and holding a hand above his eyes to get a better view. Maria squinted at the sky. This wasn't possible, surely?

The clouds in a *very specific* spot on the horizon seemed to be parting in a way that looked so spectacular that, if it were on film, everyone would assume CGI. They looked like a piece of stage scenery, something out of those old, early-days-of-cinema black-and-white five-minute shorts where the moon has a human face and everything is presented like a live-action puppet show. She half expected to see the clouds have lines where they folded into one another, revealing the join, but instead, they *flowed*. She looked behind her at the road, glanced down the beach to see if there were any other people; they needed to see this! Right in the centre of the spot where the clouds were moving, the sky itself was slightly discoloured, almost looking spotlit. It had to be a trick of the sun somehow, rays passing through a perfectly refracting mist, perhaps?

"Oh my *God.*" Maria laughed out loud to no-one at all, breathless and delighted. She glanced at Mr Metal Detector as he lay down his gadget to watch the view, hands on his hips. She hurried down the steps to the sand, inspired to kick off her shoes and actually feel a UK beach for the first time in years.

*This is a bloody* sign, *girl,* she told herself. *Life starts again, today.*

Later, she would remember this moment and think of how ironic that thought was.

She felt her toes sink pleasantly into the cool sand, standing close enough to the Metal Detector Man and looking at him to say, *Wow, that's amazing huh?* Attempting to share this magical moment with another human being.

Then he started pointing, eyes wide.

"*Haaahhh,*" he said, and Maria thought he didn't even know she was there. His face had become the same colour as the washed-out British sand below them. Maria looked back to the horizon.

"Oh... *oh...*"

The sky had returned to normal, the clouds now completely gone and the sun back to being a dim, late-afternoon lightbulb.

There was a figure standing on the horizon.

Standing *on* it? It looked like it, though of course that was impossible. It was impossible to tell if the ends of its legs reached the water and became submerged or if they were hovering above it somehow. It *had* legs because it was human in design—four limbs and a head—but Maria could not say it was human *shaped.* That would be a misleading description. Human limbs were never that long, human heads never that elongated and—except for a few notable exceptions in the more shameless pages of Cosmo—never that *thin,* although the word implied a lack of size. This was not the case. The thing had to be hundreds of feet tall. It was enormous.

While it was slightly transparent—Maria could see the shapes of the sky and sea behind it breaking through somehow—it also appeared to be an almost-uniform shade of white. It was solid and yet ethereal at the same time, as if it couldn't decide whether to be fully there or not.

It was horrible to look at.

It made no sound. It stood upright and did not move. It didn't walk, or waver, or glide. It just stood there, a silent and towering matte-white-emulsion colossus that took up impossible residence in the middle of the horizon. Watching the people on the shore? *Definitely.* Maria could have sworn that it was peering through her, beyond her. She expected her legs to give out in shock, but instead, she looked in confusion from the thing on the horizon to the Metal Detector Man and then to the road. Had any of the joggers spotted it too? One had: an old guy in a green tracksuit was standing with his mouth open, hands slack by his sides. Maria could hear distant shouts as people began to run to the promenade railings from all sides. She spun back to the horizon, the impossible sight beyond rational comprehension. Maria turned to Mr Metal Detector to say, *Are you seeing this?* but all that came out was a whimper. Her throat had dried up. She cleared it and tried again.

"*Can you see that?*" she whispered, not wanting it—crazily—to hear her.

"Oh my... oh my God," Metal Detector Man said. "*What is it? What is it?*" His plump, comfortably lined face made her think he was a retired bank manager or something, someone happy to spend his days on a beach with his toy and *not* dealing with madness like this. He looked like he desperately wanted her to have an answer. He was scared out of his mind.

"I think... its alive," she replied, the response arriving unbidden and without thought.

"It *is?*" the man gasped, clutching his fishing hat into a ball. "You think it is?"

*Can't you* feel *it?* she wanted to say. *It's looking right through us both, through all of us.* Fear was rising now. *It's many. It's one but it's* many.

Then...

*Where did that thought come from?*

A full-throated scream came from the promenade. It was a woman's voice. Metal Detector Man jolted as a loud *bang* rang out from behind them, followed by a screech and another *bang* immediately after it. Maria turned to see the three cars that had collided on the otherwise quiet road. Lots of people were at the railings now, standing staring or snapping photos with phones held in shaking hands. Maria closed her eyes tight, shaking too as she slowly turned back to the sea. When she opened them, the impossible figure was still there.

"It's *real,*" she whispered. Suddenly the memories of those visions of Patrick Marshall exploded back into her head and she was back there, back in *Coventry*, back in the road with the police. She tried to fight it, remembering how she was supposed to respond and going through the motions in her head.

*You are the Maria that is in this moment. On the beach,* now. *On the sand. Feel the sand around your feet. You're in the now. Breathe—*

She opened her eyes. She needed to get out of there immediately—out of the country. The damning knowledge of what she'd done echoed inside her head like an accusation. *LOOK,* she thought, *LOOK WHAT HAPPENED WHEN YOU CAME BACK—*

"We need to call the police," Metal Detector Man was muttering. "We need the army again, and they'll get the army; they'll get the, the, the navy." He grabbed Maria's arm—actually *grabbed* it—and his wiry old grip hurt even if his face showed no ill intent. "Do you have a phone? I don't have a phone. *Do you have a phone?*" He didn't wait for an answer, scooping up his metal detector and running towards the promenade. *"Call the police! Get the army! They're coming again!"*

The beach and the people seemed to fade in and out as Maria dropped to one knee on the sand. Dazed, her eyes followed Mr Metal Detector, only to see the people on the promenade suddenly stiffen upright, gasping simultaneously. Maria turned back to the sea, swaying as if she were on the water herself.

The figure was gone without a sound in the air or a ripple in the water. Strangely, *that* was when true panic seized her.

*"Did you see it?"* she screamed, her voice tearing as she turned to the people on the promenade. *"Did you all see that? You saw that? It was there?"* Most of them simply stared back, open-mouthed bovines trying to comprehend particle physics. Her panic heightened. *"It can't just be me and him! You all stopped to look!"*

Two of them finally nodded, their faces flashing from Maria to the sea, Maria to the sea.

Maria snatched up her shoes up from the sand, ran towards the steps and up to the street. She was beginning to elbow her way through the gathered people when everyone—*everyone*—cried out at once.

She nearly didn't turn around. She nearly kept *going.* Instead, she stopped in the middle of the crowd and looked at the surrounding, stunned faces. Saw the angle of their gaze.

They were no longer looking at the horizon.

Whatever they were looking at was now standing on the shore.

She stumbled slightly as she spun around on trembling legs. None of them had heard it called the *Empty Man* on the news yet but if they somehow had, everyone there would have thought the name utterly appropriate. Not from its appearance—the name suggested some kind of hollowed-out person, a man-shaped cookie jar bereft of cookies—but because they *felt* empty when looking at it.

Maria didn't know if the thing on the beach was the same thing from the horizon. If it *was* then it was now much, much smaller, though still taller than the tallest human. On the horizon it had looked more transparent, as if a larger form meant it had been stretched thin. This now-condensed version was almost completely opaque. It was, of course, white. Bright too, like white halogen light, but even more remarkable was that it somehow didn't glow at all. Even in the daytime such a light source would affect the shadows nearby, something you would never consciously notice until it wasn't there. It was like a bad Photoshop cut-out of a neon sign, cropped at its edges and laid over the beach like an animation cell over a background.

Its disproportionate limbs and head were the same as its larger form; elongated like the original Stone Man but thinner, much thinner. It was certainly *creepier*. Like the First Arrival before the Stone Man began walking, the Empty Man was bent at the waist. Its arms jutted out at an angle from its skinny but broad shoulders, unlike its stony predecessor whose arms had hung straight down. It was, by Maria's guess, at least fifteen feet tall. The whole thing had an air of something *looming.* Of something lurking in plain sight.

Now she could see its legs, or rather where its legs met the sandy surface below itself, but she still didn't know if it was actually standing on anything; its legs appeared to end at the sand but it was possible they were intangible and simply disappeared beneath the surface. Either way, the sand directly below it was completely undisturbed. She watched as the waves washed in and flowed straight through the thing's legs.

*So it... it is intangible, then?*

The thought was mind-boggling and then a fist of realisation punched her square in the brain.

*This thing doesn't need to walk through buildings.*

*Or buses.*

*Or—*

*No—*

*Transport museums—*

No. She dug her fingernails into her palms, hard. She was done crying over these things... but she felt a way she hadn't felt since the Stone Man turned its head to look at her five years ago. The thing on the beach was horrible. *Horrible.*

She used her breathing techniques again, identifying that the feeling inside her was *vengeful rage* combined with *pant-wetting terror* and anchored them in her *chest and bladder* respectively while she waited for her heart rate to slow down. Now it was time to *get the hell out of Dodge—*

Some people had moved down onto the sand, quite a few, in fact, having used the other steps away to her right. Some were almost directly below her, close to the wall that led straight down from the promenade to the surface of the beach. Most were a long distance away from the Empty Man, but some were as close as fifteen feet away, and *they were walking even closer.* Were they high? Were they drunk?

"*Stop!*" she screamed, the instinctive fear of anyone *touching* it, of *waking* it, even greater than her need to run. The people around her looked at her, startled. "*Don't go any closer! Stop!*" Couldn't they feel how dangerous that thing was?

To Maria it was as if it were *breathing* silent malevolence. She wouldn't have been surprised if she'd started hearing a hissing sound coming from it.

The people closest to the Empty Man—three men in their mid-fifties—were huddled together and taking strange, shuffling steps towards it. She wanted to scream *stop* again but the people around her began to murmur more and more excitedly.

"They're going to touch it," gasped a little old lady to Maria's left, speaking to no-one in particular. "Oh *God...*"

Maria could hear similar statements passing down the line— the people were now nearly three feet deep at the railing—and to her astonishment, a swell of encouragement began to build.

*Go on, son! Get in there!*

Others were counter-protesting and Maria tried to frantically elbow her way forwards to be part of it. She couldn't get any closer, the people in her way far heavier than her.

"*Don't do it!*" Maria yelled, the only one screaming when everyone else was merely shouting. "*It's dangerous! You'll make it walk! You'll make it start moving! PLEASE!*"

The men on the beach turned to look at the crowd. A cheer went up from the people egging them, most of them young men.

*Give us a wave! Give us a wave!*

One of the three men stopped—he looked older than the other two—shaking his head to the others and jerking his thumb back towards the promenade. The other two were incredulous. Maria couldn't hear the words, but their body language said it all. *You don't have to* touch *it. We'll just get close. This is a once in a lifetime experience, a once-in-a-human-race chance. Go back up to the street? Are you crazy?*

The doubting man looked back at the crowd once more, then shook his head and continued to walk towards the Empty Man. His supporters cheered, and Maria let out an involuntary and audible *no* as the three men drew within ten feet of the monstrosity.

*"STOP!"* she screamed, hysterical. *"PLEASE!"*

The noise of both positive and negative camps intensified, but as the three men got to within five feet of their goal, everybody suddenly became quiet, breathless with anticipation. That older guy wasn't going to touch it, but what about the other two? Were *they* going to do it? Maria continued to yell, not caring that she was the only one, fingers clawing at her cheeks.

*"PLEASE! PLEASE, STOP!"*

They'd slowed down now, confident strides reduced to little steps, and they were inching forwards like Olympic fencers, legs never crossing. Even out of touching range, they were raising and lowering their hands uncertainly as they approached. The doubter of the trio suddenly grabbed at his companions gently, but they politely shook him off. The doubter stopped moving. That was as far as he would go.

His friends drew even closer to the Empty Man as it towered before them. Its head, chest and torso were easily visible several feet above those of the men nervously approaching. Now they *were* close enough to touch it. They stopped, their hands faltering by their sides.

The crowd erupted.

Veins stood out on Maria's forehead and her throat hurt as she fired her verbal volley. The noise around her was primal. It wasn't just excitement. The presence, the sheer visible *madness* of that thing had triggered them all just by existing, and the pause in the men's progress was too much for the spectators to take.

*"DON'T DO IT! DON'T DO IT! DON'T DO IT!"* she screamed, watching the two men debate who would be the one to finally make physical contact. Were they having second thoughts? *"IT'S CRAZY! YOU'RE RIGHT! DON'T DO IT!"*

Then she watched in horror as a woman in a baggy sweater and tight leggings broke from further up the beach and ran towards the Empty Man. *She* was going to do it. The crowd saw her and leaped to an even higher level of mania, something Maria wouldn't have previously thought possible. The two men saw her as well, looked at each other and came to a conclusion. They held up their hands and lunged forwards.

The Empty Man vanished from view without a sound or a disturbance in the air.

Nothing was left to say it had ever occupied any space on that beach. Maria gasped, blinking idiotically as the crowd roared in a combination of shock, relief and disappointment. Baggy Sweater Woman pulled up short and stopped in her headlong charge. The two men started yelling angrily at her, as if her sudden movement had caused the Empty Man's departure. The woman yelled back— her words clearer as she was closer to Maria—explaining in no uncertain terms that the men had their chances, and what they could go and do to themselves and their mothers.

Excited babble began all around Maria. As she watched the argument begin to spiral on the beach, Maria could hear police sirens in the distance. No-one was leaving.

*I am,* Maria thought as a cold sweat broke out all over her body. *I'm going, and I'm going* right now.

Two parts of her mind began yelling over one another to be heard. One was recoiling in horror. *The thing had started off at sea,* it said, *so it's coming inland. It wants something, and that thing looked at you on the bus so what if* this *thing wants something from you?*

The other voice was all action. *The airport,* it said, *you have to get to the airport! We have to go* right now! *That's all that matters!*

Claustrophobia hit from the mass of bodies holding her in place, and then everything was too *close.* Mind reeling, she began to fight her way out of the crowd and towards the road, fear putting strength into her arms.

"Get out of my way! GET OUT OF MY WAY, PLEASE! I HAVE TO—"

It *was* time to run again, right now, and in the opposite direction to the Empty Man.

***

# Chapter Two:

# Eric and The Work

***

## <u>Eric</u>

In the partially destroyed suburbs of Coventry, just over a hundred miles away from the coast, Eric Hatton was finishing dressing up as nicely as his limited means allowed. Approaching forty and feeling it, he had to admit it was good to look nice for a change. He *didn't* want to admit that it was *the Work*, as Mickey called it, that was probably grinding him down more than his age. He went downstairs and checked himself in the mirror by the front door.

"Mickey?" Eric called back upstairs. "Mickey, I'm—" *Oh yeah,* he thought. *Mickey left.* His former... roommate? Colleague? Partner-in-the-Work? Either way, Mickey had moved back into the city centre a few weeks ago after finally accusing Eric of 'going soft'. It had been the end of an era, but Eric hadn't been sad to see him go.

*Mum and Dad gone,* he thought. *Theresa, Mickey... what's left?*

The Work. The Work would continue, that was the main thing. Besides, most of the things Mickey said towards the end had been bitter, cutting and generally aimed at Eric. *We never should have moved to the suburbs,* had been the usual rant. *It's your fault, pussy. Ground Zero is* in town, *that's where we need to be* at all times—

Once, Eric would have felt the same. These days…

*Why are you even still doing it?* he asked himself, even though he knew *exactly* why. He'd never stop, even if his level of passionate obsession didn't match Mickey's mania any more. He'd still see Mickey at the Ground Zero lookout point every day, standing twenty feet further away than normal. They never spoke now. Somehow the man had got hold of his own scanner, and Eric had no idea where he'd found the money. Eric had paid for everything, which was why his remaining savings were nearly at zero. Going to the pub today was a luxury but meeting an old friend was worth it. *This will help with the Work,* he told himself. *It isn't an indulgence. You've been going too hard for too long, not looking after yourself. You're running on fumes, and this will recharge the batteries.*

Luis was an old work colleague who Eric had contacted a few weeks ago, someone he'd always liked. He'd gone on a rare Facebook friend-scanning odyssey, brought on by loneliness after Mickey's departure, and realized that the man still lived in the area. Not Coventry itself, of course—Luis was in Nuneaton—but close enough for them to meet halfway, in Coventry's rural outskirts. If Luis didn't *know* it was halfway—Eric had said he *lived* in the outskirts—then that was okay. People still lived there, enough for there to even be one pub. It would be nice to just be around someone else, to be in a real, still-in-business *boozer.* Once upon a time, the idea of missing pubs and bars would have been insane to Eric, having spent most of his professional career in them; his days of jobbing work on the Midlands' music circuit were now a distant memory. Luis used to run one of Eric's favourite venues to play at, and they'd often had a lock-in after a show.

He'd shaved the beard off and picked up some nice enough, cheap new trainers as well as a new shirt and jeans at an out-of-town superstore—there wasn't anywhere left in Coventry that would even provide food other than canned goods, let alone cheap clothes—and the resulting change was pretty remarkable. He actually looked... normal. He just wished he hadn't felt so... *weird* all day—for the last few days, in fact. He'd had a headache so bad that, if it went on any longer, he'd go see a doctor.

Eric pulled his bike away from the hallway wall and, as he wheeled it outside, he looked at the grey September sky. It *might* hold until he got to the pub. He nearly didn't bother locking the front door; there wasn't much point. He and Mickey seemed to be the only people living on that street, and these were *nice houses* too—many of them close to the million-pound-listing mark, now as empty as the city centre. At least that area had a handful of people within its borders. *Coventry,* he thought, shaking his head. Truly, only the dispossessed and the mad lived there any more. The category he fit into seemed to change daily in his mind.

Thinking about the only things of value he owned—the portable scanner, the night-vision googles, the good telescope—and how, for once, they were being left at home, a rare day off, Eric locked the door. He thought about taking the mini binoculars out of his bicycle's pannier bag and leaving them at home. They were *always* in there...

*Well, let's not go bloody* crazy *here,* he told himself. *Always good to have* something. *Take them.*

He mounted his bike and pedalled away through the silent Coventry suburbs as the sky turned darker overhead.

\*\*\*

"You can tell this is Coventry. See those two old boys over there?" Luis said quietly, putting two pints on their table as he came back from the bar. "They're talking about how they actually bought some of that stuff from Steenaway back in the day. Remember those ads?"

"Heh, yeah," Eric said nervously, picking up his pint. He didn't want to get onto *anything* Stone-related. It had all been pleasant so far. Even the pub's *smell* had greeted Eric like an old friend. It was, of course, still possible to have a drink in a *central* Coventry pub but not only did you have to bring your own beer, you also had to prise the wooden boards off the windows with a crowbar to get in. The beer garden—where they'd ended up sitting—smelled fresher, of course, but that was fine too. In this part of town, the grey clouds he'd seen at home were gone. He felt good, although he wished he could block out his goddamn *headache.*

Luis had been delighted to see him, and real human warmth was a treat. The pair of them had been catching up while Eric managed to dodge questions about his living situation with surprising ease. Now Luis was turning the conversation into tricky waters.

*Steenaway.* Bastards.

It had been a year or so after the Third Arrival when Steenaway first started hawking their crap. They'd started off as features on home shopping channels, then radio and podcast ads and, as the sales rolled in, TV spots, where Eric first encountered them. This was around the same time Eric started to accept that he would never be the same again, and the anger was beginning. Those commercials were constantly on the TV because some shithead, to Eric's mind, had spotted an exploitable hole in the market, and commercials were like propaganda for Eric's rage.

*Recent events,* the voiceover had said, *have made us* all *realize that there are threats out there hitherto unheard of. But* you *don't have to be unprepared. Groundbreaking research from the highest levels of science at our labs in Switzerland has led us to the cutting edge of extra-terrestrial knowledge and defence. Presenting the Home Protector Alpha.*

The *Home Protector Alpha* cost an eye-watering—for the actual build quality of the thing—two hundred pounds. It looked like a cross between a toaster and a wireless router, except white and shiny like a huge old-school iPod. The concept was that it worked using *electromagnetic frequencies that helped counter those that leading scientists believe guide the path of the Stone Visitors.*

The Home Protector Alpha claimed to have a radius of three hundred feet *under optimum conditions.* Those conditions were not, of course, ever explained, but it was perfect for neighbours who wanted to split the cost of one and use it to 'protect' both of their houses. Despite various internet gadget teardown specialists debunking the hugely underpowered components that produced very little electromagnetism at all, as well as the pseudo-science behind the electromagnetic 'protection' elements (nobody had a clue how the Stone Men worked), Steenaway continued to thrive. Lawsuits against them died on the vine because the claims they were making about their products could not, essentially, be disproved, especially as nobody actually knew how the people the Stone Men visited actually died (despite the claims of the thousands of conspiracy theorists who said they knew otherwise).

"You believe in all that?" Luis asked, pale even for a white guy but well-dressed, well-fed, and grinning charismatically in his smart T-shirt and jeans, only a few years younger than Eric. Eric understood why Luis had left the pub scene to work in sales; he was built for it. Eric winced at the question. "All the cover-up stuff?"

"Well..." His heart raced. He didn't know what to say. So far, he'd managed to appear *normal.* But Luis was the one bringing it up, so... "Do you?"

"Actually, the Stone Man stuff? Yeah, I do," Luis said, sipping at his Guinness. "I'm not talking about the usual looney-tune conspiracy crap, obviously. *Commercial plane vapour is really chemtrails. Isle of Skye toxic spill was really an experimental chopper crash, and the 'disaster area' was to cover it up. 9/11 was an inside job so they could go after oil.* That kind of bullshit. But this..."

"Yeah," Eric said, letting Luis do the work. "And that Andy Pointer guy disappeared—"

"*Yeah,* right?" Luis asked, putting his pint down and leaning forwards. "The guy's everywhere, and then... *nothing.* I heard he died."

"Yeah, I heard that," Eric said, putting it mildly. He'd done more than *hear* it. Andy Pointer was the subject of great discussion in the forums, one of the biggest. "Some people think..." He hesitated.

*Don't. Don't get started. You don't want another Kelly Parsons situation.*

*Fuck it. He's asking—*

"... Some people say there's a recording," he said.

"What?"

"Pointer. They reckon he kept an audio diary. No-one knows for sure what's on it, and it's never been properly leaked, but..." Eric shrugged. "Someone must have heard it and said something."

"What do they think is on it?"

"The real side of things. Talking about what happened on the inside. A lot of people think he was..." Eric mimed putting a gun to his head and pulling the trigger. "Y'know. Silenced. *Because* he made the recording."

The alleged Pointer Audio was still the stuff of myth in the online forums, the Holy Grail for the Stone Conspiracy set.

"Oh. Wow... Shit, man."

He waited, letting Luis lead. He'd screwed up with this stuff the last time he'd been to a social function, meeting a group of former close friends. It was his prior attempt to be a normal person, and that had been a year ago. It hadn't gone well. They'd gone to Barrington's and, after yet another clash with Mickey, he'd spent too much money on booze out of spite. It was his fucking money that paid for everything anyway, he'd told himself. For once he was going to have some fun. Unfortunately, once full of several pints of *fun*, his old friend Kelly Parsons then got him onto the worst possible subject.

*Where do you live these days, Eric? What do you do?* He'd ducked it at first, but after a few pints of Guinness, the truth had come out. He'd *stupidly* let his true colours show, and then, of course, a rant had ensued. Her crime? Drunkenly showing concern, trying to tell him to drop the conspiracy crusade, to come back to a normal life.

*Why does everybody do this?* he remembered barking at Kelly Parsons. *What happened to, you know, to, to just having a conversation? When did everybody become my fucking* mother?

The regret the next day meant that he hadn't been out since.

"I know some people that are into that stuff," Luis said, not dropping it. "*Big* time."

*You have no idea, Luis.*

"Yeah?"

"Have you ever heard the Pointer Theory? It's crazy."

"... No?"

He had. It was his obsession and the main reason he was still in Coventry, why he hadn't gone with Mickey on his six-month stakeout trip to the 'wind farm' in Sheffield. That had been the beginning of the end for them as a team.

"Well, there's all this talk about the Stone Men being drawn to people because of their genes or whatever, right?" Luis said animatedly, making Eric think that maybe 'Luis' buddy' might actually be Luis. This was interesting, if so. "And that guy, I mean, they even said in the news, that he had a connection of sorts to it and that he helped the government out, right?"

"Uh-huh," Eric said, leaning in himself now and trying not to hide his excitement. This meeting could be an even better idea than he'd thought.

"But he was *right there* when the Stone Man arrived, right? Like, within feet of it. And the Pointer Theory is that Andy Pointer being physically present when the First Arrival happened meant that he was, y'know… connected."

"Wow. That's interesting."

While he'd been there for five years, Eric hadn't been out of the radius of Coventry in four, ever since he'd first heard the Pointer Theory. He'd had visions right before all three Arrivals—if they were coming back, he'd know. There was no way he'd allow himself to be far enough away to miss the next, if it ever happened.

*Plus,* he suddenly thought bitterly, *how else would you be down there with your radio scanner every fucking day, Eric?*

"A lot of the conspiracy nerds reckon that's the way to find out the truth," Luis said, and Eric watched his face closely to see if Luis agreed with said nerds. "Like, if you're connected… then you're on the inside, you know? Like he was. You'd know everything."

"You would," Eric said, deciding to test the waters a little. "But then, of course… if you were someone who had visions, if you were in that bracket *and* you were right there when it turned up... then you'd run the risk of being someone they came to see. Someone they targeted. And all the people they went to see died from the contact." He leaned in a little further. Not too much. "Do you think that risk would be worth it?"

That *was* the risk.

Luis stared at him.

Then he laughed.

"*Fuck,* no!" he said, picking up his pint. "Those dudes ever come back, I'm jumping on the first plane out!"

Eric sat back in his seat, forcing a smile. Of course.

"Ha, yeah, no doubt."

"So, you live round here now, then?" Luis asked.

*Shit.*

"Yeah, not too far from here actually," Eric lied.

"Where are you gigging these days? Obviously not locally."

"No, I don't do it any more..." Eric said, his face getting hot.

"Just had enough of it, then?"

"Kind of... I was, uh... gigging on a cruise ship during the Second Arrival," Eric said. His heart rate had suddenly skyrocketed. He couldn't believe what he was saying, but it was just coming out. What the hell? "It was... kind of traumatic," he heard himself say. "After that, I couldn't go back to just doing gigs. I... I kind of had stuff to find out about, you see." He chanced a glance at Luis. His friend wasn't screwing his face up in disgust or thinking Eric was strange. He only looked concerned.

"What happened?"

*Shut up!* Eric thought. *What are you doing?*

"I knew I shouldn't have taken the job, but I had to," Eric said, feeling as if a pressure valve was slowly being released inside himself, even as the voice protested. "My sister ended up single during her pregnancy and couldn't work right after Aaron was born, so I was sending her money to help out. She'd have these massive, ungrateful freak-outs. *Is the money coming at the end of the month? You promised it would,* she'd say. That was the line Theresa always used. *You promised.* And then she'd calm down and apologize... So, when Theresa started freaking out a few days before I left, I just thought it was more of the same, you know? But she couldn't tell me what was actually *wrong.* And back then, I didn't know *anything.* No-one knew about Patrick Marshall's pre-Arrival behaviour back then—"

"She was..." Luis looked as if he were choosing the next word carefully. "Connected?"

"Yes."

"She had visions?"

"No. She just had migraines. But she'd never had them before. I knew there'd be a sailing day when we'd be out at sea and I wouldn't be contactable, I mean, I *could* have paid the extra for data use out there but it was so *expensive* and money was really tight and it was only *one day.*"

"Makes sense."

Eric paused. Was this safe to talk about? He and Luis weren't close, but Eric knew him to be a good man, and dammit, he *needed* to.

"So, I get back into signal in port in Napoli on what turned out to be the day of the Second Arrival," Eric continued, rubbing his face nervously. "My phone explodes with voice messages from Theresa. She's in absolute hysterics. I had *no idea* that she would get that bad. I would *never* have gone *anywhere,* especially leaving her with Aaron..."

He could picture it now: pacing the dock under the Italian sun and slowly going out of his mind. "So much so that I had the number of one neighbour, Will—I didn't really know the guy well but Theresa had given it to me as, like, an emergency contact—and I tried calling him to get him to go round, but I couldn't get through. Then I tried to call some of my friends to go round, to drive all the way to bloody *Birmingham,* but I couldn't seem to get hold of anyone; the phone lines were either screwed or no-one was picking up, and I couldn't call Theresa either. Of course, I haven't heard the news yet; I'm standing on a dock without a TV and why would I check the headlines? I was so panicked I hadn't put two and two together at that point, even when we'd already heard about the First Arrival. When I couldn't even get through to the UK police, I really started to…"

"I'm sorry," Luis said softly.

"I tried everything. Those things, those *bastards,* they always screw with the phones, especially when they're walking. Then out of the blue, I was suddenly somehow able to get through to Will, the neighbour—this idiotic, selfish little *goose* of a man—but he couldn't hear me, and I remember screaming *get to Theresa* and he's just going, *hello, hello, I can't hear you,* then he finally fucking *can* and he goes round with a spare key…"

He remembered the words that came back to him nearly every night.

"… and he says, *Eric, I think she's boarded up the front door. The key's turning in the lock, but it won't open.*"

Luis nodded sadly.

"Then I hear him go round the back, and he says, *Eric, there's boards over the windows; did she go away on a long trip?* The idiot says, *is this burglar-proofing?* And I'm absolutely losing my shit, and then he says he's going to tell the army guys about it because they're there, and I say, *army guys?* And he says, *there's trucks full of army guys on the street now, and they're evacuating everyone.*

*They're making everyone leave, but I'll tell them right now.* And I'm screaming at him to just get in there, and he says, *I'm sorry, Eric, but they can deal with this, I'm not qualified.* Qualified?!"

"Beautiful day in the neighbourhood," Luis muttered.

"I went straight to the airport," he said. "I finally got through to the UK emergency services en route, but it was just a recorded message about evacuations in the area and which buttons I should press to get more information. Then all the flights into the UK were cancelled. I had to hire a car and drive to France, take the ferry across."

The lines of cars at Calais. How the vision of that—the sun shining off all those windscreens—had suddenly vanished and been replaced by all the faces appearing in his mind.

The old man, Henry Williams first.

Then Theresa. *Aaron.*

That was when he knew. Helpless in his rental Renault—screaming and impotently punching the roof of the car hard enough to break the skin on his knuckles, *helpless.*

"I eventually got through to a person," he said, trying to keep the crack out of his voice and failing. He looked at Luis again, checking for signs of discomfort, but all Eric saw was intrigue. "I said, *I know*, I *know where they are going,* and they..." He wiped his face, bit the inside of his cheek. "They put me through to an answering machine before I could say anything else. *What did you see? Did you recognize any details? Do you or anyone in your family have a history of autism or any other developmental conditions?* I answered them all and tried not to go crazy on the drive. The roads were gridlocked. It had taken me over twenty-four hours to get home. The street had been evacuated and Theresa was gone."

Somewhere in the telling his sorrow had turned into rage. His hands were shaking. *Get it out,* Eric thought. *Tell him everything.*

Eric realized that he *wanted* to. He could tell Luis all about the Work, how Theresa was the reason he was even in this godforsaken city.

Luis' eyes widened as the penny dropped.

"So... your sister was Theresa *Pettifer*," Luis whispered. "The Second Arrival Target... The three Stone Men, they came to the old guy, and the woman and her..." Luis realized what he was saying and stopped.

"Yes," Eric said, relieved for both of their sakes that he'd used her name and not the wonderful tabloid terms like *The Stone Woman* or *Twisted Theresa* or, worst of all, *Baby Killer.* "After her divorce, she'd kept her married surname for some fucking stupid reason. No-one even contacted me—no-one official—to say that she'd died."

Eric fell silent. His cheeks were glowing, but he felt lighter. He didn't know what to say next.

"Are you alright?" Luis asked quietly, and the sincerity in his tone was clear. Eric's growing anger vanished, and for a horrible moment, he thought he might cry, but instead was saved by the question from the man on the other side of the beer garden.

It was a moment that would forever change Eric's life.

"Hey... *hey.*" It was an old, beer-bellied fellow sitting at a table and reading a newspaper. He was calling to the glass collector and pointing at the outside TV on the wall. "Quick, the TV. Can you turn it up?"

Luis and Eric followed the man's gaze. On the TV, a woman was holding a microphone, standing in front of a beach. The caption said, *LIVE: BRIGHTON.* Standing on the sand was a spread-out crowd of people, many of whom were carrying binoculars. They looked like they were *waiting* for something, rather than watching something; they looked like the first people to get to a rock concert, making sure that they were at the front.

The tracker along the bottom of the screen didn't gel with the rest of the image, as if someone had accidentally plastered it across a light, on-the-scene weather report about a heatwave. Even so, Eric felt the electricity sting its way through the beer garden—and himself—as everyone saw the words written there. He blinked, stunned, unable to believe that he could be seeing the words after only just talking about such a thing. The timing was so prophetic that Eric felt an immediate sense of doom.

*It can't be,* he thought. *It just can't be. You can't be seeing this.*

He'd imagined this so many times that he stopped believing it to ever be possible.

The caption onscreen read:

*POSSIBLE FOURTH ARRIVAL PHENOMENA SPOTTED*
*ON SEAFRONTS ALL AROUND BRITAIN.*

No-one in the pub said a thing. Eric didn't breathe. The volume was turned up and now he could hear the reporter clearly.

*"... eyewitness reports of what has been described as 'an enormous man standing in or on the sea'. I say eyewitness, Steve, because here, at least, people have taken photographic stills or even video footage of the phenomena and they haven't shown up on camera."*

*"So, let's say what everyone will be wondering here, Liz,"* the in-studio anchor's voice said. *"Another hoax?"*

*"As always, Steve, it's hard to say at this point,"* the brunette reporter replied. *"The Home Office has yet to respond, and we don't expect to hear anything conclusive for at least twenty-four hours."*

*"A* carefully coordinated *hoax then, perhaps?"*

"*If it is, Steve,*" the reporter said, "*it's been very carefully coordinated. Reports were practically simultaneous around the country, and we have footage of, well, obviously you can't see any phenomena, but you heard the response of a huge group of strangers in that, uh, in that footage we showed just now, that was from earlier today over in Cornwall. You could hear that very audible gasp that goes up when, according to witnesses, the-the figure in the sea disappears.*"

"*And now, this, uh, incident, or similar incidents,*" the anchor asked, "*they've been spotted elsewhere?*"

"*Yes, all around the country and, interestingly, off the east coast of Northern Ireland as well, but not the west.*"

The back and forth went on, Liz relaying eyewitness accounts along with quotes superimposed onscreen. An artist's impression suddenly filled the TV. It was grotesque, a white wraith bent almost double as if to feed. What the hell was *this*?

"*So other than its, dare I say,* human *shape,*" Steve asked, "*there is only speculation that connects this supposed event today to the Stone Men? That this is a genuine Fourth Arrival event?*"

Liz shook her head. "*Until we hear anything official from Number 10, Steve, we can only speculate. Everybody here is certainly excited, and they're waiting to see if it comes back. We'll be here too.*"

The anchor nodded sagely. "*So not Stone Men, it seems, but Men of some kind?*"

"*That's the looks of it, Steve.*"

"*Any name suggestions? You can coin it right now, Liz.*"

"*Ha ha, well, I don't have any myself, but one person here called it the Empty Man. How does that work for you?*"

"*That'll do just fine, thanks, Liz.*" The anchor paused for the briefest of moments as a producer confirmed they were ready. Eric had the craziest sensation of knowing exactly what he was going to say, a moment made even crazier when he was proven right.

*"We can now go to Mark a long way inland, just outside of Coventry."*

"Oh my God…" That was Luis. Eric didn't look at him. Instead, he froze as he looked at the reporter standing in front of a mixed police and military blockade. It appeared to be in the middle of a dual carriageway into the city, and the air rang with beeping horns. Presumably, there were a lot of halted cars behind the camera. There were several civilians standing around shouting in protest, but Eric wasn't interested in that. His heart raced as he tried to figure out the exact location; they were closing off the city already, then? Was that blockade further inside than he was? *No.* No, that was the A444, he recognized it. The reporter was practically in Nuneaton. That meant Eric was still inside!

*"Thanks, Steve,"* said Mark, his tone sombre. *"As you can probably hear, a lot of people are understandably angry about being held up and quite a lot are genuinely scared. Firstly, we want to let people know that, of course, anyone who wants to* leave *the city can do so, although you won't be allowed back in until we've been given the all clear. This is, as we're being told, just a precaution at this point—"*

*"Mark?"* Steve interrupted. *"Sorry, Mark, have they said anything about what's happening at Ground Zero?"*

Eric listened, the blood gone from his face.

He listened to Mark explain how the airspace around Ground Zero was still—as it had been for years now—restricted and any distant footage was *too* distant to see anything except the city skyline. The only reason the news crew were there was *because* the roads into Coventry had been closed as a potential Fourth Arrival safety measure, due to the sighting on the coast. Eric was trapped in a nightmarish dilemma, frantically trying get a grip and figure out how to save the situation. He knew that, if this really was a Fourth Arrival, the phones and internet could start playing up anytime now. This meant that the broadcast he was watching could be his last chance to get information. He tried to focus even though his mind bellowed at him, *THIS IS IT! SOMETHING IS REALLY FINALLY HAPPENING. THOSE THINGS MIGHT BE ON THE COAST, BUT SOMETHING MIGHT BE COMING TO GROUND ZERO, AND YOU HAVE TO GET THERE NOW NOW NOW—*

Where had his vision been this time though? Where had his shakes been, the convulsing? No, that didn't matter. What *did* was figuring out how to get back into the city centre. This was really *it.* Out of nowhere, a question popped up in his mind.

*Am I prepared to risk becoming a Stone Man's Quarry? Am I really?*

He was. He stood up and stumbled, grabbing the table for support. He looked at Luis. The other man's face had gone completely white.

"I'm really sorry, Luis—"

Luis blinked at Eric as if he didn't know who he was. Then he came to.

"Uh… no, it's okay, I have to—" Dazed, he pulled his phone out of his pocket, his hand shaking, but Eric was already turning and walking away from the table, thoughts breathlessly focused on getting to Ground Zero as quickly as possible… and what that might mean.

*Even if you're targeted,* he told himself as he rushed outside and mounted his bike, *you might be safe. The Chisel can stop them.*

That made him feel better. The Chisel *had* saved everyone's bacon. Whenever he got too close to the Work and felt overwhelmed—even though he would never trust his government as far as he could throw it—they *had* managed to halt the March of the Stone Men originally. And they'd used the Chisel to do it. Maybe they were bringing it to Coventry even now, if it wasn't already inside Ground Zero itself? As he began to pedal, his grip on the handlebars trembling, he remembered that was where the Chisel had been the last time he'd had seen it.

Where he, and the rest of the world, had been told what happened to the Last Stone Man.

Not in person, of course. Eric had seen the press conference on TV like everyone else.

***

*Eric and Mickey. Before things became unpleasant.*

*The TV on, both of them hushed and breathless. They watch as the Prime Minister approaches the podium.*

*"I told you," Mickey says for the twentieth time, unshaven and unkempt as always, hair sticking up in various directions. "I fucking told you. Kelly was* right." *Eric says nothing, because Mickey had* told *him. Eric knows all about Curtis Kelly: a former small-time blogger— a former nobody—in the awful and wide-ranging world of online celebrity and nerdery who, out of the blue, posted an article about a government initiative that protected the greater populace from 'outsider interference'. He'd received his information from a 'high-up source' and speculated wildly about what the Chisel might be and how it might work. It was thin on details and heavy on sci-fi fanboy levels of fancy—including ideas about wormholes and 'cross-species genetic melding'. The press used more direct language: 'alien sex fantasy'.*

*It would have been dismissed as another conspiracy theory to add to the towering stack of Stone-based bullshit that Eric has sifted through over the last five years... but the name Kelly had used:* Project Chisel... *It turned out to be the only germ of truth in the entire thing, but enough for Curtis Kelly to find himself stopped at security at Manchester Airport as he prepared to board a plane to Tenerife for a holiday with his family. That interception became a lightning rod for Curtis' original article and a staggering mistake, in Eric's opinion, for a modern, internet-savvy government to make.*

*Kelly's original blog article had exploded. As more skilled and higher-profile journalists took up Kelly's crusade, the government's repeated denials sounded weaker and weaker. The internet's claims became more varied, so much so that, at the time, Eric had no idea what to believe.*

*The Chisel was being built at a wind farm near Sheffield that is a cover for a military research facility.*

*The Chisel had been in development ever since the First Arrival.*

*The Chisel had been designed to take advantage of weaknesses that had been identified in the Stone Men's cellular structure.*

*The Chisel worked on the basis of soundwaves.*

*It had continued until, to Eric's delight, the official memo was anonymously leaked.*

*The one with the words* Project Chisel *and—the clincher, of course—the phrase* fourth incident prevention *in the same paragraph. That graduated the Chisel from the online circles in which Mickey and Eric moved to the front page of the tabloids. After that, further denials were pointless.*

*And now, here they are: the Prime Minister himself, and more importantly, the Chisel. Eric can't believe his eyes.*

*The interior of the Ground Zero building has never been shown to the public before. Eric is disappointed by what he sees: a circular room, the ceiling very high, the walls almost startling in just how normal they are: magnolia white, conference-centre-dull uplighters, fire-exit signs. Nothing to say the place was built on the spot where an alien race had turned up.*

*But the room* is *large enough to house the Chisel itself.*

*"Just look at it," Eric whispers, not looking at Mickey. The Chisel is enormous, gleaming under the specially assembled floodlights to the podium's right. It's impressive, to say the least. To Eric's eyes, it looks like an engine. Or rather, an engine the size of two Range Rovers, covered in actual gold parts in places that make it look like lunar equipment; those strange, form-free hunks of machinery covered in sheets of tinfoil-looking material. A lunar engine, then, with a massive, flattened funnel-looking thing at one end.*

*The PM opens by talking about the difficulty of balancing national security and careful distribution of information in a time of crisis.*

*"Get on with it," Mickey snaps. "How does it* work?"

"We regret having to call this press conference under these circumstances," *the Prime Minister says,* "and while we would have liked a little more time to complete our findings, it would be pointless to deny the elephant in the room and pretend that our hand hasn't been forced."

*"Jesus," Eric says. "That's a surprising admission."*

"I present to you," *the PM continues,* "the miracle of British engineering that enabled us to remove the threat of the Stone Men, as intentional or unintentional a threat on their part as they may be: the Chisel. You will have to forgive the pun name, our R and D teams started using it and it just sort of stuck." *He gives a classic politician chuckle, and Eric is delighted to see that it isn't returned by the assembled press.* "After a lengthy stop-gap measure," *the PM says,* "which I will come to in a moment—this device before you will enable our continued safety."

*The wave of gasps and murmurs from the press is followed by a barrage of questions, almost as many as the ones in Eric's head. The overall nature of them is:* How did you manage this? How did you carry out this research? *One reporter is singled out by the Prime Minister.*

"Make it louder, I can't hear," *Mickey barks, and again, it grates on Eric. Again, he says nothing and does as he's told.*

"Is this the device that caused some of the Stone Men to go home so early in the Third Arrival?" *the reporter asks.*

*A damn good question, Eric thinks; everyone in the country had seen (back when the media were still allowed to broadcast live footage from the then-uncovered Ground Zero) five of the freshly returned Stone Men vanish one by one before the final two started walking. Something had sent them away, everybody knew that. The final two had walked across the country, side by side, before the highly controversial emergency powers over media coverage had been granted. To maintain public order in a time of crisis had been the frighteningly dystopian justification to months of protests afterwards, before people realized the Stone Men weren't coming back and stopped caring... although coverage rules regarding Ground Zero were quietly passed through parliament, becoming permanent. In a stroke of sheer good luck for the government, the walking Stone Men—the last Blue and the original Grey—had been heading through a rural area at the time of the blackout. This made it far harder for Eric and anyone like him to track a legitimate path of damage like the obvious ones left through urban and suburban regions. There was no civilian footage of their disappearance either, thanks to the evacuation of populated areas in their path, but there were many kooks popping up out of the woodwork to confirm that yes, they'd felt them leave.*

*Don't George Mykos this one, you bastard, Eric thinks, watching the PM shift uneasily. The government line on the original Stone Man (or as Eric and his cohorts on the online conspiracy forums believed it's rumoured codename to be,* Caementum*) was that it vanished somewhere on the outskirts of the Peak District, just outside of Rochdale. According to the government's bullshit, the remaining Blue was discovered to be aiming at the home of one George Henry Mykos, a small business owner, divorcee and father of three who—according to the Home Office—committed suicide upon discovering that he was to be visited. The Blue had vanished after that. Of course, Eric knows, George Mykos had no history of mental illness. But at least there was a story regarding the last Blue. What about Caementum's unidentified Target and disappearance?*

*There was the talk on the forums about the path of destruction left by* Caementum's *march. When people mapped the points of damage—a smashed hedge here, a flattened tree there—it seemed that Caementum's path had to have suddenly kinked to the west (something previously unseen in any of the other Arrivals). And isn't it strange, Eric remembers, how if the path had continued straight on without kinking, it would have gone straight through the site of a brand new government-funded wind farm site? One erected inexplicably in the middle of the Ladybower Reservoir? Of course, the sheep didn't listen. All they cared about was that there hadn't been a Fourth Arrival yet. Hypernormalisation at its finest.*

"We can now confirm," *the Prime Minister was saying, reading from something out of sight behind the podium's raised front,* "that the first Stone Man was, in fact, under our custody for some time after the last of the blue Stone Men departed, seemingly of their own volition, as you know."

*Amazingly, none of the press asks a follow-up question, waiting in shock for the Prime Minister to continue. Eric can't believe his ears. This was the* last *thing he expected. A confession?*

*"Are you fucking—" Mickey starts, and now it's Eric's turn to bark.*

*"Quiet!" he snaps.*

*"We managed to devise a system," the Prime Minister says, his eyes still on his prepared speech,* "that enabled us to keep it in one place long enough to carry out full and in-depth studies of its cellular structure. That is all I am at liberty to divulge on that matter at this time. This was vital in the development of the Chisel, which would have been impossible without it." *He pauses for a moment.* "There are people who... preferred to remain anonymous that gave their lives to help us achieve this information, and how this happened is also classified information for the time being. Some of the names you already know; there are several that you do not. They are the silent heroes of this country, and while the privacy of their identities and their families' identities must be honoured, I would be remiss if I did not show them the nation's respect."

*"LIAR!" Mickey yells, jumping to his feet with characteristic overreaction, and this time Eric doesn't shush him. The Chisel continues to shine under the lights, devastating and ominous, the finest product that a bullshit wind farm in the heart of the Ladybower Reservoir has to offer. Eric and Mickey listen as the Prime Minister fields more questions. Yes, the leaked reports were correct: the Chisel worked on the basis of sound. Yes, it was perfectly safe and non-radioactive. No, the frequencies it used weren't harmful to humans, and a surprising side effect of the research was potential benefits to the field of dentistry, of all things.*

More lies, *Eric thinks. The PM is playing it smart. No way that thing doesn't harm humans. He's keeping the real details of that sucker secret so our human enemies can't use it against us, but here's a bone to get the press off his back.*

Where is the Stone Man now? *several reporters yell at once.*

"Yes," *Mickey hisses, sitting down. The Prime Minister sighs heavily. Here is the hard part, it seems.*

"You said that after the blue Stone Men left," *the reporter asks,* "you managed to retain the original Stone Man for a long enough period to conduct your research. We were told that it disappeared on its way out of the Peak District. So firstly, can you admit that was a lie, and secondly, can you reassure the public as to where that Stone Man is being kept now—safely—and what further research is being conducted upon it?"

*The PM nods silently as if to say,* uh-huh, here we go. *He shifts awkwardly at the podium. Eric moves to the edge of his seat, his whole body tense.*

"There will be no further data coming from the original Stone Man," *the Prime Minister says, of course ignoring the request to acknowledge the lie,* "but research will be continuing into the vast swathes of data that we procured from it." *He looks up, an almost desperate expression on his face.* "I will stress that we have so much data it will take years to complete sifting through it."

"Why?!" *Eric cries, echoing the yelled questions of the reporters and not realizing that perhaps he and Mickey aren't that different after all.*

"There will be no further research coming," *the Prime Minister says, his head held high now, his jaw set, ready for the backlash,* "because we no longer have the Stone Man in our possession."

*Both rooms are stunned into silence; the one at Ground Zero and the one in which Eric and Mickey sit.*

"Upon first test of the device..." *the PM continues,* "the Chisel, uh, here... we..." *He pauses, takes a deep breath.* "We discovered that, uh, the design was far more successful than we initially anticipated, or we overestimated the structural integrity of the Stone Man itself. In fact, while we have since identified the fault and recalibrated the device, it was the test fire of the Chisel that caused the recent, brief national power outage."

*Both rooms remain breathless, waiting for him to confirm that which they assumed—so much so that everyone misses the confession about the Big Power Cut. The Prime Minister coughs nervously.*

"Its... physical structure was completely destroyed," *he says. His eyes are focused squarely on the middle distance. Eric doesn't know whether to be delighted or devastated, but his jaw hangs open either way.* "Its remains... returned themselves to their point of origin in much the same way as they did in previous visits as... no trace of its physical form was found at the testing site or its immediate surrounding area. We can only assume they were..."

*He pauses again, not wanting to say the last word.*

"... reclaimed."

*Pandemonium ensues at the press conference. Neither Eric nor Mickey speak for a moment.* They fucked up, *Eric thinks.* They really did.

*Then Mickey says words that Eric never thought he would hear.* "Look at him," *he mutters.* "He's... he's telling the fucking truth."

***

*Is this real? Is this real?*

The questions rattled in Eric's mind as he pedalled his bike unsteadily towards town, relieved that, if there were any further internal roadblocks, they weren't on the backroads he'd deliberately taken. Sweat pooled around the band of his boxer shorts as he pushed the pedals as fast as he could.

*And what the hell were they saying? Stone Men in the sea but not made of Stone? White ones?*

The one thing he was trying not to think about—the gamble he was taking—was pushed to the back of his mind. One good thing about his plan—if it worked—would be that he would at least finally get an ending, one way or another. Besides, right now he was so excited and afraid that he didn't feel tired at all. He felt— ironically—alive. Then something shifted in his brain, and he hit the brakes, screeching to a halt. He lifted his head, listening to the silent city.

*What was* that? Eric thought. *Wait. THERE—*

He felt it. There was a distant tugging sensation in his head leading him forwards; gentle for now, but enough that he couldn't deny its existence.

*Oh shit,* he thought. *This is real. This is real. Maybe I'll see that guy in my head again.*

Eric had only had one vision outside of the Arrivals, and it was the one that drove him mad the most; it had occurred during an incident now imaginatively referred to as the Big Power Cut. A year ago, the entire national grid had gone down for a few seconds. Had it occurred in the middle of the day the story would have been a lot larger than it was—and it *was* large, with everything from Al Qaeda to a Fourth Arrival getting the blame before it all died down again—but in the twenty-four-hour news cycle, a gentle reassurance from Downing Street got people's attention back onto whatever the next hot topic was. Since then, of course, the government had explained about the existence of the Chisel, how it related to the Big Power Cut, and—although they didn't mention it by name—what had been going on at Project Orobouros. The purpose of the 'wind farm' at the Ladybower Reservoir.

That must have been where the screaming man was, the one Eric had woken up in the middle of the night and seen in his mind. At the time, he'd desperately wished he'd been able to go with Mickey up there and scope the place out, but even Mickey had come back with nothing. But Eric wasn't having a vision *now*, so that meant this couldn't be—

No. That didn't matter. There was simply no time to waste on such thoughts. Eric followed the pull, heart racing, letting it lead him forwards, even if he knew where it was most likely drawing him. He was in the city centre, the permanently-dead streets and buildings rising up around him like a concrete prison, when he noticed the young woman walking slowly along the side of the road. She was bent at the waist as if in pain.

Eric heard her quiet sobs as he drew closer. Did she need help? Was she just another nutcase? The latter was certainly possible; very few of the people left inside the city centre were safe to approach.

*You don't have time for this!* Eric told himself. *The Arrival could—*

But she looked hurt. He couldn't just leave her. Cursing his inconvenient sense of common decency, Eric pedalled towards her. He could check quickly, and *call* for help if it was needed, tell an ambulance where she was. The city still had a few. He pulled up alongside her.

The woman was in her mid-twenties, a skinny, scruffy brunette in an old blouse and jeans—most likely homeless, as the few remaining people in the city centre were—and she didn't look up at all when Eric stopped next to her.

"Miss? Are you okay?"

Nothing.

He repeated it a little louder. "Miss? Are you okay?"

The woman continued her wobbling steps up the street, oblivious to Eric's presence. Okay then—one last try, and then he would leave.

He put the bike's stand down, dismounted, reached out and touched the woman's shoulder.

"Miss—"

It was like he'd tried to grab a stray, frightened dog.

Her eyes immediately snapped open and she fell upon Eric like an octopus with knuckles. Her screams were an almost rhythmic repetition.

"Aah! Aah! Aah! Aah!" Her bony hands and knees hammered Eric's body and head, a nasty blow catching Eric's temple as a knee connected sharply with Eric's hip bone. Eric staggered backwards on his bike, more surprised than hurt, his legs going over the bike's front wheel as he retreated, causing him to fall. He gasped as he hit the concrete, feeling a *crunch* beneath his hips that somehow didn't hurt. He managed to turn his head at the last minute to avoid more serious damage, but even so he was lightly stunned at the impact. Black spots danced in front of his eyes while he tried to blink the world back into focus, wincing in pain as he watched the woman running away up the street. Eric couldn't believe it.

*Crazy fucking bitch!* he thought. *What's her problem—*

There was no time for this. No time at all. Cursing himself for stopping, Eric untangled himself from his bike and got to his feet, groaning as he swung his leg back over the frame, bruised hip protesting. The pull in his head was urgent now, heightening his already peaked sense of time ticking away. Then he saw the bike's front wheel and realized what that *crunch* had been. The wheel's rim was now badly buckled, rendering the bike un-rideable. He couldn't believe it.

"*FUCK!*" he screamed into the sky, dismounting and throwing the bike to the ground. Then for good measure, he picked the whole thing up and threw it across the road.

*There's no time for this,* Eric thought. *Get running! That's the only option!*

Then he realized that his mini binoculars were still in the bike's pannier bag. He rushed over, fished them out and stuffed them awkwardly into his back pocket. With some more industrial-grade swearing, Eric started running. Puffing and blowing—but not too much, he cycled everywhere after all, and his fitness was good—he reached the on-ramp down to the ring road more quickly than expected. Along the way, he passed the woman again—he crossed to the other side of the road—and expected her to hurl abuse. He certainly had some of his own ready, but she didn't even look up. She was back to shuffling along, head down. Shaking his head angrily, he pumped his limbs, legs aching as he began to approach the Ground Zero lookout.

# Chapter Three:

# Eric Hears the Horns

***

### Eric

Eric was unsurprised when he breathlessly approached the lookout point and saw twenty or so people standing there. There sometimes were regular folks with the same idea, binoculars and scanners in hand, whenever a hint of a Fourth Arrival was on the news.

Ground Zero lookout point wasn't an official name. It was just a spot on one of the elevated parts of the ring road where it was still possible to get a view of the place. All of the nearby roads leading anywhere truly near to Ground Zero had been closed off and guard points installed. As Eric gasped in air, wishing he'd brought a water bottle, he could see that they'd put extra personnel on them today. It was incredible that the ring road wasn't permanently cordoned off years ago, but that would mean admitting publicly that Coventry was now dead. The view didn't show much anyway.

The lookout point was probably about a thousand feet away from Ground Zero, overlooking the overgrown mess that used to be Lady Herbert's Gardens, a small public green space.

From here, the side of the large Ground Zero building could be seen. It looked more like a temporary office building than a top-secret zone. Why spend a lot of money on something that might get flattened by a new Arrival turning up out of the blue? Shortly after, they'd drained the water from what had been Coventry's Millennium Place. The water had been a failed experiment, impeding the Stone Men's Third Arrival by precisely the number in the facility's name, so the Ground Zero building had been erected, a nondescript structure ostensibly designed to house and aid further research into the Stone Men's point of Arrival.

Initially, there had been an influx of what Eric dismissively referred to as conspiracy theorists—he did not actually consider himself a part of that particular family—into the all but abandoned city centre, camping out in the area around Ground Zero. After a few months, of course, nearly all of them had become bored and left.

Amateurs.

Eric's lungs screamed as he scanned the crowd. A horrible thought occurred to him. What if they were all there for the same reason as him, trying to 'claim' the effects of the Pointer Theory for themselves: aiming to be present at the locus of Arrival, and thus to achieve the same connection to the visitors that Andy Pointer had? No, as he drew closer, he realized that they were all standing in a familiar fashion: heads bent, shoulders tense, holding themselves, shuffling on the spot. He passed a hairy guy with a polo shirt and a heavy beer gut, bent over slightly just like the woman from earlier. What the hell was that about? Eric stood behind the crowd, looking up the ring road and saw three or four more spaced-out people heading his way, all shuffling along in the same manner. Panic struck him, and he tried to calm down.

No-one ever said anything about Pointer being affected like this, he thought. But this is maybe like the visions and things, people being affected differently? Eric wasn't sure he believed that. It's okay, he told himself. You're still on. This doesn't affect the Pointer Theory.

Eric had stopped maybe ten feet back from the loose gathering, sweaty and breathing hard, and not just from the run now. All of it—the people, and the strange, faint, GPS-like feeling in his head that was whispering to him—meant belief. This was the place to be. He looked around wildly. Eric had never experienced an actual Arrival close up. Now one was coming here... and he might be about to get on the inside of it all. There was a palpable sense of awe. It was happening. He'd made it... now, could he get any closer?

Visible from here, at a much shorter radius from the building, was the metal fence, and beyond that today stood a few armed guards. There were always blockades on the road leading in, but maybe if an Arrival did start, it might be chaos and then... who knew?

Wait, wait, Eric's brain asked him, what the fuck are we doing up here?!

He'd thought he was meaning to head past the lookout point and down the off-ramp—he doubted he could get closer but he wanted to try—but somehow, he'd followed that damn GPS feeling in his head on autopilot. That wasn't the plan... and yet, it didn't seem to be telling him to go any closer. What did that mean? Nothing ever arrived on the ring road. His headache was splitting. He wiped at his face, panicking. What should he do? He turned on the spot, feeling helpless and imagining time slipping away—

Pop.

What the hell was that? Eric staggered back a step. It had felt like a sharp slap in his mind. Something was happening.

Stay calm, he told himself. Look around.

He did. He spotted an older man standing at the back of the assembled group.

That's it, said his brain.

Most of the people here were right up against the lookout point roadside barrier, but this guy was the furthest back. He was black, wearing a suit... and his hands were behind his back. He was observing the scene like a schoolteacher overseeing a playground. He was the only person there, other than Eric, who wasn't a distressed semi-zombie.

More importantly, he was also looking right at Eric... and Eric realized that he'd felt the popping sensation when he'd looked at the man.

Holy SHIT, Eric thought, but then caught himself. He had to stay cool, check it out quickly—something had brought him to this man after all—and carry on. He could find out if this stranger was a Pointer guy too, while he was at it. But what would he do if this man was a Pointer guy? Eric raised a hand in greeting. The man didn't return the wave, but he did nod, that slow-eye-blink-with-tip-of-the-head gesture that only the most laid-back of people can use successfully.

GET ON WITH IT, Eric told himself. He jogged over. The suited man waited patiently.

"Hi," Eric said.

"Hello," the man drawled. Eric wondered if the guy might be drunk.

"What, uh... what brought you here?" Eric asked.

The man looked at Ground Zero. "Thought something might be going on," he said, unconsciously scratching at his stubbled cheek.

His voice was deep but a little hoarse, like he was or had been a heavy smoker. "Seen people heading this way. Don't see many normally. All of them were like this." He flipped a hand at the slowly growing throng. "But I notice that you don't seem that way."

"No, I'm..."

Eric didn't say, I'm feeling a strange kind of psychic link to you, and do you know anything about that? That was too weird, plus it sounded like a bad pickup line.

"Want to see if those Stone things show up," the man said. "They're slow, is my understanding. Take a while to start walking too. Never seen one myself though. You? You don't seem like..."

"Sorry, I've got to be quick, but I wanted to ask—" Eric began, but then he realized what was happening.

Connections, he thought, kicking himself with amazement. You know what this is! You read about this: people being drawn to other Stone Sensitives. That was true; he had read about it, and it was amazing to be experiencing it, but he had to just ignore this and fucking go—

"They're saying there are big giant white things out at sea," the man said, as if Eric hadn't spoken. "Or there were; now there's a lot of little ones all round the coast. Someone said on TV, it's like the few big ones split into lots of smaller ones."

"So they say," Eric said, even as the thought somehow made Eric think of insects. "Well, nice to meet you, anyway." He began to sway but offered his hand as he did so, meaning to give a quick shake and then run. The man nodded and took it.

"Jesus!" Eric screamed as a jolt of electricity shot through his arm and caused him to fall to the ground for the second time in half an hour. The pain of the fall paled in comparison to the stabbing shock.

"Fuck!" the man shouted. Eric looked up to see his new acquaintance had jumped back a foot, holding his own arm. Eric gripped his too—Christ, that had hurt—and glanced up from the ground at the shuffling crowd; they hadn't even turned at his cries. The man's lazy eyes were now alert and glaring at Eric reproachfully.

"What the fuck?" the man asked.

"I know nothing about it!" Eric barked back. "What the hell did you do?"

"Nothing!"

Eric got up, flustered, but his brain was already going to work as his arm throbbed, the pain starting to disappear. Connections or not, he'd never read about anything like that. This was brand new phenomena.

He didn't know what to do. He probably couldn't get closer anyway and here—

The glaring man suddenly thrust his hand out. "Do it again," he said.

"No!"

"It's not going to kill you, is it?" the man said, pointing at his hand. "Look at those people. Now look at us by comparison. Want to figure out what's going on here?" He pointed at his hand as if to say, Here's a clue.

Eric turned back and forth on the spot, flustered.

"Jesus—"

He stepped forwards and gripped the man's hand firmly with his own.

Nothing happened. The man nodded slowly as if to say, Okay then, and let go. He produced a hip flask. He took a small pull and grunted slightly as the liquor hit his throat. Eric noticed the frayed edges on the man's jacket cuff, the ground-in dirt on the sleeve, and put two and two together. The suit had fooled Eric. The man was homeless too.

The shock was wearing off, and Eric made the decision to get running again; he realized that his headache was even worse.

"Harry," the man announced, interrupting Eric's thoughts.

"Eric... Listen, how do you feel?" Eric asked, wincing. "Any different?"

"Not really, apart from my fucking headache getting worse."

"Mmm. Same here... Wait, you had a headache too?"

"Yeah, really bad—"

Then they all felt it.

A cry went up from everyone gathered there, Eric and Harry included, although theirs wasn't as pained and desperate as the already amped-up crowd around them. Immediately afterwards came the wave of little sounds; the skittering, scratching noise of tiny detritus coming from all around as a light wind blew ominously across the concrete. There had been zero wind a moment ago.

Then the pressure dropped.

Eric's ears popped slightly. The air became colder. Everyone was now standing ducked slightly, as if there were low flying birds around their heads. Blood thrummed in Eric's veins as he pulled out his binoculars. In hand, he looked through them at Ground Zero; the guards were on their radios.

"Anything?" Harry asked urgently. Despite his laid-back demeanour, Eric realized that Harry was scared.

"No," Eric breathlessly replied. "I just wish I could get... Wait, can you feel that?"

Harry nodded in surprised reply, eyes wide, jaw clamped shut.

The shuffling people around them began murmuring louder.

"Don't like it," Harry muttered, backing away slightly. The growing, shuffling party moved forwards now, all of them tight against the railing. Harry looked at Ground Zero. "Something's... coming. It's coming here now. Isn't it?"

"Yes," Eric whispered.

The Stone Men are coming.

The growing breeze flicked dust against his face in sharp little pings.

"Oh," hissed Harry. "Oh. Oh shit. Look. Look."

Eric quickly looked through the binoculars but discovered that was actually doing him a disservice—what he was seeing was so big that to zoom in close was to miss it. The skittering sound increased in volume as his jacket fluttered in the wind, goosebumps popping up on his arms.

"Oh... it... it-it..." he stammered, and then gave up. He didn't have the words. He let his jaw hang open, his arms limp at his sides, as he realized that he'd been wrong all along; this was different. Eric watched the Fourth Arrival truly begin and understood that this was not like the other Arrivals, and this would not be a Stone Man.

The sky above Ground Zero began to change colour.

Not the whole sky. The view above Coventry was still the same washed-out late September grey from the city outskirts to the horizon.

But the sky directly above Ground Zero looked as if that region of air were water and someone was pouring greyish-black ink into it that dissolved and spread. That idea might conjure an image of clouds but that would be inaccurate. This darkness spread as slowly and evenly as a dispersing liquid but looked as controlled as paint leaving a roller. It wasn't opaque. Eric could just make out the buildings behind it.

"Fuck… fuck…" Eric gasped, watching the blackness grow and grow, a shadow emerging out of nothing. The distant yells of Ground Zero guards floated over to them as the light wind continued to blow, and Eric realized that the blackness was forming edges, symmetrical ones.

"It's a triangle," Harry croaked, stating the now-obvious, but it was an immense understatement. It was an impossible triangle, spreading out evenly. Its shape was still uncertain, its edges uneven, but it was clear what it was becoming, growing to a single upward point. It made no noise at all as it grew. The breeze, the distant yells of the guards, and the incessant babbling of the Shufflers were all still clearly audible.

It seemed to have reached maximum size now—if Eric had to guess, he would say about sixty feet—and hung there in the air as if it had been there all day, pointing towards the sky.

"I don't believe it," Harry croaked. "It's really happening."

"Let's try to get down there!" Eric gasped, the wild idea taking him—Stone Man or not—as the wind blew harder. "Come on!"

"What? You won't get past the blockade anyway!"

"You know it's gonna be all hands on deck right now!" Eric yelled. "At least one of the blockades has got to have just emptied! We won't get past the fence, but we can get close!"

"Bollocks! You want to get closer to that?" Harry jabbed a finger at the thing hovering impossibly in the sky, a giant triangular shadow that dominated their sight. "Does… Jesus, does anything about that look like a good thing to you?"

Then the triangle began to move downwards.

Watching something of that size moving unassisted in mid-air was incredible. Eric checked the building. Yes, personnel were running out of Ground Zero—soldiers and civilians and people in white coats pouring out like ants seeing the kettle of boiling water descending towards their nest. Eric watched, rapt. The base of the triangle passed through the building's roof harmlessly, proving to be as much of an intangible dark shadow as it looked. Eric wondered if it would keep going, descending into the earth, an immense black arrowhead moving in the opposite direction to which it was pointing, but its movement suddenly stopped. Eric couldn't see the bottom of the shadowy shape any more, but he guessed that its progress had ceased when its bottom edge reached the ground.

He suddenly began to feel very afraid. That moment of touchdown, of Arrival... Something went through him. Now he wanted to run.

"Is the Chisel in there?" Harry whispered, startling Eric. The question was a good one. Was it? Eric didn't know. No-one knew. A lot of people online thought it was in Scotland.

"I don't... know," Eric whispered, squinting through his binoculars. Oh shit, he thought. Is that what this thing has come for? Is it some sort of Chisel-neutralising device? Hazmat suits were being distributed frantically down on the site. No-one seemed to know what to do, which wasn't surprising. About a third of the black triangle jutted out of the top of the building, looking like some kind of ill-conceived, mid-eighties architectural addition. "Ground Zero is the place the Arrivals always happened," Eric whispered. "But those white things were out on the coast, so why is this..." He didn't want to say triangle as it sounded too stupid: why is this triangle here, as if he were complaining about an inappropriately parked steamroller. "Why the fuck is it here?" he finished.

Harry's gaze was glued to the giant black shape. "Like you said. This is where they come—"

A noise filled the air, so deafening both of them covered their ears, screaming in pain. It was so loud that they couldn't even hear each other's cries.

The Horns, Eric thought wildly. This is what they sound like.

The Horns were legendary on the conspiracy forums. Eyewitnesses at the First Arrival had described the incredible rasping, bassy sound. There was video footage of it but all that could be heard on there was distortion. Here they were, live and in living audio and Christ were they loud. The descriptions hadn't done them justice. It was like hearing a foghorn underwater and up close. He glanced at the Shufflers—no change.

A cold snap suddenly hit, so harsh even the Shufflers flinched. It was freezing.

Several small drops of blood dripped from Eric's nose as his headache peaked sharply with a snap, and then the Horns cut out abruptly. There was a tumbling sound that Eric realized was the Ground Zero building's front wall collapsing. The shadow had become a solid mass. It was no longer a triangle; it had become an elongated prism shape: a giant, uneven Toblerone bar, maybe eighty feet long. It was no longer see-through in the slightest. The thing was made of a very familiar-looking, stone-like substance textured greyish-brown. Its texture, while it did indeed look like it was made of the same mysterious material as the Stone Men (nothing on earth existed that was even close to that substance, but dammit if it didn't look like stone), had markings all over it. Not patterns, because patterns repeat. To Eric's eyes these looked random: looping trenches and arcing shallow lines intersecting all over its surface. Eric couldn't see an inch of it that wasn't covered by a groove or intentional-looking dent. Screams emanated from Ground Zero. Clearly there were people still inside the building— or out of sight behind the Prism—who had been injured by the falling rubble or anything else that might have impacted human flesh in the instant the Prism appeared. Amazingly, only the front wall and roof at the front edge of the Ground Zero building had been damaged. Clearly, when dealing with Stone Men, the government had decided to try to build the place Stone Man strong after all.

The Prism filled the Ground Zero compound and extended a little way beyond it, smashing the fence; one of the guards had been standing just inside the mesh fence. He was squealing in high-pitched agony, cries that quickly began to gurgle and ebb. He was on the ground, stuck half-under the front of the Prism, flattened from the waist down. Eric watched in horror, but his mind was screaming at him.

*THE FENCE IS DOWN! IF YOU CAN GET PAST A BLOCKADE, YOU CAN GET INTO THE GROUNDS, OH MY GOD—*

"Let's get out of here! Let's go!" Harry barked, grabbing at Eric's arm, even as Eric began to turn, intending to make a run towards the nearest blockade.

"I'm gonna try to—" Eric shouted, before both men froze.

They'd felt the rumbling begin. They looked at the chaos at Ground Zero, the soldiers now pointlessly setting up and aiming mortars at the thing and waiting for the signal. They heard an approaching helicopter, but the rumbling was in the ground *below* them.

"What *is* th—" Eric began, before realising where the rumbling was coming from.

Something was coming up the ring road's off-ramp. *Several* somethings.

Several *big* somethings.

***

# Chapter Four:

# Maria Listens to the Radio

***

## <u>Maria</u>

*They're everywhere. Get out of here. They're everywhere. Get out of here.*

Maria gripped the rental car's steering wheel tightly, rocking a little in her seat. She'd been battling the same chant since she'd run from the beach. She'd jogged rather than ran back to the car, because a run could turn into panic and then the chant could turn into a scream. She'd fought too hard for too damn long to let that happen.

*They're* not *everywhere. They're on the coastline. You prepared for this and you have a flight all ready. Just get to the airport, and you will be gone in no time.*

Then she'd hit the traffic.

Within thirty minutes of driving, not only were the small streets around town almost gridlocked, but it seemed a lot of people had the same idea as she did. A lot of the Midlands cities had developed Arrival protocols for transport and evacuation, but— despite some half-hearted efforts from activists and vague promises from local politicians—the coastal areas hadn't. The Stone Men had never walked that far. Now the errors of complacency were clear. In the age of social media—even with sketchy and rapidly worsening communication signals—the news of the beach Arrival had spread like wildfire, and nothing got the country off their backsides like a good old-fashioned Arrival. People had learned not to take *any* chances. Everyone on the coast was now heading inland. Most of the cars around her contained full families, and all were at least half-full of possessions. She tried to ignore the connection of being in another traffic jam during an Arrival.

*You've allowed for a* lot *of time,* she told herself. *You'll make the flight. It's okay—*

It didn't help.

The shops and businesses lining the streets turned painfully slowly into trees, business parks and the occasional short row of crash barriers as she moved out of town and onto the dual carriageways. All the while something inside her *knew* something was up. It was bouncing off the walls in there, smashing itself into bloody bits like a trapped and panicking animal.

*We have to be* way *the heck out of here,* it told her. *Antarctica. The moon.*

The radio was cutting in and out so badly that it was unlistenable, making her more on edge. She turned it off.

Three hours later, she'd only covered twenty miles. Her tank was getting low, but the road sign told her that she could refuel in one mile. It also told her that she was about to pass the town of Louth.

A pang of guilt lanced its way through her.

*Ruth.*

Yes, that was where Ruth lived. There was no time to think about that. Except of course, there *was*, but that was just a *detail*.

Eventually, she reached the petrol station, a large one by rural standards: twelve pumps. The forecourt was packed. She was four cars away from a pump when her brain suddenly barked at her.

The force was so great that she cried out. That had been like an electric shock. The people in the car next to her—three kids and their young, hip but tense-looking parents—turned to stare at her, startled by her sudden movement. Then they all suddenly arched in *their* seats too.

Noise filled Maria's car. But her windows were up. As she screamed and covered her ears pointlessly, she realized the noise *wasn't coming from outside.* The people at the pumps flinched and bent double, trying to ward it off, and Maria thought, *Here it is, here it is, and no I don't want to die, no—*

The noise was low and bassy and brassy and rough and *oh,* it was *loud.* It was like having an out of control truck bearing down on you in slow motion, the sound of its blaring horn still deafening but slowed to a whale-like moan. Maria's brain physically throbbed.

Then it stopped. Everything returned to normal. She gasped and drew in a series of rapid breaths as the parents in the nearby car started doing the same, trying to comfort their crying children in the back seat. Maria tried to steady herself. There was no point in asking questions that she didn't have the answers to. This was just more weirdness and the plan hadn't changed.

*But this never happened before,* she thought. *This is worse; this is going to be worse—*

The rest of the forecourt slowly got back on track, calling to each other and asking what they thought had just happened. The enormity of the situation was beginning to sink in. That had been a demonstration of a raw and far-reaching power far beyond anything anyone had seen before, but even *that* had felt like a glitch, a hiccup. The stuttering, just-warming-up growl of a V8 that hasn't been taken for a spin in a while.

Maria tried the radio again. White noise. She checked her phone, but its data wheels were merely spinning pointlessly. It was like trying to use it just after midnight on New Year's Eve, the network overwhelmed with everyone trying at once.

*That,* she thought, *or something else is affecting it.*

The cars began to move. Eventually, she reached the pump and refilled her tank, hand shaking on the nozzle, and went into the shop to pay. The hubbub inside was far less, the usual stoic public British silence. She grabbed some water and got in line; it was maybe twenty people long. Behind the counter, one of the attendants had a little radio that was chattering away—either his worked or the signal had come back—and Maria's straining couldn't hear it from her place in line. There was a sudden, deafening roar that came from one side of the building and then shot away into the distance. Everyone looked through the window and saw three fighter planes disappearing over the horizon.

"Got to be going to Coventry," a red-faced, barrel-chested man further up the line muttered to the middle-aged fellow in mechanic's overalls standing next to him. The way the man had spoken so close to the other's face made Maria wonder if they were friends. She was thinking about asking if they'd heard anything new, when the young, well-groomed man two people in front of her gave a little triumphant cry; the crappy sound of smartphone-speaker audio made its bass-free way down the line. Everyone straightened up to listen, and some frantically pulled out their phones to see if they had anything, Maria included. No dice.

"Hold it up! Turn it up!" Maria called. The man with the phone looked surprised but did as she asked, holding his Samsung straight-armed in the air. "Thank you," she said, reddening a little. Maria was close enough to see the screen. The line stopped moving. The people at the counter stopped serving and nobody cared. Those who couldn't see listened, and it was like hearing that noise all over again. The effect was the same.

Another statement. Another signal that the world as they knew it was about to be smashed.

Maria wasn't going to be flying anywhere.

"... brings the, the total of... planes to... two..." The middle-aged and suited anchor drew out the *oo* of *two* in a gentle whisper. It was as if he was reluctant to move onto whatever was next. The presenter listened to a voice in his ear, looking distressed.

"Uh... we're hearing unconfirmed reports of a... third..." he stammered, "but we'll... once we have..."

"We have a feed from the latest crash site, Martin," his female co-anchor said, "and we obviously understand that this may be upsetting to some viewers so... this is us giving, this is, of course, uh, fair warning..."

The feed cut to the smoking wreckage of a commercial plane. It was wingless and tailless. Only the broken main cabin lay mainly intact at the bottom of a blackened scar in the earth. Rescue and clean-up crews swarmed around it.

"Let us assure you," Martin said, speaking over the footage, "our chopper pilots that are, uh, providing this feed for us are keeping very low but, uh, we don't know how long we're going to be allowed to bring you this... the Civil Aviation Authority are confirming that all flights are immediately grounded until further notice." Martin sounded uncertain, weak. "We'll update you as soon as we have information, uh, as to who or what brought the planes down, but...

*uh, I'm being told that... Number... yes, Downing Street has announced that a statement will be forthcoming within the hour..."*

Maria's plan was defeated. She physically gasped at the thought. The feeling of being *trapped* began to creep up her neck again.

*You can do this,* she tried telling herself, uncharacteristically kind and supportive. *Hey, come back. Okay, so you can't fly out.*

Her mind whirled as she screwed her hands into fists. What other options were there? She found the centre of the growing whirlwind, the stillness. *Take it in stages,* she thought. *Small steps, just like Dr Harris used to say. Can you sail out, maybe?*

It was possible. She was still near the coast, and on the right side for Europe at that. She'd need to get to a port—

The news continued, and it almost felt as if God were laughing at her thoughts.

*"And... we are getting now-confirmed news of ..."* He paused again, and Maria didn't think he was listening to a producer this time. She was hearing a man getting the same sinking feeling as her. *"... and an incident with a ferry to... Calais..."*

*Oh my God,* Maria thought. *Oh God, no.*

*"The... it appears that the ferry has... the SeaWays ferry,* Yonder Sails, *has been abandoned by all hands, including passengers, and that..."*

A longer pause. Maria didn't dare to even breathe.

*"We expect to be able to... Okay, it seems that the lifeboats were not detached and that those on board have... jumped over the side and the ferry itself is still..."* There was another pause. *"That water is very cold, and we don't know about the ages of the passengers yet; we haven't been given the manifest because, as you know, like a lot of you, we're having, uh, a lot of intermittent technical difficulties and*

information that's, uh, confirmed *because, uh, obviously we have to be very careful, but...*"

It was awful. It was just awful.

"*... but there are survivors in the water and the authorities are trying to rescue as many as they can... There are unconfirmed reports of... trouble with other vessels. Coastguard and navy resources have been stretched thin by, uh... Okay, an update... Yes, the* Yonder Sails *is unmanned right now and adrift, and they're wanting to get that under control asap to make sure it, uh, doesn't drift into the path of another vessel. We expect to have confirmation any minute now of the shipping lanes being closed... that's as well as the earlier statement from Ryan Whoberley of Eurostar that their Channel Tunnel routes are closed until further notice as a safety precaution...*"

Maria felt cold. Her knuckles were white on her clenched fists.

*The shipping lanes. The planes. All off-limits. She was trapped.*

*They're closing us off,* Maria thought. *The Stone Men, their masters. They're doing something to our minds when we try to leave by any means. The people jumped off the ferry... Did the* planes *come down because the people on board, the pilots—*

She felt her bottom lip start to go.

"*We'll update you as soon as we have something more concrete about what's happened in... Coventry, something has happened at Ground Zero... We're not sure exactly but there have been unconfirmed reports of an Arrival and—*"

The image of the newsreader froze along with the sound. A few seconds passed and the dreaded Spinning Disc of Buffering appeared over the image. A moan of dismay went up from the line, as if their team had just squandered a chance on goal. The man continued to hold the phone over his head, and after a minute, someone at the counter engaged, and then the line was moving once more. The news didn't come back.

Maria paid and walked back to her car in a daze. She dropped into the seat and started the engine, trying to focus, to make a new plan, but nothing would come. Then the tears did, and she couldn't stop them, jamming her fist in her mouth as she headed into the slow-moving traffic once more.

*Higher ground* was the only plan left.

*Think of something better once you've calmed down,* she tried to tell herself, but it wasn't enough. She was stuck, oh Jesus, she was stuck, and it was worse than she could have ever—

The radio gave mainly white noise now as she crawled along. Her phone's bars would intermittently come back, but who could she call? The internet was working so slowly that by the time anything even started to come up, the signal had gone again. Whenever radio speech kicked in—Five Live seemed to be the strongest signal—she turned the radio up.

"—*more information you can call Quinnair directly for a statement, the number, uh, should be on our website now,*" the announcer said. He sounded young for talk radio, maybe his early thirties. "*They have asked us to remind you that they will only be taking calls from immediate family members of passengers,*" he said. "*That noise, that, uh,* sound, *seems to have been heard around the country, a lot of you are saying you heard it, and I apologize for my outburst because we heard it here too and it was, well...*" He paused, obviously overwhelmed. "*It looks like the traffic is going to get worse as that sound seems to have caused a lot of accidents, uh, very quickly on that note, Sandy with the traffic... Please remember, it's best to stay off the roads right now...*"

"*Tim, I can't stress that enough,*" said an older woman's voice, obviously Sandy. "*You won't get far today. I've never,* phew, *I've never seen anything like this in my career. Here we go, it's a long list...*"

She reeled them off. Maria realized this wasn't running-away traffic, this was from people doing seventy-plus miles an hour on motorways when *that* racket had slammed into their brains. Sandy was suddenly interrupted.

"*Sorry, Sandy,*" Tim said, "*but we've got... we've got Stephen Bannatyne, and he's just, uh, he's in our helicopter on the outskirts of Coventry. I understand that we may not actually be allowed in, uh, in Coventry airspace right now, Stephen...*"

*Cov,* Maria thought. Her hands shook on the wheel. *Oh, sugar.*

There was a burst of white noise. It ended and Stephen was talking, his voice distorting over a low-level whine in the background that had to be from the chopper blades.

"*... see Nuneaton being evacuated as we came through,*" Stephen said, "*and quickly, they've had their protocols ready for some time, but central Coventry seems to be almost empty other than a gathering right by Ground Zero, perhaps trying to see the Arrival, and we ourselves are quite far away from it.*"

*Arrival,* Maria thought. *It. We're quite far away from* it. *What was* it? She felt cold. Stephen's voice was thin, breathless. The man sounded *scared.* What the heck had turned up?

"*The structure is very large,*" Stephen said. Maria almost felt relieved. Not a Stone Man, then, but... a structure?

"*We're just outside of the ring road,*" Stephen continued, "*but I don't know how much longer that's going to be the case as we're now being... escorted by two air force Harriers and they're telling us to move—*"

"*You can't get any closer?*" Tim asked. "*A ground broadcast?*"

"*No, Tim,*" said Stephen, and dammit if he didn't sound just a little bit testy. Maria didn't blame him. "*Access to the ring road has now been blocked off, and of course, any route to Ground Zero was shut down the moment the Arrival occurred—*"

"*Still no information on the Chisel being deployed?*" Tim asked, interrupting.

"*No, although there's a lot of talk on social media that it has, in fact, been deployed and is en route to... Wait, I'm seeing, there's, there's something moving down on the ring road, I think...*" There was a pause. "*Hold on...*"

The *hold on* was almost off-mic. The background whine filled the silence.

"*Stephen? Do we still have you?*"

"*Yes, I'm here, Tim. We've been moved on from the airspace; we're heading back out of the city centre now. Things seem to be going into lockdown. We're going to see how far out we have to go. They might peel off shortly and let us—*"

Stephen's signal broke up.

"*Stephen? We'll get Stephen back as soon as we can and...*"

A quiet idea popped into Maria's head, one that she hadn't allowed in for years.

*You could go to Coventry*, it said. *There will be people at Ground Zero who know more than the public know.*

No. They would make her a guinea pig. Her name would be on record as a First Arrival Encounter, and they had her eyewitness statement—although she hadn't told them that it had *looked* at her. They'd kept calling. People tried to come to visit. It had been another reason she'd left, dropped off the grid.

*That was five years ago*, she thought. *They might be able to protect you. You could stop running. You could come* home.

And she *was* trapped. Her head swam, leaning towards the idea as hungrily as a double shift worker reaching for the snooze button.

*No*, she told herself. *I have to...*

With perfect timing, an exit was approaching, its path as packed with cars as the main trunk road.

Louth.

Ruth.

*Last chance,* she thought. *You could stay at Ruth's, regroup at least. The roads will be quieter tomorrow. You have to accept you aren't going anywhere today. You can get out in the morning—*

Maria let out a yell of frustration and rocked back and forth in her seat, yanking herself against the steering wheel.

*Didn't you really, really want to make it right with Ruth anyway?* she asked herself. *After this, you're never coming back for sure, right? The exit for Louth is right there. Take it.*

Then she realized that something was happening on the radio. She'd been so lost in her thoughts that she hadn't even noticed it.

*"—in the air, maybe a hundred feet or so up, and apparently in greater number now than earlier, although they are apparently gone again..."* Tim cleared his throat. *"We have that eyewitness recording, do you have that ready... yes... okay, here it is again—"*

*They?* Maria turned up the radio's volume dial with a shaking hand. *Something's been in the air? A they?* Where was this coming from anyway? Coventry? Tim was still in the studio and sounding like a man both horrified and eager, knowing that he was a part of a terrible piece of history. Maria didn't know his surname. She didn't normally listen to Five Live apart from their movie podcast. *"And before we play this, we'd like to add that we're getting a lot of texts now saying you can hear us again, so thank you for letting us know. Uh, apparently texting is better than email because we're still having some trouble with that."* An unpleasant thought crept into Maria's head.

*They're doing this. Are they doing it on purpose? Are they trying to stop us communicating?*

She didn't think that would be the case, didn't think they really gave a damn if people communicated or not. She remembered the words of her old philosophy professor at university.

*Does the fisherman care if the maggots in his creel are talking to one other, trying to formulate a master plan to escape?*

Was she—was everyone—so helpless?

"*Here's that recording again,*" Tim said, "*made earlier just outside of Bridlington.*"

Bridlington. That was on the coast. Wherever the audio footage had been recorded there was a lot of background noise. Cars, people shouting to one another. It was a child being interviewed, a boy maybe five or six years old, being prompted just off-microphone by a faint woman's voice nearby, presumably his mother.

"*The man... it was a man and there was another man,*" the kid said.

"*There was more than one? For sure?*" That was the reporter's voice, a woman.

"*Yeah.*"

The kid suddenly started talking again, away from the mic, as if he were moving around. The reporter moved to pick up his speech.

"*—wasn't there,*" the kid was saying, "*see-through. It was up there and it went in and out, like a... uh...*"

"*Like... flickering?*" the reporter asked.

"*Yeah. There was another man too, more men, the same.*"

"*In the air? How high in the air? As high as... as a house?*"

"*No, higher. Two houses on top of each other.*"

A pause. When the reporter spoke again, her voice shook a little.

"*And what were they doing?*"

There was a pause.

"*Nothing,*" the kid said eventually. "*They were just standing in the air. Then they went away.*"

The reporter's voice started off-mic as she replied. Maria understood why. The woman would be looking around herself. Unsettled. Creeped out.

"*So they stood in the air and then they just disappeared?*"

Pause.

"*No,*" the kid replied, and sounded like he was starting to cry. "*They moved first.*"

Pause. Someone ran past in the background and yelled something.

"*They moved... moved how?*"

"*Lower. They moved lower down.*"

The background street noise cut abruptly as the live studio feed came back. Tim, the radio anchor, was quiet. It was horrible. Maria couldn't help herself; she looked out of her window too. Nothing in the sky, but as her gaze fell upon the other stationary cars she saw that every adult out there was looking at the sky too. A few people had even stepped out of their cars.

"*We now go to, uh... Kevin, in, uh... Kevin?*" Tim said quietly, clearly unsettled and needing Kevin to help him out.

"*Hi, Tim, very interesting audio there of course, but there aren't a lot of witnesses around here in Bournemouth, I'm afraid,*" said Kevin, saving Tim's backside by giving his location. There was chaos in the background of his feed. "*Even those we've spoken to were in a hurry and didn't want to be recorded. Many corroborated the idea that the, uh, figures in the sky and on the beaches don't seem to show up on camera—*"

Maria would remember that line for the rest of her life. People can see them, but cameras can't? That didn't make any sense; she knew the human eye worked the same as a camera, picking up light, so why wouldn't it—

The answer came to her.

*We're perceiving them directly with our brains, not our eyes,* she thought, hand over her mouth. *We're 'seeing' them on some other level. Maybe they don't even really look like that. Maybe that's all our brains can handle, the best we can do. Oh my God…*

Her stomach clenched as Kevin, the new voice, continued.

*"Obviously, a lot of people here are very upset, and not just because they're being evacuated again,"* he said. Car horns beeped in the background. *"We've tried to speak to some of the military, but there aren't any answers forthcoming—"*

*"Kevin, I'm sorry,"* said Tim, butting in as yet another new plate had to be spun, *"but we've got to go back to Stephen in Coventry again as something is happening—"*

*"YES, TIM,"* said Stephen, breathlessly, and the hairs on Maria's arms went up when she heard his raised voice, her knuckles whitening against the steering wheel. There was no increase in background noise that required him to talk more loudly. Stephen was excited… or scared. *"THERE'S… WE'RE TRYING TO FIND A CLEAR SPOT TO LAND AS A PRECAUTION BECAUSE SOMETHING IS DEFINITELY HAPPENING. THERE'S BEEN A-A NOTABLE DROP IN PRESSURE AND IT'S…"* He paused. When he came back, it was clear—he was terrified. *"IT'S COLD, IT'S SUDDENLY BECOME VERY COLD—"*

*"How far away are you from Ground Zero now, Stephen?"* Tim asked.

*"PERHAPS ABOUT A MILE. WE'RE SETTING DOWN NOW IN A… A FOOTBALL FIELD, THERE'S NO-ONE HERE AND… WE MIGHT HAVE SEEN SOMETHING AT GROUND ZERO. OUR LINE OF SIGHT WAS BLOCKED BY OUR ESCORTS, BUT WE GLIMPSED THE*

*STRUCTURE, AND IT WAS LIKE A LARGE TRIANGULAR SHAPE, VERY LARGE... WAIT..."*

There was a moment of silence from both men, Stephen checking whatever he was checking and Tim waiting patiently. He could allow a full five seconds of dead air before the emergency broadcast signal took over.

*"THERE'S—"* His voice vanished, as for a brief moment, all Maria could hear, all *anyone* could hear, was that deafening sound again. Maria screamed, unable to even hear herself as she clutched at her ears. Around her, the people who had stepped out of their cars bent over in pain. Some of the vehicles around her twitched slightly, bumping harmlessly together.

*"Oh Jesus, make it stop—"* she screamed, the words cutting off abruptly as she realized that the noise was over, and much quicker than before. That had been a little *brap* by comparison. She looked through the window, wild-eyed and gasping, as the exit ramp to Louth loomed closer. She had to call Ruth *now.* With a shaking hand, she unlocked her phone; she had bars, but would the signal actually—

The noise happened again. She dropped her phone as her hands flew up to try to block out that terrible sound. This time, it *wasn't stopping—*

*What if it never stops,* Maria thought, crazily.

Then it did, yet again, and Maria cried out in relief. Was this going to keep happening forever? She remembered that *pain plus resistance equals suffering*, and this time, she openly let the tears come as she fumbled in the footwell for the dropped phone. Tim came back to her speakers, gasping himself.

*"Uh... uh... sorry, everyone,"* he said, breathing hard. *"Uh, I need a moment, and... I know that's a cardinal sin in radio... uh... ha ha..."* Tim was rallying magnificently, but his fear would not be masked.

*"You… call us, text us, let us know what you experienced."* His speech became more rapid, his voice stronger, falling into a rare moment of radio sincerity. *"We're in this together, please don't forget that. Don't be frightened, or at least try not to let fear get the better of you, and we* will *get through this. Talk to us, we'll talk to you, and we're on this non-stop so stay with us. Everyone okay here?"* There was a pause as he checked the studio crew. *"Okay. We're good."*

Maria paused, oddly comforted by the moment. Maybe they *would* get—

*"Stephen, I think we have Stephen back,"* Tim said, *"Stephen did anything happen there?"*

*"YES, AND HOLD ON, TIM, BECAUSE I CAN SEE SOMETHING IN THE DISTANCE—"*

*"Stephen? Stephen, have you landed?* Are you safe?" Tim interrupted, actually stopping Stephen delivering the story to check that his colleague was okay. Suddenly a deafening drone buzzed over Maria's car, passing beyond her in a matter of seconds. She jerked forwards, looking through the windscreen as a military helicopter flashed onwards across the sky. Heading to Coventry?

*It* has *to be,* she thought. *There's something there, a structure. An Arrival. It's not just the coast. Nowhere here is safe. Go to Ruth's—*

Stephen was yelling into the microphone.

*"YES, WE'RE ON THE GROUND, BUT THERE'S… IT'S HARD TO TELL, TIM, BUT IT'S QUITE HIGH UP, IT'S LIKE… I CAN SEE IT IN THE DISTANCE, IN THE AIR—"*

*"What can you see?"* Tim asked urgently. *"Is it the triangular—"*

*"NO… THIS IS DIFFERENT, IT'S, IT'S* LIGHT, *IT'S MOVING, LIKE A FLICKERING, BUT IT'S VERY FAINT AND HARD TO SEE… IT'S ALL ALONG THE HORIZON—"*

*It?* Maria thought. *It's… WHAT IS IT? WHAT IS IT—*

"*IT'S MOVING,*" Stephen yelled. "*I THINK IT'S... MOVING TOWARDS US.*"

There was silence from both men.

"*Stephen...*" said Tim, trailing off, being handed the verbal baton and fumbling it. "*Stephen... Stephen, get... get— just get away—*" Everyone else in Tim's studio began to yell the same thing. Microphones moved quickly, making crumpling and popping sounds. Maria's heart was pounding, the phone call forgotten. Muffled cries came from the cars around her, yelps of dismay, of agreement, frantically urging Stephen to get out of there.

"*WE'RE TAKING OFF,*" Stephen yelled. He sounded harried but composed now, keeping people informed, doing his job. *This* was heroism; this was courage under fire. "*IT'S APPROACHING VERY FAST, IT'S BEHIND US NOW, BUT IT'S...*" He paused, as the background whine became louder, the feed of his voice becoming choppy as the helicopter rose. "*THIS THING IS HUGE, IT'S EVERYWHERE, ITTT—I—AU—G—*" Stephen's feed began to break up, but the in-studio audio was still clear.

"*Stephen,*" Tim yelled over the barking voices of his colleagues in the studio, "*what's happening? What's coming—*"

"*IF IT REACHES US,*" Stephen yelled, "*I DON'T KNOW, I DON'T THINK WE—*" He paused as something rattled, the chopper bumping in the air as it rose quickly. "*IT... IT'S NEARLY ON US, WE'RE NOT GOING TO... OUTRUN IT.*" He was still going even though he barely had the breath for the words, his voice high and gasping. "*IT'S HERE, HERE WE GO, HERE WE GO. AH, AH, IT'S TOO FAST, IT'S, AH, OH GOD—*"

Stephen's feed went completely dead.

Maria's hand flew back to her mouth. There was silence from the studio. After a few seconds, someone let out a muffled wail, as if they had their hand over their mouth too. Tim came to the mic with presumably nanoseconds before the dead-air emergency broadcast kicked in. He sounded concussed.

*"We've lost the link to... Stephen Bannatyne... We don't know what's happened. Let's hope he's alright. He..."* Tim gasped, then sniffed before saying something inappropriate to the situation. He was a national radio anchor, his words were pure speculation, and Stephen Bannatyne might have family who could be listening.

*He's talking to the people in the studio,* Maria thought. *Stephen Bannatyne's friends and colleagues.*

*"He might be alright,"* Tim said. *"It could be electromagnetic; it could just be something interfering with our broadcast equipment. I mean, that's been happening all day."* He took a deep breath, remembering the millions of people listening. *"We'll let you know as soon as we know anything about Stephen and what's happening in Coventry..."* He paused, listening to a voice in his ear. *"Okay, we're going to the phones."* He coughed.

Maria sat very still. *All along the horizon,* Stephen had said. He hadn't been talking about the structure. This was something new. Even Tim didn't seem to know what it was. Something to do with light—

*"We have Ashfaq Jilani over in south-east London,"* Tim said. *"Ashfaq, where were you, and did you hear—"*

She heard sirens and turned in her seat. The traffic in the opposite lane was reluctantly parting, protesting and beeping as a convoy of vehicles made its way through the Red Sea of traffic. It was two police cars and what looked like two military personnel carriers. She watched them make their noisy way into the distance, the traffic closing shut behind them like the teeth of a zipper. She felt a sensation of dark certainty and impending doom.

Maria saw that her phone had bars again. She snatched it up and dialled Ruth. She desperately needed to hear a friendly voice.

It rang—Ruth's number at least still existed, then—and Maria waited.

Later, she would wonder what might have happened if she hadn't called.

She never would have met Linda.

She never would have headed north.

She never would have had the worst night of her entire life.

Ruth—Marcus' only sister—answered the phone.

***

"Ruth? Ruthie—" That was as far as she got.

"*Oh my God!*" Ruth yelled, recognizing Maria's voice immediately. "Holy *shit,* the wanderer returneth! And you do it now, of all times? God*damn!*"

It was a total show, put on for Maria's benefit—Maria could hear the shake in Ruth's voice and knew the woman was freaked out too—but it still meant a lot. This was Ruth's way of saying, *No matter how you left, I won't treat you any differently.* It was unbelievably good to hear her voice.

"Hello, Ruthless," Maria said. "Are you okay? What's happening? Do you know?"

"Nothing happening here, but where are you? Are you still in Europe? I heard you were in Europe."

"I'm in the UK, Ruth," Maria whispered, and even as she told herself that she was only going to Ruth's to regroup, she knew it was a lie. The situation was set: she was stuck. The tears ran silently down her face, worse now thanks to Ruth's immediate warmth.

"Oh... oh. Where? Where are you?"

"Not far from you," Maria croaked. "Just outside Louth."

"*What?*" Ruth cried, so loud that it hurt Maria's ear. "Is that why you're calling? Oh my *God*, get here *now*."

This was already going differently than Maria had imagined. Warmer. Easier. No guilt.

*She's Good Family. This is what that feels like.*

"I know you were in a very dark place," Ruth said, "but *Jesus, you vanished on us*. Not a call? Not once?"

"I'm so sorry, Ruthie. Oh God, I'm *so sorry I just disappeared*, and I'll tell you all about it, but right now, I need to—" The tears took over and turned into sobs.

"*Shit,* sorry, no, wait," Ruth babbled, climbing down quickly as always. "*Sorry*, look, forget that shit. *I love you I love you I love you*, okay? Sorry."

"It's okay—"

"I just can't believe I'm talking to you. Is this your new number?"

"Yeah."

"Where are yyyyyyyyyyyyyyyyyyyyyy—" Ruth's voice became a sonic flatline. It took about thirty seconds to come back. "—hello? Hello?"

"Hello? I'm here," Maria said, relieved. "The signal—"

"Yeah, our TV has gone down too, keeps going in and out. We heard something happened in Coventry. Have yyyyyyyyyyyyyy—" This time it took a full minute for her to come back. Maria checked the radio; it wasn't quite white noise again, but the signal was so bad that their words were inaudible.

"—fucking iPhone shit, *hello?*"

*I'm talking to Ruth,* Maria thought. *I'm doing it. The only way out is through, remember?*

"I'm here, I'm here, look, before this goes out again, I'm coming to you, okay? I'm on my way. I don't know what I'm going to do next, but I need to…"

To do what? She didn't know.

"Get here. Same address. Can't wait, I need the company too."

Ruth needed the company? But where was Jason?

"Okay… Ruth? Aren't you scared?"

There was a pause on the line.

"A little," she said, all the showboating gone from her voice. "But we were fine last time. Nothing happened here. And the Chisel or whatever it is can stop things again, right?"

"Okay. I'm on my way," Maria said, not giving her honest answer.

"I'll wait heeeeeeeeeeeeeeeee—" The line locked up again. Maria waited a minute or two then hung up. A few feet ahead of her car, the exit to Louth. She licked her lips nervously.

*You're stuck here because you screwed up again,* the Chimp hissed.

She closed her eyes, took a deep breath, and flicked on the left indicator with a badly trembling hand.

*I did,* she thought. *But it's done now, and I'm doing the best I can. Leave me alone.*

She wasn't truly angry yet—wasn't ready to *fight* yet—but soon, Maria would be the angriest she'd ever been in her entire life.

***

# Chapter Five:

# It's All Along the Horizon

### ***

### <u>Eric</u>

Four military vehicles were coming up the off-ramp. Small, open-topped cars with armour plating and exposed roll-cages. They looked, to Eric's uninformed eyes, like Jeeps, only constructed slightly differently. He was relieved to discover that it was 'our boys' and not 'their Stone Men', but he still knew the rumours.

*Our boys are just as capable of doing bad things as theirs, he thought.*

"I don't like this," Harry said quietly.

"Me neither," Eric agreed, but his brain was already working.

*If they're up here, then maybe a blockade is empty—*

Once the vehicles reached the level surface of the abandoned ring road they stopped a few feet away from the unmoved crowd of Shufflers. Several of the soldiers got out and stood by their transports; all of them had machine guns of some kind on straps around their necks.

"Look at the hardware," Eric muttered.

"Looking," Harry muttered back. "Fuck *this.* Guns..."

One of the soldiers brandished a megaphone and raised it to his mouth.

"*The immediate surroundings outside of Ground Zero are now a restricted area,*" the raspy, distorted voice barked through the bullhorn. The soldier sounded out of breath and *very* stressed out. "*It is unsafe for the general public. Please return to your homes.*" Eric watched as the gathered Shufflers ignored him utterly, not even looking up. Eric noticed how some of them were in neatly ironed shirts or dresses, clean-shaven or well-presented. Of course, being homeless didn't automatically mean becoming some unwashed stinking tramp but having your own space and electricity and hot running water meant a certain freshness to someone's appearance. Most of the better-presented people must have walked all the way there from the very outskirts of Coventry, Eric realized. It made the scene even more bizarre.

*Why these people?* Eric thought. *Hell, why me and Harry, even?*

Then suddenly, *Mickey,* Eric thought. *Is he here somewhere?*

"*I repeat,*" the soldier said, once his first volley had accomplished nothing. "*Return to your homes or you* will *be moved.*"

Nothing.

The soldier with the megaphone looked concerned; Eric didn't think anyone in Ground Zero had seen the demeanour of the Shufflers closely. Megaphone Man nodded at the others, and they began to spread out, walking in amongst the Shufflers, intending to grab them. Eric and Harry were further back; none of the soldiers were nearby yet. Eric hopped from foot to foot, terrified of making the wrong decision. Should he run now? Head back up the ring road and get off further away?

*Then you could double back lower down,* he thought. *See if any of these guys have left a blockade unattended.*

That sounded like a great plan. A *great* plan.

"Let's get out of here," Eric muttered, tapping Harry on the arm and beginning to head back along the ring road. Harry started to follow—Eric guessed it was simply because Harry couldn't stay there—but Eric didn't think Harry would be down with the plan once it was explained.

"Come on, move!" Eric heard a soldier bark behind him. He turned his head to see the soldier advancing on a trembling and moaning man, one notably smaller than the serviceman. The Shuffler didn't even look up. The soldier reached the Shuffler, towering over him, trying to intimidate before using force. *"You can see what's going on, we have a job to do! We have orders, so don't fuck about!"* The volume level began to rise all around them as similar exchanges were taking place; none of the Shufflers were responding. They looked distressed—most of them had gone red in the face—but never seemed to actually *look* at the soldiers, like they were trying very hard to stayed focused on the Prism and nothing else.

"Let's *go*—I really don't like this," Harry muttered, and then the soldier they'd first been watching decided he'd had enough. He lifted up his hand to grab the little man, perhaps not the normal approach, but then this was rather a unique situation.

"*Don't,*" Eric whispered.

As soon as the soldier even brushed the Shuffler, the smaller man turned at lightning speed and went at the soldier with a hysterical screech. Startled, the soldier released the Shuffler's shoulders and went to raise his weapon—whether he meant to fire it or just threaten, Eric would never know—as the Shuffler fell on him with the surprising force of a lunatic, hard enough to knock the soldier off his feet.

This broke the spell.

All of the Shufflers began to scream. It didn't make sense; there were only about twelve soldiers and around fifty or sixty Shufflers, which meant only twelve of the Shufflers were being grabbed at when *all* of them started to scream. It was as if some kind of group defence took over, a pack instinct shooting through them all at once. Suddenly it was *pandemonium* on the Coventry ring road as the Shufflers began to attack the soldiers. The seven or eight infantrymen who hadn't been immediately dragged to the concrete quickly broke free and began to try to get back to the vehicles. The problem was that they'd been standing right in amongst the group, overconfident and flustered and hoping to get this crappy clearance job done quickly. That attitude would be their undoing as the Shufflers closed in. The ones right on the outskirts of the group were now *running in* to attack, completely cutting the soldiers off from the transports. The drivers, still seated in the cabs, leaped to their feet and produced sidearms, expertly bracing them on the edge of the open-topped vehicles' windscreens. Taking aim, they began yelling to their comrades; the screaming on that patch of tarmac was so loud and chaotic that Eric couldn't make any of it out.

*They'll never shoot, these are civilians,* Eric thought. *Even if there's been a media blackout here since the Arrival, there might still be people here with smartphones, they'd never—*

A Shuffler grabbed blindly for one of the soldiers' guns.

The shot might have been accidental. The serviceman may have felt he'd unexpectedly found himself in a life-and-death situation and made the appropriate choice. Eric didn't know. The machine gun fired a single round and shot the Shuffler in the chest. Another soldier fired into the air at almost the same moment, presumably in an attempt to scare the people back, but it was a *spectacularly* bad piece of timing. As the two shots came in rapid succession, the now-standing drivers in the vehicles—with no other orders incoming—made a judgement call, hearing gunfire and the cries of their comrades.

They began shooting.

"*Shit!*" Eric yelled, pushing Harry in front of him with a hard shove in the shoulder. Harry didn't resist, and the pair of them fled in the opposite direction, dashing away along the raised ring road. Arrival or not, getting shot dead wasn't in the plan. The air around them filled with the smoky tang of gunpowder as Harry began to slow a little already, wheezing and spluttering, but Eric pushed him again, urging him forwards. They'd only gone maybe twenty feet.

"*Come on, move!*" Eric yelled, echoing the soldier from earlier. A sharp pain slapped across the top of his left shoulder, worryingly coincident with a sharp *crack* from behind him. He didn't dare stop to check it, but the shock of what might have happened washed over him as he ran. His shoulder began to feel wet.

*No,* Eric thought wildly, refusing to believe it. *No fucking wayeeeeeee—*

Then the internal Horns sounded once more.

As much of a shock as it was, that alone wouldn't have been enough to stop them, but a *wave* of something unseen rushed up behind them, striking them square in their backs and lifting them off their feet for a moment. It was enough to make them look back. They could see that the Shufflers had stopped attacking, as docile again as before, and had turned back to the Prism. The soldiers had stopped firing, both in surprise and, presumably, fear.

The Horns had also stopped. The blast had been short, less than a second, but they'd sounded *different.* Not quite as loud, not quite as certain... a little ragged, even? And what had that wave been?

"Keep running!" Harry gasped, and he was right; it wasn't time to analyse. They ran along the ring road towards the off-ramp—or rather slow jogged, thanks to Harry's lousy pace—and then the Horns sounded *properly.*

Eric had time to hear it fully, to comprehend the sheer *force* of it, before a funny thing happened, and he seemed to go deaf. It was as if his brain had said, *No, that's it, you don't need this,* and shut itself down. He saw Harry silently yelling, the exaggerated mouth movements of his screams were easy to read as his finger jabbed towards Ground Zero.

*Look at that thing,* he was saying.

Eric looked. He could still see the Prism, but something was different. What was Harry pointing at? Then he saw it; it had been hard to make it out against the grey sky.

*Oh shit,* Eric thought. *Oh* shit...

A large dome had appeared around the entirety of the Prism.

*Anytime you like, lads,* Eric thought, desperately. *Anytime you feel like dragging the Chisel out here and pulling that trigger—*

Unlike the blackness that had preceded the Arrival, the dome's transparency was such that Eric struggled to see it in the first place. The only reason he could was because its surface—while perfectly round—seemed to *move* upon itself, a faint turning light.

Then that wave—*wind?*—hit them face forwards and knocked them a slight step backwards. Another wave washed into them, *through* them, and it *was* like warm air. Harry and Eric exchanged a rapid glance, thinking the same thing. It wasn't going to—

They stared at the dome of faint light. Was it... *moving?*

Their horrible intuition proved correct. The dome was spreading outwards from the Prism, and they were far too close.

They turned and ran. Even Harry moved faster than ever as the air pressure began to build around them. Eric no longer had any idea what the soldiers and Shufflers were doing because he still couldn't hear a thing, but he could *feel*. His feet pounded the pavement, his shoulder screamed in a distant way that said, *I'll catch up with y'all real soon, just gimme a few minutes, buddy, and then you'll feel me real good.* The air pressure continued to increase, making it hard to breathe. He looked over his shoulder as he ran, compelled by horror. The dome had already begun to reach the edge of the road—it had grown that far already?—and the injured soldiers were running for the  vehicles while their drivers started them up. Eric turned forwards, pumping his legs and arms with everything he had, pulling ahead of Harry but grabbing his arm and yanking him along.

*Run, you old bastard,* Eric thought. *RUN!*

He was wheezing himself now as he took another desperate glance. *The thing was into the ring road itself now and still coming.* Like the blackness before it, the edges of the dome weren't destroying anything but passing through everything harmlessly. Maybe they would be okay—

Then Eric saw that the Shufflers were on the other side of the dome's edge. They must have scrambled forwards the minute the dome appeared. They were okay?! They seemed angry again, riled up, but unharmed.

*The dome didn't hurt them!* Eric thought, elated. *This could be okay; they're fine, they're fine!*

Then he saw the dome reach the soldiers.

They exploded.

*No,* Eric thought madly, watching the sight before him and thinking that he was finally going to go insane. *That's not an explosion. It's a bursting.*

A memory flashed through his brain: a video he'd once seen of a water balloon being pricked in slow motion. Not the speed of it but the *movement* of the liquid.

Eric ran but couldn't look away, moaning soundlessly as the soldiers popped like that water balloon. They turned to red liquid inside their clothes, liquid that popped out of their sleeves and collars as it released, flying lazily outwards in all directions. *Pop.* The worst moment was when Eric realized, from his vantage point, that he couldn't see where *most* of it went; logic kicked in, unbidden, and he understood that due to gravity most of the blood, most of the *men,* would have burst straight out of the bottom of their combat trousers.

It was the worst thing he'd ever seen and would remain so until the next morning.

The vehicles began to slow as the feet that had been briefly planted onto their accelerators ceased to exist. The dome was still spreading. *The dome was still fucking coming, and it was moving faster than they were running.* He plunged forwards, and as he yanked Harry yet again, seeing how his chest was heaving and pitching, Harry's eyes caught his. He'd seen the soldiers too. Seen the dome's speed.

Still running, he shook his arm free of Eric's hand and stopped dead. He stood still, ribs expanding and contracting as he soundlessly wheezed under that strange deafness. Eric ran forwards an extra foot or two, instinct superseding logic, before realising what Harry was doing. He lunged back and grabbed at Harry again, trying to drag him on, but the older man pulled away, eyes screwed up and mouth wide as he continued to hitch in air.

*Come on! COME ON!*

Eric lunged again, but this time Harry took a step out of reach, shaking his head wildly, sweat flying.

*WE HAVE TO—*

Eric watched the dome rushing up behind Harry. In the strange, oppressive silence—as it grew more terrible, huge and *fast*—the lack of any noise made it look as if it didn't require any effort to move at all. It was as large and relentless as the sea cresting onto shore.

There was about four seconds before it was upon them.

Harry was staring at Eric, holding his ribs as he breathed heavily. Eric froze, gasping, caught. Behind Harry the dome rushed on, looking almost beautiful as Eric watched its lethal, on-rushing surface dancing with that faint and swirling light.

They weren't getting away. It was just too fast.

Eric's bottom lip began to tremble, and he couldn't stop it.

Harry suddenly lunged forwards himself, grabbing Eric's hand and holding it tight. He cupped his other hand over the top and looked into Eric's eyes. To his own surprise, Eric immediately put his free, pale hand over Harry's dark one, gripping it hard. There were only seconds left. Harry's eyes were shining, damp. Eric felt warmth, and a tension bled out of his shoulders as he let himself become still, feeling like the entire weight of another person was leaving his body. It was a sensation unlike anything he had felt before.

*Okay,* he thought. *It's alright. Theresa.*

The dome reached Harry and Eric closed his eyes.

Pins and needles flashed over his skin.

He kept his eyes closed. And kept them closed. And kept them closed.

*Surely the bastard must have hit us by now.*

There was a *pop*, and then that was it: *sound.*

Eric could hear the now-calm breeze and the birds around them chirping hysterically, letting each other know what they thought of the unnatural things that had been going on.

*No... way,* Eric thought.

He opened his eyes.

Harry was standing with his shoulders hunched up, eyes shut tight as if that would protect him. He was alive and apparently unharmed. In the distance behind him, the Shufflers were pacing back and forth, their aggression heightened.

Delirious, expecting to turn and see the wall of light coming back towards them, Eric spun and looked over his shoulder. *Yes!* The dome was accelerating away from them, out across the rest of the city!

*Oh my God, oh my God,* Eric's mind yelled. *We're alive, we're alive—*

He began to yell, frantically shaking Harry's arm by the hand.

*"Harry! Harry!"* Harry opened his eyes. *"Harry, it's okay! Look!"*

Harry stared at the dome as it headed out and away, passing through concrete and buildings in the distance as if they were merely an illusion. He panned his head left and right, taking in the horizon as the dome rushed outwards in all directions. He let out a heavy *hoof* of breath that he'd been holding in, so much so that he bent at the waist.

*"Fuuuuck,"* he said. "Oh fuck. Oh fuck. That was... oh *fuck.*"

Eric started to laugh with relief, ignoring the questions that his brain was spinning out: How were they alive? What were they inside now?

Those could wait for a moment.

Harry looked at their still-holding hands. So did Eric.

There were an awkward few seconds of silence.

"Uh..." Harry muttered.

That did it. Eric gripped Harry's hand even tighter and patted it hard as he started to laugh. Harry shook his head, smiled and began to join in; for a moment, the laughter was *only* relief, then joy as tears started to run from both of their eyes. They had just stared death right in the face and lived, and even though they were complete strangers, they'd done it together. The handshake turned into a heavy-armed hug in the middle of the ring road, and Eric didn't even feel his wound as they bellowed with a hysterical laughter powered by fear—a fighting response *to* fear, to the horror they'd just seen unfold—because they both knew the same truth.

*We're not out of this yet.*

Later, Eric would think that this was the moment that he and Harry became friends.

Friends to the end.

**✱✱✱**

# Part Two:
# The Empty Men

*"You must be willing to face your shadow. It's the one thing that follows you everywhere. Some days you can't see it, and you think you've outrun it, but it continues to reappear."*

**—David Goggins**

# Chapter Six:

# Terrible Warmth

### ***

### <u>Maria</u>

It was seven p.m. by the time Maria reached Ruth's house, and the sun had now set. Shortly after taking the off-ramp, the radio signal had stopped altogether. Maria—someone who had *always* followed the rules of the road—broke a decade of safe driving by constantly checking her phone's internet as she went.

Nothing.

Three times, fighter jets had screamed overhead, all heading in the same direction. By the time Maria's hire car pulled up on Ruth's drive, her shoulders, neck and upper back were screaming with tension... but she'd kept it together.

Ruth was already emerging from the house and running towards the slowing vehicle with her arms outstretched, her cascades of wavy brown hair bouncing. She was wearing her around-the-house gear: jogging bottoms and an oversized T-shirt. Maria actually laughed as she stopped the car and got out, holding out her arms in return. Ruth rushed her, wrapping Maria up. Ruth was big. Tall for a woman—five foot ten to Maria's five foot two. To

Maria's skinny frame, it felt like being hugged by a soft and nice-smelling wrestler.

"Holy *shit*," Ruth said, bringing another laugh from deep inside Maria. How the hell had she ever allowed this person to be absent from her life? "It takes the end of the world to get you to show up. Is that what I need to do to keep track of you, you part-time bitch? Arrange a major international incident?" It was still showtime, but as Ruth stepped back to look at Maria, surprise and shock flashed over her face. She'd seen how much weight Maria had lost. In true, wonderful Ruth fashion, she addressed the elephant in the room, effortlessly making it okay.

"Well, Christ. I know it's probably awful, horrendous trauma that's done it, but I was in Primarni the other day, and it's official: I'm a size sixteen. And I'm like *gym or trauma, gym or trauma*, and I'm thinking I'd like to know your secret just so I can weigh up the options—"

Maria let out a big laugh, a real *belly* laugh, her first in years, but it was too loud, cracking too quickly. She bit down on the tears, and Ruth responded, blissfully, in the right way. She pretended not to notice.

"Are you hungry?"

To her surprise, she was. They went inside.

She managed to finish a bacon sandwich as Ruth sat opposite Maria at the kitchen table, talking a million miles an hour about nothing, manic free association. Any discussion of Maria's five-year disappearance was conspicuous by its absence. Maria knew she would have to start the real talk.

"Ruthie," Maria said quietly, interrupting the babble. "Have you got any news here? The radio and my phone have been giving me nothing."

"No," said Ruth, putting on her breeziest smile, meaning she *was* scared. "Next to nothing. Radio's barely working now, and the TV feed went out a little while ago; I've left it on just in case, but it's only blue screen right now. Same for the internet and phones."

"Where's Jason?" Maria asked. "At work?" *Was* anybody working that day, with everything going on? *Some* people would have to be, surely? Emergency services? Jason was in the mortgage business.

"He was at a conference up north... I spoke to him this morning." The smile dropped. Ruth blinked.

"He'll be okay," Maria said. She reached across the table and squeezed Ruth's free hand. "He's either holed up somewhere there or on his way here. You know that."

"He's... he's inland. He's not near the coast."

Maria didn't take much comfort from this but said nothing. Stuff was happening in the middle of the country now, and she thought that those white *things* were moving inland. She didn't think anywhere was safe. She never should have come back to this godforsaken—

"That's good," she said instead. "Did you... try to leave?"

"No," Ruth sniffed. "Jason told me to, before the phones started playing up. I told him that I didn't want to run—we never did before—and now it's worse; it's... the roads. It's too late, isn't it?"

Maria felt cold pour across her back but caught herself. Right now, this wasn't about her.

"For the moment, I think. Yes." She couldn't believe she was saying it. "I... missed you."

Ruth smiled sadly. "I missed you too."

"I wanted... to let you know that I love you, and I'm so sorry for just..."

"Oh, honeybun... you have nothing to apologize for. Nothing." Maria heard the affectionate term, and just like that, she was briefly back in the old days, surrounded by warmth. Then the knowledge of the loss of it in the present struck her like an ice-cold shower. It was hard to breathe.

"I... I spoke to Marcus last week."

It was like a punch in the face. Maria's grip on Ruth's hand went slack.

"Oh, yeah..." Maria said automatically. "How is he?"

"He's good."

"That's... good."

"He mentioned you. Said he'd seen you?"

"Yeah, yeah, he did," Maria said, her eyes on the table as her temples throbbed. *Marcus.* Hearing Ruth say his name—hearing his *sister* say it—was somehow awful. It wasn't like he was dead or anything, and God forgive her for thinking it, but she sometimes wondered if maybe that would have been easier. She'd thought he was dead once, before it turned out he was fine; he wasn't inside the Transport Museum after all on that terrible day. But by then it was too late because she'd already lost—

Maria cut that train of thought clean off, forcing out words instead.

"We... met up. About a month ago. Had a talk. It was my idea. I thought it would be... I wanted to... I thought it might be worth it."

"Yeah. Yeah."

"Did he... say much about it?"

"He said it was good to see you. But he... he said it was... difficult."

It *had* been difficult. And a very bad idea in the end.

She'd been feeling stronger. What had she been thinking? She'd just picked up the phone one night and called him. They'd talked, and it had been *good,* so good, and she could tell that he'd felt the same. She'd asked him openly: Could we put the past behind us? We've grown; we've changed. And they *had,* they really had. Could they meet? He'd said yes. She'd told him there was the issue of a three-hour flight to Barcelona. He still said yes. *I do a four-hour round trip for work every day,* he'd told her, and that had been a surprise. Marcus commuting? She'd been so excited for his arrival, sixteen again. Could this be a new start?

Seeing each other had been entirely different. The pain came rushing back the second she saw him at the airport, and she knew that they couldn't do it. She would always look into his eyes and feel that terrible, desperate sadness first and foremost, and he would always do the same. But he'd come all that way, and they should at least have a drink and catch up, it might be okay...

They'd been drunk within an hour, screwing in his hotel room upstairs within two—her crying silently, holding him tight against her so he wouldn't see—and within three, they'd agreed it had been a mistake. He'd left, taking an early flight home. For the next month, Maria felt like she'd been hollowed out, scraped clean of all progress and dragged back to square one.

"It was difficult. Yeah."

"So, you don't think you'd... see him again?"

Maria knew how badly Ruth wanted them all to be a family once more, but for a second, Maria hated her guts. What was Ruth doing to her? Suddenly, Maria was back *there*, back on that *bus*, back lying on the pavement, knowing what was happening and desperately hoping that somehow an ambulance would get there in time, knowing it wasn't possible but *still* hoping they could save—

"No," she said, and it was a squeak. Ruth's hand tightened on hers.

"I'm sorry, I'm so sorry, love."

*And now you're trapped here,* the Chimp suddenly screamed. *Get OUT, RUN—*

*No,* she told herself. *Talk about it. Get the* fucking *poison* out.

Then Maria was telling Ruth things that no-one but Marcus had ever known, things that came from somewhere so deep down that she shook as she spoke.

"I'd decided her name would be Anna, did I ever tell you that?" Maria's eyes went to her cup of tea.

*Marcus was right,* she told herself, punching away at her very essence like no-one else could. *Even babysitting kids in summer school was too much in your condition.*

"I'd decided beforehand that I didn't want to hold her, once they'd... that used to be the normal way, you know, in the sixties and stuff? They took the babies away straightaway. And now, a lot of people think that you should have time with your baby, that it's better for you... but I'd already decided. I couldn't hold her, Ruth. I couldn't do it. I couldn't *do* it."

"Sweetheart..." Ruth breathed.

"I'd been so *relieved* when I found out Marcus was alive," Maria continued, not hearing her. "The police told me about the Transport Museum, and they knew about the bodies that were coming out so they'd assumed the worst, so when he got to the hospital to see me we were just hysterical... but I was so broken afterwards and so was he, and after *that*... we *tried*, but..."

"I know. I know," Ruth interrupted, stopping Maria before she could speak her darkest truth, her darkest thought: That she wasn't strong enough to save them. That she was a coward. "We've been so worried about you since the split. No-one even knew where you were."

"I'm sorry," Maria sobbed.

"*No,* I didn't mean—"

"I'm doing better now; I have a job. I don't make very much, but that's okay because I don't go out. I don't eat a lot. I miss my old job, the yoga, but I think about getting up in front of a room full of people again and I physically start shaking..." She shifted in her seat uneasily, the spell of honesty broken. "... I don't go out," she repeated, giving up.

"You did the right thing coming here. Coming to me."

"It was a vision that triggered the miscarriage, Ruth," Maria said, amazed at how easily it came out. "I saw one of the people that the Stone Men came to see, I saw them *in my mind.* Like they said in those *Be Prepared* ads. Did I ever tell you that?"

"... No."

"I told them that was the only time it happened. But even *that* wasn't true. I saw them *every time. All of them.* I never told anyone. Isn't that awful?"

"No," Ruth said, sighing. "I did the same."

Maria couldn't believe it. She stared at Ruth like a simpleton.

"You... you had visions?"

"The second time a little, and also on the Third Arrival."

"Why didn't you tell anyone?"

"I told Jason. He told me not to say anything, and I thought he was right."

Maria blinked.

"I always felt so guilty that I didn't..."

"Don't. You don't know anything about what's going on and neither do I. Those ads dressed it all up *very* nicely, but would you trust the government?"

Those ads. The ones for the *Be Prepared* appeal. The ones they played *non-stop* after all the fuss died down from the Third Arrival. They'd created an *enormous* turnout, according to the news. They'd been so ubiquitous that Maria—everyone—could almost remember them word-for-word. The voiceover had been a woman's, warm and jovial.

*Did you notice anything unusual, different or strange about yourself during the First, Second or Third Arrivals? Then we want to hear from you. You know the old saying, there's no such thing as a silly question if you don't know the answer? Well, there's no such thing as a silly application to the Be Prepared appeal. We don't know if or when we may be visited again, and we need the help of the public to make sure we're as prepared as possible. That means one thing... knowledge. Knowledge we can't obtain without your help. We're doing well but to be able to forge a better, coherent defence, we need to learn about our enemy, for your sake and the sake of, potentially, our descendants. If you or anyone you know experienced any unusual visions, rhythmic sounds or mental connections at all during any of the previous Arrivals, visit bepreparedbritain.org or call us on—*

They'd tried to call her, but she'd left by then. She assumed they'd read her incident report. They tried to contact her in Barcelona too, but they didn't try *that* hard; presumably, they'd only wanted the people that they thought could *really* connect with the Stone Men. They hadn't known that Maria had visions every single time. The *other* old question came to Maria, the one that she'd responded to by running away.

*Could they have helped you?* she thought. *It turned its head to look at you. Could you have helped* them *to help you? Get to Coventry, find a military blockade somewhere, you could—*

"I didn't trust them, no," Maria said, "but maybe... what if that was a mistake?"

"It wasn't," Ruth said firmly. "Stuff has been going on in Coventry all day, but even before everything cut out, they tried to keep a lid on—"

"*Wait,*" Maria barked suddenly, making Ruth jump. "You said you left the TV on?"

"Yes," Ruth said, her hand on her chest as she calmed down.

"It's a DVR, a digibox?"

"Yes."

"Do you think you can rewind it?"

\*\*\*

That's the thing, Maria thought. That's what Stephen in the helicopter saw before he died. It got him as it appeared.

The TV showed a distant aerial shot of Coventry city centre.

The shifting, shimmering *thing* covered it like an impossibly big single segment of bubble wrap. It made Maria think of a giant parasite, something that had clamped over the city and was in the process of sucking it dry. It was hard to see against the dark sky, especially with the lower-resolution feed that the camera delivered at night, but it was clearly there. It was like the now-dark sky was slowly churning.

"*—this anomaly, as we're calling it, arrived several hours ago in Coventry and seems to be there to stay,*" said the studio anchor's voiceover. "*This is the closest the military are allowing us. We don't know how long we're going to be able to bring you even this much, but they seem to be rather busy.... Susan Brownhill is there.*"

"*I'm here, Joshua,*" said Susan, sounding as if she was in a helicopter. Maria thought Susan had to be insane to be anywhere near Coventry after what had happened earlier.

"*Thank you, Susan,*" Joshua said, "*and I know I speak for everyone watching when I say, do stay at a safe distance...*" He paused, presumably realising that no-one had *any idea* what a safe distance really was.

"*We're about to be moved, Joshua,*" Susan said. "*We've received word that another strike will be carried out any moment now and we can't be in neighbouring airspace.*"

*Forget the airstrike*, Maria thought. *We've seen them try that sugar on the Stone Men and it didn't even make them wobble. Where's the bloody* Chisel?

Susan seemed to read Maria's mind all the way from Coventry.

"*Still nothing on the Chisel either, Joshua,*" Susan said, "*though that may be due to the technical problems we're experiencing. One rumour is that the Chisel is in fact* inside *Ground Zero but we're trying to get a confirmation from Downing Street on its status. We're hearing that there's a lot of unrest over the government's delay in resp—*" She stopped talking. The dimly shimmering bubble filled most of the screen as Susan's helicopter hovered.

"*Susan?*"

"*We're being moved, Joshua,*" said Susan, her voice flat, and the image began to turn away from the deeply unsettling bubble hanging over the city. They cut back to the studio just before Ruth's TV turned blue.

"That's where the feed ended," Ruth said. Maria noticed that her eyes were wet.

"Jason will be fine," Maria told her. "I promise." It was a pointless thing to say, a promise Maria didn't believe, based on nothing.

"I saw this earlier, it just got me again, that's all," Ruth sniffed. She breathed in sharply to steady herself, looked at Maria, and burst out laughing.

"What?"

"We're *fucked*," she laughed. "We're totally fucked!"

Maria stared at her, horrified… and then started to laugh too. What other choice was there? Laughing at it felt… like a victory?

"I have an idea," Ruth chuckled, wiping at her eyes and crossing to the living-room drinks cabinet. "Let's drink and talk. Rum and Coke. *Full sugar* Coke. I think today is the one day you don't have to worry about drinking and driving if we come up with something, but *fuck* knows what that's gonna be. If we come up with an idea before you're too plastered to drive at night in two mile an hour traffic, then you go do that. If not, you stay here, keep me company and wait this out. Deal?"

Maria felt the rising panic at the idea but also anger that she couldn't just be there for her friend, couldn't just be *present.* She knew what she was supposed to do—*find the bloody wisdom to accept that which she cannot bloody change*—but she was just so *sick* of running.

"Screw it. Let's get drunk," she heard herself say, but she was glad she was sitting down. "I'll take mine neat. On the rocks."

Ruth grinned and slapped her on the shoulder. As ever, it rocked Maria sideways a little, but Maria didn't mind. She was grinning. This wasn't just a proposed party; it was an act of defiance. If Maria was going to die, she was going to die here, with someone she loved, having a good time for the first time in… years.

*In your Stone faces, you bastards,* she thought.

"Ruth?" Maria asked suddenly. "Did you feel them before they got here? Even before I left Spain to come back for the funeral, I didn't feel right. I felt like I needed to come home, and I never feel that way. Did you notice anything?"

"I did," Ruth sighed. "I couldn't sleep. I kept looking out of the window, thinking something was in the garden. I put it down to work stress." The moment of levity was nearly lost, but Ruth saved it. "Look, you probably need a shower after today, right? Why you don't you do that, and I'll make the drinks," she said, forcing a smile.

"That's a plan." Maria stood, and Ruth's showgirl kicked back in as she headed to the kitchen to get the ice.

"And, if at any point, y'know," she said, mock-breezily, "if at *any* point you feel like, I don't know, *filling me in* on the last few years, I'm all ears, and if you *don't,* y'know... thaaaaaaat's all just fine too," she said, theatrically examining her fingernails. She then shot Maria a sideways glance straight out of a fifties spy movie and sashayed through the door, causing Maria to laugh out loud.

That was how the worst night of Maria's life began.

***

Maria woke up in the middle of the night with a screaming headache and a terrible need to pee. It wasn't even close to sunrise, and it felt like her hangover was already well underway. She hadn't been drunk for a very long time. The recent night before flashed through her mind—too many rums and even some dancing to S Club 7 in the living room. It had been great, the fear and chaos forgotten for a while and locked outside the door, but the nausea made her wish it had been a *little less* fun. She threw the covers off and rose out of bed on autopilot, the unconscious, automatic part of her brain at the wheel, driving her to the bathroom saying, *Don't worry, I got this.* Afterwards, she headed back to the bedroom.

Something had changed. She knew it even before she walked through the door.

Maria went to the bedroom window. She had to see. Something inside her knew that there was something out there. That's what had woken her up—

That didn't make any sense. What time was it? Her bleary eyes fell on the LED screen of the alarm clock next to Ruth's spare bed, reminding her dazed mind again—*Ruth's house, oh yeah, how much did we drink?* It was midnight. What time had they gone to bed, then?

Her arms suddenly broke out in gooseflesh and a bolt of electricity shot down her spine. The room swam into focus, and she realized that her hand was reaching for the curtains. The dreamy combination of pale moonlight and dim streetlight cast a faint nimbus around them against the darkness.

*Why am I opening the curtains?* she thought. *What do I expect to see?*

It felt like a nightmare as she tried to stop her hand, the drugged effect of her hangover seeming to make her a mere observer of her own actions. She shivered and it wasn't from being cold, even if she was only in her underwear and T-shirt.

*Don't open that curtain,* she thought. *Don't touch it.*

She watched her hand sleepily clutch and drag the curtain sideways. Moonlight, streetlight, all gentle as the faces of the houses on the other side of Ruth's terraced street stared back at her, devoid of light or movement. It was midnight, after all. The single visible streetlight glowed a faint white, dim enough that the stars in the cloudless sky above could be seen. It looked eerie, but peaceful. Nothing after all, then. She could just go back to sleep.

But she didn't. She waited and watched as the muscles in her back and neck grew tighter.

*Please,* she thought. *Let's go.*

Why was every fibre in her body beginning to whisper, *Run?*

She saw the first movement in the street below.

It was a glimpsed reflection in an opposite window; she initially thought that it was somebody waking up and moving around inside their house. Then it grew clearer, and her still-waking brain wondered why the person behind their window seemed to be coloured such a solid, smooth shade of white? No, it was a reflection—

*Then* she was awake. Wide awake, her breath rasping in her throat.

An Empty Man was making its way along the street.

It made no sound, and its progress was no faster than a leisurely walking pace. It was still hunched over like the one she'd seen earlier on the beach, arms still at that slightly akimbo angle. Its elongated head didn't turn or even bob as it moved, and she realized that was because its legs weren't moving at all; the thing *glided.* Its feet remained invisible, the ends of its legs vanishing into the street like a stick puppet as it slowly made its way along the road. Even in the dark, its bright whiteness somehow—*somehow*—still cast no aura of light, created no shadows on nearby objects. Watching it almost hurt her eyes... her *mind* when she looked at it, as if her brain were being asked to comprehend something that simply couldn't be and was feeling pain as a result.

Two more followed soon behind it.

They weren't moving in a line or any kind of visible formation; the first was almost in the middle of the road, the second close to the row of houses opposite, and the third only slightly closer to Maria's side of the street. All of them were standing stiff-limbed yet moving in that same slightly hunched pose. Their freakishly tall and thin bodies looked like waiting vultures, their thin, too-long arms angled out and away. That feeling she had on the beach, that cold sensation of something *lurking,* came back tenfold. She tried to let the curtain drop and move away from the window, but she couldn't. She wanted to call to Ruth, but her throat had closed. She felt a fear like nothing she had ever experienced in her entire life, worse even than when she was on that bus with the monstrosity bearing down upon her. She heard herself desperately hoping for salvation.

*They might pass. They might pass. They might—*

The first one stopped dead just before it disappeared from sight. The others continued to slowly gain upon their stationary companion. Time stood still.

Then the first one began to move towards a house on the opposite side of the road.

She put her hand in her mouth and bit down as the Empty Man made its creeping, silent way over to the house's white front door, strangely framed by it for a moment and blending in so much that it almost appeared to vanish. She moaned into her fist in horror as the Empty Man reached the front door and simply passed through it. It was as if the laws of physics didn't apply to it, which of course they didn't. Maria tried to imagine that thing now being inside someone's normal, regular house, and couldn't. It was *in* there amongst their ordinary books and ornaments and keepsakes and memories.

Then she saw that one of the remaining two had also stopped.

The one at the back kept on moving forwards, while its remaining companion had come to a complete halt by another house across the street. It stayed there. And stayed there, long enough for its companion to almost draw level with it.

Still it didn't move.

Its companion passed it.

*Still* it stood there, frozen to the spot.

*It... might... vanish... like before...*

The stationary Empty Man had stopped directly opposite Ruth's house.

*Please.*

It started to move across the street towards her.

A rhythmic sensation began to beat in her brain as she watched helplessly. It hadn't pivoted to face her; it was simply moving sideways. Maria realized dimly that it would meet the house somewhere in the middle of the front living room wall. It disappeared from sight out of the bottom of the window frame, and after a moment, she understood that even at the slow, ponderous speed it was travelling, their visitor would now be inside the house, directly below her.

Her body wanted to curl into a ball but the thought of her friend in danger gave her back her control, and she darted on her tiptoes to the bedroom door, scuttling like a rodent spotted by a hawk. She crouched as she cracked the door slightly, expecting the Empty Man to be standing there, its hunched form looming and waiting.

There was nothing there.

The upstairs hallway was a darkened tomb with only the dimmest of light coming from the tiny window in the far wall; it illuminated the short bannister and staircase that led to the downstairs hallway. Maria listened, trying to hear clearly over the rushing blood in her ears. No sounds from downstairs. Ruth's bedroom was away to the left, out of her line of sight.

*It could have gone straight through the other wall,* she thought. *You saw the Stone Man walk straight through houses. This could be the same.*

She didn't think that was true. That *rhythm* was still going on in her brain, and so she knew the thing was downstairs. What was it doing? Was it waiting for them?

*Ruth,* she reminded herself. Ruth was asleep, blissfully unaware. Maria had to get her, wake her up—

She would have to do it very, very quietly.

She willed her legs to move over the threshold with a superhuman effort. Having watched the Empty Men treat solid mass as if it were mist meant that the floor below her seemed as reliable a footing as a cloudbank. That thing was beneath her feet, *right below her.* Could it see her footsteps?

She took two slow, shaking and silent steps out of the spare bedroom and looked towards Ruth's room. Her door was open— Ruth always slept with the door open, had done since she was a child—and Maria could see her bed. Ruth lay on her side, knowing nothing of the visitor downstairs. Too far away for Maria to whisper awake. She would have to go and *wake* Ruth. As Maria began to step along the hallway, she looked back to the bannister and saw the Empty Man's head rising straight up from the floor below.

It was only a glimpse because she made a choking sound and fell backwards through the open door of her bedroom, onto the floor. The thing had been inexorably rising vertically, as if it could defy gravity. The little boy on the radio had been right, then; they *had* been high up in the air.

*HIDE,* her mind screamed.

Without thinking, her eyes locked in terror on the rising Empty Man. Maria kicked out with a spasming foot and hooked her bedroom door shut. It was pointless, but instinct was instinct and the urge to *hide*—to bury herself twenty feet deep if she could— was all-consuming, even if she knew that no matter how deep she dived, that thing could effortlessly pass through anything to find her. She heard herself whimpering and moaning softly as she crawled across the floor and then under the bed, hiding her face like a terrified child. Even as she did so, she thought, *THE CUPBOARD, YOU SHOULD HAVE JUMPED INTO THE CUPBOARD,* and in her panic she poked her head out. Maybe she still had time to make it? One glance told her it was too late for that. The Empty Man was now silently gliding in through her bedroom door.

As thin as it was, it still seemed to fill the room, that impossible non-casting white light permeating its entire being. It was completely opaque now, and its height was staggering. Its head was higher than the doorframe and disappeared slightly into the ceiling even at that awful semi-crouch. Her reeling, observing mind threw up a thought. *It's shorter than it was before, even shorter than it was on the beach, the* beach, *they're splitting and multiplying and shrinking and its INSIDE A ROOM WITH YOU—*

Her terror was so complete that she couldn't even move to yank her head back under the bed. *This is what it's like,* she realized. *This is what it's like for mice and rabbits and hedgehogs and* prey *when they are so scared that they can't move.* On it came, into the room, tall and impossible. Maria closed her eyes tight, imagined herself away, away.

The Empty Man stopped moving.

Maria waited, the prey frozen before the hunter.

It stayed there, hunched as if it were already reaching for her.

She couldn't dare hope. Doom was certain. Hope was foolish.

Still it stood there.

She knew—terribly—that she *couldn't* run now. It was too close to move around. Then the thought came, automatic and awful:

*Please. Take someone else. Leave me alone and take someone else.*

It didn't move, of course, but as that thought came and went it took a little something of her with it, some kind of internal and permanent defeat. She watched and *felt* the thing examine her, assess her, reach *inside* her. It was a sickening warmth that reached through her body. It was disgusting, warm the way fresh vomit steams. Her paralysis broke for a moment and she thought about the window above the bed—that could be an exit that wouldn't mean having to pass that thing? She wildly imagined jumping to the street or hanging by her fingertips. But *Ruth...*

*Please leave me alone,* she silently begged. *Oh, please.*

The warmth pulled out of her. The Empty Man began to move away.

It glided backwards, without turning, towards the door. Not a retreat; she could not imagine a situation where those things would ever *retreat.* It reached the door and began to disappear through it as Maria realized that she had a reprieve. The window. Once that thing had left, she could climb out, hang—

It was gone.

But if it wasn't looking for her, then it was looking for—

Her paralysis flew away, and she abandoned the window, turning away from salvation and darting out from under the bed to help Ruth. She froze as she reached the door. What if she'd been lucky? Never mind how she could even begin to stop it, what if whatever the hell that thing was doing to her, whatever it was using to *look,* had simply glitched, and she was about to throw away a one-in-a-million chance to escape? The thought of that terrible warmth coursing through her bloodstream again—through her *mind*—was almost too much to bear, but willpower just managed to beat fear. She cracked the door open once more, wanting to wake up from the nightmare but such relief would not come.

She heard sounds coming from Ruth's room.

It sounded like coughing, but a shorter, shallower version, getting cut off partway through. She stepped into the hallway once more, expecting another Empty Man to be waiting around the edge of the doorframe. There wasn't one. The only Empty Man was the one she could now see standing at the foot of Ruth's bed, framed by the open windows and pale moonlight streaming through. Ruth was making the sounds. She hadn't moved, hadn't even rolled over, and instead was making those strange half coughs as she remained on her side. Did she know that thing was there? Did she feel that horrible warmth—

The Empty Man uncoiled itself, its head and shoulders releasing as it reached its full height, its head almost *completely* disappearing through the ceiling now. Maria suddenly struggled to breathe, wanting to yell out to Ruth, to wake her up, but all that came out was a strangled squeak. Maria staggered deliriously towards Ruth's room with an act of superhuman will as the Empty Man suddenly began to *spread,* opening sideways as if it were an image in a funhouse mirror. Its already-distorted form became wider and wider, like a python dislocating its jaw in order to swallow an entire springbok. The Empty Man spread until it was almost as wide as Ruth's bed.

It then smothered her friend.

It fell silently upon her like a crashing, heavy wave, beginning its fall from the very top of its tall, stretched out body and pitching forwards, tipping almost straight down upon itself. Starting at her feet, it *poured* itself along and across her sleeping form. The parts of her that were covered by her blanket were, of course, hidden from Maria's view, but the parts that weren't—her head, her right arm, her right leg, both of them splayed and sticking out from under the covers—became covered in white. It wasn't a neat coating, the way chocolates in boxes are wrapped tightly around a tasty centre; the Empty Man lay upon Ruth's body like poured honey, loose and thick. Some places were thin enough that Maria could still see Ruth beneath the thing. Even in the darkness she could make out the outline of Ruth's closed eyes, her lips, as they stood out behind the thing's whiteness.

Then Ruth opened her eyes. She saw Maria standing there, *just standing there,* and Maria realized that she had frozen. This couldn't just be fear. That thing was doing something to Ruth, and she was feeling it too.

"M'ria?" Ruth mumbled, trying to sit and failing as she made that choking sound once more and simply twitched on the spot. For a moment, Maria saw her veiled eyes screw up in sleepy confusion. "M'ria…" She shifted slightly once more, trying harder. Then she tried harder still. Ruth couldn't move either.

"Maria?" Ruth asked again, clearly this time, as fear began to wake her fully. Her attempts to speak turned back into that strange guttural noise in her throat. She looked at her own arm, saw the whiteness hanging on it, *around* it, saw Maria's cowering form standing, sobbing uselessly in the doorway. "*Maria,*" she gasped, and it was as if it were all she could say. "*What issis—*" Her words slurred, and she suddenly began to pitch uselessly on the spot, looking as if her strongest attempts to move barely even registered in her unresponsive muscles.

"*Ruth!*" Maria yelled, a verbal Heimlich manoeuvre that finally popped the stuck and choking word free; her limbs became hers once more. Limp and weak but *hers.* She had to get a weapon and hit it, hurt it, it was killing Ruth—

She frantically scanned the room, hoping against hope that there was something in there that she could use, trying to find *anything* solid or heavy or sharp: a book, a high-heeled shoe—

Her eyes fell upon Ruth's field hockey stick that she had propped in the corner. She still played; they'd even talked about it earlier before their world became this incredible hell. Maria lunged for it, snatched it up, and leaped over to the bed where the Empty Man and Ruth lay together on top of the mattress, Ruth lying in state with that thing as her terrible shroud. Maria's shaking hand threw back the sheets, exposing the creature in its entirety. The bottom of the Empty Man was still embedded in the floor, bending forwards at knee-height to reach over Ruth's body. It covered every inch of her. Maria looked wildly for a part of it that she could hit without harming Ruth; The Empty Man was wide like a sheet where Ruth's legs were slightly spread apart, lying on her side with one leg forwards and one back as if frozen mid-step. In between was a large section of Empty Man with nothing of Ruth underneath.

*There—*

Maria swung the hockey stick overhead and brought it down onto the Empty Man's form with everything she had. It passed straight through without even a pause and bounced back up, powered by the mattress' springs.

Maria blinked, stunned, and fruitlessly repeated the action, getting the same result. Nothing.

Then she had to get Ruth *out* of there, *NOW—*

Maria's hand plunged through the whiteness, gripping Ruth's wrist tight in an attempt to pull her free. Immediately that disgusting, sickening warmth surged through Maria with devastating force, far more powerful than before. There was no sensation of touch, of Maria's hand passing through the thing's body; the feeling was suddenly buried *inside* her mind. Maria's stomach and lungs bucked and heaved with involuntary spasms that drove her to her knees, nausea completely sapping her strength. She gagged as she felt the Empty Man looking *through* her again, terribly alert and aware. The violent spasms rolled her onto her back like a dying and gasping fish, her hand so limp that she couldn't hold on to Ruth any more. Maria's arm flailed blindly but fruitlessly, instinctively going in for another attempt to save her friend, even if the Empty Man in her mind had left her too weak to pull a Christmas cracker. She had to save Ruth—

Maria's hazy eyes tried to focus on her target, trying to get her spasming arms to obey, and she looked up to see that something dark was beginning to form around the edges of Ruth's eyes. She was beginning to gurgle too.

"*Akk. Akk. Akk. Akk.*"

Those darkening sockets were looking right at Maria. She could see that Ruth was aware of what was happening. Maria sobbed in frustration and anguish as she continued trying to crawl forwards, trying to shake off the Empty Man's influence, even if the wavering distance to Ruth's rattling body seemed to be the length of five football fields. Something began to flow from Ruth's nose, her mouth, something dark but not as thick as blood as it began to run freely now, pooling against the side of her face where it lay on the mattress. It quickly overran the edge of the bed and began to pour onto the exposed laminated floorboards.

*IT'S KILLING HER,* her mind gibbered. *SAVE HER, SAVE HER—*

Even so, the fluid ran across the floor towards her and she saw that it *was* blood after all, blood that had been somehow watered down by other fluids. Maria's useless limbs tried to grab for Ruth again as she watched the pauses between her friend's twitches get longer... longer. With horror, she realized what was happening: the twitching wasn't from any kind of physical struggle with the Empty Man. Ruth was choking.

Her hand finally plunged into the whiteness, grabbing Ruth's arm once more—

*Come on—*

The nausea rinsed through her veins again like a power wash; the effect of the second blast so much worse than the first that Maria began to vomit uncontrollably. Her whole body jerked backwards so violently that she covered the short distance across the room, her head careening off the wall behind her with a bang.

She saw stars, but even as she fell to her knees, she still tried to reach Ruth, but realized she could barely move.

*COME...ON... M'COMIN... RUTH—*

It was too late. Ruth's wide eyes found Maria's again, still knowing, finally dying. Ruth's fingers began to spasm, *no,* to form a fist...?

Ruth's violently shaking finger pointed towards the door as her dying eyes bored into her friend's. She was telling Maria to run.

Doing so must have taken the last of what she had; Ruth's hand became still as she let out a heavy final breath. She stopped moving. Maria bellowed uselessly, a deep scream-moan of pain as the whiteness began to slowly pull away from Ruth's face. The Empty Man was beginning to reassemble itself, its awful work now complete. It pulled back with the speed and grace of a funeral director unveiling the beloved dead. The fact of Ruth's death hit Maria with the concussive force of a riot cannon.

*Just let it take you,* she thought. *You've been running for five years. Is there even any point now—*

The Empty Man had slid back down to Ruth's waist now, reforming, still bent at the waist.

An angry, counter voice spoke up. *DO YOU WANT TO DIE THAT WAY—*

No. She didn't. But her limbs felt as if they weighed several tonnes each.

Now the Empty Man was back to Ruth's ankles and Maria realized she could at least *see* clearly again. She tried to move her legs. The Empty Man's residual influence over her had faded a little; still there, still an incredible weight, but her limbs were becoming her own once more.

*GET UP,* she commanded herself.

*Okay,* came the weak response, but her body couldn't comply. Not yet. The feeling was fading, but she still couldn't truly move.

*DON'T PANIC,* she told herself. *DON'T PANIC, WAIT, WAIT—*

Her pulse blasted against her temples as the Empty Man began to straighten up. Maria counted to five in her head, and it seemed like an eternity.

Then she tried to make two fists. Her hands responded, and her grip was tight. Small steps. Small steps, like the man said. Could she get her feet under her?

She could, and her shaking foot flattened against the floor.

*Use the wall to stand,* she told herself, intense and trying to stay calm, an eager coach trying to coax a personal best out of their star athlete. *Push back against the wall and slide up.*

The thing's influence was dimmer still. The world went grey as she pushed herself upright at the waist with her hands and got her back against the wall, her wide and terrified eyes locked on the reforming Empty Man. It had now uncoiled entirely away from Ruth's body, bent at the waist and still rising. It would be whole in a few seconds. She had to *push*, it was now or never—

Feeling as if she were squatting twice her bodyweight, Maria gasped and stood up, gibbering to herself as the Empty Man's head came up last, sitting low on its hunched shoulders. It was ready once more.

But Maria was *up.*

*GO,* her mind screamed. *GO! GO! GO!*

She rolled sideways and around the doorframe, snatching a final glance at her friend's body as she did so. Ruth's eyes were still wide and staring.

Maria hadn't saved her friend. The magnitude of such failure was incomprehensible, and now she had to run again—

The thing at the foot of Ruth's bed began to move slowly away, and then Maria was lurching towards the top of the stairs like a drunk Tin Man, oil reaching her joints with glacial speed as she lurched down the stairs, crying silently. She nearly fell down the stairs, and then she was opening the front door and plunging out into the night, beginning to bellow. Lights were coming on in a few houses, their formerly sleeping inhabitants woken by the noise, and as Maria's feet hit the cold concrete, it occurred to her that there could be more Empty Men outside. They were heading inland after all, and no-one knew how many there were. She bolted down the street as fast as she could, clothed in nothing but her underwear and T-shirt, frantically scanning the street. There were no Empty Men in sight as she managed to break into a lumbering run, screaming into the chilly September night. Her feet were already turning numb.

She didn't know how long she ran, but eventually, the pain in her stomach made her drop like a stone on the front lawn of someone's house, the light coming on in the bedroom at the sound of her wheezing cries. A woman's voice was asking her frantically what had happened, was she alright, and then arms were around Maria. She tried to push the woman away frantically even as this stranger told her it was alright, that she was safe, but Maria knew that just wasn't true. She would always have to run, so would this woman, the pair of them, or go into that whiteness like Ruth.

A whiteness of her own rose up quickly behind Maria's eyes, and when she awoke hours later, there were two men in suits staring down at her.

***

# Chapter Seven:

# Eric Takes One For the Team, the Boys Hit the Club, the Exit Interviews, and Eric and Harry See the Light

*** 

## Eric

"I thought we were going to die," Harry said. "We didn't." It was an obvious statement, but it needed saying. The soldiers' deaths replayed in Eric's mind as they stood on the ring road, getting their breath back, staring at the Prism. The sky was darkening as the sun began to set, the Barrier's gently churning surface sitting in between them and the clouds above.

"The soldiers—" Eric said, looking back up the ring road and waving a shaking hand in the direction of the bloodied military transports.

"No. Not now," Harry hissed, closing his eyes. "Later. We've got to plan."

"Okay. Okay."

He breathed out heavily, equilibrium returned, and looked at the dome in the distance. It was a long way away now, maybe a mile even, and still going. *Wait...*was it?

"Harry... do you think it's stopped moving?"

Harry turned to follow Eric's gaze—pointlessly, the thing was all around them in a circle—and squinted. The thing was so fucking hard to *see*. He began to crane his head backwards as his eyes traced it all the way up.

"It's like a big... microwave plate cover," he said, not answering the question. He looked at Eric. "Do you think they're going to cook us?"

"Who knows, but do you think it's still *moving?*"

"... Don't think it is, you know," Harry was saying, but Eric wasn't looking at the Barrier any more. "Should we go and find out? Good to know the lay of the land."

The question of *direction* brought Eric's brain back online, understanding that the moment of imminent death had passed, and an incredible truth slammed home. He spun to look at Ground Zero. Harry didn't notice.

*There's nobody guarding Ground Zero any more. Oh my God.*

He was already walking towards it, but then he hesitated.

*Are you crazy?* he thought. *Look at what just happened! What if you're standing around here, and that Prism puts out another one of those dome things? One that* does *kill you.*

It was a fair point. Anything he might find in there would be worthless to him if he were dead. His eyes scanned Ground Zero. Had the Prism damaged it... *yes!* He already knew that the Prism's arrival had burst through the fence, but the rear corner edge of the Prism had smashed a gap open in the Ground Zero facility wall as well. It was as if the back of a giant heel had come down upon the front of the building, and now, a small, dark opening into the facility could just be seen behind it, looking like a small cave mouth. It didn't look particularly safe to pass through—the rest of the wall could crumble inwards at any moment—but it was an opening.

*This isn't the kind of Arrival you expected,* his brain countered. *There's no Stone Man—that's why you didn't get a vision... so Plan A is out; there's no Pointer Theory to test—*

"Harry," Eric whispered. "We can actually *get into* Ground Zero..."

Harry scoffed.

"We'd be torn to pieces. *Look* at them."

The Shufflers, Eric saw, had all moved down off the ring road. Even in their mania, they apparently understood blockades. *Or maybe they'd been waiting,* Eric thought. Either way, they were packed in tight all around the exposed parts of the Prism, so much so that others, some Eric hadn't seen before, were now spread around the rest of the Ground Zero building itself. Their demeanour had worsened. They were all pacing on the spot, turning and breathing heavily, growling like dogs. The influence upon them had clearly been heightened by the energy wall's passing. To get through the gap, they'd have to get past the Shufflers.

"Saw what they did to the soldiers—"

"But the soldiers *grabbed* them—"

*"Look at them."*

As they watched, two of the Shufflers—a man and a woman— connected with only minimal force. The man roared and went to grab at the woman, but she ducked under his hands, screaming, and went at his throat with her teeth.

"Shit..." Eric gasped.

The man, though larger, fell backwards, punching at the woman's head and bellowing, but she held on.

"Don't look," Harry said. They both averted their gaze until the screaming stopped. "You can't get in there. *Yet,*" Harry said.

"You have *got* to be joking," Eric gasped, genuinely stunned by his response. "You want to just go *that* way?" He pointed to the horizon.

"I'm not sure we'd survive if we tried going in. Look, that's the only part of the building that's crumbled," Harry said calmly, his face blank. "Even if it's not, those people are all around it. *We can't get in there.* Why would you want to, anyway?" Before Eric could give a very lengthy answer, Harry pointed a finger at Eric's left shoulder. "Plus, we have to fix *that* before we can do anything."

Eric was confused for a moment then remembered that *crack* that he'd heard. Taking a deep breath, Eric followed Harry's finger and looked at his own shoulder. That was a mistake, as he saw the missing chunk there just as the adrenalin was wearing off. The shoulder pad of his jacket had burst open and was soaked with his blood, as was the ragged patch of shirt beneath. With all of that fabric and redness, Eric couldn't see how bad it was or how deep, but it was a mess, and the pain was arriving now, dull and warm.

"Oh…" he breathed. He'd been shot. *Madness.*

"Don't think they were shooting at us," Harry said, inspecting. "Probably a stray bullet. We have to check it, clean it and close it up," said Harry solemnly. "That can get infected very quickly, and you're bleeding badly."

"I… I don't care, I need to…"

"Eric. Look at me." Eric did. "Now look at them." Eric did. "Now answer me honestly: do you *really* think we would survive trying to get past them right now?"

"I…"

Harry hesitated, then put his hand on Eric's good shoulder.

"Whatever it is, man, it's going to have to wait. And we *need* to clean that and close it."

*No…*

He was so *painfully* close. But Harry was right.

Eric looked up at Ground Zero and actually fought back tears as he swore a solemn promise under his breath.

*I'll be back soon, you bastards. I'll be back.*

The pain in his shoulder began to worsen.

"Uh… are you a doctor or something?" Eric sniffed.

"I only did St John's, back in my day," Harry said, fishing in his pocket and producing a stack of napkins that he'd liberated from a Starbucks. "But I can clean this and dress it, reckon I can stitch it too, but I'll have to go to my place and get supplies." He folded the napkins into a thick pad and pressed it onto Eric's wound. It *hurt*, badly, but Eric put his hand on the napkins to keep them in place as his shoulder throbbed.

*St John's? Volunteer ambulance?* Eric thought. *How did this apparently community-minded man end up on the street?*

"Actually…" Eric said, and paused. He never told anyone about his stashes. He didn't want anyone taking them, and also… well, it was embarrassing. Real *prepper* stuff. "I have some… stuff stashed very near here." He sighed. "Change of clothes, spare sleeping bag, rucksacks, some emergency canned stuff, that kind of thing. First aid and medical stuff too. It's really close by." Harry looked surprised. Eric reddened. "I'm over this way a lot, okay? So it makes sense to have stuff here, if I need it. And you never know what's going to happen when you're dealing with all this, how badly you could get hurt." He didn't mention the other four stashes he had, spread out in an even radius around the abandoned parts of the city centre.

"Oh. Okay. Where?"

Eric had to think about it.

"Nearest one is probably inside Kasbah. Someone had broken in a while back." Harry looked at him blankly. *Of course,* Eric thought. "Sorry, you might remember it as the Tick Tock Club."

"Ohhh... right."

"But we need to be quick, okay? Let's fix it and plan our next move."

Harry suddenly jerked his head to say, *Let's go then,* and started walking in the right direction. Eric fell into step alongside Harry, wincing as his shoulder burned and listening to the silence. He watched, amazed, as the energy wall continued to churn above them in the sky. Harry, looking very serious, pulled out the hip flask again and took a deep pull. Eric noticed. If Harry got drunk, could he carry out minor surgery?

It wasn't like he had much choice, was it?

After a few minutes, they were down the relevant off-ramp and back at street level. Eric kept looking for movement, for any motion that told him they weren't the only people still alive in the city. He was incredibly tense and restless, and his shoulder throbbed with every step.

*The fucking Stone Men were simply indestructible by all accounts,* Eric thought. *Does the fact that they used that dome thing mean that the Prism is vulnerable? By the way, you know you're walking* away *from Ground Zero, right?*

It wasn't until they were walking up the slight incline towards Kasbah that Harry suddenly spoke.

"Why are we *alive?*" Harry muttered, eyes still on the road. "Why didn't it kill us?"

Eric considered the question.

"Stop a second," he said. They did. Ahead of them, a large dirty white building rose up on the left-hand side of the road. The place was huge, and an independent venue at that. When it was still in business, Kasbah would have been classed as a super-club in any other city. They were standing by the high fence that created a barrier between the street and the enormous outdoor bar area of the nightclub. *A barrier,* Eric thought. *Is that what the thing above us is? If so, is it keeping everyone out or keeping us* in?

"Listen," he said.

"Don't hear anything."

"But you *do* hear *something*," Eric said. *"Listen—"*

Harry sighed, rolling his eyes... but then his eyes widened as he *did* hear it.

"Birdsong," he said.

"Right," Eric said, wincing as he pointed with his bad-shoulder arm. "Birdsong. The *birds* are alive. *We're* alive too, so that means *that* thing," he said, pointing into the sky, "is *selective*. It's not just a wall of killing energy. Now, it might have been set up to kill humans and not other organisms, and somehow, we were just lucky... but that seems a little *glitchy* for those Stone guys, don't you think? I don't get the impression that the stuff they make and send has a lot of holes in it." Harry looked up at the sky. You had to squint to see the Barrier directly above against the white clouds.

"Sounds right to me," Harry said quietly. "Assuming that's the case, then I'm asking again: why are *we* alive? Those soldiers hadn't gone crazy like those people standing around near Ground Zero, and neither did we. But the soldiers died, and us and the crazies didn't."

Eric winced again at the memory of the soldiers. "Yeah... that's my point. I think that means we *have* something. Something different to both of those groups."

"Soldiers would all be from different places," Harry said, shaking his head. "Different parts of the country, different backgrounds. They'd *all* just happen to be inside some unique, *killable* bracket?"

"I don't know about the soldiers, but I think the difference between us and the Shufflers is that you and I... well, I think we have something a little extra."

Harry's slack face didn't even twitch.

"Go on," he said softly.

"Harry, I *felt* you when I got up to that lookout area. I didn't get that from any of those people, or the soldiers for that matter. Remember when we shook hands? And we had that jolt?" Eric said, waving his hand for emphasis. "That meant something. I met a friend for a drink a few hours earlier and touched him, and nothing like that happened." *Luis,* Eric suddenly thought. *Would he be like the soldiers?* No. Surely, he had moved outside of the city centre and was safe. That thing couldn't have travelled that far out.

*At least, not yet.*

"Okay, I met up with him before things started to happen in Coventry," Eric continued, "but things had already started to happen on the coast. Those things... people on the news were calling them the Empty Men."

"Think they're coming this way?" Harry asked out of nowhere, sending a chill down Eric's spine. The thought hadn't occurred to him at all. He'd been too obsessed with what was going on at Ground Zero. "There's more than one of them, isn't there? The big ones dividing into smaller ones? I can't see them staying out at sea. Maybe they were waiting for *that* thing to turn up," he said, jerking his head towards Ground Zero, then upwards. "Or for *that* thing." It was harder than ever to see now against the almost-night sky. Eric didn't have an answer. What Harry was saying made horrible sense.

"I... I don't know. Maybe. One thing at a time, Harry," Eric said, trying to relocate his train of thought. "Okay, cards on the table," he said, looking Harry dead in the eye. "When we met, I asked why you'd gone to Ground Zero. You said you followed the people. I don't think that's true. I think you felt something. I think you were drawn there. *I* was drawn there. So be honest with me."

Harry's inscrutable expression wavered for a moment, eyes shifting.

"Did you see anything?" Harry suddenly asked. Eric was confused by the question. "In the first three Arrivals," Harry explained, "I did."

Now it was Eric's turn to use a poker face. The question was standard water cooler chat or dinner conversation now. *Did you ever see anything?* He'd always managed to laugh convincingly and say, *No, only pink elephants around closing time,* and it would be met with a polite little chuckle. People who *knew* Eric stopped asking after the Second Arrival.

*Tell him the truth.*

"Yes," Eric said. "Yes, I did." It made him feel naked.

"You see the blond fella? The old fella? The woman? That lot?"

Eric nodded as the lump started to form in his throat.

*Not this,* he thought. *Not now.*

"Yes," he croaked, blinking fast. "All of them."

Eric knew Harry meant during the Arrivals. He didn't mention the vision he'd had during the Big Power Cut a year ago.

The big man, screaming.

Harry pointed at the empty nightclub.

"Me too," Harry said. "Let's get inside." Harry saw Eric's crestfallen face and gently turned the younger man's good shoulder. Eric allowed himself to be led like an obedient child.

"The front door," Eric grunted, clearing his throat. "It's… *uhh…* the shutters are down but they aren't locked."

Harry grunted slightly as he bent to lift the shutters. They rattled upwards, suddenly deafening in the near-silent street. "Okay. Show me where your stuff is."

***

The whole club had an unpleasant, musty smell to it, and when lit only by Eric's phone torch the place felt like a crypt. There were two old wooden chairs in the cloakroom, and neither man had spoken a word since they came inside. Not even when they saw the hoodie and jeans and accompanying pair of trainers. They lay in a pool of thick dried blood just inside the club's doorway. Nearby there had been a sleeping bag, a bottle of water, and a bong. Despite the empty houses and apartments nearby, many with beds, it appeared someone had still used the empty nightclub as a sleeping space. Eric looked at the very recent remains with a morbid curiosity; he would imagine that vaporizing an entire human body would mean an incredible amount of liquid, but it appeared that after the initial *bursting,* contact with what he now thought of as the Barrier meant that remains were desiccated and fried at the same time. The circle of blood was congealed, almost burnt-looking, and only a foot or two in diameter at that. He observed all this, felt nothing and realized that he was probably in shock.

He eyeballed the three remaining jackets still hanging, incredibly, inside the cloakroom, and wondered if any of them would fit.

*You need a replacement,* he thought. *Yours is totally shot.*

He nearly got the giggles then but caught them. If he started losing it…

Harry was fishing through Eric's extensive first aid collection.

"Got antibiotics here," he said. Incredibly, Harry's eyebrows were raised.

*Wow*, Eric thought. *You've impressed him enough to change his expression.*

"You even got rations. Sterile gauze, sterile water... you really did well to get all this."

"Thanks," Eric said, then added, "Not just this either. I have at least another four elsewhere, I think."

"You don't mess around."

"No. I don't mess around."

Harry nodded and waved the antibiotics at Eric.

"You'll need to take two of those a day for the next two weeks." He handed them to Eric along with a bottle of distilled water and two other pills. Eric recognized them. Prescription-grade painkillers. "Those'll make it easier when we do the stitching, so take them now," Harry grunted. "Gonna hurt regardless, though."

Eric turned a nearby wooden chair around, gingerly removed his jacket and shirt, and sat with his back to Harry. He hadn't dared look at his shoulder yet.

"Got to clean it first," Harry muttered. "Looks like it didn't do bone damage. Very shallow. Skimmed the top. Flesh wound."

"It doesn't fucking *feel* shallow—"

Harry poured fire into his shoulder.

"*Fuck*—"

"Gonna give those pills a few minutes before we stitch," Harry interrupted, putting down the alcohol and leaning against the wall. "Can I ask you something?"

"Uh-huh."

"Why did you stay here?" Harry asked.

"Oh... well, this is the place you have to be if you want to try to monitor communications. They're mostly encrypted, so it's very hard to—"

"Sorry, that's not the right question," Harry said, waving his hand. "I mean... why do you care so much?"

"My sister was Theresa Pettifer." It came straight out now, zero hesitation. *I really must be in shock,* he thought.

Harry's eyes widened slightly. "Jesus," he said. "I'm sorry to hear that." He scowled. "Sorry, not that she was your sister, I mean what happened with the, you know, her and the kid—"

"It's alright," Eric said, saving Harry from further fumbling. "Don't worry."

"But... I thought you'd be on the inside with them, after that?"

Eric regarded Harry carefully.

"How'd you mean?" he said quietly. His tone was dark.

"Family connection, I mean," Harry said. "Like... you'd want to work with them? Help find out what happened..." Harry trailed off, unsure if he was out of line. Eric relaxed slightly, shaking his head with a bitter smile.

"Harry," he said, "I wouldn't trust those fuckers if *Jesus* endorsed them."

"Okay... why?"

Eric shifted in his chair, wincing slightly, and stared at the ceiling.

"They're liars, Harry," he said with a sigh. "I realized it right after she died. D'you know, I couldn't even speak to anyone to find out any concrete information? The police kept saying I had to wait to hear from the military. I just kept calling, and when that didn't work, I started going down to the station. On the third day, I caused so much of a scene—I was really going nuts, I mean, *where was her fucking body, man?*—they arrested me for public disturbance and put me in a cell. Word must have got to someone, because that night, someone came to see me. A woman. Military." In his mind, he saw the white walls, the inside of the thick metal door painted blue, the one with the hatch at eye level. "I will never forget that conversation. Long as I live. Changed my life." He sniffed. "Not in a good way."

"What did she say?"

"I knew it as soon as my visitor told me her name," Eric said, ignoring the question and lost in the memory. "She had this very *strong* air about her, despite being old enough to be my mother and about five foot nothing. Her face said, *I am used to people doing what I say because I am very good at what I do.* You know that thing about women in the army having to overcome sexism? That they have to work twice as hard and have to get twice as good as the men just to be treated the same?" He smirked bitterly. "It spoke volumes that someone of such a high rank came to see little old me. She was a *brigadier.*"

Harry raised his eyebrows, looking impressed.

"One look in those eyes and I *knew.*"

He remembered them. They'd been like sharpened points mounted on the iron shield of her face.

"Knew what?"

Eric let out a long, steady outbreath and realized that, in the telling of it, maybe the demon was a little smaller.

"Straub, her name was. Brigadier Straub. And I *knew* she was going to lie to me. It sounds like a cliché, right? *I could see it in her eyes.* But I could. The rest of her was this mask of fucking *duty,* and whatever those bastards had done to Theresa, they thought—or *she* thought—it was for the greater good. I don't think she *regretted* it as such." He wagged a finger at thin air, that bitter smirk back on his lips. "But it still *weighed* on her, oh yes. Even her. That's why *she'd* come to see me and not some lieutenant or some shit. I almost respected her for that. At least she didn't send someone else to do her dirty work, her penance."

"What did she say?"

"She starts in with the *I'm sorry for your loss,* and *I'm here to answer any questions that you might have.*" Eric scoffed, shaking his head. "She didn't sit down, I remember that. And I'm just lying on the bunk-bench, looking like a half-starved wreck because that was exactly what I was—I don't think I'd eaten since I'd been back in the UK—and I just start yelling at her to cut the bullshit. I yelled so much that the cops kept coming to the hatch to ask if everything was okay. Every time, she calmly tells them everything's fine and they leave. I called her everything under the sun, and she just stood there. Bitch didn't even flinch."

"Did... did she *answer* anything?" Harry asked. He was leaning slightly forwards now, fascinated.

Eric shook his head. "Not in any significant way. I rattled about twenty questions off at her, not even pausing to actually let her bloody answer. Every time I asked one, I thought of something else. And she just stands there until I'm done, and then she just takes this breath and goes into this... this fucking *speech.* This *timeline,* and I knew it was bullshit from the first word, but I wanted to at least hear the story they were going to peddle. She says that the Prime Minister was going to make a Second Arrival statement tomorrow, but they wanted to tell me first, in person, *out of respect.* I nearly laughed at that. They claimed that Theresa had already come forwards; she knew they were coming for her and volunteered to meet with the Stone Men for the good of the country. She'd been in intense distress due to the unexpected 'cot death' of her son. *That* was supposedly due to the Stone Men's connection to the mother; the child's body had been too fragile at that age to handle it. They claimed *full and spontaneous organ shutdown.*" Harry shuffled on the spot awkwardly at this mental image but said nothing. "She said that Theresa sadly took her own life in custody—while briefly unsupervised—due to her distress.

"I said that I wanted to see the bodies, and Straub gave me the poker face routine. *Unfortunately, that's not possible, as we need to do a full autopsy. We need to learn more about the Stone Men and any reasons why Theresa may have been chosen.* She said because they didn't know enough about any potential pathogens linked between the Stone Men and my sister and my nephew, they would have to cremate the bodies. Such blatant *bullshit,* you know? That was when I started screaming. *I'm the next of kin, I don't give my fucking consent for you to cut my family open.* Straub tried to calm me down, and when that didn't work, she gave it to me straight: They didn't *need* my consent. It was a matter of national security. That's when I *really* lost it. The police came back, and Straub looks at the guy through the hatch and says, cool as a cucumber—I won't forget this—*This will take as long as it takes, officer. I don't expect to speak to you again.* Ice-cold bitch, that one, but very good." He *hated* Straub—it was a rage previously unknown to the old Eric—but there was that strange grudging respect at the same time. "Then I just pleaded with her to tell me the truth, Harry. I *begged.* She just watched, the eyes saying it all, and only once did that poker face falter. I caught her *out,* man."

Harry folded his arms at this and cocked his head, waiting.

"*How did she volunteer when the neighbour told me she'd barricaded herself into the house?* I asked her. Straub was *good,* man, didn't miss a beat. They must teach Advanced Bullshit at officer academy or something. *Yes,* she says, *Theresa told us she'd done that. She'd had to remove the boards in order to get out, apparently it took her quite a while.* She didn't realize she'd just walked right into my set-up. *Okay, I said, then why, when I got there, was the door off its hinges with a caved-in section by the lock? That door had been smashed in from the* outside. *What was that about?"*

His lips twisted involuntarily as he recalled it. *That's what hate does,* he thought. *It* twists, *makes your body turn in on itself.*

"And she blinked a few times. Just a few blinks, but for Straub I think that was a huge tell. I'd just told her about a big screw-up. In all the chaos, someone hadn't done their job. Must have assumed someone else was dealing with the clean-up. They'd evacuated the street, there were no witnesses, and there were far, *far* more pressing things to deal with than making sure the door was removed from the scene. Or maybe what she said next was *planned* to be the official line, but it got lost in the mess. *It must have been looters,* she said. *We've had many unfortunate reports of evacuated houses being looted before the owners could return. I'm sorry, that must have been a lot to deal with on top of—* and I didn't hear the rest, because at that point, I lost it and tried to go for her. It was a good thing I was still cuffed to the bed."

Eric didn't mention that he meant a good job for *his* sake. He knew that a military woman would have probably had more than a few tricks up her sleeve, and Eric wasn't an experienced fighter by any means.

"She stood there for about five minutes while I ranted and screamed. Then she made her excuses and left. Once they let me out of jail, someone in a suit, *two* someones, came to my house a few days later. I watched them through the window upstairs until they left. After that I started... getting into this stuff more and more. I started to go a bit off the rails, if I'm honest. Started looking at forums all night, message boards. Reading about the *billions* the Stone Men caused in losses to the country and what that might mean."

Eric looked at Harry and actually whispered the next part out of idiotic habit. There had never been anyone listening in the past and, almost certainly, no-one listening now.

"If the government could identify who the Stone Men were heading to see, surely it made sense that they could cut out the middleman, the middle *Stone* fucking Man..."

Harry nodded again, that same sad, knowing movement. "It'd make sense to get things wrapped up quickly," he said, finishing for Eric. "Take the Stone Men's Targets out themselves."

"The Third Arrival did a lot to quell that theory," Eric said. "After all, only two of them started walking that time, remember? The original Stone Man and one of the blue ones. The government must have taken all of the people out super-quick that time and maybe the last two slipped through the net. The blue one that went after George Mykos, and the original one that vanished and went home somewhere up north. Whoever *that* one was after must have had a lucky escape. We never got *his* name."

"Yeah, I heard that theory before," Harry said. "You really think that's true? The government was—"

"Of course," Eric snapped, trying to keep his irrational anger down. Even the *question* annoyed him. What did these sheep *think* had hap—

*Stop being a petulant teenager. You're a reasonable man who has been asked a reasonable question.*

He physically forced himself to calm. "I do, Harry, I do. Think about it. It worked out beautifully for them. If they can get to the people—the word they use on the forums is *Quarry;* it's kind of a dark pun—before the Stone Men even start heading their way, then they can whack them and bundle them in with all the usual religious or fear-based suicides that happened every time the Stone Men appeared or claim that they had visions and went crazy.

Best of all, *maybe they don't have to say anything as so many people die or disappear in the mess when those things come.* Look, I don't imagine the Illuminati making secret, Machiavellian plans; I think that, most of the time, the truth is far more boring and mundane than we like to admit. I think it's as simple as corrupt or weak people saying *yes* to things they should say *no* to. But you know why I believe in *this* theory, and it's not just because of Theresa and Aaron? The motive. This isn't for money or to please the toga-wearing overlords of their secret satanic pedo-cult or whatever. In their minds, this was for the *national interest.* I think they could justify it because for once they truly believed they were doing the right thing. Stopping chaos, protecting the economy against collapse. That's why I believe it. They think they're the good guys."

"What if they are?" Harry asked quietly, leaning back against the wall once more. Eric looked up sharply, his eyes blazing.

"What?"

"They told lies. Did very bad things," Harry said, his face as inscrutable as ever. "But what if it really did *save* more lives?"

"I've asked myself that many times, Harry. Here's the response I have, and it's the reason I do what I do: *I know what the press said about her.*"

Eric's voice was now low and breathless.

"They said she had a drinking problem," he whispered. "That she killed her kid in a drunken rage. They even came after *me* briefly, but I guess there wasn't enough of a social media response, so I was dropped. They said George Mykos was a recluse and hinted that he was a sexual deviant. That wasn't the military, no, it was the papers, *but if they'd told the truth, then those people would have been truly remembered as heroes.* They made Patrick Marshall a hero, but they couldn't do it with the others, as that would have been too suspicious. So, they let the vultures pick at their bones."

Eric stood up and started to pace, ignoring the pain in his shoulder. "Straub stood in front of me—while I grieved for my dead family members—and lied to my *face,* Harry. That's what they do; they lie. They lie to the whole damn country. Case in point: do you remember the Panama Flu thing?"

Harry shifted on the spot. Eric could see he was making Harry uncomfortable, but he was determined to make the truth understood.

"When they offered all the free jabs?" Harry asked. It had been all over the news, the strain finally reaching the UK after causing havoc in mainland Europe. The government responded by announcing a national immunity-booster programme. "You can't be serious. That was real; I knew two people who had it."

"That's what I mean, man. That's part of whatever they're working on. Whether the flu was real or not, there was something else in that response that they didn't tell you about. Did you get your booster?"

"Yes, I did, didn't want that shit to happen to me—"

"Then you *should* be concerned. I didn't go anywhere near that crap. It's all over the forums. They think it's really called the Kindness Protocol." He suddenly fished his phone out of his pocket, remembering something. "Here, *here.*" He thumbed the screen, found what he was after, and thrust the device into Harry's hand. On the unlocked screen, Harry saw at least eight audio files and more seemed to continue off the bottom of the phone's display. They were labelled O'REARDON 110, 111, 112. Harry looked back up at him, confused. "Folder is triple encrypted. You're the only other person that *I* know, other than Mickey, that have heard these. I paid thousands for them on the Dark Web, cleared out my savings. Dynamite *before* the Prime Minister's confession at the press conference, when they admitted they'd had the Stone Man under lock and key. Rendered the tapes almost worthless. If I leaked these now, it'd only cause a ripple, but I'm waiting until I have—"

*—proof of what they did to her—*

"… Until I've finished completing a dossier. They don't give away much, but it proves the kind of thing that was going on up north. The people they were interviewing."

"How did these get out?"

"Someone named O'Reardon. We think she was a psychologist—the tapes seem to say so—but she's in a mental institute in Northampton now, and no-one can get to her. Something happened up at the 'wind farm' in Sheffield, and we don't know what, but she somehow leaked some stuff. Most of it was pointless email logs, but somewhere in all the mess were these tapes. They're interviews, initial assessments, on-site mental health checks, outgoing interviews. The best one on there is the one with someone called *Sophie Warrender*, 127. Listen to it—"

"So, once you got into all this… that how you ended up on the streets?"

"I made a choice. I sold my house, Theresa's house, took the money and went all the way off-grid. *Yes,* there were some very, very difficult times. Antidepressants didn't really touch the sides, let me put it that way." Eric had only kicked them a little while ago, realising as he mentioned them that he'd hadn't thought about them for a while. *Shows how much they were working.* "That's where I met Mickey. He wasn't… he wasn't a very nice person. But he got me up from absolute rock bottom, probably because I was as passionate about the truth as him, and he thought I might be useful. And today I was trying to…" He sighed. "There's a difference between coming forwards and ending up on a hitlist for the next Arrival or being *indispensable* and on the inside like Andy Pointer was. That would have been worth the risk."

"What do you mean?"

"The Pointer Theory—ah, it doesn't matter."

He sighed again and threw his hands up.

"I can't stop, Harry. Even if I wanted to. I promised her, after she died, and I've got to keep *one* promise for once."

There was an awkward silence.

"I'm very sorry to hear about what happened to you," Harry eventually said, and even with his blank face and flat voice, Eric could feel that he meant it.

"Thanks." *More* awkward silence. Dammit, why didn't Harry ever *talk?*

"Did you ever tell anyone about your visions?" Eric asked.

"No."

"Why not?"

Harry shrugged.

"Didn't want anyone to think I was fuckin' crazy."

"Huh," Eric said. "Maybe I should have tried that."

Harry snorted quietly, breaking a smile, and things were okay enough. Eric's weariness began to heavily settle in. He didn't know if it was from the painkillers or the blood loss or just the ridiculousness of the impossible day. Harry was still holding Eric's phone.

"You can listen to the audio if you want," Eric asked. "You should. It's only a few minutes. Well, apart from Linda Wyken, 117—she doesn't shut up."

Harry shrugged in agreement.

"Might as well. Something to listen to while I stitch you up."

Eric didn't ask the question he was thinking. *Then what?*

"Okay," he said. "Harry, I need to get to Ground Zero after that—"

He hadn't had any visions, so he didn't think that any Stone

Men were coming, but time had passed. Maybe he could get past the Shufflers now—

"You'll need to rest it—"

"I can't do that."

He could though. He was so damn *sleepy.*

"Mmm. Guess it doesn't matter." Harry said. "Probably gonna die anyway."

"... Maybe. Why do you think that?"

Harry thumbed along the list of audio files onscreen.

"You had visions. I had visions," he said, "and like you say, that thing seems to be selective in who it kills. Not us, not the birds. So, it's either defective or it's pre-programmed. If it's the latter, then *that* means we've been kept alive on purpose. That means they want us for something."

Eric's skin went cold.

"So that's *two* things that scare the living shit out of me," Harry said, sighing and rubbing his bristled face as he pushed *play.* Background noise from whichever room was on the recording began to filter out of Eric's phone's speakers. "The fact they *want* us in here for some reason. And the fact that everybody else has been kept out."

The near-silence in the room was eerie, punctuated only by the scraping of chairs on the recording.

"... Do you think the pills will have worked yet?" Eric asked.

"Don't know. Try moving it a little."

Eric did. It was very painful but dull now, more distant. "Might be okay," he said.

"Okay. Good," Harry said, fishing in the huge box once more and producing the surgical needle and thread. "Still going to hurt like a bastard, though."

***

PROJECT OROUBOROS.
O'REARDON 117: LINDA WYKEN.
EXIT WEEK SESSION 2 OF 5.


Four? *Bloody hell... then we're done?*

*Good. The 'exit interview' was horrible. I want me saying that on the record. I think you have all been extremely ungrateful. I know I'm going home, but there was just no need for that. The last session in the cabin was upsetting enough as it was. Seeing him like that... and then the exit interview? I thought the timing was very unfair. You could have at least given me a few hours before all the threats started. It was like being reverse indoctrinated or something. They put the fear of God into us. You may be monitored, all that. Treason? Ungrateful bastards. I signed an NDA, didn't I? I came here to help. Let's just get this done with and get these bloody things off my head.*

*Dr Garrett said you wanted me to start with the business that happened just before the Third Arrival. The vision I had. My only vision, I should add. I only had dreams before that. But it was the vision that made me call you.*

*Eh? What's the point in describing it? You know who I saw, what he looks like...*

*Fine. My vision was of a big guy. He was crying... wait, is that what these things are for? Electrodes? When I talk about this, what are you measuring—*

*Fine. Uh, the vision. Well, I kind of panicked and it vanished, but later, it happened again at the house and again at night, and I just knew that it was real. I could feel that man as if he were in the room. I ran into the back garden, screaming, freaking out, but I was also frustrated, and I just shook my fists at the sky and asked the... well, this really does sound stupid but... I asked the world where the hell this man was, so I could find him to get rid of him. I just tried to feel where he was. And then... I did. It was the strangest thing I've ever felt in my life. I must have stood there for about ten minutes, letting it come to me, sharpening it. I could tell I was homing in, the way you can tell that a lift is moving downwards.*

*And then BAM, the feeling stopped, and yes, that's when I had the... What was the word Dr Gopal used...? Interference. Oh, God. It was horrible, this awful sound in my head, and it hurt. It was really short though, because the second it started, I let go of whatever I'd connected to, ping. Like I'd been holding on to something hot. It was... a bad sound. Do I have to talk more about that? Okay, good. Well, I should have felt even more freaked out by that, but as it happened, I felt a bit better for some reason. Then later, when the Third Arrival actually happened, I didn't feel bad at all. No visions. Nothing. I watched it all on TV like everyone else, before they shut down all the coverage anyway. A few days later, I saw the ad on TV, the Be Prepared appeal one.*

*(Pause.)*

*I didn't call straightaway. I felt silly. I didn't think I would be what you were looking for. I mean, even the other signups here, they'd seen several faces, but I'd only ever seen one, so I didn't think I'd be... So anyway, I kept putting it off. Well, there was always an excuse, wasn't there? But... you know, eventually my daughter starts working and gets her own place... and four years later, I'm sitting at home alone again with a glass of wine feeling a bit low and the ad comes on the TV. For some reason, I think, stuff it and I called the next morning. They asked me the initial questions, describe the vision, etc. Then I went to London for the interview. Three hours. Family history questions, even those little cards from the start of Ghostbusters... Zener cards. They said I'd only just caught the annual intake date. I asked why they only took annually. I mean, I thought they'd want as many as possible. They said the number of people that accurately fit the criteria, at the level they want, is quite low. Is that true?*

*Mmm. I guess that's a compliment, then.*

*I was surprised when I got here. I'd expected to see soldiers in uniform, not the, you know, the polo shirt and jeans combo thing. I mean, it made sense, trying to keep it looking all civilian. Then they took us into Office Six to sign things, and then to the waiting room... Does this matter at this point? Garrett said you'd want to watch me talk about all this... right.*

*I was... nervous in the waiting room. Nervous. No-one else looked comfortable. One guy was sitting there with his arms tight around himself, rocking back and forth and that blonde woman, whatshername... Warrender. Sophie Warrender. She just stared out of the window, dabbing at her nose because it was bleeding.*

*I felt a little out of my depth because whatever was affecting them wasn't affecting me anywhere near that level—all I had was a headache that started when I came on site. That didn't make any sense at the time; the Arrivals were supposedly over after all. I know now obviously Warrender was on a whole other level to me. I mean, she's in Strachan Group now though—she's not going home—so I'm guessing she must be the bee's knees... is she?*

*Come on. That's got to be okay to tell me? I heard people using a codeword the other day, you know. Dispensatori. That's Sophie Warrender, isn't it?*

*Fine, fine. So, I'm in the waiting room. A woman comes in, and she's in a different uniform, and I rightly assumed she was in charge. Either way, a woman in charge in the army, good to see, right? It's just unfortunate to see that this one is a total pain in the arse. And that's swearing. Hello, she says, and thanks us for volunteering. We're operating almost completely in the dark, she says, but if it turns out you can help, then we can talk about what happens next, and if you can't we'll be extremely grateful for your time, and either way, you get paid. I think that was supposed to be a joke to lighten the mood, but I don't think she regularly made jokes. My name is Brigadier Straub, she says. Welcome to Project Ouroboros...*

*I was nervous as hell when she finished. She laid out all of the consequences that would happen if we broke our NDAs and talked— didn't appreciate that either, frankly—and then she says we're going to the main hangar, so we need to put on our hazmat suits 'as a precaution', which made me feel even worse, before you ask. And she says... ah, how did she put it, it was so... that was it. She says what you're about to see may frighten you, but if you stick to the rules, you'll be safe. I didn't know what to think. We just got in the van. It wasn't far, so I presume the van was for cover, you know, keeping the hazmats from view. It was hot. And I felt...*

*Hmm. This is gonna sound stupid.*

*(Pause.)*

*It was creepy. Not because of... you know... but it was actually the lights. The ones in the roof. It was so dark except for... it was the way those huge lights were concentrated on the centre, creating this weird... halo effect over that thing in the middle. That wasn't light. You know, when I was a kid... do you have time for this? Does this count? Brain responses, yes. Okay.*

*My grandmother used to like to wind us up before bed—the exact opposite of what she was supposed to do, I know, but that was my babunia—by telling us scary stories. She was Polish on her mother's side. Her stories were always about the Dark Things. We'd always say tell us about the Dark Things, Babunia, and normally, she'd be too tired or in a bad mood or just wanted to watch Eastenders or Parkinson or just couldn't think of a story. She didn't do it very often. She could be a grumpy sod, to be honest. But when she did tell us those stories... they were brilliant, just brilliant...*

*(Long pause.)*

*I'm telling you, Doctor. That thing in the hangar is a Dark Thing. I could feel it. I could feel it as sure as I'm sitting in front of you right now.*

*(Pause.)*

*Okay. So I saw the cabin, obviously. Driving itself in a circle. Little window in the side, like a big metal caravan, only uglier. I remember seeing light from inside the window and noticing, just before it turned away, that there were curtains hanging in there. Curtains, I thought, what on earth? Is someone inside there? Is someone living in that? But the funny thing is that I knew there was someone in there. Once I was that close, I could feel it. Even little old me could feel it.*

*(Pause.)*

*I... ugh, look, I don't want to describe what was following behind the cabin. You know I don't like talking about it. I get these dreams sometimes... Look, can't I just go home today rather than tomorrow....*

*(Pause.)*

*Fine. I assumed that... thing had been there for a long time. The Third Arrival was years ago, and I could see how all the walking had worn a deep groove into the dirt, separate from the cabin tracks.*

*I felt stunned. Everyone else was the same, totally silent. Watching that thing walk—as terrified as I was, as terribly exposed as I felt—was... indescribable. It just didn't look possible. It was silent. Totally silent. I wonder how the hell they dared show us this, but then I remembered Straub's threats on the way in. Nothing compared to the ones on the way out this morning, mind you—*

*What? No. I don't like to refer to it by name. Not when I'm this close to it. I know that's stupid.*

*(Pause.)*

*Jesus, fine. Fine. (Deep breath.)*
*Walking behind the cabin was the Stone Man. Okay?*

\*\*\*

Eric jerked awake, gasping in air and frantically looking around himself. He'd passed out? How long had he been out? How much time had he lost—

Wait. Something had woken him up. What had it been?

Then Harry was suddenly leaping to his feet in a flash, crouching slightly as if he was expecting something to hit him. Eric's phone fell to the floor, the audio from one of the leaked recordings coming to an end. Harry had been listening to them while Eric was asleep, then.

*"What is it? What is it?"* Eric hissed, but Harry put a finger to his lips.

*"Shhhhh! Shhhhh! Wait! Wait!"* he hissed back. Eric's chest cramped from the panic, and his fucking shoulder was buzzing at him, no, *barking*, and *oh yeah*, his waking brain finally remembered he'd been shot and stitched up. Still shirtless, he glanced at the wound; it was now neatly dressed, the far less painful part of the job completed while Eric was unconscious. Now the painkillers were wearing off, and the healing wound *did* hurt like a bastard.

Eric listened, alert. He couldn't hear a thing. After a moment—

"Harry."

*"Shh!"*

Still nothing.

*"... Harry."*

Pause.

*"What?"*

*"What woke me up, Harry? What's happened?"*

Pause.

*"... I don't know."*

Pause.

*"... Was there a noise?"*

*"... No."*

Pause. Eric realized something.

*"Harry. I really need a piss."*

Harry's eyes searched the room. He didn't respond.

*"I don't think anything's here,"* Eric said. *"Do you?"*

Harry straightened up and lowered his hands.

"No, actually."

"Okay. I'm gonna go and have a piss in the gents, and then we'll talk about it when I come back."

"Right you are."

Harry let out a sigh and leaned on the wall, trying to calm down, and once Eric was on his feet, something shifted in his head, and he immediately pitched sideways.

*"Fuck—"*

He managed to turn just in time, letting his good shoulder hit the wall, but doing so left his head unprotected and it collided with the plaster. As the world flashed white, he suddenly knew what it was, what was coming.

*Oh, no—*

The vision hit him stronger than it ever had before.

*It's the Barrier,* he thought, his perception being taken over by something outside of himself. *It's stronger because we're inside the Barrier—*

Then all he could do was *see* as his body fell to the floor. He tried to say Harry's name, but he could hear the man choking a few feet away; the vision was hitting him too.

*Oh my God,* Eric thought. *Here it is—*

It wasn't a glimpse of a person. It wasn't even a face.

The vision was *bright*—an incredibly bright light—and while he frantically tried to breathe, part of Eric still tried to see *through* the light, to clear the lens flare that was clouding his mind's eye.

Then he understood what he was looking at. The light wasn't a blurry image.

The vision was of the light *itself*.

It hung there, filling his view, and as his mind spun, he understood that it was… round? Maybe not spherical, but circular at least. Triangles and prisms and circles, it was turning into *Stone Sesame Street*, but he understood that this light was a physical object of some kind.

*As physical as light can be,* he thought. *This* exists *somewhere.*

Somewhere out there, that light was waiting.

*It's close by… and it's* female, Eric suddenly thought, electricity in his veins now. *That light is female.* He knew it even as he simultaneously thought, *How can light be female, you fucking bellend—*

Then it was gone, and he could breathe. The black cloakroom ceiling stared back at him.

"You see that?" Harry gasped.

Eric nodded, incapable of speech, his shoulder flaring back into his awareness. He sat up gingerly and saw Harry's wide eyes. One of them was a little bloodshot. Eric didn't say anything about it. "Did you see that light?" Eric wheezed, noticing that something seemed to be pulling at his scalp, much worse than earlier that day.

"Yeah… maybe we were seeing the Barrier," Harry said, holding his head. "Maybe that's how it looks from far away."

"Maybe," Eric said, "but I don't think so. Didn't it feel smaller than that to you? Like it was *inside* somewhere?" He held his hands up as soon as he said it, seeing Harry already starting to bristle at his unwise choice of words. "Not inside bloody *Ground Zero*, I'm not *hinting*. I just mean... didn't it feel on a smaller scale to you? Like it wasn't city-sized?" He didn't ask, *didn't it feel female?* That was too silly.

"Don't know," Harry said, resting his head against the wall and breathing out wearily. "Wasn't super clear to me. I only realized that it was round just before I stopped seeing it. Did you see that? That it looked like a circle?"

"I did. I actually got that straightaway; it was pretty clear to me." He felt strangely bad for saying it, like he was starting a psychic dick-measuring contest.

"Hmm. In that case," Harry said, straightening up with an old man grunt, "what I meant to say was, *I* actually saw it *very* clearly. I could pick it out of a line-up. I could tell you its exact diameter." Eric realized this was Harry's idea of a joke and faked a chuckle before looking at his watch. He was surprised to see that it was ten p.m. He'd slept for several hours and it would be dark by now. "Why'd you let me sleep so long?" He felt wide awake, more than that... *electrified*. And what was this goddamn feeling in his *scalp?*

"You have a bad wound in your shoulder and needed sleep," Harry replied. "And those antibiotics can really knock you out— you'd only be groggy and useless if I'd woken you. Plus... I was listening to your tapes," he said, nodding at Eric's phone. "Got through a few of them."

"What did you think?" Eric asked, genuinely intrigued.

Harry sighed and shook his head; it wasn't denial though. Eric was learning how Harry used body language and understood what this meant. *They're real, and it's too much.*

"There won't be a lot of light now," Eric said, testing his shoulder a little, "and I worry that if we try to get to the edge of the Barrier in the dark, we might walk into the thing because it's so—"

His scalp tugged sharply at him. Harry gasped at the same time.

"Jesus, feel that?" he asked.

"Yeah!"

"Mm." Harry shifted awkwardly.

"It's okay, Harry," Eric said. "I feel it too, man. It's definitely real." He knew from bitter experience that, once you'd had a few crazy visions that turned out to be legit, it was far too easy to start reading into everything, to have every thought, every hint of instinct and decide that it *meant* something. It became very hard to trust your gut.

"I want to try to get out of the city, but..." Harry said, pretending to be interested in something on the floor. "Look, I don't have much left, generally. But I would really *hate* to not find out what that thing is. That vision was like... what the fuck *was* that?"

"You don't have to explain to me. I understand more than you know." The pull was starting to feel almost irresistible. Didn't it feel like it was pulling him towards Ground Zero anyway? At least in that direction? And he *had* to know what that light was, especially if it was as close as he felt. Ground Zero could come next, even if he had a hunch that the Shufflers would almost certainly still be blocking the way in.

*And if that light can be somehow extinguished,* he thought wildly, *maybe we can stop this shit in its tracks—*

He caught himself. *Extinguished.* The kind of word he thought Straub might use.

*One step at a time. Find the light. Get a move on.*

"Can you feel which way it is?" he asked breathlessly, snatching up his shirt and pulling it back on.

Harry looked up for a moment, trying it.

"Not sure," he said. "You?"

"Not sure either," Eric lied. "Let's get outside and check."

Harry grunted an agreement and pointed to the backpack that was propped against the wall. "Found a backpack in your stash," he said. Eric nodded. You never knew when you might need to move your stuff, and a bag was easier to cart around than a box. "Threw in the food, the distilled water, topped yours up too. Made up a mini first aid kit, packed the antibiotics too. Torch. Thought it might be best to be prepared."

"Okay, yeah, that's fine," Eric replied, pulling a clean T-shirt out of his stash. He hadn't seen it in a while; it had been one of the ones he used to sleep in a while ago, an unimportant one he didn't mind stashing. It had been a joke gift from a friend, the words I'M NOT A GYNOCOLOGIST BUT I'LL TAKE A LOOK splashed across the front. A little inappropriate for the end of the world, but at least it wasn't covered in blood. It was certainly better to have the kit with them than not... and then it suddenly crossed his mind that Harry had had ample opportunity to leave with all of Eric's stuff while he was asleep. He hadn't. Eric paused, fingers still on the hem of his T-shirt. Pathetically, maybe Harry was suddenly the closest thing Eric had had to a friend in a long time. Panicking as he felt his weary, shell-shocked mind start to get emotional—off-task—Eric scrabbled for something to say. *Thanks for sticking around?* Too weird, too out of the blue.

He copped out.

"Uh... do you mind carrying the pack? My shoulder—"

"That's fine. It's not heavy," Harry replied, hefting it onto his back. "Let's get out of here. You can lead. Think you got a better bead on this than I do."

"We'll see."

They stepped outside and headed towards the light.

# Chapter Eight:

# The Spooks and the Goodmans

### ***

### <u>Maria</u>

"—ria. *Maria.*"

She awoke. Everything rushed back at once. *Ruth,* she thought, *Ruth—*

There were two men in suits in the room with her, saying her name even as she pushed backwards on the bed in a tangle of sheets and limbs. One of them grabbed her wrists, holding them firmly. She started to yelp and struggle as he tried to soothe her.

"Maria, it's alright, *you're safe, you're safe—*"

She wheezed as she took in her surroundings—another spare room perhaps, decorated as if intended for a child. Posters from TV cartoons, colourful wallpaper. A worried-looking older couple stood in the doorway behind the two suits. She recognized the woman; Maria had passed out on her front lawn. The woman had tried to help, and she'd run because Ruth, *Ruth—*

"Maria. *Maria.*"

The other suit moved quickly to the door and gently ushered the couple away, whispering something quiet and soothing. They accepted it with that rapid *of course, of course* nodding movement, at which Maria herself was all too good. Suit Two closed the door, and Maria looked at the guy holding her. His grip was like a set of handcuffs. He was about average height, white, younger than Maria, clean-cut. His blue eyes bore sternly into hers.

"Maria. *Stop.* You're alright."

She looked at the curtains; it was still dark outside. What time was it? Who the hell were these two? Had they found Ruth?

*Do they have her body?*

"Did you find—get your *hands off me*—" She pulled ineffectually away again, but Suit One did as asked, holding his hands out as if to say, *Okay, look, I'm cooperating. See?* "Did you find *Ruth?*" she sobbed, pulling the sheets up to hide her minimal clothing. She felt exposed. "Is she dead?" she added. The question was pointless. Of *course* Ruth was dead. Suit One did a good job of appearing saddened when confirming it.

"Mrs Wicker. Your former sister-in-law. I'm afraid so."

Maria moaned softly, face in her hands.

"I'm sorry, Maria, but we need you to stay with us. Okay? We have a few questions, and then we're going to leave you alone."

"Who are you? How do you know my name?"

Suit One nodded. "You told Mrs Goodman last night," he said. "She told us. Take a moment. We're very sorry to have startled you, but we are tight for time here and we have to be quick."

*Mrs Goodman. The woman.*

"Mr and Mrs Goodman called the police last night," Suit Two answered, standing by the door. He was a big guy, older and sporting a crew cut, but his voice was soft. "She was lucky to get through. The landlines were working a little better than mobile phones last night, which isn't saying much. We don't have many people who have experienced what you have and survived. Police are pretty overwhelmed right now, but you warranted special attention—"

"Did they come here?" Maria barked, leaning forwards. *"Have those things been through here?"*

"Yes. A few hours ago, and we need you to breathe slowly, Maria," Suit One said. "Mr and Mrs Goodman saw them, as did several others."

*They came through here? While I was unconscious?*

The thought chilled Maria's bones.

*"Did they come in the house?"* she hissed. *"Were they in here?"*

"No," Suit One said. "Maria, you're *safe.*"

*No, I'm not,* she thought. *None of us are.*

Old instincts kicked in, and she tried to breathe her way down to calm. Suit One saw it.

"That's good, Maria."

"Miss Constance."

"Sorry?"

"That's what you call me. Miss Constance. That's my surname."

"Okay, of course," Suit One said. "I'm Stanton, this is Kenpas." Suit Two nodded in acknowledgement.

"All right," Maria said, her voice almost steady. "I'll answer your questions, if you answer some of mine first."

Suit One sighed heavily at this, wiped his tired face. "There *are* lives at stake and time is of the essence. If you'll cooperate, I'll answer what questions I can, but we need to be quick. Fair?"

"Fair," she said, but her mind was already flying back to thoughts of Ruth. "Have you... *have* you found her body then?" A horrible follow-up occurred to her. "Did you tell Jaso—did you tell her husband?"

"Yes and no," Stanton said quietly. "Recoveries are happening now. They're taking a long time—it's hard for our vans to get through most of the traffic. We can't get through to Mr Wicker."

Maria couldn't handle the second part. She fixed on the first.

"Recoveries?" Her voice was a squeak as she heard the word *vans* and thought about what that meant. "How... many people have died?"

"It depends how you look at it, Miss Constance. We have a national event going on here. Percentage-of-the-population-wise, it's small—"

"One went into the house opposite Ruth's," she told him, interrupting. "Did you know that?" Stanton glanced at Kenpas, who was already leaving the room and muttering something into an enormous handheld device. A satellite phone, perhaps? *They* were working properly, then?

"We didn't yet, no," Stanton said. "Thank y—"

"So that's two on the same *street*," Maria whispered. "Maybe there were more? Where are those things now? How many are there—"

"Stay with me, Miss Constance."

"And *this* street. Did people...?"

"Yes."

"How many...?"

"Three hundred people live on this road, Miss Constance."

"*How many died on this street?!*"

"One. One person died."

A vision of Ruth's dying moments swam horribly into view, and cold assessment came with it: the spasming was from the fluid, the blood, the choking. So how could it have been holding her there and making it happen if it had been less dense than mist? How could it affect *Maria* the way it had? She remembered the sensation as she'd come into its aura of effect, remembered feeling it *move* inside her mind.

*They work on our thoughts,* she thought. *They are thought made manifest.*

Could it have been making Ruth purge *herself* then? Forcing her brain to send her body into some kind of internal super-overheat?

*What if they come back—*

She felt sick.

"Where are those things now? Tell me. Where are they?"

"We've had witnesses describing them disappearing again and others describing them appearing further still inland." He paused. "A lot further inland. I'm sure you've figured out that they're no longer just along the coast."

"So, they *are* walking inwards?" she asked, knowing that *walking* wasn't the right word. They glided. *No,* she thought, finding the correct description. *They creep.*

"It... we believe so," Stanton said. "Broadcasts are sporadic, but this has been on the news so I can tell you: there have been sightings as far inland as Birmingham. Which is pretty much as far inland as you can get before you start heading out again."

*Birmingham. Right on the doorstep of Coventry.*

"How many are there?" she asked him, her voice dead. "I saw three. There are a lot more than that, aren't there?"

"We don't know an exact number."

"Guess!"

"I couldn't. There's... there's definitely a lot more."

"Can I... are the flights still grounded? Boat lanes closed?"

"Yes, but I'd forget about getting into Europe. France has announced that they're not allowing anyone with a UK passport into the country anyway. Spain is expected to do the same shortly."

*"What?"*

"Emergency powers." Stanton shrugged. "Like before, this is a UK-only event. I think they're worried that if any of *us* go there, some of *them* might follow."

It was awful, but it made sense. Continental Europe had seen the previous Arrivals. They had their own people to protect. There might be sea in between here and France, but she was certain that even the Stone Men could just walk right along the bottom of the Channel and pop up the other side. The Empty Men, though... they wouldn't even have to do that. They could just drift across. A vision came to her: a sea full of Empty Men, moving like a terrible wave, those hunched shoulders leaning forwards as they pushed onwards towards the continent.

"If that's all, Miss Co—"

"When were they last seen?" Maria spotted a clock on the wall. It was three a.m.

"Locally? A few hours ago," Stanton said, sighing and fishing inside a small bag on the floor. "Nationally... we're getting updates every time we manage to access the network." He produced a small tablet. "Your full name is Maria Constance?"

"Maria Autumn Constance, yes."

Stanton tapped the tablet a few times and his brow furrowed slightly. Kenpas re-entered the room. "Still got connection issues," Stanton muttered, turning slightly to Kenpas and sounding like a dentist asking his assistant for more suction as he added, "Do we have any more swab kits?"

"Radford might have taken the last lot," Kenpas said softly. "If not, maybe there's one in the KS box. Lemme check." He left the room as silently as he'd entered.

"We're gonna need to do a quick saliva swab and a blood sample just to make sure we have you on record," Stanton said. "It'll help us figure these things out."

"What? For DNA? You want to check my DNA?"

"Don't ask me, I'm just doing what I'm told." Stanton's face was professionally blank. "You don't have to give it to us—I'm legally obliged to tell you that. But we're trying to draw a picture of why some people have lived and some haven't after... close encounters. Please forgive the term. DNA might be a part of it. It takes about three minutes to administer the test, if that. Afterwards... we'll need you to describe what happened, I'm afraid. It might save lives," he added quickly.

The thought of doing so was awful... but there was hope of salvation in the suggestion, however terrible. Here was a way she might save someone after all.

"... Okay."

"After that, you'll be good to go," Stanton added, gesturing towards the window.

"Go... where?"

"Wherever you like," he said, not unkindly. "We can't take you anywhere ourselves, but we can arrange a ride to a women's shelter. Then you can figure out what to do next, but you might have to wait here a few hours until you get picked—"

"Why haven't they used the Chisel yet?" she asked.

Stanton paused. "I don't know," he said, finally, and put the small tablet back in the bag. "We'll wait downstairs while you get dressed. Mrs Goodman said she put some of her daughter's things here; she's about your size." He pointed to a small pile in the corner, including a pair of battered-looking trainers. Maria could see the logo on the T-shirt: *Hard Rock Café.* There was also a pair of grey jogging bottoms and a cardigan. "Don't worry," Stanton added, noticing Maria's gaze as she regarded the child's wallpaper. "Their daughter is at university. Don't let the wallpaper fool you."

Maria's head swam. She was going to a women's shelter? She suddenly felt very tired. She truly had nowhere to go. She remembered how she'd felt in that room.

She'd been ready to die.

And what was the point of any of this? They were all screwed, *screwed.* They couldn't even touch the Empty Men; they were literally untouchable.

*No*, the Chimp whispered, *you have to run harder than ever.*

*Oh really*, Maria snapped back. *How's that been working out so far?*

But she was so *tired.* All of her strength was gone. The Empty Men were everywhere. She couldn't stay at the Goodmans' house, and *Ruth was dead...* She could sleep at the shelter. Maybe the Empty Men would just come and take her, and she wouldn't even wake up. Well... at the very least, sleep would be good. Then she could deal with things, make decisions, and with that thought, she convinced herself that this thinking was the truth.

"I'll get dressed and come with you," she heard herself say. Her voice was cold. She would rest, regroup. Make a new plan. This was *smart.* Okay.

"I'll see you downstairs," Stanton said and left the room. Maria got up and pulled on the clothes and shoes as if in a dream, disconnected from her body. She realized she could hear the muffled sound of Mr and Mrs Goodman talking quietly but earnestly to one another in the bedroom next door. She could imagine it: *I don't know; they said they were from the government. That poor woman, she said something about her friend—*

They didn't need *any* of this. She had to go. The Goodmans had helped her and she was profoundly grateful, but by the time she'd dressed herself, she already knew that she would leave without saying a word to this very kind couple. The guilt she felt over Ruth's death meant she couldn't even look at them.

The Goodmans were the second people in twenty-four hours who had been kind enough to take her in; for the second time, confusion and fear had come with her.

There was a small knock on the door.

"You decent, love?"

It was a woman's voice. Mrs Goodman.

"Oh," Maria said, turning bright red as the walls closed in. She couldn't do this. Not now. "Yeah... yeah." The door opened, and Mrs Goodman nervously entered. She was only a little taller than Maria, a little heavier, a little older, with a thick shock of long black hair. This woman's kid was already twenty-one? Mrs Goodman must have been a young mother. *The Goodmans.* Maria had heard the name and had visualized them completely wrong. Mrs Goodman's nightwear was a pair of her own loose-ended jogging bottoms and a Duran Duran T-shirt.

"Hi," she said kindly. "I just wanted to check you were okay before you left. You don't have to go with them, you know. You can stay here a bit. I... I got the gist of what had happened from what you were... you know, screaming about. I can't even imagine."

"Yes," Maria croaked, shuffling on the spot. "Yes, I'm sorry about that. I'm so sorry to have bothered you—"

"*No, God,* no. You'd just seen... *ah,* seriously, it's not a problem, and you're more than welcome to just sleep here, have a few *days* even, *God*—"

"Oh, *no, no,*" Maria babbled, anxiously playing her part in the classic English Dance but truly meaning it. The thought of inconveniencing these good people with her continued presence sent ice down her spine. "It's okay, they're going to take me to my sister's," she lied.

"Are you alright?"

"Shaken up," she lied again, "but I'm okay."

*I could have been you*, Maria thought. *In another world without Arrivals, I could have been you.*

"Yeah," Mrs Goodman said. "Yeah." There was an awkward silence as Mrs Goodman checked the door and suddenly stepped very close to Maria. *"How did you get away?"* she stage-whispered. *"Did you run? My husband has a very bad back, you see. He can't run. We don't know what to do if they come back. We didn't even* hear *them before. I'm so sorry, but I have to ask, I have to. I'm so* scared."

It felt unreal. Maria couldn't believe that Mrs Goodman was asking, but the woman had done Maria a great kindness. Plus, Maria realized, her host was terrified.

"I just ran," Maria whispered back. "I ran away. I'm... I'm sorry." She was. "I have to say... you knew what had happened, what I was running from. You still took me in?"

"Oh," Mrs Goodman said, looking embarrassed and trying to wave the oncoming compliment away. "Of course. I think about my daughter being in the same situation and... I haven't heard from her," she said, eyes wet. She was breaking and telling the stranger *her* fears. "I know the phones are bad, but I haven't even had a missed call."

Would the Goodmans sleep once she was gone? *Could* they? Would Mr Goodman, perhaps, stand by the window and keep watch while Mrs Goodman slept fitfully in their bed? Or would they lie together and hold one another tight as the Empty Men made their creeping, silent way down this street once more? Perhaps towards the Goodmans themselves this time?

"I'm *so* sorry that I bothered you," Maria whispered, shame and gratitude mingling powerfully within her.

Mrs Goodman just nodded gently, wiping at her eyes before breaking into outright sobs. "Oh God, I'm sorry, you don't need to be seeing—" she began.

Maria couldn't stand to see it. She reached out suddenly and pulled this stranger against herself, biting her lip hard to hold her own insane tears back. Mrs Goodman's tears turned into open wails, muffled against Maria's bony shoulder.

Maria wished it was only a moment of humanity in the midst of chaos, and half of it *was*, but mainly it was because she had nothing left. She held Mrs Goodman and tried to escape the thought racing round and round the inside of her skull like a stunt rider on a Wall of Death.

*Could me being in this house,* she thought, me *having* been *here... could that bring the Empty Men* to *them? The same way I brought them to Ruth?*

That couldn't be true. If it was—if she found confirmation of this later—she would kill herself. She knew it. But if it *was* true, then all of the women in that shelter were going to be in big trouble.

As it was, the question would be moot.

Maria would never reach the shelter.

# Chapter Nine:

# Into the Light

\*\*\*

## <u>Eric</u>

They felt the cleaner, thinner night air outside Kasbah and something effortlessly lit up in Eric's brain as he looked in the direction of Ground Zero. Even Harry stiffened and drew in a breath. They knew which way to go.

"Jesus," Harry muttered, rubbing at his neck, his ratty suit actually looking passable in the dark.

"Yeah." In the near distance the buildings were shadowy hulks, the few functioning streetlights in the city creating little light. Somewhere amongst them was a new edifice; the Prism was waiting in the night. "It's so much stronger and clearer now that we're outside... Do you think it's because of the Prism, and the Barrier?" Eric asked, scalp pulling him onwards.

"I do," Harry said. "Never felt it like this before." He pointed off towards the high rises, squinting. "That way, right?"

"Definitely." The difference outside really *was* remarkable.

The pair of them fell into step, Eric frustrated by Harry's slower pace but not saying anything. He wanted to move more quickly but Harry wasn't in great shape. Eric felt warm; one of the jackets in the cloakroom fitted him nicely, replacing his damaged one.

As they walked, Eric left the torch switched off, wanting to stay hidden. The Barrier, the great *they,* was all around them, after all. Harry looked uncomfortable, and Eric thought it wasn't just his stiff-jointed walking pace. Eric realized that he knew nothing about this man, even if Harry now knew *Eric's* innermost demons. As they made their way through the dust-and-leaf strewn streets of the city centre—occasionally pointing at certain street turnings when they felt compelled to follow them—Eric kept thinking of things to try to ask, if only to take his mind off his frustration, his desire to *run* into the city. Then Harry did it first.

"Feeling's getting stronger."

"Yeah," Eric said immediately. "My headache's getting worse. Nose is running too."

Off to their left in the near distance they caught occasional glimpses of the Prism through the jungle of concrete, ugly and vulgar-looking.

"Bleeding?"

"No, I don't really get nosebleeds, but it's running like I've got the flu."

"No headache here," Harry said. "But I can feel it in my *bones.*" He pointed to the left. "Take this turning. Whatever it is, it's further ahead, but this will be a little quicker. Bring us out farther down." He was right; they were moving into an area Eric knew very well. Up ahead, above the row of shops, rose the St Joseph building.

*Wait,* he thought. *Is it* inside *the St Joseph?*

He felt a faint stab in his brain. It was like running your finger over a smooth roll of tape and finding the end of it. He stopped walking.

"Look at the St Joseph building. That one," he added, pointing, just in case Harry didn't know its name. "Anything?"

Harry squinted.

"Maybe," he added, "but I always seem to be a step behind you on this. If you're getting a feeling, then let's keep an eye on it."

"Okay," Eric said, feeling strangely flattered by Harry's deference. Willing admission of submission by a colleague in *any* department is a great compliment to men, no matter how pointless. They continued to walk, and after a few minutes, the answer was clear.

"It's definitely in there," Eric said. "The St Joseph building—"

"Yeah, I know," Harry replied, a little quickly. "Head's starting to hurt, and it's worse when I think about that place or even look at it. Has to be something to do with why we weren't killed," he said, doubling down on his statement from earlier. "Different levels maybe, but we're still in the same kind of bracket." He paused. "The tape," he said quietly. "Speaking of levels and brackets. *Dispensatori...* that was someone called Sophie Warrender, possibly?"

"Yes?" Eric asked, intrigued. What had Harry made of it all?

"Well, the woman on the tape seemed to think that *Dispensatori* was like a codename for this Sophie Warrender person. Wasn't confirmed but..." He shrugged. "If you're one up from me and this *Dispensatori* was the business... how high up do you think they were? What do you think she could do?"

It was a question Eric had considered many times.

"I've no idea. Maybe she was the best hunter in the pack, finding Quarries easier than—"

He broke off in surprise as they turned the slight bend. The St Joseph building rose up before them.

A man was standing there, frozen partway through the process of opening the building's door. Before Eric could say anything, Harry suddenly cried out.

"Hey! Wait!" The *wait* was unnecessary; the guy had stopped dead in his tracks as soon as he'd seen them.

"Hold on, Harry," Eric murmured, thinking of the sudden violence of the Shufflers up on the ring road. The guy ahead of them was big, bigger than both Eric and Harry, stocky like a rugby player.

He was standing half-inside the door, looking at them with his arms at his sides.

*He hasn't said hello back,* Eric thought. "We don't know if he's alright," he hissed.

"If he was like the others, he'd be up on the ring road still, wouldn't he?" Harry muttered. "But he's down here instead."

"Or he could be taking out witnesses," Eric muttered back. It was unlikely, but it *was* possible.

"Do you want to turn around, then?" Harry whispered. The building was probably a hundred feet away, and the guy still hadn't moved.

"*No,*" Eric sighed. He thought about the heavy torch in the backpack and wished it was in his hand.

"Okay then," Harry whispered, and raised his hand. "Hello?" he called, his voice echoing off the buildings either side of the dead street. "We've been hiding out since that barrier thing went up. We don't know why we're alive. Do you know anything?"

"No!" the man called back. His deep voice had a northern twang to it. *No* came out like *Nur.* "I've been wandering around for hours! All I found was a load of crazy people on the road watching that thing!" As Eric and Harry drew closer, the big man's features became clearer in the dark—older than Eric but younger than Harry, albeit with a decent head of hair. His face was jowly but lined, as if he'd had a rough few years, and he wore a sweater with a shirt underneath. No jacket.

*Got to be someone's dad,* Eric thought.

The man raised his thick, sausage-fingered hand in greeting.

"I'm glad to see people. I'm glad to see *you*," he said. "Sane people anyway. Have you seen the people up there?" His clothes looked clean, new even. Too clean and new for him to be Hardcore Homeless, at least.

"Yeah, we have," Eric replied. "I'm Eric, this is Harry."

"John. John Bates. Did you do a different tour?"

"No, we still live here—"

"You did the *tour?*" Harry asked, interrupting. The distaste in his voice was clear.

Some enterprising bastards had realized that, outside of the quarantine city centre, immediately around Ground Zero, there were people who would actually *like* to have a fun day touring the destruction. Technically, there was no harm in it, and why shouldn't people make some money? There'd been public murmurings and outraged opinion pieces in the press, but the national economy was still in a huge slump. The government was distinctly wary of saying no to new businesses in the years immediately after the Third Arrival, and a lot of people felt that anything that got money moving and created jobs was a good thing. Eric could, in a sense, see their point... except he'd been in this city for quite a while. He'd *seen* the damage the Stone Men had done and had spent time around the lost people who had been destroyed by them—those who lost their homes and jobs and communities and Wednesday-night darts teams. All the things that linked up intricately to make the tapestries that people called their lives. This wasn't some World War Two tour of history that happened in the

1940s. This was a destructive event that had happened only five years ago.

"Yeah," John said. "I do a blog... I'm retired, sold my plastering business. Now I write about abandoned places. Theme parks and towns and hospitals, that kind of thing. Been doing it a few years now, just for fun. People kept requesting that I do Coventry, so I did. I wouldn't have done the tour *otherwise*," he added hastily.

"Why would anyone want to read about the tour?" Harry asked, the dark tone in his voice confirming Eric's suspicions that Harry was a lifelong Cov lad.

"It was for my *blog,* I told you," John repeated, bristling a little. "People like to read my stuff, and they wanted to hear my take on this place. It's not my fault if they want to read what they want to read."

*Don't let this get testy,* Eric thought. *Not now.*

"You were on a tour bus?" he asked. "What happened to the rest of the tour? Are they with you?"

The man held his hands up as he tried to find the words, and then simply shook his head. "No. Only me."

"How many people?" Harry asked quietly.

"There was only about six of us on the bus, the tour was d—It was empty." His voice shook a little as he talked. "We weren't even anywhere *near* Ground Zero. I didn't see that big pyramid thing until about an hour ago. I had no idea what was happening. There was this huge, horrible noise. The driver had to stop and then it happened again and then something was suddenly passing through the bus and I saw the driver just... *burst.* Then this light passed through me... There was just clothes left on the bus..." He coughed and took a deep breath. "I tried to head out of the city but once I got a few miles away I saw the edge of that *thing.* Where it stopped. I couldn't go any further." He waved his hand at the faintly shifting movement in the sky above. It was an incongruously camp gesture for such a burly man. Eric and Harry stepped forwards as one, eager.

"You saw the edge of it?" Eric asked.

"Yes," John said, biting his lip. "I got all the way up to it. This close." He held up his thumb and forefinger. "Up close it's... it's like water. But *thin*. Like a waterfall but thinner than a waterfall could ever be."

"Jesus..."

"I don't know where I was though. I don't know the area."

"You tried to get through it? Did you touch it?" Harry asked.

"I *wanted* to," John said. "But every time my hand got near..." He shook his head. "I saw what happened to the people on the bus. In my head I saw them. And I thought..." He didn't have to finish. Eric would have thought the same. "I got a stick though, broke one off a tree. I poked it."

"What happened?" Eric asked, lightheaded with excitement.

"That thing was *solid*," John said, a tinge of awe creeping into his voice. "Like concrete. Stronger, I mean, this thing was so *dense*. It felt like it was fifty feet thick, even though I could see straight through it. I've never seen anything like that in my life. I didn't know what else to do so I headed back into town. My phone isn't working, and I've heard helicopters. I think I've heard jets a few times, but I've always been in the wrong place to see them. Then I just..." He sighed again, shaking his head. "You're going to think I'm crazy."

"You felt something pulling you here, didn't you?" Eric asked gently. "Did you *see* anything?" He tapped the side of his head for clarification.

"A little bit," John said, looking relieved to hear the question. "Like... like a glow. Like a roundish light. It wasn't clear though." He gestured to the door that he was holding open with his foot. "I got here, and the lock was already busted open. Do you think other people got the same idea and got here first?"

"Actually, no," Eric said, looking at the gnarled point in the metal doorframe. "Shine your light on it; you can see it's been like that for a while. Someone broke that lock a long time ago, probably looking for a place to live."

"Huh," John said, shrugging. "Good job. I wouldn't want to have to bang somebody's head in there if they were planning on jumping me." It was a strange thing to say, but Eric knew that even decent men sometimes felt an unnecessary need to prove themselves to new people.

"How far up do you think?" Eric asked Harry, seeing him already gazing up at the building, wincing a little. Eric could sympathise. The painkillers were starting to wear off and that was just his shoulder; his head and nose and neck were throbbing almost in time to a beat.

"Five floors? Six?" Harry looked away. "*Shit*, can't concentrate like that too long."

"Yeah, my head is hurting," John said, sounding surprised. "What do you think—"

"Wait!" Harry hissed. "What the hell is that?"

"What do you m—" Eric started, and then he heard it too. There was a noise somewhere off in the distance, a faint *hiss* that was getting louder, and now it was suddenly so loud that it was unmissable. "Shit! Get inside!" It was filling the air.

All three men dived for the open doorway with such panicked speed that they all became temporarily bottlenecked there, a Three Stooges routine made reality. Eric yowled in pain as his shoulder pressed against someone's body.

*"Get off! Get the fuck off!"* John barked, but it was lost as the air all around them became a sudden, deafening roar. A nanosecond later, the roaring sound passed over the building, and there was an almighty *KABOOM* that seemed to split the world in half. Eric's ears were ringing immediately. The only thing he'd ever heard that was louder were the Horns, and they'd been *inside* his head.

"What the fuck was that?" John bellowed as all three men untangled themselves and ran back outside. Even over the ringing in his ears Eric could hear that roar fading away into the distance at unbelievable speed.

"Airstrike!" Harry yelled. "That was *our* guys!"

Eric looked into the sky, scanning the area, but that faintly turning, rippling thinness still remained in place. The strike had done nothing.

"Was wondering when they were going to try that!" Harry added.

Eric let out a long breath. "That won't be the last, so—"

"Let's get upstairs. Come on, *go go go*; you don't want to be out there," John said, darting back in through the doorway. He repeatedly waved his arm at Eric and Harry as if they were children needing to be rushed back into a classroom. "If they *do* break through, that thing might collapse, and you'd be standing right under it." Harry and Eric didn't move quick enough for his liking. "Come on! Oh, right, suit yourself, I'm going up," he said, already striding across the building's lobby towards the stairs on the opposite side. Eric looked at Harry, a little stunned.

"Fuck *me*," Eric muttered.

"Stress," Harry replied. "This is too much for some people to deal with."

"Come on," Eric said, patting Harry's shoulder and heading towards the stairs. "Before he starts *banging heads*."

Harry smirked a little and followed.

***

At six storeys, Eric was certain they had the right floor. The throbbing in his head had become an orchestra composed entirely of kettle drums and, somehow, falling anvils. He was about to check if Harry was okay—the man was wheezing behind him on the stairs—when John called to them from behind a set of double doors.

"Hey!" he yelled. "I think it's this one! Are you there? Come here!"

Eric wondered what daily life had been like at John's plastering company. He reached the double doors and held one open for Harry, the older man rounding the stairs corner a few seconds later. He was breathing hard.

"You okay?" Eric asked. Harry gave a thumbs up as he passed, and Eric left it at that. He thought maybe Harry had stopped worrying about his health a little while back. The hallway they were now inside was as pitch-black as the stairwell they'd just left, or rather it would have been if not for Eric's now-in-use torch and the light from John's phone. He was standing about six apartments away, waving them over frantically.

"*Here,*" he hissed. "It's this one; I think it's *this* one."

So did Eric. He could almost *see* the rhythmic waves of... *something* emanating from that doorway. His nose was bleeding now. "This lock is busted too," John whispered, pointing at the splintered doorframe. The door itself was shut, the fireproof kind that created a good solid seal when closed, but a strong shove would swing it open. "I think most of these are like that in here. I was checking on the way." Eric wasn't surprised. This was the case in most of the halfway-decent high rises around the city now, and for a sting of a moment, Eric hated John and his ignorance. For all Eric knew, the guy could live an awful existence, but his playing tourist for the day—away from his nice, normal, completely imagined cosy life and safe retirement plan—just pissed Eric off.

"Yeah," he said instead, "lots of people looking for places to stay. Lots of them left the city over the last few years."

John was nearest to the door, so Eric was expecting him to lead the charge. The man's physical bulk blocked most of the doorway.

"Ready?" Eric hinted.

"Oh, I'll shine the light," John said, stepping back slightly. "You go first, and I'll shine it over your shoulder so you can see."

Harry coughed a little in the background, and it almost sounded believable. John looked at him in the dark but didn't say anything.

"Thanks, John," Eric said, sighing and turning to the door. "Sounds like a plan."

"Are you sure you don't want to keep an eye on the hallway while we go inside, John?" Harry asked. For a man with a naturally deadpan voice he was reaching a whole new level of flat.

"No, no," John said quickly. "One in, all in."

There was no point delaying. Whatever had drawn them, whatever they had come to see, was inside that room. It was feet away, and they all knew it. Eric looked at Harry, a shadow behind the torchlight. The man nodded.

Eric took a deep breath and pushed the door open.

Or rather, he *started* to; he'd intended to slowly push it all the way open, a controlled reveal that meant he could jump back the second any danger might rear its head, but as the light suddenly flooded the hallway, they all screamed and jumped back. Light like they'd never seen before.

Light that pulsed and moved.

As the door opened, the screaming began.

"*Hello?! Is someone there? Help me! Please! Please, God!! PLEASE! PLEASE—*"

It was a young woman's voice. She sounded scared out of her mind.

Eric had time to take in the state of the studio apartment—duvets on a mattress shoved in the corner, a half-eaten Pot Noodle sitting next to it, a suitcase, light fittings with no bulbs in them, a huge stack of books against the opposite wall, a single door off to the right, leading to what Eric would later find out was the bathroom—before John was barging past him and leading the charge inside.

"We're coming!" he yelled.

Eric followed, his mouth hanging completely open. The Prism had been one thing but what they were seeing was *right there,* inside a fucking Coventry *flat?* The world spun for a moment—shock, the blaring pull in his head, the fact that it had been *a really bloody crazy day*—and Eric realized that he was starting to fall backwards just as Harry caught him.

"Sorry," Eric said.

Harry just nodded, stunned, not even looking at Eric. Even though they'd technically already seen it, they hadn't expected to see... *this.*

"*Hello?! Hello?*" the girl yelled, spinning towards the sound of their voices. "*Is someone there? I'm in here. Please help! Oh Jesus, please help me!*"

"*Shit...*" John breathed, tottering himself now and then actually falling onto his backside. He didn't say another word, remaining on the floor with one hand clamped over his mouth.

"*Help me!*" the woman screamed. "*Please help me! Call somebody! Smash it!*"

On the opposite side of the room, over by the half-wall window, was the young woman, imprisoned while seated in an old deckchair. She looked to be about twenty-five, thin and tall like a runway model, with limp, pale and dirty-looking blonde hair. She was wearing a baggy T-shirt and jeans. Her black socks both said 'TUESDAY' even though it currently wasn't. Her face was red and wet from the screaming and her open mouth quivered as she squinted towards the sound of voices.

Surrounding her, at perhaps about four or five feet in diameter, was a gently pulsing dome made of bright golden light.

Now that he saw it in person, rather than in a vision, Eric could see the way it slowly expanded and contracted ever so slightly. It would flicker over solid for the tiniest fraction of a second and then flash back to its resting state: a sheer, nigh-translucent gold. If Eric looked very closely, he saw super-tight little contour lines, so close together and thin they could almost be mistaken for a haze. Later, when he thought about it, the only word that he could think of to describe it—even when he knew what a hateful, terrible thing it was, when he would remember that room and want to scream— was *beautiful.* It was incredible. It didn't *shimmer;* it *breathed.*

Seated as she was, the dome cleared the woman's head by about a foot. She wouldn't have been able to stand up inside it, but as they entered the room, she fell forwards out of her deckchair and onto her knees. She pushed her hands against the dome, her palms visibly flattening against it as if it were made of glass.

"*Jesus Christ, get me out of here!*" she bellowed, fresh tears springing from her eyes. "*I don't know what this is!*"

"Don't worry, we'll figure this out, don't worry, don't worry," John babbled as he got unsteadily to his feet, but then his hand went straight back over his mouth. He squatted down a few feet from it, out of touching distance, staring.

She was squinting, Eric realized, somehow struggling to see them from her side even though they could see her clearly. Harry continued to circle the dome, stunned; the city-wide Barrier was distant, harder to grasp. Here, there was no filter. Eric saw how the bubble disappeared into the floor. It appeared as if, were he to run downstairs into the flat below, he would see the rest of it.

*Stop being amazed and say something, arsehole.*

"Hi," Eric coughed. "Can you hear us? I'm Eric…" He drew closer but still maintained a safe distance. The girl might have been touching it from the inside but that didn't mean touching its *outer* surface was a good idea. "We're going to… try to get you out of there…"

"*Call the police! My phone—*" A phone was lying on the windowsill five feet away. John fumbled his own phone out and looked at it, then grunted and snatched hers up too.

"Still nothing," he said to Eric.

"You can't break out?" Harry asked her, squatting down next to Eric. His breathing was still laboured.

"No," sobbed the girl, sounding a little calmer, if still scared out of her mind. "I've been trying for hours. I've been kicking and kicking—can you hit it with something?"

"Yes, we can. Do you have anything heavy?" Harry asked, looking around the room fruitlessly, eager for something he could metaphorically and literally cling on to.

"There was a sledgehammer!" the girl said eagerly, jumping up from her knees in her haste and forgetting the limits of the dome for a moment; her head bounced off the inside of it. It didn't seem to hurt her; she barely blinked. "In one of the rooms on the fifth floor. Someone must have scavenged a load of tools and rope for some reason. I don't remember which flat number—"

"I'll go," said Harry, already up and walking towards the front door.

"You sure?" Eric said, thinking of Harry's physical state, but the older man flashed a thumbs up as he left the apartment.

"It was on this side of the building, same side as me!" the girl called after him. Eric noticed that John was now crouched much closer to the dome than he was before. Was he about to do what Eric thought he was about to do?

"What happ—" Eric began, and caught himself. "What's your name?"

"Jenny, I'm Jenny," the girl gasped. "Jenny Drewett."

"Hi, Jenny," Eric said, thinking of old movies and how the characters would talk to people who are traumatized. How the hell did anyone handle new and difficult situations in the days before movies?

He drew a little closer himself. Was that... heat he could feel coming off that thing?

"This here is John," he soothed, "and the guy about to have a heart attack on the stairs is Harry. What happened, Jenny? Was it— *John!*" Eric barked, and John jerked his hand away from the dome as if he'd been stung, a child caught doing something wrong. Jenny Drewett yelped in surprise, her hands flying to her mouth, but John hadn't touched the golden, breathing surface.

"Sorry, man," Eric said, breathing out, relieved. "But we don't know what it does."

John's face reddened. "I wasn't going to *touch* it," he lied, an edge of petulance in his voice. "It's not quite the same as the other one," John said. "This looks different."

Eric winced. He could have slapped the man.

"Other one? What other one?" Jenny moaned. "Was it something to do with that big blast? There was a massive bang just now—"

"There's been an *Arrival*," John said, helpful as ever, "but don't worry; we're here now—"

"The government is trying some new stuff," Eric lied, interrupting quickly, "but they haven't used the Chisel yet, we think. When they do, we're going to send those Stone fuckers packing again, and we're going to get you *out* of there, okay? Now tell us how you ended up in here. Did you come here on a tour too? Are you homeless—"

"No, I have a *job*," she snapped, frustrated. "I work in Northampton. I have a *car* downstairs. I commute. I came here in the summer." Her head dropped. "People had said that there were places, clean and warm ones and some still had power. I just thought that if I brought supplies and didn't spend much for a few months then I could get ahead of... I have a *lot* of debt. I started to save money, I was nearly done, I was nearly fucking *done*," she hissed, slapping at the floor to punctuate her frustration. "No-one at work knows about this. I don't even normally 'live' in this part of town. I'd originally got myself a nice house out in the suburbs, I'd even found the spare keys in the back garage, so I didn't have to bust the lock. There were still a few places nearby to buy food, but they all closed soon after I got here." She was spiralling but Eric wanted her to keep talking. This would calm her down. "I even had friends around here trying the same thing. One was a lawyer! He was trying to save for a house deposit! But they left months ago. I was going to do the same in just a week or two, *fuck!*"

"How did you end up inside *there* though, Jenny?" John asked, bringing her back on subject.

"It's been... I had a bad few weeks then a very bad few days," she said, shifting slightly as if she was embarrassed. "A few days ago, I started feeling this... *urge* for a change of scene. Which is just stupid because my place was fine. But I just felt... I just *felt...*"

"Like you had to be in the middle of Coventry?" Eric asked.

Jenny nodded... but then she cocked her head. Her eyes suddenly became distant, glazed. She looked as if her brain were trying to understand the concept while her mouth told the story.

"But as soon as I got here," she whispered, "I just suddenly started to feel trapped. Scared. You'd think I'd go straight back to the suburbs again, wouldn't you? But I didn't. I felt the opposite... like it was unsafe to leave. It didn't make *any* sense, but as soon as it came to actually leaving the flat, I would panic. I stopped feeling like I couldn't leave here and started knowing it. I turned my phone off because work kept calling. It all got worse. I thought at first that it was maybe depression or something—it's not been easy living in Cov... One day here became three. I kept thinking about that door and how I couldn't lock it. I wanted to get the tools from that other room, find some wood and nail the door shut! But by then I was too scared to go and get it. I'm not *crazy*, though," she added quickly.

"I know you're not, Jenny," Eric said, pretending to be calm when all of his brain was screaming, *The Quarry Response, here it is again, for real.* He'd heard it in Theresa's voice, and then had read about it online—the pre-visitation fear phenomena seen in the previous Quarries. Goosebumps popped up all over his entire body.

If Jenny was having the Quarry Response, then she could be Quarry. And if she *was* Quarry... could that mean the actual Stone Men were coming back?

Adrenalin shot through his veins.

*Hold it, hold it,* he thought quickly, trying to stay calm. *Look at the situation. It looks like whoever's running the Stone Show seems to be trying either a new plan or is at the second stage of an existing one. The Quarry Response in Jenny doesn't necessarily mean that Stone Men are going to be rocking up any time soon. Plus... answers or no answers, let's take a moment to acknowledge the fucked-up nature of getting excited because a girl has potentially been handed a death sentence.*

That did it. Eric pushed aside his unrelenting need to know, and as he did so, he realized that his headache seemed to have stopped. It was as if being this close to the girl or, more likely, to the dome around her—this *mini Barrier*—had pushed him past some kind of threshold. He looked at John and noticed that his hands had stopped shaking too.

"That's right, you're not," John was saying. "You were looking after yourself; you were managing your stress." He didn't get it.

"Yeah, *clearly*, I was doing *great*," Jenny snapped. "Worked out just fucking *great*." She pulled at her hair and breathed out. "*Sorry*, I'm just..."

"It's okay," John said, but looked deeply offended at his role as comforter being rejected.

Eric shuffled a little closer, staying on his knees but still keeping a good three feet between himself and the ball of light. An image suddenly struck him as he looked at Jenny's terrified face, one he had only ever imagined but that was as strong as any true memory: Theresa, sitting at home, holding her infant son and waiting for a Stone Man to walk down her street. It was so strong and sudden that he drew in a sharp breath and nearly reached out to the girl, to try to push through the light, but he stopped himself.

"I'm listening, Jenny," he said, his voice quiet.

He had to save her. He had to.

"After a while, I was just going mad," Jenny said, clenching her fists in frustration. "I even climbed under the mattress just to try to feel safe and then I'd feel like I couldn't *breathe* and I'd burst out and sit in this chair and try to calm down. Then back under the mattress... I've barely eaten for two days. After a while I was so exhausted that I sat down here, and I must have passed out. And when I woke up, *this...*" She stopped, stunned all over again by her own reality. This was *impossible* after all, even in a world that had seen walking men made of Stone and white giants standing on the sea. "And I was myself again, but then I was *trapped...*"

Eric thought frantically. Her tears were winding up once more. "Jenny—"

"I'm inside *this fucking*—" She suddenly started kicking at the barrier, lying on her back. *"Get me out, get me out, GET ME OUT!"*

John's eyes widened in panic, looking to Eric to come up with something as Harry saved the moment by bursting into the room carrying a filthy-looking sledgehammer. He was puffing and groaning the way only an alcoholic homeless man in his fifties carrying a ten-pound sledgehammer up several flights of stairs can.

"Okay, I've got it," he wheezed, and of course John jumped to his feet to take it from him, his assumption immediate and unspoken. Eric actually thought it was the right decision, given John's size.

"We're going to smash it, okay?" John said, holding up the hammer. "We're going to smash you out of there *right now.*"

Jenny stopped kicking at her barrier.

"Can you move right up against the side?" John asked as he hefted the sledgehammer in his hands, all business now. This he *understood,* this he could deal with. "If this breaks in one go, then I don't want it to swing through and..."

"Yes, yes," said Jenny eagerly, scrambling as he asked and getting as far away from John and the sledgehammer as the sphere allowed. She curled up against the inner wall, drawing her knees up to her face. This was happening so fast that it felt like nobody dared breathe. Even Harry shifted from foot to foot.

"Hang on, love," Harry said quietly, and Eric suddenly found himself wondering again if Harry had kids somewhere.

"I'm going to do a half-power one first," John said, his eyes on the dome's surface. "Just to see what happens, okay?"

Jenny nodded and John set his feet, drawing in his breath, gaze laser-focused on his target. Then he made a little *whup* noise and swung the sledgehammer out, up, over and *down* in an expertly smooth arc.

The hammer's head smacked into the side of the dome with no sound at all.

Eric gasped and his face turned pale.

He saw the speeding, heavy, metal hammerhead stop dead in its tracks with zero accompanying noise and experienced what many addicts refer to as *a moment of clarity.* There had been so much power even in John's 'half-power' swing, and yet, it had been effortlessly absorbed as if it were nothing. Before then—even the earlier airstrike had been distant and unseen—Eric had still held out a small modicum of hope. The country had survived the Stone Men, after all. Now, however, he understood.

They were completely out of their depth.

He was suddenly terrified. He and John exchanged a glance; John was pale.

"Okay. Now you know how hard you have to hit it," said Harry, speaking a little too loudly, obvious that his words were for the girl's benefit. "Now really *twat* it."

John blinked a few times, and then rallied magnificently. "Probably better to cover your eyes, love," he said to Jenny, speaking softly. She did as he asked. John snuck a quick, frightened glance between Eric and Harry—the strength of the barrier had rattled him, and *he'd already touched the city-wide one*—and Eric showed John his clenched fists, nodding encouragingly. The hairs stood up on his arms. He tried to believe.

*Okay, let's fight,* he thought. *Let's show them what we've got. Smash that bastard.*

If they could smash this, then maybe, *maybe...*

John took two steps backward and mounted the sledgehammer on his shoulder, his knuckles whitening, eyes intensely focused on the dome. He took several heavy breaths, trying to pump adrenalin through his body, and then rushed forwards, lips pursed and making a hissing sound. He torqued his upper body suddenly and *powered* the heavy hammer downward, snapping forwards sharply at the waist to add every possible ounce of his body mass to the speeding lump of metal as it whooshed home.

Eric winced instinctively as the sledgehammer's head met the golden surface.

There was a deafening shattering noise.

Eric opened his eyes, elated.

The dome was completely intact and unmarked. He heard a slightly distant and hollow *bang,* as if metal were being dented.

He looked at John, confused, but John was looking behind himself, holding his shoulder. Eric followed John's gaze to the gaping hole where the window's glass used to be. The distant *bang* that had followed the *smash* was from the sledgehammer landing on an abandoned car or something in the street below. Possibly Jenny's car, in fact.

"Did it..." the girl asked, stunned. She uncovered her face and found her answer, looking at them through a golden filter once again. "What... happened...?"

John turned around in a daze, a vein pulsing in his forehead. Eric couldn't tell if the man was shocked or embarrassed or both. "It just... it bounced off," he whispered. "I couldn't hold on to it, it came back too..." He winced, his hand gripping the back of his shoulder. "*Ahhhh...* Christ..." He stumbled against the other, intact, windowpane, his other hand now going to his lower back. "Fuck *me...* sorry..."

Harry darted forwards and squatted down worryingly close to the dome; he was only maybe two feet away.

"*That* didn't work, no," Harry said softly to Jenny, his face unreadable. "Going to find a way to fix this though. Going to put our heads together. All of us, you too."

"Okay," said Jenny, nodding quickly, trying to be brave. "Okay."

An idea hit Eric. They might not be fucked yet. Not quite.

"Downstairs," he said to Harry. "The ceiling. I'll go and get the hammer back from the street and we'll try to smash through the ceiling below us. Who knows, maybe this thing is wedged in the floor, and if we smash the floor *that* might free *this* and then we're a step further forwards. That would be something, right?" He said this last part to Jenny.

"Right. *Right*, yes!"

"Alright," Eric said. "Me and John might be able to get her out from underneath. Harry, you rest up a minute and stay here with Jenny. You sound like you're about to keel over."

Harry snorted but John was already limping towards the door while trying to hide his physical pain. "Good idea," he said, disappearing from sight, his heavy boots thudding rapidly down the hallway. Eric grabbed his torch and hurried after him.

**\*\*\***

# Chapter Ten:

# The Killing Fields

***

## <u>Maria</u>

Even with the sirens on, they were only moving about twenty-five miles an hour. This was lightspeed compared to the rest of the traffic.

After she'd had her first middle-of-the-night shower for a while, it had taken several hours for Maria's ride to arrive. It was a police car rather than an unmarked spook car. Constable Foleshill was in his mid-thirties, pale and exhausted, and not much of a talker. That suited Maria just fine. The Goodmans, saints that they were, had left her alone in the living room after Stanton and Kenpas had gone. The couple had triple-checked that she didn't need to talk, of course. They'd even made her a cup of tea before they returned to bed. She'd dozed fitfully on the sofa, falling into awful dreams about Ruth and the Empty Man.

"Miss Constance?"

"Yes."

"Constable Foleshill. You ready to go?"

*To go to a women's shelter,* she thought. *I'm ecstatic.*

Then she reminded herself that she was lucky they were even giving her a place to stay.

"Yeah. Let's go."

She'd never ridden in the back of a police car before. Almost immediately after leaving the Goodmans' street they hit the traffic.

Even Foleshill's police sirens did next to nothing for their progress, the dense lines of cars opening and closing even more reluctantly than before. Occasionally, they'd see other police officers standing by their cars on the hard shoulder, sometimes talking to drivers who'd stepped out of their vehicles to ask questions. These police all had firearms, a completely ordinary sight in many parts of the world, but not England. At one point, Maria passed a parked army personnel carrier, its purpose unknown, but the soldiers inside were carrying some heavy artillery. Every now and then a helicopter would pass overhead, far too regularly to be normal.

*It's like a warzone,* Maria thought, but then corrected herself. A war meant both sides could fight.

By the time they reached the now-stationary dual carriageway it was around seven thirty a.m. and the sun was well into its ascent. The traffic was worse than anything she'd seen so far; cars stretched as far as the eye could see in both directions. This wasn't some knee-jerk movement of people away from a scary few sightings on the beach. This was a populace who knew of at least near-enough neighbours who'd been killed by untouchable Empty Men. They were getting the hell *away.* Maria wondered if they knew that the Empty Men were heading inland now and that their cars might be heading towards them.

*When it comes to survival, people just act,* she thought. *Do they know where they're going? Do they have a purpose?*

She caught herself again; *she* didn't have a clue what she was doing. A women's shelter?

*You're in shock,* she told herself. *Try to be still.*

But she was also scared out of her mind.

Both lanes eventually stopped moving entirely; Maria assumed there'd been a major smash up ahead. She looked, face slack, through the front windscreen. An army transport was parked on the hard shoulder, and several soldiers were attempting to move a large and presumably broken-down van out of the road. The big squaddies were struggling to shift it, so Maria assumed the van was loaded to the maximum. This was what had been blocking the left-hand lane, at least; something further up was presumably blocking the right. Maria idly guessed that the military had been called in to help take up the slack, the usual services overwhelmed. One of the soldiers saw Foleshill's car and gestured that he wanted to talk.

"D'you mind if I have a word with this fella?" Officer Foleshill asked, turning and looking at Maria through the metal divider.

"Can I get out and stretch my legs?" Maria asked, lying about her reasoning. Maybe these guys had information. Officer Foleshill had politely refused to put the radio on, saying it wasn't working, but Maria thought the answer would have been the same regardless. If Foleshill was going to talk to these guys, maybe she could wander close enough to listen in. But then why did she care? She was running away to hide in a women's shelter after all.

"Afraid not," Foleshill said politely but firmly. "Even in slow traffic, I can't let you out of the car in the middle of a dual carriageway. Kind of frowned upon."

She didn't have it in her to argue.

"Okay."

"I'll be quick." He got out, leaving the back doors as locked-from-the-outside as ever. Maria watched as Foleshill walked over to the soldier and shook his hand, looking between them and the cars slowly crawling by. Had any of the people in this traffic jam seen an Empty Man and lived? Was she the only person here who had seen one up close?

The thought that she actually wanted to die—that she'd had enough—was shocking but not surprising.

The approaching sound of a motorbike interrupted. She turned her head to watch it heading towards her along the line of traffic, the rider's pace the envy of all who watched. He was little for a guy—maybe about five foot six and wearing an overly large leather jacket and baggy jeans—and his weaving little bike meant he moved faster than jogging pace. Maria watched him with idle curiosity until the bike came level with her, maybe six to eight feet away horizontally. The bike was a smaller, scrambler-style thing to Maria's eyes, a little bigger perhaps than the sort of bike you see people using for big jumps in arenas full of mud.

Then the biker's helmet suddenly turned ninety degrees, and he looked straight at her.

A funny electric charge shot through Maria's body.

The biker felt it too; he wobbled slightly and snapped his helmet forwards, grabbing at the handlebars to steady the bike, but he kept going. Whatever spell that little jolt had cast was broken, and Maria realized that the biker was leaving.

*He even looked at you,* Maria thought. *Did you feel that?! Tell the Foleshill you want to catch him!*

Then the first distant scream started.

Remembering it later, Maria would realize that she started to feel something a nanosecond before she heard that first person yell.

The scream came from a long way down the road behind her; she lunged to the rear windscreen. The cry had made everyone else notice what was happening, setting off a tidal wave of yells, one utterly alien to anything she'd heard before in her life as almost everyone in the vicinity was inside sealed cars. The muffled-by-glass screams of hundreds of people all at once was remarkable.

To the police car's passenger side, the dual carriageway was all metal fencing. Perhaps preventing access to some industrial unit of considerable size, it continued up and over the curve of the hill, blue and tall. On the opposite side of the carriageway, beyond the roadside barrier, was a common sight in many parts of England: fields broken only by hedges, stretching away into the distance. It was a grey early morning and the sun was still low enough in the sky that the light had a misty, waking-up quality to it, making the endless green look slightly dreamlike. A sudden addition, however, had just inserted itself into this rural scene that made the whole thing look like a nightmare. Maria thought wildly of the imagined vision of the Channel she'd had at the Goodmans' house.

Ten or fifteen Empty Men had appeared in the field on the opposite side of the road. They were in an uneven row, slowly making their way across the grass towards the cars. They were identical in posture, in height—shorter again than the one she had seen in Ruth's house but still taller than the tallest human—and their number, their slender length, their whiteness against the grass made Maria think crazily of wind turbines in a field, turning silently and endlessly. On they came, bent and… The word came to her like a gunshot, triggering her into action. *Hunting.* That was the word. She knew they could appear and disappear but… they could just show up out of *nowhere* like that? There were so many. How many more of them were out there?

*Is this happening* everywhere? her brain screeched. *Stanton said they had already passed; they're in the* Midlands *even, so where are these coming from? Are they just going to* keep *coming?*

It was another nightmare. She looked beyond the front line of the Empty Men; yes, the fields a little further away contained even more of the white creatures, flanking along the dual carriageway.

Flanking it as far as she could see.

Maria grabbed the back-door handle and pulled at it in a frenzy, instinct overriding the knowledge that the door was locked from the outside. She started to scream, her voice hoarse, looking desperately for Constable Foleshill and the soldiers, but the military men were yelling and rushing forwards towards the advancing Empty Men. Foleshill remained in place, barking into the radio attached to his chest and looking almost as white as the Empty Men themselves. She bellowed to him with all of her might.

*"Foleshill! Please!"*

He couldn't hear her over the chaos in the road. As people saw the Empty Men, panic spread through the lines of cars and vehicles that were now emptying quickly, the air filling with screams. A family of four raced past Maria's window, laden with bags, the adults dragging the children by their hands. Escape by car would be impossible now, the road a blocked graveyard of abandoned vehicles.

All attention was on the Empty Men. Maria screamed and banged frantically on the glass for rescue, but none was coming. Foleshill was so lost in his shock and terror that he might as well have been on another planet.

Terribly, Maria realized that she was trapped.

# Chapter Eleven:
# The Bubble Bursts

***

### <u>Eric</u>

Eric and John didn't exchange a word until they were on the equally dark fifth-floor hallway and entering the room below. That lock was busted too, and the light that hit them wasn't as dramatic as the reveal upstairs—less of the bubble was exposed down there— but it was equally as eerie.

This living room was even more empty than Jenny's, perhaps due to the decorating that appeared to have been interrupted some time ago. There was still a stepladder against the wall, the floorboards were bare, and the walls had been painted a dark, cosy colour that was hard to identify. There were still abandoned paint trays lying on the floor. Emerging through the ceiling—and of course causing no damage to the plaster surrounding it—was the bottom half of the barrier, breathing silently. This, at least, confirmed that it *was* spherical. Most of it had obviously been formed on the floor above to allow space for Jenny to fit inside; the visual result was that of a giant, avant-garde light fitting, a sun tunnel swelled to ridiculously outsized proportions.

*She's inside* that, he thought, horrified, *and we're all inside the Barrier. We're all dead meat—*

"Okay," Eric said. "I'm going to run downstairs for the sledgehammer. Drag that stepladder over."

"This isn't going to work," John said quietly. He stared at the light, not moving. "This little one might look different to the other one, the big one, but I still think she's going to die."

"Well, fuck me, John, let's not write her death sentence just yet, eh? I'll be back in a second." Eric headed out but stopped by the door. "Please don't say anything like that around her, will you?"

John looked at him blankly. "She reminds me of my eldest daughter, you know," he said, and Eric saw then how scared the man was. He wondered if they'd underestimated the level of damage the madness of that day had done to John.

"She reminds me of my sister," Eric said suddenly, meaning it. "So let's... let's do our best then, mate, eh?" he said, forcing a smile. "Let's keep it together. Back each other up. Okay?" John nodded and gave a feeble thumbs up. "Grab that stepladder, and I'll be back in a minute. Please don't touch that thing."

He jogged down the stairs and out of the front door, quickly finding the sledgehammer resting on the bonnet of a Honda Civic; presumably Jenny's, given that it was the only vehicle around. *Talk about lousy luck,* he thought, grabbing it and turning to run back into the building before he heard the noise.

It wasn't a loud sound, but it reminded Eric of those moments in movies when they show you a huge explosion from very far away. It was so gentle that Eric assumed, out of old habit, that it was from a distant car's speaker.

Then he remembered how rarely he heard any cars in Coventry city centre, and that, in fact, nearly everyone inside the Barrier was probably dead.

"*Fuck—*"

He ran back into the building, lugging the hammer with him. He took the stairs two at a time; the hammer was only a ten pounder, and he barely noticed its weight in his haste. On the landing of the fifth floor, he could hear the muffled sound of Jenny and Harry shouting over each other upstairs. They'd obviously heard it too, but they sounded more alarmed than hurt. Eric charged through the fifth-floor apartment entrance, swinging his torch's light into the room.

"*John—*"

It took Eric a few moments to realize what had happened. The weird light from the bubble mingled with shock and the sight of the remodelling paraphernalia, leading to instant confusion. His brain asked all the wrong questions, spotting the wrong things while simultaneously denying the truth.

*Why was the painting done in a such a haphazard and uneven fashion? It's thick here and thin there, and... how did they manage to get so much of it on the floor because it nearly covers the* whole *floor, in fact, and* hey, *they've left their rags on the floor and they couldn't have left* that *long ago because the paint is still wet and glistening and even running in places and* look *there's a pair of shoes on the floor, that one's full of paint—*

He cried out in horror. John's sweater was crumpled against the far wall, drenched in paint.

*That's not paint.*

Eric staggered, feeling his gorge rising, but something else was urgently poking at his brain, what was it—

"*HARRY!*" he screamed, the words ragged as he staggered into the hallway, sledgehammer forgotten. "*DON'T TOUCH IT! GET AWAY FROM IT RIGHT NOW, GET AWAY!*" He lumbered up the stairwell and into the darkened upstairs hallway, watching as, to his immense relief, Harry's face leaned out of Jenny's apartment. Harry threw his hands up silently in question, but all Eric could do was shake his head. Harry began to move past him, but Eric grabbed his arm.

"*WHAT WAS THAT NOISE? WHAT HAPPENED?*" Jenny screamed from inside.

"No," Harry croaked. He gently removed Eric's hand from his coat sleeve. He hurried away down the hall. Eric choked suddenly and threw up as Jenny's frantic *what happened, what happened* continued from the apartment like a stuck record. He wanted her to shut up.

*Don't take it out on her,* he told himself. *You'd be even worse.*

He hadn't liked John, but who deserved *that?* As he coughed out the last of his puke, Eric suddenly remembered that the last thing the man ever said was about his daughter.

*Don't forget the other thing he said,* Eric thought. That the edge of the city-wide Barrier was now solid. Were they *all now just really, truly, fucked?*

They couldn't give up. They had to try to get out of there as soon as possible and try to—

His obsession interrupted his flow of thought with a question.

*Was he really going to leave an* open *Ground Zero behind?*

Harry approached once more, having inspected the apartment below. He bent and put his hand on Eric's shoulder.

"In for four," Harry said. "Hold for seven, out for eight." Eric tried to breathe as advised. *Man,* it was difficult. "He touched it?" Harry asked quietly.

"Uh-huh," Eric gasped. "I warned him not to. He said a few times about how it looked *different* to the other one. Maybe he thought he was okay to do it. Maybe he literally couldn't resist." He realized the whole hallway was dead quiet. "She's not talking.

Better go in there." Harry helped Eric back to his feet and the pair of them went inside. Jenny sat on the floor of the sphere prison next the deckchair, shoulders slumped.

"John's dead, love," Eric heard Harry say softly. There was no point in lying. "He touched the outside of it."

"He... he what?"

Eric looked at the hateful ball of light as Harry reassured Jenny, watching it pulse and softly turn around her. He caught its reflection in the remaining windowpanes and looked past them into the black Coventry night beyond.

That was when he realized they had a perfect view of Ground Zero.

With all the drama and visual wonder of the bubble, he hadn't noticed this earlier but there it was—the shadowy hulk of the Prism lay just a few blocks away. They had a clear sight line. He wanted to go and get his binoculars out of his bag then realized there wouldn't be much point in the dark...

The idea struck him—slightly ironically—like a sledgehammer. He nearly jumped in the air with excitement. How long had Jenny said she'd been there? He desperately tried to remember. A few days, right? That should be fine, no way the battery would be—

He glanced over to the windowsill, looking for something he thought he'd noticed earlier. Yes, there they were. A set of car keys. The Honda logo sat embedded in the main key's black plastic.

He snatched them up, already turning towards Harry to explain, and as he did so, he accidentally passed within about two feet of the bubble, closer than he had been so far. Later he would wonder—he would wonder over and over—why he allowed himself to get so close. A blunder in his haste to talk to Harry? Was he used to its presence already, even with the fresh memory of John's death?

As he passed by the bubble, he felt his skin pull towards it, a movement so sharp and quick that it almost hurt.

He cried out, jumping away, and the sensation immediately died. Someone shrieked and Harry looked at Jenny, but she had barely moved. The squeal had been Harry's.

"Fuck's *sake*," he hissed, breathing out as he saw that Eric was unharmed.

"Wait," Eric snapped, already moving forwards... but carefully. That had *stung.* "Harry... how close have you been to this thing?" Harry blinked a few times, considering it. Then he held his hands about two feet apart, maybe less. Closer than Eric had just been. "Did it hurt?" Eric asked.

"What? No. Not at all."

He could try approaching more slowly maybe? Eric's pulse raced as he inched forwards, holding out his left hand.

"Harry," he whispered. "Tell me when I'm as close as you were." He felt a stinging warmth slowly begin to creep into his hand—up his *arm*—as he moved as close as he'd just been. It was easier to take now that he was prepared for what might happen.

"Don't get too close," said Harry nervously, getting to his feet.

"What's happening?" Jenny said.

"I don't know," Eric said, being honest, lost in what he was doing. The stinging became worse. Eric gritted his teeth as he moved within a foot of the bubble.

"*There*, that's as far as I got," Harry said, quiet and intense. "Don't go any closer. *Stay there.*"

"Wait, just wait," Eric whispered.

"What are you trying to prove?" Harry barked, misunderstanding. "*Yes*, you dare go closer than me, don't be fucking *stupid!*"

"It's not that, it's not that," Eric babbled, trying to concentrate as he took a deep breath and moved his hand within six inches of the thing's surface. The *stinging* moved up several levels to *burning*, but didn't get worse than that, and Eric's hand was unharmed.

*What am I doing?* he thought. *What the fuck am I doing—*

Jenny suddenly pressed forwards against the bubble's inner wall.

"I can *see* you," she breathed, her eyes gazing at Eric with wonder and—it was bright in her eyes, bright as the bubble itself— hope. "I can see you! What are you doing? *Keep doing it!*"

"*Whatever you're doing*," Harry hissed, "*whatever you think makes this okay, that will be what John thought. This is what he did! Don't you realize?*"

"I...know..."

"Don't *touch* it!" Harry yelled. He jumped up to stop Eric, but the younger man's free hand shot up in the universal sign for *stop*, halting Harry in his tracks.

"Don't touch *me! Please,* Harry," Eric hissed, barely able to get the sentence out. He was sweating heavily. "Please, Harry, please. *Wait...*"

Harry shuffled anxiously on the spot as Eric moved so close now that he was practically touching the bubble.

Its golden texture changed colour underneath Eric's hand, a step or two down on the Pantone chart. It was brief, but it was *there.* Jenny saw it too.

"*You're doing something!*" she breathed, her hands and face pressed right up against the insides now. "*It's changing!*"

*"Don't go any closer!"* Harry yelled, but Eric almost laughed. He suddenly *knew* Harry didn't have to worry. It was obvious. As his hand burned like fire and its flesh stayed intact, Eric knew that the sphere was as much a threat to him as antibacterial soap. He understood it then: he *was* different to John. Different to Harry.

*"Harry... it's... okay..."* he whispered.

As Harry gasped and lunged forwards far too late to stop him, Eric pushed his hand all the way home.

There was a sound like bacon being thrown onto a red-hot skillet.

Eric felt nothing beneath his hand. This was because the bubble's surface had opened up to allow his hand through; he'd pushed so hard that the rest of him nearly fell face-first onto the solid, breathing light. The sizzling sound had been made by the emerging perfect hole that had opened up around his hand, the bubble suddenly giving way like a pair of trousers splitting from a sudden bend.

*"Jesus!"* Harry yelled behind Eric, the *sus* of *Jesus* coming out like *sufff* due to his hands being clamped over his mouth.

Jenny's right hand shot out to grip Eric's. She held it so tightly that it hurt.

*"Can you get me out?"*

Their eyes met, and as Eric had that moment again—a sudden, desperate *need* to save her—he panicked as he realized how close he'd been to losing his concentration. He stared at the hole, not answering. The opening of the bubble had been accompanied by a matching sensation in his brain. He couldn't think about that, he had to stay focused—

The burning in his arm was now racing through his blood like liquid fire. His hand began to shake in Jenny's grasp; his eyes briefly darted to hers. The expression on her face told him that she saw his gritted teeth, the veins bulging on his forehead. She put her other hand around his as well, relaxing her own death grip as she did so. Her fingers were soft, her touch became light, and Eric's goosebumps were not just from the fire in his veins now.

*Concentrate,* he thought. *Fucking concentrate!*

"You can do it, you can do it," she coaxed, but her voice was eager.

*That's... good...* Eric thought, *but... what... do ... I... do... now...*

"That's right," Harry urged, squatting down about a foot behind Eric. "You can—" He stopped, and Eric could have sworn he *heard* the idea occur to his new friend.

*No, Harry,* Eric thought, *not* now *for God's sake—*

Sweating profusely now, Eric didn't dare look away from the hole he'd made, not wanting to break his concentration. Out of the corner of his eye he could see Harry's hand start to come up too, palm out, moving towards the bubble. They weren't the same! If Harry touched that thing—

Eric couldn't break his concentration to stop his hand; he didn't know how he'd got this far and didn't know if he would be able to do it again. He tried to speak, but all that came out was a strained gasp. He couldn't even shake his head.

"Hang on, Jenny," Harry said quietly. "We're going to get you out."

*No, Harry,* Eric wanted to scream. *For fuck's sake no—*

Harry took a deep breath.

Eric's free hand flashed out, limp as a noodle, and slapped feebly at Harry's arm. It was the lightest touch, a *brush* more than a slap, and that was all that Eric had been able to muster. It was enough to let Harry know. Harry looked at Eric, looked at the bubble, put two and two together and suddenly darted back a foot.

"Fuck me," he said, holding his hand to his chest. "Fuck *me.*"

Eric knew he was running out of steam. He could only take a little more and he had to make the hole big enough to get her out. Should he move his arm around, widening it? The bubble started making that sizzling noise again and Eric realized that the bubble wasn't designed for this. Whatever he was doing was not supposed to happen, the bubble's *purpose* didn't include Eric Hatton fucking around with it.

*Is it... breaking... down?* Eric thought, hope fluttering in his chest as he shook with effort. Jenny heard it too.

"It's breaking, Eric. It's breaking!" She scanned the walls all around her as her grip tightened on his hand again. "Keep going, *keep going!*"

He began to turn his heavy arm in painfully glacial circles, as if it were moving through clay, or concrete that just got stirred up. He gritted his teeth and visualized the hole getting wider, *wider.*

*"Go on..."* Eric suddenly heard himself grunt through gritted teeth, the words seeming to give him strength, *pushing* the hole open with his will. *"You... bastard..."*

The hissing got louder, and the circle spread open. It was now about the size of a dinner plate, and Eric's body felt as if it were gripped by a boa constrictor. He screamed now, throwing his head back, but he knew horribly that the hole would have to be twice as big if they were going to get Jenny out of there. He would have to take even more.

"Eric, you're bleeding," Harry breathed. "Your nose."

He cried out and tried to circle his left arm again.

It wouldn't move.

*"Come!"* Eric screamed, finding his voice in his desperation. *"On!"*

"Eric?" Jenny's voice was small. *"What's wrong? You can do it—"*

The sizzling sound began to quiet... and stop.

Eric heard it and his belief wavered, just for a moment. It was a critical doubt.

There was a sharp *pap* sound, and Eric realized two things. The first was so crazy that it took a few moments to even register in his brain, and *that* was when he realized the second: he was going into shock.

*So* this *is what it's like, ah yes,* he thought, delirious. *That's so weird.*

His hazy mind looked at his arm.

*Nope, still can't get it.*

He looked at the bubble, now perfectly sealed over once more. There had been a light *thud* from inside the bubble. He looked at Jenny. Her eyes were wide, and both of her hands were now over her closed mouth.

*That's good. You* really *can't blame her, but man that girl can yell for England.*

Eric was surprised he wasn't yelling too, especially as his eyes went back to that arm for a second time. He looked at his severed hand lying on the floor next to Jenny, seen through a lightly swirling and breathing sheen of deadly beauty. He realized that she must have been holding it when the bubble snapped shut, and then dropped it.

*Click.* There it was. Everything dropped into place in his mind and he understood what had happened. He was dimly aware of Harry yelling.

*"Shit! SHIT! ERIC!"* he bellowed.

*Hell of a day it's been,* Eric thought.

*"Harry,"* he mumbled as he fell sideways, fading from consciousness to the sound of Harry rushing in too late to catch him. Mercifully, the darkness took him before the perfectly

cauterised stump that used to bear his left hand bounced off the side of his face.

# Chapter Twelve:

# The March of the Empty Men

***

## <u>Maria</u>

Maria watched helplessly through the glass of the police car window as the soldiers rushed to the roadside barrier. They knelt, raised their rifles and began firing at the Empty Men as they inexorably advanced across the field, utterly unfazed by the deafening gunshots that rang through the air. The soldiers must have known that shooting at the Empty Men was pointless; eyewitness reports would have told them that those things couldn't be touched by physical objects, let alone bullets.

*"Foleshill! Foleshill! Foleshill! Foleshill!"*

Amazingly, he glanced at the car and saw her. His expression was blank in his bleached face, and Maria frantically banged against the metal grille. She watched, stunned, as he turned his terrified and vacant face away to look back at the Empty Men, hands by his sides.

*"No! No! Foleshill! Foleshill!"*

When she looked back, the Empty Men—horribly—were already closer than she thought they would be. Where it reached the edge of the dual carriageway, the field was slightly lower than the road's surface, ending in a hedge and then a short ditch. The Empty Men were already nearly at the hedge, mere feet away from the still-pointlessly-firing soldiers. Were those things moving faster than when she'd seen them? Or was it just something to do with the proximity of so many people?

Were they *hungry?*

She had to get out of that car, *now—*

*"Foleshill! Please! Foleshill!"*

Then he was looking at her again, sweat on his forehead, and she pressed her face right up against the dividing grill. *"Please!"* she screamed, her face pushing into the black metal. *"They're coming, they're coming, please, let me out!"*

He blinked twice, and then he was staggering towards the car.

*"Yes! Yes! Thank you!"* Maria cried. The door opened and she burst free into a nightmare scene that rang all around her with screams of men, women and children. The madness of the people's cries was now in high definition. She barged past Foleshill and ran for her life, joining the human stampede. She would never know what became of PC Foleshill or the soldiers. She didn't remember hearing any more gunfire after she started to run.

For some reason—perhaps a sheep mentality or just an instinct to get out from the potential pitfalls of wingmirrors and left-open car doors, of which there were many—the majority of the screaming masses ran to the hard shoulder first rather than heading straight down the alleyways between the cars. A lot of people realized that it may be worth trying to climb the high blue fence on the left and ran towards it. The idea of doing the same flashed through Maria's mind, but she dismissed it quickly; one panicked look told her that it wasn't going to work. Not only was it tall at well over ten feet—which may as well have been Everest for Maria—but the top of it ended in some twisted anti-climb configuration, and there were no visible handholds. Some people were trying unsuccessfully anyway, and others were already trying to push their children up. It was a scene of pandemonium and blind panic.

*They do something to our minds just by even seeing them,* she thought. *Something we've never known before.*

She knew it to be true. She felt it too. Some part of the people there—part of their brains, buried deep inside on some evolutionary level—*knew* the Empty Men and their purpose. The planet had never seen them before, but it was as if people somehow understood their threat level instinctively, the Empty Men's presence setting off deep-rooted survival processes that fired like thunder in their minds. All the people could do was try to hang on as their bodies responded.

With a wall of Empty Men to the right and a nigh-impossible-to-scale fence on the left, Maria and the breathless runners had only three options. They could try to hide, an idea which those too old or infirm to run *were* trying; Maria glimpsed at least one old couple hunkering down by the side of their car in the midst of all the sweaty, hairs-up-on-end chaos. Option Two was to face the Empty Men. She saw a few individuals, those either too scared or too crazy to run, standing and watching in awe. Some of them even moved towards them with their hands outstretched. It was if they intended to make first contact for the greater good of the human race. The rest of the bellowing, panting masses were going for Option Three: trying to get to the end of the fence before the Empty Men reached them. Maria realized as she ran that, if they made it, they *could* jink left and start running away from the Empty Men rather than along their flank. They'd at least stand a *chance* of getting away.

It was time to *go.*

She ran over to the fence and pelted along it, realising with horror that the shoelaces of her borrowed shoes had come undone. There was no time to stop and tie them. Her loose laces whipped at her calves. She glanced to the right; for a brief moment, her heart leaped with hope in her chest as the Empty Men seemed to have vanished. They were gone! Then *no,* the top of many awful, elongated white heads slowly rose into view, following the curve of the ground back up from where it had dipped below the edge of the road.

*Why do they do that?* she wondered wildly. *Why do they follow the line of the ground when they can rise straight up? They could just float at whatever level they like.*

There was no time to analyse as here they came, creeping along as fast as the people were running and keeping perfect pace. Maria could see that, long before she or anyone around her reached the end of the fence, they would be within a few feet of touching distance. She strained harder and pushed on, her breath like metal in her throat as the end of the fence still seemed so, so far away. She glanced at a movement to her right and saw a woman—young, maybe not even thirty yet, in a plain T-shirt and jeans—run out from between the cars, a small boy running with her, and *oh God, her hair looks just like Ruth's, it's even styled the same.* The connection was unbidden and instant in Maria's mind at the sight of those thick curls. *She's even the same height as Ruth,* Maria thought deliriously.

The woman fell over suddenly and landed *completely* on top of the child, most likely her son. She cried out in pain, the kid's yelps muffled by her fallen body, as the two of them lay between a big jeep-type vehicle that Maria didn't recognize and a black Mercedes. Maria ran ten steps further forwards and, *oh God,* she realized she was stopping and turning around and running over to the fallen woman. She couldn't help herself, images of Ruth flashing behind her eyes. The sight of the road as it stretched away down the hill was unreal at this distance, a spray of humanity emanating out of an endless line of metal, hundreds if not thousands of people behind her now running just like the people around her. Horror of horrors, *the fields back there were full of Empty Men as well,* flushing a wave of people from their cars like rats out of a sewer.

*What the hell am I doing?* she babbled inside her head. *What the hell am I doing?*

Maria reached the woman and crouched down. She'd run through the streets for hours the night before to get away from these things, and here she was effectively running *towards* them? She grabbed at the woman's hand and tried to drag her to her feet. The woman was slim but a lot taller than Maria, outweighing her by a good margin, and *no,* it wasn't Ruth, she knew that, this person's face angular where Ruth's was round, but that hair, just the *same,* and Maria had to save her—

Dazed, the woman pushed against the Mercedes, helping Maria, even though she didn't seem to be aware of where she was. Maria saw why; she had a huge welt on her left temple from her fall.

"Come *on!*" Maria screamed, pulling with all her might, and the woman got a knee down and stood up. Her kid gasped in air as the woman's weight fully came off his ribs. The boy was almost a carbon copy of his mother, with a flawless feminine face and those goddamn curls. He had to be seven at most, and little for his age. *"Get up, get up!"* Maria barked as the kid started to curl into a ball and cry. She looked up, seeing the Empty Men reach the cars now. They towered above them like ghostly prophets of doom, a dozen or so faceless Jacob Marleys come to tell all present of the terrible fate that lay waiting for them. She'd seen that fate, and it *was* terrible. They didn't weave between the vehicles, of course; they just kept coming, the roofs of the cars passing through them at around stomach height.

"*Come on!*" she bellowed again, letting go of the mother's hand and grabbing her shoulders as she swayed, stunned. "*Snap out of it!*" Maria thought about slapping her awake, but the woman already looked concussed. The Empty Men were maybe ten feet away now and coming on fast. In a few seconds, Maria would have to leave these two to it, her attempted moment of kindness done.

*You can't let those things take you*, she thought. *Kill yourself first.*

She looked, desperate, at the kid curled on the concrete, crying. She didn't have a free hand as she was still holding his mother's weight upright. *What the hell did she do—*

"*For fuck's sake, GET UP!*" she bellowed, and kicked the kid in his backside. The boy let out a little *ah* of surprise and looked at Maria. She pointed away to the Empty Men. They were close enough now that the kid, even from the floor, could see their heads. He looked at his mother, blinking the life back into her eyes.

"*Mum!*" the boy yelled, scrambling to his feet, eyes now wide, crying forgotten. Something came back online in the woman's head as she saw her son, darting down for him and gripping his hands to pull him up. Maria watched as, a few feet to her left, one of the Empty Men suddenly moved sideways in that manner she'd seen through the window at Ruth's. It widened itself quickly then fell forwards between the cars and *down* onto someone that Maria couldn't see, transforming in that terrible, collapsing, *liquid* motion. As it descended, the screams of whomever it had chosen peaked and then turned into a horribly familiar rhythmic choking sound. Maria could hear it even over the noise and yells all around her. Mum now looked like she knew what day it was, and the Empty Men were upon them. It was time to run.

"*GO!*" Maria yelled and turned away from the pair, her eyes firmly on that seemingly endless blue fence and the only hope of salvation that lay at the end of it, when suddenly it seemed to be getting farther away.

Maria was utterly confused. She was moving backwards. Something was *pulling* her. She jerked around and saw the sky.

*They have you,* she thought. *Oh God, THEY HAVE YOU—*

"*Get down,*" the woman hissed in Maria's ear. "*They'll fucking see you!*" She'd pulled Maria back by the neck of her cardigan and the three of them were crouching on the road by the Mercedes' tyres. Maria wriggled like a caught wildcat.

"Get off me! Get off me! Jesus Christ!" she hissed, bewildered and trying to get away, and then the woman's big hand was over Maria's mouth. The woman's son was tucked under her opposite arm, her other hand over *his* mouth, both of them held under her arms like rolls of carpet. What was this crazy bitch doing? Why didn't she run? Didn't she know *hiding doesn't work?*

Maria struggled harder but this girl must have been doing her crossfit because her wiry frame was as strong as an ox. Maria was half a foot shorter, exhausted, unfed and underpowered even for her size. She wasn't going anywhere, even if the woman had a hard time keeping hold of her. "*Get off! Get off! You're going to get us killed!*" Maria hissed frantically behind the woman's hand, and then her captor *actually dug her nails into Maria's face.* She couldn't believe it.

"*Shut up,*" the woman hissed back. "*You're going to get my son killed. Shut UP!*" Maria hated her in that moment, hated her for making Maria helpless again, but then she saw that the Empty Men were literally all around them in the labyrinth of cars.

Her entire body went cold, and she screwed her eyes up tight, willing herself to be away from there, to be invisible. In her mind, she was running, running along that fence, and she opened her eyes again because maybe they'd be gone but *no.* One was moving forwards to her right, one was coming into view from their left, and one—the worst— had stopped dead just in front of them, right in between the roadside barrier and the car they were crouched against. From ground level, they positively *towered* above them, giants of impossible death, as silent and deadly and permanent as the grave.

*They're still shorter again,* Maria realized with horrified wonder. *There's more of them, but they're getting smaller as that happens.*

Maria wriggled her legs backwards, trying to tell the woman to get *under* the car, but there was no response; the woman's eyes were wide with madness, her freeze instinct leaving fight and flight in the dust, and her son was visibly vibrating with terror under her hand.

*See?* Maria wanted to scream. *Do you see, you moron? Do you see why you* always *run?* But now she was frozen too, watching that awful, spindly white shadow in front of her. Though it looked as if its back was to them—the head was hunched, facing away—Maria knew that didn't matter.

It saw them. Maria felt it.

That sickening puke-warmth began to leech into her again, and once more, Maria mentally curled up into a ball and willed the Empty Men away, *away,* that pathetic, pleading thought coming to her again just as it had in Ruth's spare room.

*Please leave me alone. Please.*

The warmth crept further in, searching, and Maria knew now the right verb truly had come to mind as she'd watched them make their creeping march across that field: *hunting.*

*Please,* Maria pleaded, *for the love of God, leave me alone.*

She felt the woman stiffen; she felt it too? They were checking her?

*"Fucking LEAVE ME ALONE!"* Maria screamed, unable to hold it back. Then—unbelievably, lucky sevens coming up a second time in a row—the Empty Man began to move away, falling back into line with the others. Maria felt the woman's body behind her give a little pitch as she gasped, unable to believe it, but her grip tightened as if to say, *Not yet, not yet,* and that was just fine as Maria had zero intention of going anywhere just then. The Empty Men were now ahead of them; running to and along the fence was out of the question, even as the other Empty Men were approaching to the right. In that moment, the only way to go was forwards. The *next* moment's decision could be made in the next moment.

*I survived twice,* she thought, desperate and pleading. *Twice I've been checked, and I've lived? So, I* can't *be whatever they're after, right? Does that mean I don't have to worry about them?*

The Empty Man that had been to their left now suddenly darted forwards and to the right. Moments later, more of those awful gurgling screams began. The woman's grip loosened, and she was pushing Maria away, getting to her feet.

*"Let's go,"* she hissed, bent at the waist. *"Stay down low."* She started to move back down the road for some reason. It made no sense; more Empty Men were approaching across the fields to the east, and even though some had now moved past her to the west, at least the fence ended that way up ahead. If she ran up the hill as fast as she could, she might be able to get over the rise before the next wave of Empty Men reached the road. Maybe the traffic would

be free flowing after that point? Maybe she could get into a car and escape by going straight ahead after all?

*Or maybe I don't have to worry about them,* she thought. *They aren't taking everyone—*

She wasn't going back the way she'd come. No way.

*But what if, even when I get up there, the ones that are coming—*

The woman was already moving away back down the hill, scuttling behind the Mercedes to get into the maze of cars, presumably to avoid detection. To her credit, she looked back at Maria, her bloodied forehead still swaying. She was almost certainly concussed. A mix of approaching and disappearing screams echoed around them. Maria glanced towards the fence; the Empty Men that had passed them continued westwards, the three that had been nearby now catching up with the others.

"Come on!" she hissed. "This way!"

"I'm not going that way!" Maria hissed back. The woman simply nodded in response.

"Thank you," she said, and turned away, that disappearing hairstyle twanging at something in Maria's stomach. She ignored it, turned and ran in the opposite direction, and then she felt a *pop.*

She stumbled like a sprinter who had been poked in the back right after the starter's gun. What the hell? On instinct—perhaps already knowing on some level—she looked at the wave of Empty Men moving towards the fence.

The one that had stopped by her earlier—the one in the middle of the trio—had stopped once more.

Maria staggered backwards, her rear hitting the side of a Ford Focus, and she briefly turned her head to see an old woman sitting in the passenger seat. She was unconscious or dead and the driver's seat was empty, the door on that side wide open. Maria turned back to the Empty Man.

She watched as it began to glide sideways in the direction of the fleeing, concussed woman and her son.

Eyes wide, Maria looked down the alleyway between the rows of vehicles at the woman's hunched and disappearing back. She was already a good thirty or forty feet away. Even bent over, she was *fast.*

"*Hey!*" Maria yelled. "*Lady!*" The woman didn't stop but she turned her head as she ran. "*It's coming, it's coming after you!*" She pointed. The woman's face became a mask of terror.

"*Mum! Mummy!*" the boy yelled as the woman quickly straightened up to see. She was on the near side of a Toyota Yaris, the Empty Man almost at the far side of it already and coming on fast. The woman screamed, scooping the boy up in her arms as, for some reason, she turned and began to run back towards Maria. She was fast, yes, very fast even with the weight of her son—Maria's guess about some sort of athletic regime had to have been correct—but the Empty Man was already nearly through the Yaris and gaining, definitely increasing speed as it came, and the woman found an extra burst of speed. Maria realized that, for *some* ridiculous reason, she was holding out her hand to the woman as she started to run too, looking backwards like a relay runner waiting to take the baton. The woman's terrified eyes looked into Maria's... as Maria realized that the Empty Man was getting left behind. *The woman was going to do it! She was going to get away!*

The Empty Man began to flicker, and Maria wondered if this meant it was giving up, bested by human speed and drive. If this was true—if they could beat them this way—then PureGym was about to have the best year of their corporate life.

The Empty Man vanished and then reappeared right in front of the woman as she bolted headlong. She'd chosen the wrong moment to look behind herself; the second she turned her head forwards was the same second that the Empty Man made its reappearance right in her path. She screamed, skidding to a halt, and the boy slipped out of her arms, sliding down her body to the ground. Torn between picking her son up and defending him, she swung a pointless punch at the Empty Man that passed straight through it. She shuddered involuntarily as her arm went into the Empty Man's space, a violent movement that caused her to stagger sideways against a nearby car.

The Empty Man bent forwards and engulfed her son.

Maria screamed too now and ran towards them, hearing herself yelling a similar phrase, out loud this time, as she drew closer. *"Leave him alone! Leave him alone! Leave him alone!"*

The Empty Man paid no heed to Maria as it went to work. The boy's mother simply bellowed like a wounded beast as she fell to her knees and began clawing pointlessly at the intangible white figure now draped all over her son from foot to forehead. Her knuckles were immediately turning a ragged red, scraping against the tarmac as they caught nothing in her attempts to free her boy. Her efforts quickly ebbed as the Empty Man's influence took hold. She spasmed violently, a small spray of spittle flying from her mouth as she fell sideways again but then almost immediately... wait... she was *getting back up?*

Her son was bucking on the spot and his head was facing towards his mother, mouth open, eyes pleading. Then she was scooting her shaking arms under him, her body gagging and spasming, *and her son was in her arms and she was standing up,* jerking wildly as she turned on the spot, desperately trying to see with her glazed eyes which way to run. *How was that possible?*

Of course, the Empty Man just moved with the boy, hanging from his pitching and choking body like disgusting see-through icing.

*You're useless,* Maria thought, watching helplessly as the woman held on to her son with the Empty Man all around him. She *can do it. You could have done the same if you weren't so—*

The thought trailed off as she observed how the woman's arms passed through the Empty Man, gripping only her son's body inside it. The Empty Man was so much bigger than the child that it hung down like a sheet, touching the road and disappearing through it slightly. The mother dropped to a knee, her head rolling back on her shoulders.

*That's it,* Maria thought, *she can't take any more either.* But she moaned and stood up again as fluids began to leak from her son's eyes and mouth. Maria felt the distant residual effects of the Empty Man and, in a moment of terrible clarity, realized that she'd been right: the Empty Men made their victims do it to themselves. *We can't touch* them, she thought, *and they can't touch* us... *but they can affect our minds.*

A movement to her right snagged her attention; another Empty Man was approaching, heading straight for the mother. Maria halted dead in her tracks about ten feet away as the woman bucked and heaved a final time and dropped to both knees, finally unable to take any more, her son spilling out of her arms as she landed face down. His movements had stopped. His mother blindly scrabbled around, feeling for him, unable to clear her vision. She twitched violently and fell backwards, banging her head so sharply against a car's window that she cracked the glass. Stunned, she looked up from the concrete, her eyes suddenly widening and seeing Maria, who understood at a glance that what she'd seen and read in films and books was an actual thing: a person could, in a moment, go completely insane.

"*Help him,*" the woman squeaked, and then her tall frame was briefly blocked from view by the solid whiteness of an Empty Man.

A moment later her body suddenly became clear once more as it became tightly wrapped in the intangible drape of the Empty Man's embrace. Once it had collapsed onto the woman Maria could see her face, her open mouth choking. Her shoulders spasmed once more, and she fell flat, twitching as the purging began. The other Empty Man upon her dead son had finished its work and was beginning to reassemble. They were beyond help, even as Maria had to tear herself away, telling herself, *No.* There was nothing she could do here.

She turned and bolted for the brow of the hill. Away to her right and in the distance, she could see that the next approaching wave of Empty Men was much closer. She'd given away even more time, but now she didn't think it even mattered; she'd seen one of the things appear exactly where it wanted to once it was close enough to detect its prey. Could they detect her?

*Maybe better to worry about that when it happens*, she thought.

She ran for dear life, unaware that she was moaning softly as she pelted along the roadside crash barrier between her and the fence, a rush of people swarming around her. Maria jumped over or around anyone that fell. She wasn't stopping again, not now, no matter how *different* she thought she might be. All the while, the Empty Men poured towards her from the fields to the east. The odds of the traffic suddenly opening up as she reached the top of the hill were slim to none, and worse... how long did that wave of Empty Men go on for? Was it ahead of her all the way to the tip of the UK? Was it even *possible* to get ahead of it? If not, then running was pointless; trapped between two waves of Empty Men and trying to escape would be like trying to outrun a closing circle. It didn't matter; again, the job of *this* moment was to get over the rise and see where she was in the *next* moment. She tried to find an extra burst of speed, to tap deeper reserves as she ran alongside the fleeing mass of humanity towards the top of the hill.

Precisely *because* it was so gentle, the view before her was a steady, slow reveal of bad news, bad news, *worst* news, and only a small piece of good news. *Bad news*: the high fence on the left didn't end for quite some way ahead, perhaps a good straight minute or so of running. *Bad news:* the traffic ahead was just as jammed as it had been on the approach. No-one would be able to drive her away at speed. The line of stationary cars continued to the horizon, and worse, the cars were now abandoned, panicked people charging and screaming ahead of her exactly as they had behind her. The reason for this, of course, was the worst news.

The fields to the right were full of approaching Empty Men as far as the eye could see.

From her vantage point, she could see well into the distance; they formed a white line that stretched on until she could see no further. The approaching wave would easily reach her long before she got to the end of the fence. The only bit of *good* news was that she could now see how the road started to veer to the west, keeping in between the two waves of Empty Men, but that didn't happen until after the fence. She kept running, thinking crazily in her blind fear. Could she just let them pass? She'd survived them twice, maybe she didn't *have* to run?

She didn't want to find out. A high scream came from a few feet away to her right, in amongst the cars; it was the biker that had passed earlier, now brawling with a larger man. In fact, the brawl was ending, the larger man now astride the bike's seat with his head down, trying to restart it while the little biker's fists rained ineffective blows down onto his back. The larger man aimed a kick backwards at the biker, catching him square in the stomach and knocking him down and out of sight. Suddenly the biker was back on his feet and tearing his helmet off. A thick mop of short brown hair popped into view and Maria realized that the biker was not only a woman, but that she looked like somebody's mother, complete with small red stud earrings. Her cheeks were flushed with anger and pain. As Maria looked at her, she felt that funny *bolt* again, making her stumble as she ran.

*A connection,* she thought. *Didn't you read something about that happening with the previous Arrivals—*

She stopped, stunned for a moment, chest heaving as she gasped for air. The biker must have felt it too because she immediately turned Maria's way, but only for a second before she charged back up behind the man stealing her bike. Swinging her helmet by its strap she powered it as hard as she could into the man's head, David's sling felling Goliath once more. His limbs went instantly limp and the man slumped sideways, taking the bike with him. The woman looked at Maria and frantically beckoned her over.

"*Come on!*" she yelled. "*The road goes left down there! We can make it!*"

*No way,* Maria thought. *This can't be hope.*

Maria ran to the woman who was already down on her knees, pushing the unconscious man's big leg off the bike so she could pull it upright. "Help me with this!" she barked. Maria crouched to grab hold of the seat to assist in uprighting the bike. Glancing down the road, she realized their chances were even slimmer than she thought. On a clear road, they could have made it, but with so many open car doors blocking a speedy exit along the roadside barrier it would be a tall order to get away in time via that route. Maria knew their much better chance would be to ride on the clearer hard shoulder, but that would mean physically lifting it off the ground and *over* the roadside crash barrier. As Maria helped get the bike upright, she realized that wasn't going to be possible. It wasn't the biggest bike, but it still weighed a tonne. Even with two of them lifting, they wouldn't be able to get it into the air. The only way now would be to weave; they'd have to wind their way in and out of the labyrinth of doors.

Once the bike was upright, the woman jammed her helmet on and immediately swung her leg up and over the seat, pressing a little button above the throttle. The bike burst into tiny-engined life. "Get on the back!" she yelled, even as Maria was already swinging a leg up and over the seat. The bike's suspension bounced a little as she leaped on and grabbed the Biker Woman tightly around the waist. "Not there, grab the handle on the back of the seat!" the woman yelled as they pulled away, whipping her visor up so Maria could hear her. "Hold on to *that*, not me. I can't steer with you like that!"

Maria did as she was told, and then they were off, zipping alongside the barrier. Within seconds, they'd reached the first open door blocking their path.

"*The door—*" Maria barked but the woman was already slamming on the anchors, veering right at the first available bonnet-to-bumper gap between two cars. Now they were in the canyon between vehicles as they raced so close to the cars that Maria shut her eyes, certain that her knees were going to connect with a wing mirror or a bolting person at any moment. She chanced a glance to her right, hardly daring to. They were getting ahead of the wave of Empty Men but not by much and now those things were closer, looming again. The motorbike reached another open door, and the woman braked again, snaking them sharply to the left and back out to the barrier.

They progressed this way, speeding and slowing in short bursts as they moved in and out of the cars and lanes like a horrible real-life version of *Frogger*. Still it wasn't fast enough. The Empty Men were silently coming. They were close enough now that Maria could see the second wave at its full height, rising up from road level having now crested the ditch.

They weren't going to make it. Maybe she would, though—

As they whipped back onto the barrier side once more, Maria spotted something she hadn't seen earlier—something wonderful, blissful.

The crash barrier ended before the fence did.

She hadn't seen it from her earlier vantage point on top of the hill, either due to haste or a rush of bodies blocking it or any one of a million reasons *that didn't matter because there it was,* and if they could *just* get a little further down, then maybe they could—

"*Here we go!*" the biker yelled, and at first Maria thought it was a cry of triumph before realising that the woman meant *this was it, win or lose.* Maria looked ahead: yes, the road *did* pull away to the west, but she watched the approaching wave from the east and saw that there was an obvious point, looking at the speed of their approach, where road and approaching Empty Men would meet. Though the fence ended, it was simply replaced once more by ditch and high hedge. Another nigh impossible barrier to cross to get to the open field beyond in time. There would be no escape.

She was going to have to ride through them.

Maria closed her eyes and flattened her face against the Biker Woman's back, trying to pump herself with adrenalin as the biker opened up the throttle. Maria watched the blur of the breathless people to their left, moving too fast now for any of them to act on the stealing-the-bike idea that she saw flash across many passing faces. She looked to her right; the Empty Men were a few feet away, *right there,* and in a few seconds, she would be able to put her right hand out and trail down the middle of all of them. They could leave *these* Empty Men behind as the road curved away from them, but the bike wouldn't outrun the ones ahead. Surely the Biker Woman was able to see it too—

*"Go as fast as you can!"* Maria yelled over the rushing wind. *"We have to go through them!"*

*"I know—oh God, here we go!"* the woman shouted back, torqueing the throttle to maximum as the engine squealed. The Empty Men immediately to their right became a blur, flashing past like enormous white fenceposts and drifting away a little as the road curved.

*Can they sense us at this speed? Hunt us? Flash into our path like the other one did?*

They became a white wall as the bike's speed increased further, the downward slope of the hill helping the motorcycle's momentum along the hard shoulder.

*Top speed,* Maria thought. *About as good as it gets for testing this theory.* Her pulse raced as she tried to remember what she'd thought, what she'd done. Had she closed her eyes? Yes… but she'd wanted them to *leave her alone.* That was it! But she'd thought the exact thing with the boy and his mother, even yelled it out loud and it didn't work—

Maria realized that if they took Biker Woman at this speed, they were both dead. Maria wasn't wearing a helmet. The crash would kill her.

*Then you'd better think about them* leaving you alone *as hard as you can,* she thought, *because in a few seconds you're going to hit that white wall and find out the hard way if you're right.*

She screwed up her eyes, remembering that *pop* as the woman ran away from her. Could it be something to do with touch? Maybe it only worked if she was touching someone—

She quickly released the seat handle and threw her arms around Biker Woman. This time she wasn't corrected and instead the woman bent forwards slightly at the waist, leaning into their speed. The line looked endless; Stanton said they'd been seen as far as Birmingham—

There was no time to think about that. The line of Empty Men was rushing up to them, to swallow them whole, and Maria's world began to fill with white as she prepared to crash into them at around sixty miles per hour. *Could the Empty Men even snag the two of them at this speed—*

Yes. Even before they were in them, Maria felt the sickness begin to leech into her body. They sensed her, both of them perhaps, as the woman in Maria's arms tensed up either in reaction to their probing or from bracing herself. Many must have sensed Maria at once; the strength of it was staggering. There was no way that speed would save them. There were too many, their grip already too strong, and in a moment, Maria would be *in* them, engulfed by that white wall. Her arms started to go limp and Maria realized that she simply couldn't take it and hold on at the same time. Her spine felt like water. She was going to fall off the bike. She cried out as the awful nausea washed deeper into her and the bike wobbled—did the biker feel it too?—and the thought came unbidden, one forgotten in the fear and nausea.

*LEAVE ME ALONE,* she thought, wishing it with all her being. *LEAVE ME ALONE—*

The Empty Men engulfed the bike. All Maria could see was white. She closed her eyes and felt herself begin to pitch helplessly sideways.

Suddenly there was no nausea. Shouldn't it be worse than ever? She found her grip, tightened her arms, opened her eyes—

Then she could see nothing but the road, the abandoned cars, the few running people that had managed to clear the ditch and hedges who were now fleeing to the east, the gloriously empty hard shoulder stretching endlessly ahead. She looked behind her; the line of Empty Men was disappearing from view, shrinking as the bike sped away. Biker Woman screamed, a primal cry of joy and relief. Maria joined in.

"*We did it! We* did it!" she bellowed.

"*We did! We did!*" Maria agreed, feeling like crying with relief as she looked behind herself again and watched the Empty Men disappearing.

Except this time, they were *literally* disappearing.

The line looked like it had stopped moving; they began to flicker on the spot. They looked like a hologram that was breaking down, the light source running out of juice. Maria blinked, and they were gone. She couldn't believe it.

"*Oh my God!*" she yelled.

"*What? What?*" Biker Woman yelled back over her shoulder.

"*They... I think they've gone!*"

Biker Woman considered this for a moment.

"*Maybe enough of them got here!*" she shouted. "*I'm not stopping. If they come back, we'll wish we'd kept going!*"

Maria suddenly realised how wrong she had been about wanting to die. Oh *God,* she'd been wrong. She breathed and breathed and realized that she didn't want to die at *all.*

*But what now?* she thought.

"*Where* are *we going?*" Maria yelled, even though at that point it didn't matter any more than it had that morning; they were away, they were *alive,* and they were *moving.*

"*It's complicated. I'll tell you when we* do *stop,*" Biker Woman bellowed back. "*If we can get away with it, I'd like to not stop at all, okay? But I have to close my visor now; I can't see at this speed!*"

That was fine by Maria. Whatever got them out of here quickest.

"*Go, go, go!*" Maria yelled, suddenly starting to laugh like a lunatic. It wasn't good laughter; it was the kind that could very easily break into desperate tears. The biker kept the throttle fully open as they followed the steady curve of the hard shoulder at what felt to Maria like a million miles an hour.

# Part Three:
# On the Inside

*"It's always in the transitions between one phase and the next phase that people fall apart."*

**—Robert Downey Jr**

# Chapter Thirteen:

# Eric's Separation Anxiety, Harry Paints a Picture, and the Prism Goes To Work

***

### Eric

First, something cold and wet. Then the voice. Eric recognized it, but who was in his bedroom? He and Mickey didn't *do* visitors. They just weren't living that kind of life. *Come round for heated-up beans tonight at our place. Well, we say it's our place, but we don't actually know whose place it is. Bring a bottle. In fact,* don't, *Mickey has a* really *severe drinking problem.*

"—ric. Come on, man, come on…"

He opened his eyes and realized that his bedroom ceiling had changed colour. It felt really early, and Eric was absolutely exhausted. His shoulder was burning like a son of a bitch. There was a mix of outdoor and indoor light—big windows letting in a little sun but with the added megawattage of a halogen lamp—

*The light,* he thought. *The bubble. The girl. The Prism. Ground Zero.*

*My fucking* hand—

He shot upright, the water that had just been dripped upon him flying from his face. Harry jerked backwards from his crouched position, startled. Eric immediately waved the stump of his wrist in front of his face like a nightmare that didn't end upon waking. He'd lost his hand. *He'd lost his hand.* This was real. The brutal reality in front of him would not change.

He moaned gently, even as he felt the taking-care-of-Stone-business part of his brain beginning to construct pathways to get him back on task.

*Yes, sir,* Eric thought, delirious. *That's some British-trained obsession there.*

Harry approached again.

"Easy... easy, man," Harry said, holding out his swaying hands in what was supposed to be a calming gesture. Unfortunately, this had the opposite effect; in displaying both of his still-connected hands, it felt crazily to Eric like Harry was taking the piss.

*What's he gonna do next,* Eric's blasted mind thought, *fucking Jazz Hands? Harry Two Hands. Sounds like a gangster name.* Eric rolled over and looked at the bubble behind his friend. Jenny was slumped against the far side of it, her head down. Her feet were drawn as far away from his now-amputated hand as possible. Eric moaned when he saw it, longing sluicing through him. He couldn't tell if she was defeated or just asleep. Harry darted around behind him, putting his hands under both of Eric's armpits to prop him upright against the wall. Eric cried out as his shoulder jarred and got his first real whiff of Harry's suit; it was musty and thick. Not dirty as such, just... lived in.

"Sorry," Harry grunted. He headed over to one of the backpacks and rooted through it for the painkillers. Eric continued to stare at his stump. "Hold on, just hold on," Harry muttered, and Eric thought about telling him that his shoulder was somehow hurting far more than the amputation. *That* barely hurt at all. Shouldn't he be in shock or something too? Maybe that didn't happen when aliens do it to you?

The stump was blackened almost as if it had been cauterized but didn't smell like burnt meat. It didn't truly look like it either. That would have perhaps been uneven, ragged. The amputation was so neat it could have been cut by laser. It was so perfectly even and uniformly black that he couldn't see what was end-of-bone and what was end-of-flesh. Eric started prodding it in a daze, feeling nothing but the dim sensation of pressure. Harry turned to see this, holding pills in one hand and a bottle of distilled water in the other, something Eric would now never be able to do himself.

"No, *Jesus*," he said, pulling Eric's good hand away from his left. "Don't do that. Leave it alone, okay? Take these. Time for antibiotics anyway." He pushed the pills into Eric's good hand and unscrewed the bottle. Eric plopped the pills into his slack mouth like a simpleton, and Harry tipped the bottle to his lips. The distilled water tasted like warm, sanitized piss but Eric swallowed it and the pills. "You wouldn't wake up," Harry said. "Kept talking in your sleep."

Eric looked back at the bubble, at his perfectly severed hand lying palm down. *Thing from the Addams Family taking a rest,* he thought, his mind still doing cartwheels. *Doing a plank.*

"... Does it hurt?" Harry asked.

"No. Doesn't hurt."

Pause.

"Are you okay?"

"I think so."

"Do you want to... what do you want to do?"

Was Harry slurring his words? Eric had absolutely no idea what to do. They couldn't get the girl out—he'd lost his hand trying—and they couldn't get into Ground Zero either. He'd lost his hand. He'd lost his *hand.*

"I don't know, Harry."

"Are you... are you left-handed?"

"... No."

"That's good then... that's a big deal."

*He's right,* Eric thought. *That* is *a big deal. I'll never play the guitar though.* That struck him as funny, so he decided to say it aloud. Maybe he could finally get a smile out of Harry?

"I'll never play the guitar though." The delivery was half-baked, and Harry's face didn't even twitch. Then Eric remembered the situation wasn't funny at all. *Get it together,* he thought. *Now.*

"How'd you *do* that?" Harry asked, breathing out heavily and sitting down in front of Eric. "Whyn't you... let me help you?" Eric could clearly hear the slur in Harry's voice. The man was now drunk.

"I didn't think you *could* help, Harry," Eric sighed. "Did *you* feel anything? When you were that close to the bubble?"

Harry shook his head. "Nope. Should I have?"

"Well, I did when I walked *next* to it, so if you got close and didn't, then I think we really are different with this..." He trailed off, staring at the black lump that used to have a hand attached to it. He fell silent for a moment, the obsessive, unrelenting part of his brain desperately aware of time and already trying to make plans, compassionate as ever.

*Fuck your hand,* it commanded. *You've been out for* hours. *The sun is up now; it's early morning. You have to—*

Wait. Jenny.

"Is Jenny okay?"

"Yeah," said Harry, looking at the girl. "She went very quiet after you passed out. Think she dropped off not long after that. Let's talk, you know..." He waved his hand hazily in the air.

*Harry,* Eric thought angrily. *You being plastered right now is really the last thing I need. That* we *need.*

He suddenly felt like he was going to cry.

*You just lost your hand,* he told himself. *You're allowed.*

But he didn't; he stood instead, swaying a little, and moved nearer to the bubble to look at Jenny's sleeping face. She looked peaceful for the first time but wouldn't be once she awoke. Let her sleep. Eric noticed how young she was. Too young to die. Not as young as Aaron but—

For a moment, Eric's hand was forgotten. He felt helpless.

"We can't get her out of there, Harry," he said quickly, dragging the world back into focus. He felt nauseous but thought maybe that was his body processing the adrenalin, shock, whatever. "I don't think... *uhh...*" He wiped at his face. They had to work. *Time,* always time. He could worry about everything else later. "I don't think that even if we managed to cave the floor in from underneath that... that bastard is going to somehow break, do you?"

"Not after all this, no," Harry slurred. "Gonna need a better plan."

Eric suddenly was wide awake, his nausea forgotten. He *did* have a better plan.

"*Harry,*" Eric said, turning to grab Harry's arm to get his attention but seeing his stump bump against it instead. The sight turned him cold.

"Hang on a second," Harry said, interrupting, but his tone was gentle. "Hang... hang on. I need to make sure I'm clear about something first, alright? You sure you're okay?"

"What? *Yes,* I mean it doesn't hurt, and really, maybe I'm not *okay,* but... I just can't deal with that now. Later. *Listen—*"

"There's something... important. Got to tell you, man."

"Can this wait?

"Eric... please?"

"Jesus, *fine,* what's so fucking important—" Eric hissed, exasperated, his words cutting off as he threw up his hands and realized that he was only throwing up a hand and a pseudo-wrist. "Oh..."

"I need you to *know...* that I don't care if I get out of here," Harry said, his head and his gaze lowered. Eric's petulance vanished. "Okay?" he continued. "Been thinking about it while you were out. I've... I've kind of changed my mind. When I started watching the people yesterday, watching the... what did you call them... *Shufflers* head into town, I was just curious. Well, curious and I had this feeling..." He waved a hand vaguely in the air as if to say, *You know what I mean, you had it too.* "It was the most interest I'd taken in anything in months. *Months.* And I'd... *ahhhh...*" He sighed again, and this time, it was a soul-sigh, his truth brought to the surface like a shadow-thing held in the light, protesting and squirming. He fished in his pocket for his hip flask and began to unscrew the cap. "Actually, gave up long before *that.* Ten years before, fuck it, ten *years,* that's the truth..." He took a pull on the flask and closed his eyes. Eric couldn't tell if Harry was relishing the spreading feeling of warmth or hating the helpless, pointless, endless craving for the dopamine hit. "This has been the first twenty-four hours in... I've no idea how long that I haven't spent eighty per cent of it fully drunk. That make sense?"

"Yes."

Harry nodded and examined the flask closely, stroking it with his thumb as he spoke.

"I was a married man, Eric. Wasn't a good husband, but I worked hard. What do you think I used to do? *Guess.*"

"I don't know, Harry." Eric suddenly really wanted to know. "I *couldn't* guess... The suit, I mean... Stockbroker? Accountant?"

Harry chuckled darkly at this, and Eric wanted to snap, *Well, don't fucking ask me to guess then,* but that was childish, petulant. Yes, it had been a rough twenty-four hours, but the man was talking about dying. There was no need to be a dick.

"Was actually a painter. Don't mean a decorator, I mean an *artist*. I made a living from it. Never made megabucks, never a Damien Hirst or a Banksy or that lass who had the shitted-up bed. But I made a good living, had a nice enough house, decent car. Nice wife. Nice kid. *Great* wife and kid. But a lot of *free time,* Eric. Free time. Idle hands." He held up the flask and gently shook it at him. "Know what I mean?" His head swayed as he spoke.

"I get you."

"She *asked* me," Harry said, and there was that soul-sigh again. "She *asked* me if I'd get help. Said I would. Didn't. *Meant* to. Then she stopped asking and started *telling* and then I still didn't and then she left with the kid and I *did* go and she came back and for a while... everything was great. Then I'd get back into work, and I'd miss a meeting, miss a sponsor one-to-one, and there'd be another excuse, and then she's leaving me again. Then I would hate myself *so bad*... it was a dance. She did it with me for a few years. Wouldn't have done it if she hadn't loved me. After a while, you know..." He jerked a thumb over his shoulder and blew a short raspberry. "She moved to Europe. Already had family there. In hindsight, that's one good thing that came out of all this; she and my kid aren't in Britain for *this*. Takes away a little guilt, and that's *the* thing, Eric. The knowledge that I could fuck something *so good* up *so badly*... Anyway. One thing led to another, and I ended up in Coventry. I hadn't, y'know... *admitted it to myself yet.* What I wanted to happen. I just let the days bleed together, and then one day, I saw that I was down to my last seven bottles. I saw that and *click,* just like that, I knew. I could finally admit it."

"Admit what?" Eric asked, knowing the answer.

"I'd *decided*... I decided... that when the last bottle was finally gone, I'd go to the top of a building like this one and jump off the fucker, take care of business. And I wanted to be dressed nice when I did it. Have *some* dignity about the thing." He brushed what was either dust or dandruff off the suit's shoulder pads. Eric wondered how much dignity Harry would have when his body was a ragged combination of whisky stink and smashed blood and bone from the impact, but kept his mouth shut. "I still had this suit in my things," Harry said, inspecting his arms, "wrapped up in a bag. I got married in it. So, I started wearing it every day in case, you know, I got up the guts and chugged all of the booze just to get it over and done with. Then one morning a bunch of loonies appeared to be roaming the streets and I felt weird shit in my head and I thought, *Hey, if you follow them maybe this will all get decided for you.* Know what I mean?"

Eric did.

"For a little while there, in all the excitement, I was actually thinking about getting out, trying to escape," he said, chuckling bitterly. "Survival instinct, maybe. I got all amped up about trying to live and thinking about how we could make it away from the city. I didn't think about Lucy or Oggy at all, for the first time in *years.* Probably why I've been sober. I had something else to worry about." Eric assumed, from the way he said the name, that *Oggy* would be a daughter—maybe not her real name but an affectionate term—the tone unique to fathers talking about their girls. "But now I've been sitting here looking at this poor girl in this fucking *thing*," he spat, waving a loose hand at the bubble, "and I've not been able to think about anything or anyone else but those two. So, I had a drink and I remembered. I remembered my *original* plan. And I started to wonder..." He trailed off again, shrugged, and then turned his damp eyes towards Eric. "... What the hell I was doing worrying about *anything?*" He grinned suddenly. "*Ahh,* but there's a sting in the tale," he said, wagging his finger. He fished into his jacket pocket, swaying slightly, and pulled out a small key on a keyring that said I HEART EARLSDON. He dangled it at eye level theatrically before tossing the key to Eric. The younger man tried to grab at it with both hands, but it sailed through the gap where his left hand would have been and gently landed on his chest. "Fuck. Sorry," Harry muttered.

"Christ..." Eric sighed, feeling incredibly sorry for himself. "It's okay, it's alright. Finish what you're saying, Harry."

"That *key*," Harry said, pointing with drunkenly inaccurate aim towards the key, "opens my garage. The address is written on the other side of the key fob." Eric looked; there it was, written in biro. "When I first came here—when I still had a car—I brought all my unfinished stuff with me. My work. Before things got really bad, I *finished* a lot of it. All of it, I think." The word *finished* still came out as *funnshed.* "I could sell pieces for a few hundred quid back in the day. There will still be people—dealers—that will vaguely remember my name. Not many, but enough. When I'm *dead,* Eric, those paintings will go for at least a grand, or maybe *several* grand at a push. There's forty-plus pieces there, Eric, that's a *lot.* I'll make you this deal. Okay? Okay?"

"What you got?" Eric breathed, feeling sleepy but intrigued.

"Give them to Oggy," he said. "She'll be eighteen this year. In return, I'll help you do whatever you want to do. I mean, I don't think I can do things like you with…" He waved a hand at the bubble.

"Well, I didn't let you try—"

"You felt it when you were close," Harry interrupted. "You're higher up the Stone food chain than me, we both know it. Some people just *are*, right? That's why, when the Stone Men are in town, some people get nothing, some people get a bit of a vision, and some get the whole movie and have weird things happen when they touch even lower-down people like me. Right?"

"Yes."

"Whatever you were doing to that bubble *wasn't supposed to happen*, you know. Maybe you're a little different altogether. Did you hear that thing? The noises it made when you were opening it up?"

Harry was right. Eric hadn't had long to think about it in the brief time he'd been awake, but the memory of that hole magically opening beneath his hand—at his *will*—struck him hard. It had been like having a superpower. What did it mean?

*Maybe*, Eric thought, *it means you have a fighting chance—*

"I did, Harry, but look what it did to me," Eric said softly, holding up his stump. "I don't think we can stick that in the win column."

"But *it didn't like it*, did it?" Harry hissed, leaning forwards and stabbing a finger downward into the floor. "Sounded like it was really grinding its gears trying to *stop* you. Look, look what's gone on already! The lines have been drawn!"

"Lines? What lines?"

Harry's face screwed up in drunken annoyance, and he theatrically waved his arm towards Jenny. The change was upsetting to see; Harry's cool exterior had loosened in such an embarrassing way.

"Class divides," Harry murmured. "Isn't it obvious?"

"Indulge me."

"Everyone else died when the Barrier touched them. *Poof.* They're *dead, boom*, gone. Okay?" He counted *one* on his index finger, holding it out. "Go up a level to all the people that are alive then, starting with the Shufflers. They lived, but something got to them, made them act funny. But *we're* not like that. So, there's another level again, another divide." He held up two shaking fingers. "Then there's you and me, right? We're one up from them because we're alive too, but not mental." Three fingers. "But then you're picking up shit that I can't, and you can also do stuff that I can't by the looks of it. So, go up another level to *you*, okay." Four fingers. "Then, top of the class, there's *her.*" He pointed at Jenny with all four fingers and added his thumb. "And she's inside an unbreakable bubble. What do you do with your most precious possession?"

Eric didn't answer, suddenly completely fascinated and not wanting to interrupt Harry's flow.

"You put it inside a *box*," Harry finished, spreading his arms wide. He paused, and Eric thought he was just breaking off for a moment, but then Eric heard it too: a distant but familiar approaching sound. It quickly became a roar, and they knew what was happening. They both covered their ears, Eric remembering to use just his remaining hand for his right ear and his shoulder for his left, but Harry didn't bother. The sound hit a crescendo and there was a *BOOM* before the jet noise raced away into the distance. Another airstrike. They weren't giving up then. As Eric rushed to the window, he saw Jenny turn over in her sleep but, amazingly, not wake. She had to be exhausted beyond measure. Eric looked at the sky, saw the faint swirling of the Barrier still hanging above.

"Been a few of those while you were out," Harry muttered. "You didn't wake up for any of them. I got *worried.*"

"What are you saying?" Eric asked, sighing not at Harry but at the failed airstrike. He was intrigued by what Harry was saying. There was logic here, drunk or otherwise. Eric returned to the floor next to his friend.

"I might not be up there enough to be put inside a bubble, Eric," Harry said, shrugging and giggling a little at the foolish sound of the sentence. "But I'm good enough to be alive in here for some reason, maybe Level Three me is just a backup option, who knows? I think I'm going to die in here, one way or the other." He let it hang in the air, and Eric didn't know what to say. "It doesn't look good so far, let's be honest. I'm fine with that. But *you,*" he said, the waving fingers aimed at Eric now, "you look like you might have something up your sleeve that they didn't anticipate. Something they *missed.*" It was a good point, but whatever Eric had was useless if he couldn't even get Jenny out without losing limbs in the process. Even the effort of making a hole that small had half-killed him.

"And maybe you're the kind of person they don't *want* on the inside," Harry continued, "so when *you* get out, and I think you will, you get those paintings to Og—to *Olivia* Regis. She lives in Majorca with her mother; I doubt there's many Olivia Regises over there. Okay? In return, I'll throw myself in the line of fuckin' fire if need be. That's the deal." He opened his mouth to add something else, realized he had nothing then threw both of his hands up to say, *That's it.*

Eric nodded in agreement, but his brain had turned to all the theories surrounding the fate of the Quarries as a terrible confirmation came to him.

Thinking about what Harry had said about precious possessions. About putting them inside boxes.

He looked at Jenny as she slept, imagined her blissfully unaware of an army unit heading her way. Looked at the bubble.

Understood how it proved everything he'd ever thought about the government's Arrival protocols.

*Straub and her army bastards killed Theresa and the others,* Eric thought, the sense of dull horror growing in his stomach, *because* they *were 'precious possessions' to the Stone Men. That was the way to stop the Stone Men quickly.*

His hand went to his mouth as he stared at the bubble, wide-eyed.

Pictured bullets ricocheting ineffectively off it.

"The Stone Men had to change the plan..." he whispered.

"What's that?" Harry mumbled, before the sky filled with noise again. It was too quick for Eric to cover his ears. Another deafening airstrike. Both men flinched. Jenny didn't move. The chaos went on for a good few minutes—perhaps several successive strikes too close together to tell them apart—and once it died down, Harry got up and walked to the window, gazing at the sky and telling Eric what he already knew.

"Fuckin' thing's still there," he muttered. Jenny turned over in her sleep, moaning softly. Eric's mind was racing, turning to rage as he looked at that golden ball, how it proved *everything* about Straub and her crew... but now was not the time.

"What'd you say just now?" Harry asked.

"Doesn't matter," Eric said quietly, his voice shaking. There was no point discussing it with Harry at the moment. "Your deal,

Harry. I agree," he said, slipping Harry's key into the pocket of his jeans. "But there's one catch." Harry didn't say anything but gestured repeatedly towards himself, rocking steadily now. *Tell me, go for it.* "Give me the hip flask. You're not going to be any good to me fucked. In fact, you're going to be more of a hindrance."

"*Ohhhhhh,* I don't think so..." Harry hissed, a stupid smile on his face, shaking his head.

"I'll even give it back to you, if you *really* need it, but that's the deal."

Harry eyeballed Eric for a moment, looked at the hipflask in his hand then nodded and went to throw it over. At the last moment he thought better of it and handed it over instead.

"Thank you. I'll get the paintings to Oggy, I promise. Now," Eric said, sighing and leaning forwards to show even a drunk man that he *really* meant business. Fuck the hand, fuck thinking about whatever abilities he may or may not have; right now, this was what he was going to deal with. "I had an idea, before... before I passed out."

"Uh-huh?"

"I think I've thought of a way to get past the Shufflers. More importantly, if we can get *in* there... they might have something. It's a research facility, right?"

"That's what they say."

"Right. And we don't know what they know, do we? Did they *know* this shit was coming? Either way, they've been researching *something.* Who's to say they don't have something in there that could help us get Jenny out of that thing?"

"The Shufflers... they're dangerous..."

"Yes, but not more dangerous than a car. *Jenny's car.* She said she was drawn here a few days ago, and I think that's her Honda downstairs. It's not a Ferrari but it isn't a piece of shit either. We can try to push through with—"

Both men felt it. A pulse of some kind, a jolt. It hadn't been major like the Horns, but it was still unmistakable. Both men looked at each other.

"The Prism—"

They quickly moved to the window, giving the bubble a wide birth, and Eric used his good hand to pick up his binoculars from where Harry had left them on the floor. Harry stared through the glass.

"Nothing's happened?" he said, confused. The base of the Prism was surrounded by Shufflers, just like before, the only difference being that there was a good deal more of them now, maybe a third of their original number again.

They were still doing that swaying, self-grabbing movement from before. Was Harry right? Were these people in some kind of different bracket than Harry and him?

Both men flinched as a second jolt hit them, harder this time. That horrible feeling of something waking up rippled through Eric's body.

"*Fuckers,*" Harry hissed. "I'm sick of this shit—"

"Wait, Harry," Eric said, lifting the binoculars back to his eyes and squinting again. "*Look.*"

As Eric watched, all of the Shufflers by the Prism straightened up as one, stilled and then relaxed, their heads held high.

"*Jesus,*" Eric whispered.

"Christ," Harry muttered. "What are they... what are they *doing?*"

All of the Shufflers' heads suddenly flopped backwards on their necks, hanging as loose as pool balls inside a sock. Their mouths were hanging open, and through the binoculars, Eric could see that their eyes were rolling over white. Jenny's building was close enough that if the Shufflers were making noise, it would have floated over to them—especially as the middle windowpane had been smashed open by a flying sledgehammer—but there was nothing. The effect was deeply eerie. The Shufflers were looking up at the sky from their heavily angled point of view and were pressing more closely against the Prism, their arms now by their sides.

Eric wondered if part of them was conscious. It was a horrible thought. Had whatever drawn them to Ground Zero taken over their motor functions and made them walk, their conscious minds protesting *no, no,* all the way? Could the way they'd been holding themselves be some sort of attempt at self-protection, their distressed faces and anguished moaning an outer display of the inner battle to resist? Did they know what was going to happen next, then?

"It can't be anything good," Harry said, as if reading Eric's thoughts. "If the Prism wants *them,* it can't be good news for the rest of us, either."

Then Eric spotted Mickey in the crowd.

He must have taken the long way around, or become lost, or snapped at the wrong guy and been beaten up en route or *something,* but he was there now when he hadn't been there before. Even in the midst of a crowd—his short frame putting his head way below those of most of the other Shufflers—it was easy to pick him out, especially with that stupid white Top Rank T-shirt that was two sizes too big for him. It had been a freebie. Eric couldn't see Mickey's face, but he could see his movements from the back. Even if the crowd of Shufflers were several people deep and Mickey was a few layers away from the surface of the Prism, Eric didn't know how long it would be until he touched up against it, drawn there like all the others.

"Shit, that's *Mickey.* Harry, we have to go!"

But what could he do for him? Mickey was now at the front of a press of bodies, the crowd three Shufflers deep behind him. They'd have to drag Shufflers aside to get to Mickey, and then they'd be torn to pieces. The car, he could use the car—

No. It wouldn't work. They'd have to get out of the vehicle in the middle of the Shufflers.

*"Mickey..."* Eric whispered, but an unpleasant realisation struck him; he was playing a part. If he was honest, he didn't feel any more for Mickey than he did for any of the other Shufflers gathered nearby.

*But he was my friend,* he tried to tell himself... but Mickey *hadn't* been a friend. Eric knew it. Mickey had only seen Eric as another soldier that he could use.

Eric noticed the gap in the crumbled Ground Zero facility wall. He felt sick. He couldn't get to that any more than he could save his former roommate.

*I don't even know if anything will happen if he* does *touch it,* he thought. *The people at the front must be pressing against it by now, surely—*

He tried to see. They were *close*, but he couldn't see if they were actually—

Then he remembered what happened to the people who had touched the Stone Man.

He'd seen the uploaded footage just like everyone else in the world, and the Prism looked like it was built out of *very* similar material. He glanced at Jenny. Still asleep... or was she? Could that thing be doing something to her—

"Wait," Eric suddenly barked. "What's that guy doing...?"

A Shuffler on the front line had stepped all the way in and was now clearly pressing against the Prism. He was a chubby, well-dressed man. He hadn't come from the streets of Cov; where had *he* been drawn from?

*How far does the Prism's influence go?* Eric wondered, mind reeling. The Shuffler's stomach would now be pressing against the Prism as his head swung around loosely, staring up at the sky as it hung backward on his neck.

"Do you think—" Harry whispered, and Eric knew he meant the bursting death they'd seen with the soldiers. It didn't come. Eric waited then for the limpness, the collapsed noodle-limbs that came with touching any of the Stone Men. This would be followed by what was known in the forums amongst other Stone conspiracists and cryptozoologists (or what even Eric referred to as *fucking nerds*) as the GATTACA Chant. That didn't come either. Another of the Shufflers made contact with the stony surface, then another, until a small wall of people was now pressed very tightly around the Prism's base, or at least the part of it that Eric could see. Mickey was one of them. It quickly became several people deep in places. How many of them were there? Three hundred? Four? There hadn't been anywhere near that many there earlier; perhaps they had arrived at Ground Zero *after* the Barrier had gone up, heading inwards on foot from nicer areas much further out. Eric saw with horror that one or two of them seemed to be hesitating, almost fighting against themselves, before losing the battle and stepping forwards.

*Oh God,* he thought. *They* are *aware. They* do *know that they shouldn't touch it*—

So many people had pressed in now that the people at the front were flattened against the Prism by the folks behind them. Nothing happened; Mickey too seemed to be unaffected by touching the Prism if not from whatever had already attacked his mind. Eric's eyes kept being drawn back to the gap in the wall.

*If they leave...* he thought. *If they* leave... *Hold on, wait—*

The gap in the wall seemed wider than it did a moment ago. How was that possible? *No,* the gap wasn't wider, the bodies blocking it were covering less of it. And less. And less. What the hell—

Eric swung the binoculars back to the front of the Prism, finding the chubby, well-dressed guy from earlier as a reference point. He couldn't look at Mickey.

The man's head had come back up now—all of the heads of the front line were upright once more—and oddly turned sideways, lying flush against the Prism's wall. His eye on the visible side of his face was no longer rolled-over white, and was darting this way and that, as if trying to understand where he'd suddenly found himself. He looked terrified and horribly lucid.

Later, Eric would wonder what the man had been thinking. Perhaps wondering where he was? Who all these people around him were? What was the huge stone object he found himself pressed against?

Why the hell did it *hurt* so much?

Eric would assume this last part because the man's mouth opened wide, teeth bared, as he let out a blood-curdling scream. It was a sound that Eric would take with him to his grave. It was quickly joined by the other frontline people pressed against the Prism's wall—some were shrill, some were baritone. Some of them actually managed to form words—words that Eric would later be glad that he couldn't quite make out—as the sound of their immense pain drifted towards him on the early morning air. He'd heard distant cheers from stadiums before, but this was like a gunman had suddenly run onto an imaginary stadium's field and started blowing away spectators. Even through the binoculars, Eric could see the confusion and terror in those innocent peoples' eyes as both they and he realized that they were dying.

The reason the gap had widened was because those people were flattening *into* the Prism. Eric thought he could see very faint, very thin plumes of smoke; they were hard to make out, and he slowly realized from the way it rose and dissipated that it wasn't smoke at all. It was red vapour. It had seemed at first that the Prism was simply *absorbing* them somehow, but once Eric saw that vapour, he understood that the Prism was taking a million little bites of them from top to toe at unbelievable speed. A thousand times faster than the world's quickest wood chipper.

The Prism had no teeth that Eric could see, but even so, there was no doubt that thing was eating them. That was the only term Eric could think of using to describe it.

The Shufflers behind the people at the front—for those frontline unfortunates were no longer Shufflers but fully lucid humans—continued to press forwards as if they knew nothing about what was happening, their heads still lolling backwards, their eyes still white. Eric looked back to the fat man; his eye, his *face* had disappeared from view along with his hands and the front of his shoulders. All that was visible of his skull now were his left ear and left side of his head, sticking from the Prism as if someone had created a crazy art installation. A Mr Potato Head toy but with a wall instead of a spud. His back still twitched as he died, but then that vanished quickly as the Prism pulled that last piece of him into it. The Shuffler behind him, a tall blonde-haired woman, was immediately pressed against the Prism's dark, gnarled surface, either by personal intent or from the force of the individual behind her. She was well-dressed too, unlike the Shufflers they'd seen on the ring road the day before. She had to have arrived later.

The effect on her wasn't instant. She writhed calmly on the spot for a moment against the Prism wall and Eric realized that she was *trying* to get closer still, trying to burrow deep into it. Then she stopped moving and her head came up, pressing sideways against the Prism just like the man whose place she'd taken. Her visible eye blinked and her mouth opened as she began to twitch, wondering where she was, trying to pull away and finding that, of course, she couldn't as her face was already beginning to be chewed inwards. Her twitching became frantic, and then Eric couldn't watch any longer. He desperately panned around for Mickey and found him a few feet to her left, just as he reached the wall.

*"Mickey!"* he yelled, as knowledge broke through. Friend or not, Mickey had been *his,* part of his tribe, and in the moment, Eric had no doubt of it. Thoughtlessly, he turned and began to dart for the door, to run *down* there even though there was nothing he could possibly do, but Harry lunged and grabbed his arm. One look in his eyes brought Eric back to his senses, back to the window.

*Mickey,* he thought. *Please stop.*

Mickey didn't. Over the course of the next minute, Eric watched him die.

After that, he gave Harry the binoculars. Shaking, Eric sat down, stunned beyond thought. Looking up from his lower vantage point, he saw that Jenny's eyes were open, and she was looking at him.

"What's happening?" she asked, her voice flat, distant.

"They... they..."

The truth hung behind his lips, unspoken. *They've done something truly terrible, Jenny.*

But what could he tell her?

*How dare they?* he thought. *How fucking dare they?*

He looked at his severed hand, still lying on the floor of the bubble. Jenny's feet continued to be drawn up and away from it as if at any moment it might leap up and grab her ankle, scuttling up her leg and onto her mouth like a Facehugger.

Eric suddenly realized that once all the Shufflers were eaten, he would finally be able to get inside Ground Zero. To get answers, to get fucking *evidence*—

To his great surprise, as his one shaking hand balled into a fist, all that was in him now was *rage*. Not even at the government that had taken his sister and his nephew, that in itself was remarkable; he *lived* with that rage, slept with it, ate with it, every thought and emotion that made up the meat of his mind smoked from below by it. *Functional rage* was the name he used, a constant only truly noticed when something dragged it to the surface like some horrible Lovecraftian creation, albeit a pallid and impotent one.

But *this* rage was not impotent.

*They want to keep her in there,* he thought. *You tell them* fuck you *by getting her* out.

"We're going to set off for Ground Zero now, okay?" he told her quietly, his voice sounding unfamiliar and unsettling to his own ears. She flinched as he slapped the floor with each word, spittle forming at his lips and tears forming in his eyes. His voice cracked as he promised her. "Me and Harry. We're going to go in and try to find something or someone that's got better ideas or better kit than a fucking value range B&Q sledgehammer, and we're going to come back, and I promise you, we are going to bust you the *fuck* out of there. They can't fucking *have* you because *they don't get to have what they want.*" He sounded like a madman, but Jenny, to Eric's amazement, just nodded as if she understood. She saw him.

"What happened to you?" she asked him softly. "What did they do?"

Eric blinked dumbly, caught by her tenderness, a chord struck deep in the marrow of his vulnerability. His good hand went to his stump-wrist, and his voice was like a child's.

"Not this," he said, bewildered. "It wasn't just this."

"I know," she said. "It's been a long time. Hasn't it?"

She was right. She reached her hand towards him, and an ache broke through him that he hadn't acknowledged for many years. He reached out his hand to her in return and as he did so, the bubble *stung* him at close range again. He couldn't get near enough, and the moment was lost.

"Will you tell my mother? She lives in Northampton."

"You'll tell her when you—"

"Will you?"

Her eyes were pleading. It hurt to look at her.

"... Tell her what?"

"Uh... that I love her. That I thought about her." She blinked. "Her name's Felicity Drewett. Felicity May Drewett."

It was the kind of request Theresa never got to make. It was too much. Eric couldn't look at her any more.

"I'm getting you out," he repeated quietly.

"I know," she said, nodding even as her eyes brimmed with tears, terrified.

Eric would never forget her saying that.

He got to his feet and watched with Harry until the last of the Shufflers were gone. He couldn't have helped them; if they'd tried to stop the remaining Shufflers from going into the Prism, the reaction from them would have been murderous. Even so, he watched them die, his mind passing beyond horror into some new and unknown state. As the last human mouth vanished out of sight into the Prism, its choked-off final scream rang out sharply on the breeze. Silence returned except for Harry's ragged breathing.

Were he and Harry somehow next? Would whatever happened to the Shufflers work its way along the food chain to them? Were they going to suddenly find themselves shaking and crying before they began to follow the Shufflers into that thing? Would he go to sleep that night—if he lived that long—and wake up to find his face pressed sideways against a solid surface? Would his eyes see the back of a stranger's head in front of him and have time to realize where he was before the pain started, before those million bites began to whittle him—all that he was—away?

He waited. *Something* had to happen now.

*Just do it, you fuckers,* Eric thought. *Get it over with, but I guarantee, I will do my very best to make sure you* choke.

Nothing happened. The gap in the Ground Zero wall lay open before him.

He could wait, or he could move.

"Let's go, Harry," Eric said, and he didn't recognize himself in that flat, dead voice. "We're going into Ground Zero."

# Chapter Fourteen:

# Linda

***

## Maria

The hair and earrings under the helmet had been one thing; the collared blouse with patterned-wool sweater under the biker jacket was another thing entirely. It was like watching the Terminator undress to reveal that he was wearing a bunny costume. Linda not only looked like someone's mum—she *was* someone's mum. Maria would find out that her daughter was on a gap year travelling around America.

They'd ridden in silence along the dual carriageway's hard shoulder for nearly an hour, surrounded by stationary cars and blessedly empty fields. The line of the Empty Men must have been long indeed, but Maria stopped thinking it had been countrywide; they were beginning to pass cars that were slowly moving once more. Eventually, it even turned into flowing traffic, although maybe only at twenty-five miles per hour. The panic hadn't set in quite this far yet, or the Empty Men had gone through their cities much earlier, and the survivors had hit the road.

*Survivors?* Maria thought—now she'd had time to calm down and think about it—that would be the majority. The Empty Men seemed very *selective* in who they took. Even so, if they'd gone from the coast to Birmingham, they'd covered a lot of the country. Maybe what she'd seen was the last of them. A final delivery in bulk, the end of the packet all dumped out at once.

As the bike slowed to a halt by the side of the road, Maria thought of all those cars *behind* them, the ones the people abandoned. No-one would be able to get away via those roads now, except on foot or by motorcycle. They were plugging up their own transport systems.

*Are those things going to Coventry?* she wondered. *What happens when they get there? What's* happening *there?*

The woman put the bike on its kickstand and waited; Maria realized that she was supposed to get off first and did so, hamstrings yelling in protest. The biker took her helmet off and pointed to a billboard by the roadside. Her eyes met Maria's, and suddenly, Maria could imagine them smiling at her over a cup of tea, offering to clean her house while she was away on holiday. What the heck was this woman doing riding a motorbike, swinging a helmet like a sack of doorknobs?

"I'm sorry, I need to pee," she said, dismounting. "I've been holding it for ages. I'll be quick." She was well-spoken, southern-sounding.

"That's... fine, don't be silly, go, go. And thank you," Maria added, having waited all this time to do so.

"That's all right. You're welcome."

"But... where *are* we going?"

Maria had noticed on the way that the woman had taped a GPS to the handlebars. When she'd strained to look over the woman's shoulder, she'd noticed how it glitched in and out, the route onscreen vanishing as they progressed, but it seemed to be enough to get them roughly in the right direction. Somehow, at least, GPS seemed to be working slightly better than the phones.

"Well, it depends if we have enough fuel to get there, but I think we do," the woman said, looking at the cars. "The petrol stations are a nightmare now. There have been fights even. I don't really want to stop again, so if you need to use the toilet too, or think you might, maybe go after me? Are you hungry?" She caught herself and cursed—it didn't sound right coming from her. "Sorry, even if you are, I don't have much. I had a bag all prepped but... *ugh...*" She sighed heavily and actually clenched her fist as she shook her head. "I *left* it in the rush, silly cow. I've only got a pack of sandwiches under the seat, I could *scream...*"

"It's okay, it's fine," Maria babbled. "I left *my* bag in..." She remembered how she left it, *where* she left it. "... In a rush too."

"Silly sods, we are," the woman said. "Okay, I'm going to go now then, wait here." Then she stopped and held out her hand. "Sorry," she said. "Linda. Linda Wyken."

Maria took it. "Maria—*Christ!*" Both of them yanked their hands away as they got a static shock. That had *hurt.* "Sorry..." Maria said, nursing her hand. "Guess it's because we're both wearing wool..."

Linda just stared back at her. The older woman's hand was curled into a fist against her chest as if Maria might bite it. Maria suddenly felt as if Linda were considering her; she could see the cogs turning behind Linda's eyes, figuring things out.

"Is everything... okay?" Maria asked.

"Yes," Linda said quietly, nodding gently. "We've got a lot to discuss, I think."

"Yeah," Maria said, missing Linda's meaning. "I can't believe we got away..."

"Oh, me neither," Linda said. "Have you seen them up close before?"

Maria nearly lied.

"Yes. You?"

"I saw some in my village a few hours before I set off from home. They were quite far away though, maybe a hundred feet or so. I was walking, and I hid behind the car when I saw them. They were on the village green, moving towards the houses nearby, in the opposite direction to me, fortunately. There was about seven of them. I saw them and I thought..." She shook her head. Maria shuddered as she pictured a gang of them creeping their way through a genteel English village.

"They didn't come towards you?" Maria asked.

"No."

"Did you... *feel* anything when we went through them? Just before?"

"No, why? Did you?"

"... Yes."

Maria thought about actually saying what had been ticking away in her mind ever since she'd seen that spectre moving away between the lines of cars. What had been almost confirmed by the rush through them on the bike...

*It's happened three times,* Maria thought. *Tell her. It might help—*

No, she couldn't do that. Linda would then start to ask questions and say Maria had to—

"What's up?"

"Linda... I think I can make it so they can't see me. Maybe so they can't see the people *around* me too... It happened earlier. I think..."

That *pop* she'd felt as the woman on the road moved away from her, running with her son.

Going out of her range of influence.

"I mean, I think, *Leave me alone,* and I can hide but... I think it affects people next to me too. Or maybe people I'm touching. This woman in the traffic earlier, once she ran away from me, I *felt* her leave, felt those things see her..."

Linda was staring at her.

"I'm not crazy," Maria added hurriedly. "I've had those things start to leech into me, and I've sent them away—"

"I believe you," Linda said, holding up her hand. "That jolt told me everything. You're on the spectrum for sure."

*On the spectrum?*

"Did you have visions, Maria?" Linda asked. "In the first few Arrivals?"

Maria thought about Linda's face when she'd shaken her hand. How her expression had changed. The woman knew something.

"I did," she replied quietly, feeling strangely naked in admitting it. "Every time."

Linda nodded.

"Okay. Let me go and pee, and we'll talk—"

"Oh, yes, of course—"

"I'm going to take the bike with me. Keep it out of sight in case..."

"Yes. Good."

Linda half-smiled and began to wheel the bike towards the billboard. Maria realized Linda hadn't answered the question of where they were going. She hugged herself and watched the cars roll slowly past until Linda came back. The bike remained out of sight. She held a carrier bag with a sandwich inside.

"Let me give you a tissue for, you know..." Linda said, and Maria heard it in her voice: the well-practised tones of a mother saying, *Let me take care of it.* She produced a little Handy Pak of tissues from a hip pouch on her waist. Maria imagined Linda fishing in that same pouch for change as she got on a bus... but Maria realized she had to stop thinking like that. She'd just seen the woman happily brain a two-hundred-and-fifty-pound man with a motorcycle helmet, so that meant Linda wasn't exactly Miss Marple. Plus, she was too young. Mid-fifties maybe, not quite *Golden Girls* yet. Linda thrust the whole pack into Maria's hand. "Here—oh *God,* you're *freezing,* of course you are, here, here—" She began to shake her jacket off.

"No!" Maria protested, even though the woman was right; she *was* freezing. The Goodmans' cardigan was no match for the wind chill on the back of the bike in that late September air.

"Don't be silly, your hands are like ice. Here."

"Well, just until we leave so I can warm up, okay? Then you put it back on. We share."

Linda shook her head. "No, I've got better layers on, and I'm sweating in that thing," she said. "Please, love, go do your business, and we can get moving." The woman was a saint, and Maria was happy to oblige, especially as she suddenly really needed to go and the jacket was so *warm.*

"Thank you. I'll be quick. *Thank* you."

Once Maria was finished, she emerged from behind the billboard and waved Linda over. For some reason, she didn't think it was her place to wheel the bike back out again. Once Linda reached her, they both stood awkwardly, wondering how to pick up the previous conversation. Linda went first.

"Look," she said, "I probably should tell you a few things, and then you might have a few questions after I do. We've made good time. I'm starving and seeing as we probably won't be stopping for another hour, we can take five minutes to share this sandwich. I'll tell you as much as I can while we do, and then we *have* to get back on the road. Fair?"

"Fair," Maria said, relieved to be getting the holy Arrival trinity of rest and food and information. Linda fished in the plastic bag she'd brought from the bike and unwrapped the sandwich inside.

"I'm really not a government person or anything, if you're thinking that," she said, handing Maria her half of a cheese and pickle sandwich. Her stomach growled, and she wondered when she'd last eaten a meal. "I was a Be Prepared signup. Before that, I was a receptionist at a beauty spa." She paused, struck by the memory, and shook her head slowly. "I didn't think they'd want me, but they did," she said. "That's how I ended up working at Project Ouroboros."

Her expression darkened, as if recalling bad memories.

"Where?"

"It's a military base near the Ladybower Reservoir in Sheffield." She sighed. "No-one knows it's a military base. It looks like a wind farm. That's where we're headed. It's probably the only place that can help us, and I didn't like the idea of sitting at home while those things made their way towards my house." She gestured at the rolling cars. "If everyone here knew what that place was for, they'd all be going there too."

"A military base?" Maria asked. Something dawned on her. "To do with the Stone Men? Research or something?" The something grew a sliver of hope. "They have the Chisel there?"

"I don't know what they have, but I know what they *had*," Linda said, her voice low. "Well, they told everyone in the end, so you do too."

"*That's* where they had the Stone Man? Before the—"

"Yes. I was there for a while."

"Well, what were they—"

"You want to know what happened just now?" Linda interrupted, but not unkindly. "When we shook hands? Why we felt each other in the middle of a traffic jam?"

"Yes," Maria said. She felt awkward.

"Mmm. So did they," Linda sighed, and took a bite of her sandwich. She chewed it thoughtfully. "Poor Paul. I hope they got some answers in the end. That's what *I* want to try to find out. Probably a waste of time, but..." She shrugged and sighed heavily, her gaze faraway again. "I'm a part of this. We have to do *something.*"

Maria ignored the word *we*—being *a part of this* was the *last* thing she wanted to be and had no intention of making it worse—and went back to Linda's earlier comment.

"Who's Paul?"

Linda gave that self-scowl and headshake again.

"*Ugh,* I'm terrible. Getting ahead of myself. Paul was..." As she tried to find the words, Maria saw with great surprise that Linda's eyes were wet. "*Sorry.* Sorry. It's a little bit emotional." She sniffed and shook her head. "He spent four years inside a metal prison on wheels with that thing chasing him," she said, anger in her voice. "A prisoner with death at his heels, every minute of every day. Can you imagine? Some people do less time for manslaughter. As far as I know, he never did anything to deserve it either."

*A metal prison on wheels?* Maria didn't dare interrupt. *Wait,* she thought, *is Linda upset because—*

Her guess was right.

"He died, Maria," Linda said. "He's dead. He was a nice man, and he's... he's dead. I liked him a lot. Look, let me start at the beginning and I'll explain everything."

\*\*\*

By the time Linda finished explaining her Be Prepared appeal recruitment, her sandwich was long gone. Maria's was still only half-finished. She stood stiffly, arms wrapped around herself, feeling sick; the idea of arriving at some mysterious hangar and being shown her worst nightmare mere feet away, following some cabin on wheels? A lot of people hadn't believed the government's account at the press conference, herself included. How could they really have kept *that* thing in one place? Everyone had seen it shrug off hellfire missiles on live TV. Yet here was Linda confirming it. If the Stone Man hadn't been destroyed, there would be no way she would be following Linda to that place.

"But... they'd managed to get the Stone Man trapped just by getting it to follow this guy?" Maria asked, incredulous. "That's *it*? *That's* how they caught it?"

It just seemed so... simple. It was almost stupid. *Almost.*

"I didn't actually get to spend a huge amount of time in the main hangar," Linda said, shrugging. "Most of my time was spent in rehearsal rooms before I had to leave. I'm glad of that. I didn't like being around the Stone Man. I found it hard to watch." She shuddered, and Maria was sure she heard Linda mutter *Dark Things* under her breath. "The hope was, I presume, that keeping *Caementum* here—they called it *Caementum*—meant we'd somehow buggered up their process of the others returning. We had the lynchpin."

*Caementum*, Maria thought. It sounded like some cutesy corporate mascot. What was the Michelin Man's actual name? *Bibendum?*

"Either way, all public recruits there had visions of people during the Arrivals, people that the Stone Men had apparently come to see. Part of our job there was to get *better* for when—if—those things came back. I'd only ever seen one guy as I say, but some of us, the really good ones, had visions of *all* of the people. *Targets* was the word the people at the project used, and I didn't like that. Sounded like an assassination."

"Was it?"

"I didn't think so… or I didn't think so at the *time*, anyway," she said, sighing as she looked up to the sky. "Now… I don't know. I heard no-one got to see them after they were 'saved'. No-one knew the names of the Third Arrival Targets—other than poor old George Mykos—so we could never check what happened to them if we wanted to." She sighed. "But I try to picture Straub having a problem with killing a handful of people in order to stop half the country getting flattened. I can't… Oh, I don't know."

Maria shivered.

"So… what did they train you to do?"

"We did a lot of relaxation work, visualisation techniques, ESP training, stuff that a few years ago would have been laughed out of any military facility in the world. An entire field of psychology that had been written off as folklore was suddenly back on the table. *Parapsychology,* they called it. Automatic writing, mirror work, heck, they even had us work with a load of blood samples in petri dishes one day, *hundreds* of them. They'd give them to us in rows of ten and we had to pick one."

Maria remembered the Suits at the Goodmans asking her for a blood sample and DNA swab.

"So, genetics has something to do with who is a Target?"

"Has to be. As well as determining who is *Stone Sensitive…* to differing degrees, apparently," Linda added, raising her eyebrows at Maria, who tried to hide her sudden embarrassment. "The problem was that—ironically, because the whole point was that we were trying to learn how to *stop* them—there wasn't an in-process Arrival going on."

"What?" Maria cried. "The thing was *right there,* in the hangar! Why couldn't you practice with that?"

Linda looked confused then seemed to understand. "Of course," she said, shaking her head. "My fault, you wouldn't know. It was like... okay, imagine trying to learn how to use a metal detector, but you were inside a room where every single thing was made of metal?"

"Ah... but then why not take the recruits further away?"

"Because they already knew where Paul—the last Target—was. In the cabin. Hell, for a lot of us, a vision of Paul from afar had been what had got us into the project in the first place. Even *I* could describe him before I saw him, at least until I heard that noise in the garden. The military were having to train people by using someone the people could already find, see? They needed *new* Targets to train with, and without another Arrival, there weren't any. We couldn't search for Targets ahead of time either. Even the very best of us couldn't. Picture it like this." She placed the tips of her two index fingers together. "A circuit, with a Target on one end and the Stone Man that's targeted them on the other. Once they're here, their signals crossing the country, then the whole thing activates, and a few people can just *do* stuff regarding the Stone Men. Apparently, some people even get visions and intuition just *before* the Stone Men arrive... Makes me think that, even if those things *appear* quickly on our end—*ping!*—it takes them a long time *before* that to travel from wherever they left."

Maria didn't like to think about that, especially now with the Empty Men here and so many of them.

"But *Caementum* was the only one left, and it was only 'broadcasting' for Paul, at a range of mere feet, for that matter—"

"Wait," Maria interrupted, "you said that was *part* of your job. What was the other part?"

"They never explained that part of the work. I wonder if that was the more important part, sometimes. The time we spent in that monster's presence."

Maria actually backed up a step.

"You spent *time* with it?"

"Oh, yes. Not as much as the others in the end, but even I spent several hours in the company of *Caementum*."

"Doing what?"

Linda raised her hand and placed a finger on her forehead.

"They wanted us to try to read it."

"Read... you mean *communicate* with it?"

"Uh-huh."

Maria was stunned.

"Oh my *God...*"

"Rumour was a few people had briefly seen whatever the thing was seeing and, presumably, transmitting back home. I think the idea was that we could potentially go the other way: pick up signals from the other side. I don't think they even got close to that, and I certainly didn't help. They only kept me on as long as they did to be doubly sure I was no use."

*The other side.* Maria didn't like to even try to imagine it.

"You couldn't... what? Connect to it?"

"Not really. I couldn't really do anything except hear that noise when I tried. The one I heard when I was 'cut off'."

"So you just somehow lost the, the *mojo* or whatever?"

"Well, I think I didn't have very much mojo to begin with," Linda said with a sigh. "Always low level, unlike some."

*There she goes again. Does she mean me?*

"It's unsettling to talk about," Linda continued, "but I felt like they'd *seen* me." She pointed upwards. "From far away. There were... *eyes* behind that sound. Like I'd been spotted *eavesdropping*, you know? And the noise I heard was them putting a stop to that. It happened to this guy too—Ken—while I was at the project; I saw him in the canteen, and he was just as white as a sheet. Everyone was giving him a wide berth, but I asked him if he was okay. He said, *They saw me, man.* And he wouldn't say any more than that, but that was confirmation, right there. *That* was why they made us work in pairs, I think, keeping the sessions regular but short. If you stay in too long, they can see you. I wondered if maybe Ken had been doing well, and the top brass had decided to push their luck with him."

"What happened to Ken? When did they kick you out?"

"He was sent home, same as I was, after the last-ditch attempt," she said. "The *Hail Mary pass*, as our American cousins would say. They tried putting me inside the trailer with Paul."

Maria imagined being inside a trailer with the Stone Man following only a few feet away. Tried not to imagine it smashing through the metal and glass of the bus as if it were made of tinfoil and ice—

"It was one final thing they wanted to try. Straub said that if it didn't work out, then I would be sent home with their *very best wishes.*" Linda's bitter smirk made it clear what she thought of the sincerity of Straub's *best wishes.* "The Ice Queen wasn't around much really, despite being in charge, but when she *was* there, she ran a tight ship. Everyone seemed to be scared to death of her. So literally straight after that conversation, I was taken there. To the cabin. We went inside the hangar, and they put me in this special truck that they'd sent alongside it, one that drove itself too. I'd seen it in action a few times—they'd use it for food drops, and I'd seen civilians go in it as well. Once I saw someone carrying a folding massage table. I recognized that because Sarah from down the road sometimes pops round with hers and does my neck—she's a lovely girl, great masseuse." Linda blinked, shook her head, realising she'd wandered off track, and suddenly, Maria was reminded of how *ordinary* this woman was. "But on the way over to the cabin, we'd *pass* it. The Stone Man."

Her eyes became distant as she pictured it.

"They put this kind of drawbridge thing between them with railings on it so you could walk straight from one truck into the other," Linda said. "They said *watch your step*, but all I could think of was the Stone Man. Always walking, always following… anyway. Inside was… well, like a little apartment. There was a bed in there, a sink, that kind of thing. A big TV, even a multigym in the corner. It was wallpapered, but it was a bit shabby. The engineering was amazing though. You barely even knew the trailer was moving. Paul told me later that they used to have handles for him to grab onto before they'd really perfected the gyroscope base."

"What was he like?" Maria asked.

Linda opened her mouth and stopped. Then she gave a false, nervous laugh.

"Sorry," she said. "I haven't talked about this since… you know. I haven't even told my daughter. They were very, *very* clear about you not doing that… last time I went through this was with O'Reardon at the project. After the *exit interview*." She scowled, then sighed. "Okay. Paul."

***

PROJECT OROUBOROS.
O'REARDON 120: LINDA WYKEN:
EXIT WEEK SESSION 5 OF 5

*I could see Paul used to be bigger. He had that loose skin around his neck the way some people get when they were fatter once and then lost weight quickly. Pale. I was scared to death when I first saw him. Imagine having a picture of someone you've never met appearing magically in your head, and then you not only meet that person in the flesh—they're real—but they're in a prison. Yes, they said he was here voluntarily, but to me, if you only ever see someone with an armed guard—who live edits your conversations—then they're really a prisoner. But then I don't think it matters much what they call him now, does it?*

*The first meeting? It was awkward, to say the least. Making us hold hands. I know you won't tell me why now any more than you would then, Doctor. If I had to guess, I'd say it was because you wanted to see if that shock happened when we shook hands. I hope you were happy, Straub wasn't—obviously wasn't a big enough reaction for her. It hurt—a lot—but I remember the bitch looking disappointed, like Straub expected it to knock me out. What? No, I won't watch the profanity. Let's be honest. What are you going to do about it now? And the woman* is *a bitch.*

*(Sighs.)*

*Paul said it's always worst the first time, and that it would be okay after that. He was right, and he was... kind. We did the meditation exercises together but...*

*Sorry. I went away there. Thinking about him. He was just so sad. He was* broken, *O'Reardon. You people broke him. I could see it right away. And you know what's stupid? I felt bad. For him, but also for wasting you people's time. Now I'm almost glad I did. You deserve it for what you did to him. You actually put that* thing *on his neck later...*

*Hold on. I need some water.*

*So, the first time in the cabin. Paul knew I didn't have 'it'. So did Straub. She left us to it—with the guard, obviously—and neither of us said much. Then after a bit, he says,* We can sack this off if you want. *I'm shocked—he'd barely said anything until then—and then he says,* I don't think there's much point with the breathing and what have you if you're not connected. *The soldier behind us coughs to cut him off and Paul just rolls his eyes.* Oops, *he says.* Sorry, Private Pike, loose lips sink ships and all that. *Then we're just left holding hands and the room's quiet.* Sorry about this, *he says.* They keep doing it. *He eyeballs the soldier and says,* That's okay to say, isn't it? *and the soldier rolls his eyes like he's used to Paul misbehaving. He's got this... I don't know, I think you'd call it a gallows sense of humour. I think being a nuisance was the only real fun he had.*

Don't worry, *he says.* They'll bring you back here a few times, and then they'll send you home. This has happened before. Trust me, *he says,* you're better off anyway. *I said, yeah, I'd actually seen him in my head a few times, but then I heard this screeching sound. After that I didn't have visions any more. And his* face *when I said that... He'd been grinning before then, but his smile just...* vanished. *I talked more about the noise in my head, and Paul just... He just nods, all quiet, but his eyes keep going to the soldier. I'm worried now, and I ask what's wrong, and the soldier quickly says that time's up for the day and he's escorting me out of there. I'm leaving, and then Paul... He jumps up and the soldier moves fast, getting his gun up, thinking Paul is attacking, but Paul wasn't. He wouldn't be that stupid. Paul isn't even looking at the solider, he's looking at me, and he says,* It just means that they sensed you, and they didn't want you nosing in, so they cut you off, that's all. They're not coming back and you're *safe, and he's saying something else, but the soldier shouts,* Winter! *like he's telling off a kid. Paul says,* Ah bollocks, what are you gonna do? You might as well tell the poor bugger, blah blah. *He's just going off, and then the soldier pulls me out of the cabin door and that was it for that day. The next time I saw him...*

*You bastards had put a shock collar on him.*

*Actually... I have a question. Can you at least tell me this? Why did you keep taking me back there? What were you hoping would happen? It was obviously supposed to happen the first time. What was he supposed to do,* restart *me? There's a rumour he's like a battery, a booster... I know it did something to some of the others. They were moved into Strachan Group before anyone could ask them... like Sophie Warrender.* She *was moved after she went in that cabin. That was* no *surprise. Everyone* knew *she was special, old* Dispensatori. *That has to refer to her, right? We'd hear it all the time. Surely you can tell me* that. *It* has *to be; she was the only one that was really gifted, I liked her...*

*So, any chance of letting me know what the hell I was... No? Didn't think so.*

*(Pause.)*

*I heard a rumour that the Be Prepared appeal only ever found maybe six or seven that they thought were good enough, reliable enough. Is it true? Sophie* has *to be joining that list, you* can *feel it coming off* Dispensatori *in waves—*

*Sorry, fine, fine. What? Yes, I saw Paul four more times, total. We talked for longer, got to know each other. They let us do it, outside of time doing the exercises. I think the idea was that if we could make a personal connection then maybe things would... in our brains, I don't bloody know. Or maybe that I was good for him, seeing as he was, you know. Deteriorating.*

*Yes, we were friends. On my part, yes. I liked him a great deal. We'd talk about his old job. Former life. Former wife. Things like— you know that collar was the final straw...*

*(Long pause.)*

*No, I'm not alright! That horrible thing! And every time I saw him, he looked so much worse. Was it being close to the Stone Man for that long? The stress of it? Or just living in that bloody cabin? Even life prisoners get to stretch their legs in the yard from time to time! So much to do with the Stone Man was mind over matter, but that connection could go both ways. Look into the abyss, the abyss looks back into you, all that. Or did we drain him? His visitors in the cabin? I suppose it doesn't matter, like I say.*

*Once I saw him stuck in that collar, it looked like he'd just kind of given up. Done. Energy... it's a very real thing. Not like calories or whatever. I mean the energy of the mind, of intent. You see it in pack animals when they're without a pack. When I saw him this morning... for the last time...he looked like a skeleton. His cheekbones... It was clear he was dying. It was clear to anyone with eyes.*

*But he still didn't blame you lot. That's what I couldn't fathom. He was in bed, and he looked so bad that I got angry and started shouting at the guards. He stopped me, he actually stopped me. Said,* They're just doing their job, *although it sounded like it hurt when he spoke. He seemed to come round a tiny bit when we'd been speaking for a while, if briefly. We only did the hand-holding thing towards the end. And then I realized that his eyes were looking through me. Totally gone, glazed over. I said his name, and he didn't even... The soldiers were radioing for medical hel,p and I was being hustled out of the door again. I could see him just before I left; they touched his shoulder, and he was... he was slumping backwards like... He kind of breathed out but it rattled...*

*No, I don't want any more water. I want to...*

*(Pause.)*

*He'd been holding on to the end, don't you see? He was holding on to say one last thing to someone who really knew him and who wasn't military. He said it right before he died. What? Oh, you* know *what he said, it's on the CCTV...*

*Fine. He said he was sorry for everything he and Andy did.*

*I asked what he meant, who Andy was. And that was when I realized, like I said...*

*(Pause.)*

*Who was Andy? Paul had never talked about how he ended up in there, he wasn't allowed. Sure you don't know, sure.*

*(Pause.)*

*That's what he was holding on for. To apologize. It was the last thing he ever did.*

***

The sandwich was finished. Linda's unblinking gaze watched the traffic still slowly rolling by. Maria wondered if Linda had been lying a little when she'd described Paul as a friend; he'd been more than that, on Linda's part at least.

*Are you lonely, Linda?* Maria wondered. *Do you have anyone?*

She felt a sudden and strong empathy for the woman.

"Sorry," Linda said, coming back to the present. "I've been talking... I promise I'll actually ask something about who you are at some point."

"You know my name, and there's not a lot more than that, I promise—" Maria said.

"There's something I didn't tell them." Now Linda's eyes were firmly on Maria. "There's something they didn't know. I left something out. He was holding on for one *other* thing."

"For what?"

"To warn me."

"What, about the project? Where we're *going?*"

"*No*, no," Linda reassured, raising her hands gently. "I think it was about the Stone Men. He slipped me a note when we shook hands. Even as emaciated as he was, his hand was so much bigger than mine, and the note was so small that I didn't feel it until I let go. When I did, he held my gaze, and one look told me it was to be kept secret. I closed my hand around it, and he nodded at me a tiny, tiny bit. The guards wouldn't have noticed. I didn't look at it until I got back to my quarters, and even then, I pretended to have a nap so I could read it under the covers. When I did, I knew I had bigger concerns than Straub and her lot. I remembered his face when I'd said I'd heard that sound and then didn't have the gift any more. How his face dropped."

"What did the note say?" Maria asked.

Linda ran her hand through the air in front of her, outlining text that only she could see, her expression deadly serious.

"*'GET OUT OF THE COUNTRY',*" she said.

A breeze blew through them with impeccable timing. Maria couldn't believe it. She'd taken Paul's advice herself without even knowing it.

"I didn't know for certain that he was dead until the next morning," Linda was saying, continuing before Maria had a chance to ask, *Why the hell are you still here then?* "Then I *knew* he was finally gone. It was the first inarguable psychic sensation that I'd had—other than that sting of the first handshake—since that noise in my head. It was feeling the sudden hole in my mind that woke me up. He *tore* it as he left. I could even hear some of the people in the other rooms screaming a little. On one hand, I was relieved, for his sake, as he'd been in so much pain, but even so, I was crying like a baby. After a while, I just got up and went for a walk. We had the blue lanyards by then that let us walk freely in the open areas. We couldn't get in anywhere we weren't supposed to after all, and there were cameras *everywhere.* The second I stepped out of my quarters, I could see it was chaos, *total* chaos. No-one had even told us civilians to stay indoors yet. Soldiers running everywhere, shouting into radios, trucks and helicopters on the move… pandemonium. I was stopped before I even got close to the hangar. Guards sent me back to my quarters to wait. I was in there for *hours* before anyone came to see me. To be honest, it was only by chance that I saw O'Reardon again—sorry, she was one of the scientists I dealt with. When I saw her going past my window, I yelled at her through the glass. She came in and told me that *all* the civilians were being sent home. She looked strange, and I thought she was just tired, but then I realized that she barely recognized me. She was in severe shock or *something*. She was just swaying, and I had to keep repeating things to get her to understand."

"So, everyone was going home because Paul had died?" Maria asked, even more confused.

"No, no. Look, even before that day, we *already knew* that once a Target died, the Stone Man that was following them disappeared, okay? It went home. We'd figured that out; we didn't get a lot of information from the scientists, but every now and then they'd slip just a little. Nothing really important, maybe just their opinion on something, or they'd remark something to each other. We weren't stupid."

"Okay."

"And I don't think that O'Reardon would have screwed up and told me the truth if not for the chaos and if she hadn't been in such a state. I mean, she looked like she was on *drugs*. Or maybe she told me before anyone had told her not to… It was crazy, and I think a *lot* of things slipped through the net that day."

"And what *was* the truth?"

"She was talking like I wasn't even there." Linda pulled a dazed expression, mimicking the scientist. "She was babbling, saying things like, *You aren't supposed to know. They told me, they told me, it's gone, it's disappeared. It's gone* home." Linda's voice was faint now. "Obviously, I knew what she meant. No wonder the place had erupted. O'Reardon looked like seeing that huge thing just vanish had completely blown her mind. Then she kind of seemed to come back to herself a bit and said she had to see Doctor Boldfield and wandered off. I never saw her again. Later that day, I was taken home. No-one knew she told me. You're the first person I ever said this to."

"But you *didn't* get out of the country? How long ago was this?"

"About a year ago. And no, once I left the project… I didn't. I was *going* to. My mother was already sick when I went in— it was one of the reasons I nearly said no to Project Ouroboros at all, but she'd always taught me about obligation. When you can help, you should. That was her credo."

Maria reddened.

*Don't listen to that,* she told herself. *No-one* asked *you to help… but then you* did *deliberately lie and tell them that you didn't have visions. You never volunteered. You ran—*

Maria fought against that thought, telling herself that she'd *had* to run, but the counter came straight back, loud and damning in her head: the woman on the road had managed to hold on to her son for longer than Maria had held on to Ruth. Blessedly, Linda was still talking, and Maria could ignore the chill and her impending guilt.

"But after I came out, she got a lot worse and I had to look after her. Weeks became months and, well... nothing was happening, was it? *Did* he actually know something about those things coming back, or did he only think something was going to happen to me because I heard that noise in my head? Was he just delirious at the end? Look, it sounds crazy *now* that I didn't head for the hills, but this was a year ago. There hadn't been an Arrival for *four years.* Would you leave your dying mum on the advice of a strung-out dying man?"

"Well... you didn't disbelieve it *that* much though, right?" Maria said carefully, not wanting to offend. "I mean... the bike? Forgive me, but you don't seem to be the petrolhead type. I think you remembered what the roads were like in the Arrivals and prepped to have something that could get you away quickly in an emergency." She pointed at the helmet by Linda's feet.

"Actually, it's my daughter who's the petrolhead. It was hers before she went to spend a year in America," Linda replied. "Anyway. The bike was her dad's influence. I don't even have a licence. I fooled around with it for a few hours in a car park, getting familiar with it. Couldn't hurt." She spread her arms and raised her eyebrows as if to say, *And it didn't, did it?*

"Fair enough," said Maria, smiling a little herself, but she realized that Linda looked a little awkward. Was she waiting for something?

"What?"

"Um... look, you seem to have missed my point here a little bit. Don't you understand what I've just told you? What it means?"

Maria thought about it, surprised. "No, I mean, I understand the story, but what am I missing?"

"The Stone Man went *home,*" Linda repeated, seeing that Maria wasn't getting it. "Because Paul *died.*"

"Yeah…?"

*Am I being ignorant?* Maria wondered. *Does she want sympathy again or something?*

"I'm… really sorry to hear that, Linda."

*Then* Maria got it.

"Wait," she said, the air suddenly colder as a horrified feeling crept into her veins. "It went… home… because the Target, meaning *Paul*… died…"

Linda just nodded sadly as she watched Maria's cogs turn, albeit through wet cement.

"Yes." She sounded patient.

"But that means… the Prime Minister… the Chisel," Maria said, her hand slowly making its way to her mouth. "They said that… the Chisel *destroyed* the Stone Man."

"Yes," Linda said solemnly, nodding. "He did say that. Several weeks *after* the Stone Man left."

"But that means… they *lied*."

"Yes. I think it's entirely possible the Chisel is nothing more than a very necessary PR stunt," Linda said, whispering. "I think they thought the Stone Men weren't coming back again and, once rumours got out—maybe about something that they really *were* working on, something unfinished or failed—they decided to try to *own* it, to restore some of the order that's been missing ever since the First Arrival. I think they had to—look how the stock prices of every big British company skyrocketed back up the day of that Chisel press conference. *I* have. And what's more believable than the reluctant admission that a leak or exposé is true, especially when the end result is good news?"

Maria thought about the Empty Men. Thought about what might be happening in Coventry at that very moment.

"The Chisel didn't…"

The other shoe dropped, and the hand over her mouth became a gripping claw in fright.

"But that means… we're defenceless."

# Chapter Fifteen:

# Three Fists and a Sledgehammer, You Just Made the List, and an Unexpected Arrival

*** 

### Eric

Down on the street, Eric glanced across at Harry, who was marching forwards with his knuckles whitened around the sledgehammer handle. He'd grabbed it from the fifth floor on their way out of the building, and now Harry's stern gaze was locked on the Prism, the picture of determination. Drunken bravado? Outrage? Straight up bravery? Eric didn't know. He supposed watching a crowd get eaten by an otherworldly Prism is a hell of a lot better for your sobriety than a breath mint. As for himself, all he felt was anger and fear. Here he was, about to actually *walk into Ground Zero*, about to pass through the crumbled gap that the Prism had created in the wall and right into the truth. Only the day before, the thought of walking past the now-empty military checkpoint in the street would have made him giddy beyond belief. Close up, the sight of the murderous Prism looming before him made Eric fight a sudden urge to turn tail and run in the opposite direction. Then he remembered Jenny, and Mickey, and *Theresa,* and clenched his teeth in fury, and the cycle began again.

Something else was growing though—had been ever since the last of the Shufflers had been eaten by the Prism—and it wasn't just Eric's fear and rage (*or excitement to finally know,* part of him whispered*).* The air felt thicker. Whatever the purpose of eating the Shufflers had been, it was part of another stage, and it was clear that under the Barrier, the Prism was warming up. Eric couldn't think about that. He just had to get inside, get something and get out. Help Jenny.

A nasty additional thought came.

*And help yourself too, right?*

He tried to reject it, telling himself that this was about Jenny... but he couldn't deny that his head was rushing with blood. *Ground Zero. You're going inside Ground Zero.* In his wildest dreams he'd never imagined getting so far. Surely, inside would be that which he'd sought for five years: proof of what they'd done to Theresa. To Aaron.

*And proof that you might be a Target as well,* he thought, *don't forget that—*

Soon they were about twenty feet away from the base of the Prism, standing and looking up in awe at the height of the thing. Eric had been to New York City in his lifetime, seen the skyscrapers. They were taller than the Prism by a long way, but then they hadn't appeared out of thin air. Harry broke the silence by whistling through his teeth.

"Jesus," he said.

"Yeah. Whatever you do, don't touch it."

"Wasn't planning to."

"Let's get inside," Eric said, then gasped in annoyance. "*Shit, the circuits have to be ruined in there. Did you grab the torch?*" He'd forgotten it in the rush.

"Yep," Harry said to Eric's great relief. Eric held out his trembling hand for the sledgehammer. Harry gave him the torch instead. "You light the way. I've got twenty years on you, but I've also got 'n extra hand," he said. "Reckon I can do more damage with this now than you, if need be."

"Fuck, Harry. Kick a guy when's he's down, why don't you?" Eric grunted, turning back to face the Ground Zero building.

"Makes you feel any better, I think you'd still be the ladies' choice," Harry muttered back, resting the sledgehammer on his shoulder. Eric looked at the Prism's surface; the patterns gouged into it were deeper than they'd seemed from Jenny's flat. Eric thought that if he didn't mind potentially losing an arm, he could rest it inside one of the deep, sweeping lines in the Prism and still have room to spare. He eyeballed the gap in the wall between the right-hand side of the Prism and the Ground Zero building wall. It was a few feet wide, big enough to squeeze through with their backs against the remaining human-built wall without touching the Prism's deadly surface. Even that was too close for Eric's liking though. Maybe the walls had crumbled elsewhere? A quick lap of the building, larger up close than he initially suspected, confirmed that the gap was indeed the only way in. Magnetic or electronic locks on the entryways still somehow held in the event of a power outage—an internal generator? Eric didn't know enough about it.

"Come on."

They walked to the gap and shuffled through sideways, slipping past the Prism and making their way into the building. As they did so, Eric couldn't keep the image out of his head of that carved surface chewing people up. He imagined the claustrophobia and terror as lines of people pressed up from behind him, pushing his face against the Prism's deadly sides. He made his way inside as quickly as he could.

No torch was needed once they crossed the threshold into Ground Zero itself. Not only was there was enough light coming in through the gap, but some of the remaining, undestroyed light fittings still worked. It was dim, but once their eyes adjusted, they surveyed a large, high-ceilinged atrium, the left half of it completely blocked by the back end of the Prism. The right half had several doors leading into the building. There were cracks in the side walls leading up to the shattered front wall, but other than that, the rest of the structure was holding. Eric recognized the room, as bland, empty and corporate-plain as it had been when he first saw it.

"This is where they did that press conference," he said, pointlessly sweeping the torch.

"Which door you wanna take?" Harry asked. "Could be screwed here anyway... look at the security locks." There was a small, credit-card-sized metal box next to each door handle. In the centre of all of them was a black patch of plastic. A card lock. There was a small LED light above each one. They were red.

"Lights still on. Locks work?" Harry asked.

"Maybe," Eric said. "Security first and foremost. The power and the circuitry will have a backup of a backup of a backup, especially when they're at bloody Ground Zero. They'd have to allow for big parts of the building getting smashed at any time." He would have been worried about access if not for several large patches of a dried, crusty red substance on the floor. Nearby were crumpled clothes, random shoes.

"Hey, Harry..." he said, an idea occurring to him. "Do me a favour. Can you go and check through those clothes to see if we can get a key card or something? I'd do it but, you know... my hand..."

It was a cheap get-out, but in that moment, Eric was happy to use it.

Harry looked from Eric to the mess on the floor then began to search through various sticky pockets with a resigned sigh. It took a few minutes, but Harry eventually straightened up with a gasp—he'd been holding his breath—and held up a laminated card on a lanyard.

"Nice one, Harry," Eric said. "If the lanyard is clean, maybe put it on. We don't wanna lose that."

"It is, actually," Harry said, inspecting it closely. "It must have been on the outside of their clothes when the Barrier hit..." He trailed off, looking around the atrium and silently counting the clothing piles. "Fuck, *fuck*..."

"Stay with me, Harry. Let's take that door at the back," Eric said, stepping over a large chunk of rubble by his feet. His hand started to shake with anticipation.

*Maybe you* are *here to help Jenny*, he thought, *but that's not really what you give a shit about, is it—*

The sight finally penetrated. There were *so many piles*. Nearby, a pair of florescent green Crocs lay near a lab coat. A half-open wallet nearby another pile—

*Stay with* yourself, *man*, Eric thought quickly. *Don't lose it now, there isn't time. You can feel something happening around you, can't you? In the* air?

He could. That build-up of pressure was worse than ever. Something was about to happen. They needed to get Jenny out *now*, but even so, there would be answers—

Harry swiped the card against the pad. The red light turned green, and they heard a click. Oh God, they were in. They were really *in*.

"Eric?" Harry asked, and Eric realized that he'd been staring at the door, not moving. "Let's go."

"Huh? Yes, yes." They went through the door.

Beyond was a long, brightly lit corridor with a series of floor-to-ceiling glass walls. At first glance, Eric assumed they were meeting rooms, the kind employees 'rented' in advance. A closer look revealed that these were clinical in nature: laboratories. Inside were metal cupboards and tables, mounted magnification lights and test-tube racks, some of which were filled with what appeared to be blood samples. The doorway to each had a small airlock-style second doorway, with hazmat suits hanging on the inside. Surrounding the glass walls were tiny jets—a decontamination chamber, Eric supposed. Unsafe for them to go in, not knowing how to work it, or just the military being doubly safe? There were four piles of dried blood and clothes in the hallway itself, with one of the sets of clothes appearing to be military fatigues. One of the glass labs had a white coat pressed against the clear front wall, caught crumpled halfway in its fall to the floor, dried blood sticking it to the see-through surface. They walked along the corridor in silence, heading towards the exit door at the other end. All of the laboratories appeared to be identical.

"Research and development?" Harry muttered. "If the research is here, is the development in here too?"

"Could be," Eric replied. "We'll come back here and go through all the cupboards, but let's complete a sweep of the place first." They opened the door at the far end of the corridor and found themselves inside another atrium, this one with an exposed balcony level running along the perimeter. On the opposite side of the room there was a staircase leading to the balcony and a lift behind it. There were doors leading off this atrium, six on the upper level and four on the level upon which they were standing. Eric surveyed the main floor; there was a door that seemed to be leading back towards the entrance, perhaps a matching corridor running to the side of the atrium blocked off by the Prism. Based on the distance they'd travelled and their earlier sweep of the building, Eric thought that would be right.

*So, either we find something inside these rooms,* Eric thought, *or that's everything.*

They had to turn as much of this place over as possible, as quickly as possible. If they just happened to come across something like a big, prototype gun marked 'Stone Shooter' then so much the better, but even information might be something to help Jenny. He didn't think they could access the computers, but there might be documents somewhere.

"Let's get started," Eric said. "Check that door first." They did, and his guess had been correct; a matching corridor to the one they'd just crossed, with more laboratories. This was worse to look at though; more people had been in this space before the Barrier went up. What had they been thinking? Had they been trying to get samples out of here? What could have been so important that it was worth sticking around for after the Prism arrived? There were eight or nine piles of clothes in there and at least half were military. Escorts, maybe? The dried and crusty substance was all that remained of people's bodies, and it covered the entire floor of the hallway. The piles seemed bigger here too, for some reason. It was impossible not to step on the redness, but it wasn't as sticky as it looked. It really had been desiccated. Harry took a step and some of it crunched under his foot. He coughed a little and then propped the sledgehammer against the wall, bending at the waist as he dry-heaved.

Eric spotted a cardboard document box.

Red-coated dark clothes obscured it, as if someone had been carrying it—running with it?—before the Barrier hit. The lid was askew, and Eric saw paper.

*Documents. Someone was trying to get something out. Something that wasn't safe to send electronically? Or just a backup?*

"Harry, can you check the door at the other end?" he asked, crossing over to the box. "Check it leads back to the first atrium." Harry covered his mouth as he crunched his way away down the corridor. Eric bent and gingerly pushed the lid off the carboard box with his elbow. Inside was a dense stack of pages, and as he pulled out the top sheet and straightened up, he looked down the corridor. He saw now that, similarly obscured by piles of empty, stained clothes and sticky redness, there were other boxes. That was why the piles were larger.

They were trying to get them out.

The paper in his hand displayed a list of categories with names after them. The words in the header leaped out at him like an assailant.

KINDNESS PROTOCOL CV1A7IIHL4TI

How the fuck did that help Jenny right now? It didn't, but still he read.

The page was laid out in a series of vertical columns, labelled, 'CROW', 'TIN', 'LION', 'GALE', and DIGGS. Only the CROW column, on the page Eric was looking at, at least, had anything in it. Surnames and initials—SANDERS GJ, SANDERS, GK—followed a series of letters and numbers that looked like catalogue tagging. Maybe national insurance numbers, Eric wondered. The CROW column went on for the rest of the page. Eric snatched up several of the next sheets from the box; the first four were the same, a full

CROW column but nothing in the others. Then he reached the sixth page and saw the first name in the TIN column: SANDERS, GJ.

He reached into the cardboard box and flipped through the top few pages, so frantic and focused that he barely noticed how he was already adapting to doing everything one-handed. The pattern seemed to be the same, all the other columns empty. He flicked through some more and saw the occasional addition in the TIN column but still nothing in LION, GALE, or DIGGS.

"It's the atrium again," Harry called, closing the door. "Nearly walked face-first into the fucking Prism, it's right up against the door. Do you want to go through these labs, or—" He broke off mid-sentence as Eric frantically tore open the other boxes, lifting up stacks of paper and thumbing through them before moving onto the next. This went on for several minutes. Harry let him work, not wanting to interrupt such frenzied activity.

"*Shit!*" Eric spat.

"What?"

Eric slapped the last of the papers back in the box.

"These names only go from *S* to *W*," Eric said, wiping his face and standing up. Harry started to say *what names,* but then realized what Eric was looking for. *Pettifer.*

"Civilian names?" Harry asked.

"Has to be, there's enough of them here," Eric said. "Let's... let's check the other doors in the balcony room before we go through the labs." He paused, pointing at the boxes in the hallway. He hoped Harry didn't notice how hard he was breathing. "We don't leave without one of these, okay? It's important."

"You alright?" Harry asked.

Eric looked at the space where his hand used to be. "No," he said, and was satisfied when he felt nothing as he said it, his functional armour complete. "But it doesn't matter. You'll have to carry the box when we leave—it'll need two hands. Is that okay?"

"Sure, make the black man do all the heavy lifting."

"Hey, that's not what I—"

"I'm just busting your balls." Harry sighed. "Listen, I could do with a—" He made a drinking motion with his hand.

"We agreed. Let's get done in here, and you can have a swig. Fair?"

"Fucking hell. *Yes.*"

"Okay."

Harry grabbed the sledgehammer, and they crunched their way back to the second atrium. Eric could hear Harry breathing solely out of his mouth as they swept the rooms. The upper level was disappointing; it appeared to be two computer hubs—the machines were still working, but access was impossible—a cold storage for samples and two meeting rooms, but the last, large one was the most interesting. Inside were shelves stacked full of identical boxes to the ones they'd found in the hallway.

*Jenny's car!* Eric suddenly thought. *Come back with Jenny's car and fill it up with these!*

It could be done, but Eric knew it would have to be quick. His ears were starting to feel like he was on an ascending aeroplane.

"You... feel something?" Harry asked, confirming Eric's fears about time. If Harry was feeling it, they really had to move—

"I do. Let's get a move on."

"We're not going to find anything, are we?" Harry said flatly. "Anything to help her."

"... Let's just keep looking. Quickly."

They hurried downstairs to discover the remaining rooms, once opened, were much larger. The first was a garage for vehicles; there was one open-topped, Jeep-style vehicle—the same as the other three left abandoned on the ring road—and a people carrier with blacked out windows. A quick search told them there was nothing worth having inside, and also, no keys. Eric cursed under his breath; these would have been ideal for transporting the boxes. They left the garage and moved to the next room, which turned out to be a small antechamber with metal walls, a desk and a single door in the wall. Harry swiped the key card against the lock, but the light didn't change.

"Not working?" he said.

"Must not have access," Eric muttered, suddenly wanting very badly to be on the other side of the metal door.

Harry raised himself up on his tiptoes so he could see behind the desk. "I think *that* guy probably had it though," he said. Eric looked; there was a red mess of clothes back there. "I'm not doing it again. I can't."

"Fair enough," Eric said, crossing behind the desk and pawing at it with his foot. His shoe clunked up against something solid; he bent and fished it out. It was a pistol, slotted snugly into a shoulder harness. He lifted it up and showed it to Harry.

"You taking it?" Harry asked. Eric considered it. It was too heavy to just slot into his own pocket; he would have to take the harness as well, coated as it was in dried blood. It wasn't a pleasant thought.

"I... we don't know what could happen, right?"

"No. Do you know how to shoot that?"

"Think so." He took his jacket off and pulled on the harness. He'd never fired a real gun before, but he'd had a replica Sig Sauer BB in his late teens. He pulled out the pistol and the similar release switch popped the dense magazine out onto the desk. It looked full, but then he supposed there was always a bullet at the top of the mag; he wouldn't know unless he counted them all out.

*Not now. Time—*

He picked the magazine up and handed it to Harry, who snapped it back into the pistol while Eric held it. Eric thumbed the safety switch on, reinserted the gun back into the holster, and then shrugged his jacket back on over it. The weight of the weapon against his ribs made him feel a little better. Something about going in and out of those now-dead rooms had been creeping him out. He poked at the clothes again, pushing them out of the way until he saw a familiar lanyard.

"Got one here," he said. "Let's see."

It worked. The green light came on above the card pad, and there was a loud hiss from the door as it unlocked. Inside was another decontamination portal with a clear glass door at one end. The hazmat suits hung at either side but neither man noticed, only staring at what they could see in the bright white room beyond.

It was very different to what they'd seen so far.

Eric leaped back in surprise, fumbling for the gun in fear, but Harry grabbed his arm.

"*No, wait, Eric!*" he hissed. "They're not moving! They're... they're... Oh *shit,* what are they?"

There were two of them.

They filled the room, lit harshly by the glare of the strip lights in the ceiling bouncing off the white walls. On the floor were two piles of intact hazmat suits, their visors completely crusted over inside with red. Eric couldn't speak.

"Do you think... I think they're dead, Eric. Look, *look,* they're not standing up. *Look.*"

Eric was looking. He couldn't do anything else.

"What are... what are..."

They were around the same height as the Stone Man, perhaps slightly taller. They were dark grey, and at first, Eric thought they were made of the same material, but as he stared, he realized that they were constructed of something similar to flesh... then he had it. They looked as if they were made out of rhino hide. They were multi-limbed, and the way they were propped—for propped up is what they were, held upright on small, presumably custom-made metal stands to keep them in what looked like their natural position for study—with their legs, or arms, or whatever the hell they were, crossing over one another made it hard to tell initially how many they had. Then Eric had it; six legs, ending in large, knuckled nubs, making Eric think of an elephant's feet without the toenails. Their torsos were wide, perhaps five feet or so around, the same again in length. They had no faces. He had never expected to find anything like this.

"Did you hear anything about this?" Harry asked, letting go of Eric and moving close to the decontamination chamber's glass. "With your online buddies, did anybody ever talk about anything like *this?*"

"No," Eric gasped. "This is..." An idea struck him. The hazmat suits were still there, after all. There was a red button to the right of the door that led into the room with those things. "Harry. I think we can go in." He expected Harry to say no, but instead, the older man's gaze travelled to the suits and back to the glass. He was thinking about it.

Eric would always wonder what Harry's answer would have been.

The building air pressure suddenly ratcheted up sharply, and Eric slapped his hand and wrist to his temples, moaning. There was no accompanying noise, but it *hurt.*

"Eric! What's wrong? Are they doing something—"

"You don't feel that?"

"I feel nothing! Shit, what can I do? Tell me what to do—"

They both stared at the things on the other side of the glass, waiting for them to come to life and smash their way through the partition towards them. The creatures didn't move. What the hell was happening?

"Is it something to do with Jenny?" Harry gasped. "She's... I can still feel where she is, like before. I don't know if it's something to do with..."

"I don't know either, but it..."

Then he understood.

*Outside,* Eric thought. *Something is happening outside.*

# Chapter Sixteen:

# Maria Gets Angry

***

### <u>Maria</u>

"I don't want to give you false hope, Maria," Linda said, just before she pulled on her helmet. She was sitting on the bike, still concealed behind the billboard. "I don't know what they have there now, where the research has gone. I mean, I don't even know anything about you, obviously—*God,* I talk too much—"

"No, I was asking you—"

"—but you seem nice, and I don't want you to think this is any kind of sure thing."

"Well… a military base designed to deal with, to any degree, the Stone Men? Sounds a lot safer than anywhere else I can think of. Even if we *are* dealing with Empty Men rather than Stone." *As long as they don't ask me too many questions,* Maria thought. She paused. "Linda… what do you think they are? I mean… what are they here for?"

"I have absolutely no idea, love. To kill, as far as I can see."

"But they don't kill *everybody.* Only a few. Did you notice that?"

"I did…" She threw up her hands. "I don't know. I just don't know. But between you and the brains at the project…"

Maria froze. Linda was staring at her, face blank.

"Well..." Maria stammered, shifting her feet. "I don't think I want to get... you know..."

Linda looked surprised.

"But you said it yourself... you have what looks like a unique gift? I don't trust those people, but right now, but they have to be our best bet." She waved her bike helmet around. "Don't you think you might maybe have a personal *interest* in helping now? In telling the people at Ladybower what you can do, if only so you can help *yourself?*"

Maria was suddenly back on the bus in her mind, her chest cramping.

"Uh, I'm not... I mean..."

"I don't want to be impertinent but... aren't you *angry?* Don't you *want* to—"

Blood rushed to Maria's face, and she swayed slightly, hearing the children screaming, the metal tearing. Ruth choking.

"*Uh...* my friend..."

Linda saw it and immediately understood, leaning over quickly and taking Maria's hand, holding her steady. "Oh my God, oh my God, I'm sorry, I'm so *sorry,*" she said hurriedly. "I understand, don't worry. We don't have to tell them anything if you don't want to, nothing. Okay?" She stroked Maria's hand. Maria nodded, embarrassed, and cleared her throat as the road, the billboard, the cars came back into focus. "We'll go there, and I'm already on their system, so they know I'm not a loony. I'm going to claim I've had new visions, so they let us in. I'll say you're a blood relative. I guarantee that with everything going on they'll let us in—they can't afford not to. Once we're in, they'll be too busy to kick us out at least, and we can figure the rest from there. It isn't a great plan but... best bet, right?"

Maria just nodded again, trying to escape the question in her mind.

*Aren't you angry?*

"You ready?" Linda asked.

"Yes. Yes."

Maria mounted the back of the bike.

"Where are you *from,* at least?" Linda asked, starting the engine. "I've talked so much…"

"Coventry, originally."

"Oh *dear,*" Linda said, sincere. "I'm sorry to hear that."

***

Over the next hour, the dual carriageway became single lane A-roads as they headed out of motorway country and into rural areas once more, the most 'proper countryside' Maria had seen in years. Normally there would be almost no cars at all here; today, they passed fairly regularly, filled with people and possessions. The roads became so narrow that they didn't even have a white line down the centre. They rose and fell in sharp inclines between high lines of hedges, huge old trees often gnarling their way through the midst of the shrubbery. The clouds above were so dark with threatened rain that the light looked like that of early evening.

Then the bike rounded a bend, and Maria saw the first windmills. There were six or seven of them, rising above the tops of small buildings. Slightly beyond them was a very large, grey hangar.

Her anxiety began to creep in. She knew she couldn't trust these people. They'd lied, after all.

But she didn't have any better ideas.

A few minutes later, the entrance was approaching to their left, and Maria realized the base was at the bottom of a natural valley that was almost bowl-like. Nearly all the way around them, the hills rose up in a circle, one of them covered in a dense forest. Linda parked the bike on the opposite side of the road from the entrance itself—a high gate that was only slightly set back from the road. It stood at the end of a short V-shaped path between a stretch of chain-link fencing—high mesh that had been put in place of torn-out hedges. It was obvious that a lot of land had been levelled and cleared to make way for the installation. If Maria had to guess, the whole site was probably about the size of six football pitches; there was a second gate a little further in with double guard booths at either side.

*But it feels closed down,* she thought. The Stone Man was gone; it made sense.

The man in the entry gate booth didn't have a weapon in plain sight. He looked like an ordinary security guard—Linda had been right about no-one wearing military fatigues—but Maria didn't doubt he was armed. Cars still passed every few seconds. She felt nervous.

"Let me do the talking," Linda said quietly, and walked towards the booth. The man inside was a skinny-but-wiry-looking guy a few years younger than Maria. As he watched Linda approach, Maria noticed how wild-eyed and spooked he looked, as if he would have abandoned his post long ago if it were up to him.

*Something's gone on here,* Maria thought. *Something bad.*

She unconsciously started to back away. What was she doing here?

A voice inside her suddenly spoke up. *Aren't you angry?*

The man in the booth—the *soldier*—had eyeballed them all the way up the final stretch of road, his stare intense. He had an old-fashioned landline telephone handset pressed to his ear, the curled cord stretching away into a unit on the wall. His breathing was rapid, and he was listening intensely. Maria realized that, even though he was only the doorman, he was managing to have this much of a rough day. She had to get the hell out of here... but where was she going to go?

The guard said something into the phone and then put it back on the hook.

"Stop and stand there, please," he said to Linda, his voice projecting loudly and forcefully. He pointed at a faint white pavement line painted across the V of the entrance. "This is private property. State your business."

Linda literally toed the line. Did she recognize the guard? If she did, she showed no sign of it, and the guard certainly wasn't giving her the prodigal daughter routine.

"Hello, I'm Linda Wyken," she called, projecting her own voice. "Consultant R36, and..." She hesitated, started to glance over her shoulder at Maria and then changed her mind. Something was *wrong*—

Maria knew that Linda was going to reveal her secret even before she opened her mouth.

"... And I'm here to report a tactile connection class four with the civilian behind me. Civilian reports prior experience of visions across all incidences of—"

*NO*, Maria thought, *NO, NO*—

"Stop," the guard barked, and Maria thought he meant her as her legs began to tense, ready to run back up the road. He was talking to Linda. "One moment, please," the guard said, the politeness of the words *one moment, please* completely at odds with their delivery. Maria's eyes bored into the back of Linda's skull, completely stunned. She'd promised.

The guard snatched up the phone again and muttered something into it as Maria stared at Linda, *willing* her to turn around so she could say, *What the hell are you doing?* Linda just continued to look straight ahead as Maria realized what she'd done.

No-one knew where she was.

She'd walked blindly into territory where the rules and human rights didn't apply, and now, they knew she had something they might want. This was how people disappeared. She backed up a step, looking down the lane, thinking crazily that she could try to jump over the hedge on the opposite side of the road.

"Wait there, miss," the guard said. It wasn't a request. He shifted his stance; it was the subtlest of movements, but his eyes stayed locked with hers as his hips turned to reveal the sidearm he was carrying. The message was clear. Maria felt the world around her close in. Surely there was no way he would shoot her here. A car might pass—

She looked and listened. With terrible timing, no cars were in the vicinity. And of course, he could shoot. This was a national emergency, and to them, the ends justified the means.

All she could do was wait while the guard muttered into his phone. Maria looked at Linda's back and felt rage building inside her like a long-lost sister.

*Yes, Linda,* she thought. *I'm angry.*

\*\*\*

They were escorted down the short corridor of a small prefab building after being advised that they were *in the middle of a national emergency and conversation must be kept to a minimum.*

The few soldiers there looked as wary and harried as the entry guard, moving quickly and constantly talking into radios. What the hell had happened here? Was it the Empty Men?

Maria's heart had begun racing with fear as she and Linda had been frogmarched across the field. They passed large rectangular patches of dead grass where structures had once stood. Long stretches of flat plastic, several inches thick, crossed hither and thither along the ground—protective covering for power cables. The big hangar—clearly the building that, by Linda's description, had housed *Caementum* himself—had loomed ominously at the other end of the field, but much to Maria's relief, they'd headed to the far smaller prefab building instead. Even if the Stone Man was gone, she didn't want to visit what felt like its old cave. Its lair. The hangar's doors had been wide open—hadn't Linda said something about them being welded shut?—and despite knowing the Stone Man was physically gone, Maria craned her neck to see inside. She had to be *sure*. The sight was less than exciting: just a few vehicles and iron walls even rustier than Linda had suggested. *This* was where they'd kept the biggest national security secret in the world? She caught a glimpse of an immense, hulking shadow tucked into the corner.

It looked like a huge metal cabin on wheels, now as stationary and surplus to requirements as the constructions that had once stood outside.

*This place is dead.*

To her surprise, furthering her confusion about the place, she heard faint sobs; a dark-haired man was standing near the entrance to the smaller, one-storey building they were approaching, dressed the same as the others. His face was in his hands, but then he looked up briefly at the sound of people. His eyes were red, and he turned away immediately at the sight of Maria and Linda, wiping his face. What the hell—

But then they were already inside the building, heading down a corridor. The floor was plastic-tiled, the walls white and the ceiling was strip-lit. It felt like a hospital, albeit a tiny one. The corridor was simply a series of closed doors with a double-wide set at one end blocking further passage. Maria's thoughts turned back to the object of her anger: Linda. The older woman still wouldn't catch Maria's stink-eye, instead staring straight ahead... and then her eyes suddenly flicked towards Maria's and away. Linda's head then stooped slightly, eyes down. Good. Linda knew what she'd done, then.

Their escorts stopped walking.

"You'll be seen to shortly," one of them said, producing a key card and unlocking a door on the right. "In here, please." Maria stepped forwards, but the escort held up a hand. "Just her, miss." Linda walked through the doorway without a word, and Maria caught a glimpse of a room with olive-green walls, a metal bed and some kind of wall chart. Again, it felt like a hospital room. Then the escort was closing the door behind Linda, who finally caught Maria's eye and mouthed, *I'm sorry.*

Maria only had time to scowl before the door to Linda's room clicked home. The electronic lock mechanism whirred.

*A prison after all, then*, she thought.

The escorts then led Maria past the next door, and the lead trooper opened the one after that without a word, pointing towards it.

"You're going to lock me in?"

"It's standard operating procedure here. It's for civilian safety."

"*Really.*"

The escort simply gestured to the door. Maria hesitated… but there was a government-issue bed inside, and where else was she going to go? Oh, she wanted to *rest…* She wouldn't sleep, that was for certain, but *all* of her ached.

*Screw it. Screw all of it.*

She marched into the room. It had the same olive-green walls and furniture that she'd seen inside Linda's. She looked at the escorts—the *soldiers* in matching disguises of polo shirt and jeans—as one of them leaned into the room to pull the door shut.

"Someone will come and see you shortly," he said.

"How long?" she asked, hating how small her voice sounded and wondering how she'd lost control of the situation so fast.

"We don't know," the solider said. "There's a lot going on out there."

"What *is* going on?" she demanded… or tried to.

"We can't tell you, miss," he replied, and Maria had the strange feeling that she was talking to a robot. *I can't do that, Dave.* Then his dark eyes blinked, and she saw that his face *wasn't* robotic, that it was the expression of a well-trained man under great stress. He was young too, maybe not even in his mid-twenties yet. "I'll come back to check in half an hour, okay?" He paused. "I'm Private Binley." Then he closed the door.

Twenty minutes passed, and no-one came to visit. No sounds came from outside, no footsteps, no shouting, no gunfire aimed at an approaching threat.

*How far away are the Empty Men?* she wondered. *Are they even coming?* Is this place our best line of defence?

She lay down on the bed and tried to relax, to rest and be ready if need be, but she couldn't do it. Her anxious mind was bouncing off its internal walls. She desperately, *desperately* wanted booze. That was unfamiliar.

Then she heard the doors at one end of the corridor open, followed by footsteps. Several people, maybe four or five of them. She sat upright on the bed. A door opened maybe two rooms away. They were going into Linda's room first, then. There was a brief silence.

Then she heard Linda scream.

Maria jumped off the bed, every nerve firing. Linda's scream had been high, short and cut off very quickly.

There were no windows in Maria's room. She looked everywhere for something to use as a weapon. Of course, there was nothing. Oh God, she was trapped in there—

Her head felt light as she hyperventilated. Her usual flight response had nowhere to go. Another minute passed, and then she heard Linda's door open and close as the footsteps started up again. She darted over to the wall by the door like a startled cat and flattened herself against it on instinct, hoping foolishly that maybe when it opened—the longest shot ever—she could dart through the gap and be away down the hall, but then the door was opening, and she knew it was impossible. Two soldiers entered, and her blood felt like ice as she saw that Private Binley wasn't one of them. They were *huge,* far larger than her previous escorts.

Maria froze.

She *was* angry.

Something snapped. She charged.

Later, she would wonder where it came from; backed into a final, inescapable corner, she suddenly found her fight. Perhaps the soldiers were overconfident, unconcerned with a woman of Maria's small size, but whatever the reason, they were caught napping as Maria's foot connected solidly with the testicles of the soldier in the centre. He buckled, grasping at his groin, but as Maria lunged for the door, the soldier on the left caught her wrist in his hand. He wrapped his other arm around her waist, holding her tight as Maria kicked at *his* groin. He was ready though, turning his hip in towards her so her flailing foot caught nothing but thigh. The brief advantage of surprise that she had was now gone. The soldier holding her barked for assistance. She screamed as the pair of them lifted her over to the bed, set her down and pinned both her arms and legs, Maria thrashing and straining against them. One soldier took his hand off her leg to hold her shoulder down, but she dived her head towards it and bit down hard. He yelled, trying to pull away and yanking Maria's jaw and neck painfully, but she knew this was all she had left. *Click!* Her teeth banged together painfully. The guard had pulled himself free, grunting, and Maria tasted copper. She felt a small something in her mouth and quickly spat it out; he'd left some skin behind. One hand free, she thrust upward with her thumb and plunged it straight into the eye socket of the soldier still pinning her other arm and leg down. He let go suddenly, screaming.

*You're doing it!* she thought desperately. *You have another chance, you have another—*

The room was full of noise as the two now-injured soldiers—how the hell was she getting away with this?—tried to recover, but then she was up and off the bed and bolting for the door just as the soldier she'd previously low-blowed staggered to his feet and shot out an arm. He grabbed her around the waist and scooped her up off the ground into some kind of elevated hold. Her jaw was locked and now he was doing something with her arms, and she was stuck. She cried out and tried to wriggle free, but it was useless. The whole thing over inside about six seconds. They had her, of course they did, hadn't she always known that this was where fighting got you—

An older man entered the room. His polo shirt and trousers had different markings on them to the others, a series of yellow pips as opposed to Private Binley's single blue one. This *was* some kind of Ladybower-only internal ranking system then, but even without it, Maria would have instinctively known that he outranked the others. He had thinning ginger hair, a neatly clipped ginger moustache and was built like an old, wiry oak tree. Much like the guard on the gate and Private Binley, his eyes had dark circles around them, but his face was flushed. Maria glared at him and felt hate; this was the kind of thing that Linda *hadn't* seen during her time here. Whatever they'd done to Linda, whatever had made her scream, they'd happily done it to so many others while she was making friends in a cabin and doing mind-reading tests. Now they were about to do it to Maria.

"*Fuck you!*" she screamed in fury, the words coming out *futch ffoo* from her locked-up position.

"What the hell is going on?" the man barked, but not to Maria; he was addressing the guard holding her.

"She's hysterical, sir!" the guard with the bitten hand hissed. "We just walked in and—"

"Look here, there's really no need for this," the Boss Soldier said as he pinched the bridge of his nose and screwed up his eyes for a moment, the action of a man who really *didn't have time for this shit.* "There's no problem here, Miss Constance; you're quite safe." He waved a hand at the soldier holding Maria who immediately released her and placed her on the floor, stepping back. It was so sudden and confusing that Maria froze for a moment; the man's demeanour was so calm, *uninterested* in her. She watched as Boss Soldier turned to someone else now standing behind him in the hallway. "Could you..." The words were inaudible and whoever was out there mumbled something back and the higher-ranking guy nodded.

"Where's Linda? What did you do with her?" Maria yelled. Boss Soldier screwed up his face again and then relaxed with sudden understanding.

"Oh, you heard, just now—right, I see. Look, it's *fine*..." He looked at the guard with the wounded hand. "Go and get Wyken, will you...?" The guard cast a reproachful glance at Maria and left the room. "She'll be here in a second," Boss Soldier told Maria.

Maria glared at him.

"You'll see," he said softly. "It's alright, it's alright. We're very sorry to have frightened you. It may sound like a strange way of reassuring you, but if we wanted to do bad things with you, we'd already be *doing* them. We don't want to, so we're not going to. Okay? We're on your side, and you're safe from us."

Maria said nothing, looking from Boss Solider to the door, but she adjusted her clothes, shoulders rising and falling quickly as she tried to calm down. She was... safe?

"Then Doctor Holbrooks can do a quick, painless test so we can see what's what," Boss Soldier said. "Totally *voluntary,* of course," he added quickly, stepping back to allow two more men to enter the room—one a curly-haired, wiry man in a lab coat who had to be in his sixties. This had to be Doctor Holbrooks. He was pushing a small trolley on wheels with an unrecognisable device on top. The other man passed between the two hulks; he was tall too, but not as big as his escorts. This was someone Maria hadn't seen before. His face was drawn and tired-looking, but the lines at the corners of his eyes suggested that he was once, at least, a man who'd liked to laugh. He was dressed in civilian clothes unlike the others—a sweater with jeans. He extended his hand to shake hers then stopped halfway as if catching an automatic movement. He deliberately folded his arms, tucking his hands under his elbows and looking uncertain for a moment, not knowing how to finish the greeting. Then he gave up, smiled and did a kind of awkward half-bow, shrugging afterwards as if to say, *I don't bloody know.* For some reason, this immediately put Maria at ease.

Then he introduced himself, and Maria instantly realized what Linda's loud, short shriek had been: not a cry of pain, but a cry of delight, cut off perhaps by her face landing on the man's broad chest as she rushed in to embrace him.

"Hiya," the man said. "My name's Paul. Paul Winter. They want to get us prepped, and then we have to shake hands. That alright?"

# Chapter Seventeen:
# Eric and Harry Run Out of Space

*** 

### Eric

"Harry…. I think something's happening outside…."

The thought of hurriedly *leaving* Ground Zero flashed across his mind. It was hard to conceive. The discovery on the other side of the glass called to him, thoughts of the room full of boxes, it was all happening too fast—

"Come on!" Eric hissed through gritted teeth. "*Fuck,* we come back, okay?!" he yelled, realising he was shouting even thought there was nothing to shout over. He was already moving quickly to the door, furious at the interruption. "For the boxes! We can come back for the rest but on the way out grab the one I looked at. I need your hands! Don't miss it!"

"Yes," Harry gasped as Eric fumbled with the dead guard's key card to get them out. Eric stole another pained look at the creatures in the glass room, and a realisation hit him like a cold slap. This was the most incredible discovery that he could have imagined… and he was *leaving?!*

*I'm fucking coming back,* he thought. *On my life, I'm coming back.*

They frantically made their way through a seemingly endless series of key card locks before reaching the main atrium. Eric hadn't tightened the shoulder harness, so the gun was banging painfully off his ribs all the way, taking his wind even more than his lack of fitness did. Even Harry wheezed alongside with him, running with the sledgehammer in both hands until they reached the boxes in the hallway. He handed it to Eric without looking and snatched up the box Eric had been rooting through earlier.

*We at least get that one,* Eric thought, even as they reached the gap between the Prism and the crumbling concrete wall, flattening himself against the latter to slip outside. *That alone was something, but no matter what, he was going back for the rest—*

*FUCK THE BOXES,* his mind screamed, *WHAT WERE THOSE THINGS—*

They staggered outside, looking wildly for a threat.

There was nothing there.

Confused, they moved beyond the edge of the ruined fence. Eric put the sledgehammer down and raised his remaining hand pointlessly in the air to try to pick up on whatever had triggered his radar. Still nothing. They walked another twenty or so feet further forwards, scanning the area, and then Eric called it.

"Okay, false alarm, back inside," Eric hissed, even though the hairs on his neck and arms were all on end. "Must just be some kind of residual feedback from the Prism or some sh—"

They both froze as they realized that the Barrier above them had become a faint shade of grey.

*Oh,* Eric thought, *could I please just have five fucking minutes—*

"Eric..." Harry muttered, looking at something in the distance. He gently put the box down and then straightened, extending a hand and pointing. Eric looked.

*Holy shit.*

Eric slowly bent, picked up the sledgehammer and handed it to Harry who took it without a word. He quietly drew his gun from his holster, hand shaking, and thumbed the safety off. He blinked rapidly, trying to focus.

On the pavement about two hundred feet away—on the corner, near a streetlamp—silently stood three Empty Men.

They weren't moving. Neither were Eric or Harry.

The entirety of the empty space around Ground Zero started flickering like an old black-and-white movie reel. The effect was overwhelming; all of the air around them began to strobe. It was as if they'd been somehow dumped into a streaming TV show over a bad internet connection. The abandoned streets around Ground Zero seemed to be filling with a wind-free and silent blizzard.

"Over there," Harry whispered. "Look over there."

The flickering whiteness in the near distance began to solidify and thicken; the opposite street corner filled with white, forming into six figures, standing stooped and motionless but still taller than the tallest man. They were worse than Eric had imagined. When he'd heard the name and description on the news in the pub with Luis, he'd pictured something shadowy but bulky, a see-through version of the Stone Men perhaps. Five feet or so to the left of those Empty Men another cluster appeared, their feet disappearing through the pavement. Then another cluster about another five feet in front of that. And to the right of that. And to the left of that.

The Empty Men had finally come to Coventry.

Where the Stone Men had been big and dramatic, these were taller, thinner and infinitely creepier. He looked at them and got the feeling that they were looking right back, no matter how far away they were. Eric blinked, and now, where there had been no Empty Men, there were suddenly clusters everywhere, filling the street.

He raised the gun, instinctively knowing it would be useless but ready to fire if one got any closer.

"Let's get—"

Whiteness suddenly filled his vision as another group appeared four feet away from Eric's face. He leaped back a foot, fired the gun in fright, and watched in horror as the bullet passed harmlessly through the Empty Man in front of him.

"*Come on!*" he yelled, turning to bolt back inside Ground Zero, holstering the gun on the second attempt as he spun, only to halt in his tracks as he saw that his path was already cut off. They were now standing in the midst of a stadium crowd of Empty Men, and the path back to Ground Zero was full of them. With every few flickers, more arrived, the whiteness becoming more and more dense.

"*What are we gonna do—*" Harry hissed, the sledgehammer raised and ready. Eric swung his head left and right, trying to find a safe path out of there. There wasn't one.

Still they came.

They were filling every inch of space between Eric, Harry and the Prism, some of them sporting weird patches of colour or shade, and then Eric realized that it was an optical illusion; they were solid-*looking* but not solid-bodied after all. The colour he was seeing in them would be the partially visible edge of a billboard sticking out through one of their backs, the shade of grey from the stem of a lamppost emerging through one of their hunched-over necks. And they *were* hunched, bent over like Nosferatu coming up the stairs. They spread so far back that Eric couldn't see an end to them.

*A way out,* he thought, *please—*

Coventry was now the city of the Empty Men, and Eric knew that he and Harry weren't getting out of there.

As Eric watched the Empty Men, images of bacteria came to him, or the organized chaos of bees.

"They're *swarming*," Harry whispered, as if reading Eric's mind. They both cried out as another cluster of Empty Men appeared about half a foot to Eric's left. A slight sidestep, and they would have appeared right on top of him. Around them, the flickering continued, and the Empty Men continued to pour in. In moments there would be nowhere left that they didn't fill.

With lousy timing, another jolt went through both men. Eric was experienced enough now to know another vision was coming.

It hit him. It was so brief that Eric only saw a flash of olive-green walls—a room somewhere—before every hair stood up on his body and every muscle clenched hard, forcing him onto his tiptoes as Harry swore and did the same. Eric braced mentally for the fits and spasms, but they never came; it was over. The whole thing had been different. The others had been like accidentally receiving a deliberate signal meant for someone else; this time had just felt like a glitch. *That had been like the vision during the Big Power Cut,* he thought. *Not as powerful but... from the same place—*

It didn't matter. The streets around him were filling with Empty Men.

*Trapped—*

Eric noticed something in the bright white crowd about twenty feet away. A cluster of the Empty Men—one hundred? Two hundred? It was hard to tell—began to flicker again. Unique amongst the solid mass of white, they looked like a partial graphical error on a video game, a display set to *Ultra* when the graphics card could only handle *Low*. Then the flickering group vanished. The Empty Men behind them slowly moved forwards to fill the gap. It was the first time Eric had properly seen them... walk? Perambulate? They *slid.* Their legs didn't move an inch to propel their bodies forwards. It was somehow hard to watch. Even so, some of them had left.

"Don't move, Harry," Eric whispered, his voice barely audible. "Did you see them leave, over there? Something's happening. Maybe if we stay still—"

There was another flicker and six more Empty Men appeared to Eric's right. They narrowly missed him but two of them materialized right in front of Harry.

"*Shit*—" Eric cried and darted forwards to grab him, but it was too late. Harry's scream was choked off as one of the Empty Men collapsed upon him like a wave.

# Chapter Eighteen:

# Maria Makes Contact and Meets the Sleepers

***

## <u>Maria</u>

"I recognize your name," Maria said, quickly recovering from her surprise and tucking her hands under her armpits. "You're supposed to be dead! Linda told me."

Paul shrugged slightly, not in a cruel way but as if to say, *This is the first I've heard.*

"I'm not, no. I can see why she'd think that. A little while back..." The older man standing behind him—Boss Soldier—coughed slightly, and Paul rolled his eyes. "Short version: I got *better*, basically, and that isn't a joke."

"But what happened, how... how did you—"

"I'm really sorry, but we have to hurry here, Maria, and I'm pretty sure I can help make you a deal. I can maybe explain that later," Paul said quickly, eyes darting towards Boss Soldier. He towered over Maria's petite frame, but he didn't seem threatening. She felt like she was with a stressed but genial uncle. In age, he had to have twenty years on her. "As it stands, you can keep asking me questions, and Captain Mainwaring here can keep coughing—"

Maria didn't know the reference, but one of the big men by the door grunted slightly, suppressing a chuckle "—and warning me—and *I'm going to listen,* Jesus—and we waste time and get nowhere. *Or* we do the handshake thing right now and see if what Linda just told us is true. If it is, then maybe you and these guys can have a talk."

"No, thank you," Maria said sharply. "I'm not that interested. I came here to be safe, and I'm..." Maria trailed off. She realized that it wasn't going to work that way. If she shook his hand and something happened, she was in. If she didn't cooperate, they were going to kick her out.

"It's up to you," Paul said softly, but his eyes widened slightly as he said it, and she realized it was a warning. *It isn't up to you,* his eyes said. *They'll do it the hard way if they have to.* "But—I'm gonna be honest with you—even on a personal note, and I'm not one of these bastards, I'm *very* interested to test it—"

"*Tactile connection class four,* I heard her," Maria spat. "And I know how they treat people who have it. How they treated you."

"Well, I'm a little different," Paul said, already holding a hand up to the older soldier to wordlessly repeat, *Yes, yes, I'm saying nothing.* "But it wasn't actually the tactile connection we wanted to talk to you about."

*She told them what you told her,* Maria thought. *About hiding people.* She flushed hot, realising they would be very interested in that indeed.

"That was..."

They might be interested because it meant *she could do something.*

She froze, thoughts tumbling. She began to shake.

"Time is against us," Boss Soldier said, "and *I* have the clearance to tell you, unlike Mr Winter here, that we have seen the... ability Linda described once before." Paul seemed surprised

Boss Soldier was sharing information. He cocked his head towards Maria as if to say, *There you go.*

"*How?*" Maria asked. Everything was happening so *fast.* "The Empty Men have never been here before, and—*wait,* what kind of danger am I putting myself in?"

More glances were exchanged.

"To be honest," Paul said, looking stern, "if you'd been here yesterday or this morning, I probably wouldn't be asking you, and *they'd* be forcing *me* to do it. But if what Linda is saying about you is true... well, I could be helping you to be one of the less in-danger people in this country."

"What?"

"Agree to shake his hand," Boss Soldier said. "If Linda's right, then you immediately shoot right up the clearance chain. Higher even than *me.*" As if summoned, there was a knock on the door and Boss Soldier opened it to show Linda waiting outside with the soldier who had left to fetch her. She had tears all over her cheeks and a silly smile on her face. Paul grinned as he saw her but immediately forced a straight face. "After, I promise," he said to her, warmly. "We've just got to take care of some business—"

"Oh yes, yes, that's okay," Linda said rapidly, but Paul briefly stepped forwards and took both of her hands. Maria noticed that, of course, the touch seemed to do nothing. Linda grinned, but then she saw Maria and fell silent.

"Thank you, Linda, we'll see you shortly," Boss Soldier said kindly, and Linda was taken away again as Maria realized that now was the moment of truth.

"But what is the handshake supposed to do?"

Paul looked at Boss Soldier, who sighed and nodded.

"It always causes a reaction in two Stone Sensitives," Paul said, "when the Stone Men—or apparently also when the *Empty* Men—

are here. With different combinations of people, it varies, but there's always a lasting effect after they've touched me. I'm different, somehow. Got a very bad bang on the head a few years ago, and it altered some things—neurons, brain chemistry... I don't think I'm supposed to be in the plans, in the system."

"What plans?"

He pointed a finger upward.

"*Their* plans," he said. "In simple terms, Maria, it seems that I'm a battery. But I am unique, as far as we know. There's no-one else like me. When I touch other Stone Sensitives, nearly all of them get boosted. Not all of them—our friend Linda is a good example—but most. It first happened when I met Andy Pointer—you might remember him from the news—and I've been involved with all this bullshit ever since. At first, I was just here to keep *Caemen*—sorry, the *Stone Man* on my tail, but then they started wanting to try things out."

"You're going to boost me, but what does that means in terms of me being in *danger*?"

Paul shook his head. "You were in danger from the moment the First Arrival started," he sighed, "and like I said, we think you of all people are probably about as safe as it gets, although nothing is for certain when those Stone Bastards are involved. Maria..." He glanced at Boss Soldier, and then shook his head; *Bugger him*, the gesture said. "I have enough blood on my hands. If I thought that I would be putting you in more danger than you already are, I wouldn't do it."

His words were a shock, the look on his face dark but sincere.

*Do it,* said the voice in her head, loud and clear, suddenly certain and irrepressible. *You've been running for so long that you're on autopilot. You haven't truly considered that you might actually be able to help fight back.*

She looked at Paul's face... and there it was. Some sort of connection. She knew that he had it too, even if he didn't understand. She slowly cocked her head—she saw the confusion on the faces of the people in the room—and began to cross the distance between them.

*He's broken,* she thought. *But he's...*

She couldn't get it. Paul began to blink rapidly. Maria pressed on. There was a hunger in him—an *anger*—the same as hers. But she shouldn't know that... How was she doing this? What the hell was going on?

But what she said was, "*You're* angry," the wonder clear in her voice. Everyone else in the room was absent to her. "Not at these people. Despite everything... you're angry with *them*..."

Paul's eyes looked through her as if hypnotized. Maria closed her eyes, the movement as natural, fluid and automatic as lifting her feet to walk.

*It's about what they did to your* life, *isn't it?* she thought.

She heard Paul gasp slightly, and flinch, and then there suddenly was a *flow* between them, faint and distant but unmistakably there.

In his reflected anger and pain, she discovered that, yes, she was very angry indeed. *My friend Ruth,* she heard herself tell him. *My unborn daughter.* My *life*—

She blinked, the room coming back into focus, and for a moment, she could believe that she'd imagined the whole thing. One glance at Paul's red and disbelieving face told her that whatever had happened, had happened.

"Uh, well... shall we..." Paul fumbled, hand extended but not close enough to touch.

"Are you alright?" Doctor Holbrooks asked.

"Yes, it's just been an emotional day," Maria lied, her heart racing. She could talk to Paul later on about what had just happened, she hoped, away from prying ears. "I'm ready."

She held out her small hand to Paul. It was trembling. Now *he* looked scared to touch hands.

"Excellent," Boss Soldier said, and his well-spoken, clipped but hoarse voice made Maria wonder if he was posh, a graduate from officer college perhaps. Holbrooks eagerly began to unpack the contraption atop the trolley.

"Don't worry about these," Holbrooks said, holding up a set of electrodes that were attached to the device on the trolley. "They're just for measuring. Sit on the edge of the bed, please. This will take a few minutes."

***

Maria sat on the bed, her legs dangling over the side. When Paul seated himself on the cheap military mattress, Maria found herself shifting towards his weight on the opposite end. Her heart was now beating very quickly.

"Try to breathe slowly," Holbrooks said. "I'm about to turn on the machine."

"Doctor, if I get told to breathe slowly one more time today," she hissed through gritted teeth, her eyes screwed up tight, "I'll—"

"She's fine, Holbrooks," Paul said softly. "She's just scared. We all are."

Maria knew it was meant to be comforting, but *we all are* sent a jolt of fear down her spine. Again, the thought came. *What has happened here?*

She knew there was no point asking now. She was about to shake his hand. If they got what they wanted, she would find out.

Holbrooks studied the electrode boxes on the trolley table in front of him and adjusted a few settings. Boss Soldier—she still didn't have his name—stood by the now-closed door, continually checking his watch and shifting from foot to foot. The remaining, hulking guard stood in the corner.

Holbrooks looked up. "Whenever you're ready."

Paul coughed a little and then extended his hand to Maria. Linda had been right; his hand *was* big. She hesitated.

"Best of British, and all that," he said kindly.

*Do it,* she thought.

"Try not to hurt me," Maria said, not knowing why. She thrust her hand into his.

She braced, wincing in preparation for a bigger version of the shock she'd had with Linda, but it didn't come; Maria opened her eyes and was lost for words, for thought.

She saw nothing but light.

There was no physical pain at all this time, but she tried to gasp in shock and found she had no lungs. She felt no physical sensation at all. There was only light, and… She wanted to see more clearly, to take it all in, and with that thought, the view panned back to reveal a dim shape. She thought she recognized it; *after all, she'd been avoiding it for the last five years.*

She could make it out if she concentrated, trying to clarify its outline. It was Britain. And the light was now far away, glowing in the centre of the country… *What was that?*

*Now* she could feel her body. Pain growing in her head. Someone else was screaming, a man's voice, and a grip on her hand tightening… the vision before her became blurry as the image of the room in which she was sitting began to lay over it, a crossfade stuck halfway as she could see a man, a man who… *Paul.* Paul was screaming. It was hard to see him clearly, not just because of the two images bleeding into one another, but because the light in the room was flickering in and out. The lights in the ceiling were blowing. It was chaos, other people were shouting, and her *hand hurt,* her fingers were grinding together, but something was growing in her head, an *awareness.* It was building, but the *pain*—

She had to stop this, and even as a voice inside her started to shout, *NO, I WANT MORE,* she began to pull away. His grip was too strong, and so she had to come back into the room entirely to free herself, pulling with all of her strength. Immediately, the acrid, burnt smell of shorted-out wiring filled her nose as her hand popped free, Paul's scream filling the air. It trailed off as the connection was broken. He fell backwards on the bed, breathing hard, his gaze never leaving Maria. His face was bright red. Her heart was pounding—had she hurt him? *what the hell just happened?*—and she looked at Holbrooks' machine, following the smell of smoke. The readout was blackened. She looked up to see that many of the light fittings in the ceiling were now dead while the others were only just clinging to life, flickering weakly. Doctor Holbrooks was rushing towards Maria with a tiny torch.

"It's alright, you're alright," he said, but his breathing was rapid. He shone the light in her eyes. "Can you look at me, Maria? Look this way? How do you feel?"

She didn't answer. She was more confused than shocked. She'd had visions before, yes, but not like that. That had just been *easy.* And something else had been building up at the end, hadn't it? Something had been changing? Inside her head? Her top lip suddenly felt wet, and she put her hand to it in a daze as Holbrooks spoke.

"It's a nosebleed, don't worry; we see that all the time, don't worry," he babbled, sounding too excited for this to *only* have been something that they saw all the time. In the corner, the Boss Soldier was barking something into his radio and the Hulk just stood there, gaping. He'd certainly never seen anything of the kind before. *Maybe he's new*, Maria thought deliriously.

"*Jesus!*" Paul finally gasped. "That was... That was..." He ran out of words. "*Fuck!* That *hurt, fuck me!*" He nursed his hand, and Holbrooks went over with the light, but Paul waved him away. "I'm fine." He wiped his brow and stared at Maria again. "Linda was telling the truth," he sighed, speaking to Holbrooks but not taking his eyes off the only woman in the room. "She's like Warrender, but... *Christ...* Warrender was never like *that.* I've not felt *anything* like that before."

"What *was* that?" Maria asked, amazed at how calm her voice sounded. "I haven't, I mean, what I saw, that's—"

"Everything went off the charts before..." Holbrooks said, gesturing excitedly at the fried machines. "Physical manifestation—"

"We didn't finish," Paul groaned, sitting up. "We weren't done." He looked at Maria. "We weren't, were we?"

"No," Maria said, sounding amazed. "We have to go again."

"What?" Holbrooks cried. "There was *more?*"

"Yes," Maria replied. Now she was regaining clarity, she felt strangely relaxed.

"Why did you let go?" Paul asked. "Did it hurt you?"

"No, *you* did. You were crushing my hand. Not to mention screaming out loud."

"Shit, sorry. Okay, let's go again, and I'll try to make sure I don't—"

"Stop," she said, holding up her hand. While she was still worried... somehow, she also felt like she'd been on a spa weekend, as if she'd just blown off more steam than she had in years. *If they could make a drug out of this,* she thought, *they'd make a goddamn fortune.*

Plus, she'd just realized that now she had some clout.

"Let's not mess around. Obviously, you four can physically *make* me do whatever, shake hands, fine. But I think that you need me to actually cooperate to make use of… whatever the hell is going on. It sounds to me like I *am* whatever you think I am. You said that would mean major clearance. Right?" She addressed this to Boss Soldier, who just passed the look to Holbrooks. A smile crept onto Paul's face.

"You remind me of someone," he said. "He said similar things."

"Yes, *great*," Maria snapped. "I'm honoured. But I want answers before I go any further forwards." She turned to the Boss Soldier. "Actually, what's your bloody *name*, please?"

"Edgwick."

"Thank you. You're not the top person here, right? No offence meant, but you're not, are you?"

"No."

"Okay. Then I think I need to speak to whoever that is, don't I? Straub, isn't it?" She marvelled at the sound of her own voice, a tone there that hadn't been present in years. She sounded the way she used to when she taught class. She'd just touched some part of herself—embraced it for a moment—that she had previously never tapped. It was exhilarating. She felt *powerful.* Edgwick didn't reply at first, looking again at Holbrooks in another game of visual tag. "Oh, come *on*," Maria snapped, frustrated. "I *know* she's in charge. Where is she?"

"She's in the field," Edgwick said quietly, surprising Maria. "Believe me, she's been informed. She's spinning about every plate there is right now, but I would not be surprised if she weren't on her way here already."

"Okay. I'm potentially willing to help," Maria said, bluffing as she was now most certainly on board after *that*. "But I will be as *un*cooperative as possible until you tell me what is happening here."

"Alright. Bollocks, let's not piss around," Paul said, standing up. "I'm going to tell her everything and if either of you two," he said, looking from Holbrooks to Edgwick, "are opposed to that then go and get the bloody collar. This is the first breakthrough we've had in a year and, frankly, the first *ever* like that. It couldn't have come at a better time either because I think we are, to use a sporting metaphor, in extra time here, and we have to put even the goalkeeper in their half. Jesus, today we've already had one big...." His face fell, and he waved the rest of the sentence away. "Straub isn't here, Stoke is at the Chisel—"

"The Chisel?" Maria interrupted. "Is that here—"

"—and Edgwick, that  actually puts you as the *current* tip-top on base, to my understanding," Paul continued. "Permission to spill the bloody beans so we can get *on* with this?"

Edgwick's poker face—the best Maria had ever seen, but she hadn't met Brigadier Straub yet—didn't even twitch behind his ginger moustache, his eyes boring into Paul's. Then he spoke in that firm but gentle voice, a classic Brit if one ever drew breath.

"Will you want to show her the Sleepers?" he asked.

Maria didn't know what that meant, but she knew acquiescence when she heard it. Paul looked surprised at the suggestion.

"Yes," Paul said. "That's probably a good idea. See if she can... Yeah." Maria watched as Paul lowered his gaze. "She makes Warrender look like an amateur, Holbrooks." The scientist turned slightly pale, but Edgwick was already opening the door to the hallway. Paul stood up. "It's just a few doors down," he said. "Come on."

Maria was led out of the room and down the hallway to the double doors where Edgwick and Holbrooks stood either side with key cards. Edgwick nodded, the two men pressed their cards to an access panel simultaneously, and the doors unlocked. Maria thought she heard a slight hiss of air pressure releasing. Then Edgwick was pushing one of the doors open, and they were heading through, the Hulk and Paul walking a few feet behind. If Paul was big, the Hulk made him look small by comparison, but the larger man still had the worried expression of a little boy.

The hallway was different this side of the security system; only a few doors, each one with a long observation window accompanying it. The lights behind the windows were off, the rooms looked empty, and Maria couldn't see what their purpose would have been. She looked at Paul and saw he was studying the floor intently.

"Which..." Edgwick was asking, gently waving his key card.

"Uh, 14, that has the most..." Holbrooks said, and Edgwick was opening the door, and Paul surprised Maria by placing his hand on her shoulder.

"This might be a little bit upsetting," he said softly. "There's nothing bad to see in there, everything's covered up, but when you walk in there, we want you to tell us what you feel. Then we're going to come straight out again, alright? It's important, and then we're going to go through everything, okay?"

"Okay..." Maria said slowly.

Edgwick opened the door to Room 14. As soon as he did, Maria knew it *wasn't* okay. The feeling was like walking into a sauna except instead of heat, the air was thick with... she didn't have a name for it. They turned on the lights.

Even though whatever had happened had, to Maria's guess, been quite recent, the *thickness* inside wasn't from the smell of death, as the room had been cleaned and bleached to laboratory standards.

*Whatever happened in here is why everybody is so on edge.*

There was closeness, a cloying *something* in the air that came from having at least ten or fifteen body bags inside a room, and Maria wondered if anyone other than her or Paul could sense it. The black, zippered bags were laid out on rows of single metal beds, each one with a dormant, unattached life support machine and empty IV drip stand beside it. Maria covered her mouth, but she wasn't even horrified by the scene—she'd witnessed far worse in the last twenty-four hours and this at least had some reverence to it, some dignity in the way the dead had been treated.

*It's as thick as treacle. All of these people...*

"They all died within the last few hours, didn't they?" she breathed, not realising that she was walking down the centre aisle of the beds, her hands raised at either side of her. *So many in one room, all in one place,* she thought. *It's still just tangible, even though they're dead. Imagine what it would have been like if they were alive...*

It felt like walking through a kitchen where every worktop, every stove was cooking exactly the same meat in completely different ways, some with sweet, some with savoury, some with spice.

"How do you know that, Maria?" Holbrooks asked from behind her, but she wasn't listening. She stopped by one bed in particular, drawn to it.

"This one," she heard herself say, feeling calm even though her voice trembled, like an athlete at the top of their game about to compete. "This one was... this one was *strong*." She cocked her head slightly, held out a hand. "It's fading. They're all fading." *In an hour, maybe two, this room will only hold corpses.* The thought was what finally upset her—the *loss* here—and she gagged slightly. Paul stepped forwards then hesitated, but then she was talking again. "How many more?" she asked, her voice clogged, then she suddenly walked to the other end of the room and put her hand on the wall. "There's more in there, isn't there? Next door? How many are there?"

"Fifty-seven in total," Paul said. "There's a few rooms like this."

Maria realized something, spun so her back was against the wall, horrified as she raised a shaking, accusing finger.

"*You* did this," she hissed. "This is some sort of control thing. *You* killed these people." Edgwick and Holbrooks were by the door. Holbrooks she thought she could get past, but Edgwick—

"*No,*" Paul and Holbrooks said at the same time, Holbrooks stepping forwards, but Paul raised a hand to hold him back. "Not these people, Maria," Paul said, his own eyes blinking. He was struggling. "The people at this project have had to do some bad things to keep the country safe but *these* people were here, volunteering, and we tried to save them. These rooms," he said, waving his arms around, "were an attempt to save them. We thought they would..." He looked at the bagged bodies and wiped at his face again, put his hands on his hips, coughed. "I should have been... Holbrooks and his people put them into medically induced comas, Maria. It was an idea they'd been ready to try for a long time, and they thought it might work. It didn't."

"What..." Maria started to ask, but then the answer came all by itself.

*Induce a coma,* she thought. *Fake a death. But why did they need to—*

This one found its own answer too.

"The Empty Men," she whispered. "They've already been through here."

"Yes," Paul said, and his face turned pale. *He was here*, Maria thought. *He saw it.* "We lost a few soldiers too. The people in these rooms are all the volunteers that... well, it's complicated, but basically these are the people who qualified. A lot of them had left the project. Some of them had been flown back in to be put under, that's why Straub dispatched special recovery choppers to go and get—"

"Linda was a volunteer. *Wait,* these people are like me? You said I would be safe."

"Linda was on Tin *and* she was cut off. These are all Gale—top level—not like —"

"Tin, Gale... what is all that?"

Paul scowled at himself.

"Sorry," he said, rubbing at his eyes, and Maria wondered if he'd slept as little as she had. "These are terms for—"

"What do you *feel* Maria?" Holbrooks asked, interrupting. "We need you to explain, that's really important right now."

"I can feel *all of them*," she said, her brow creasing as she tried to understand what was happening to her. "All of these people, what's left of them... they had something, didn't they? Like Linda, like me?"

"Not like Linda—more than that. They certainly weren't like you, no," Holbrooks said, but Maria's attention was already caught by something else, and she was reaching out with her mind, beyond the room. Touching Paul had done *something*, even if she didn't get to finish—

"Maria? Maria, can you...?" Holbrooks' voice trailed away as Maria's consciousness was drawn out of her and she just went with it, allowing herself to ride the wave as she raised up, up, *up* beyond the entire prefab building, past the nearby hills as she once more picked up the lure of that *light* she'd seen, how far away was it—

"Maria?" Holbrooks asked, and now he was in front of her, gently holding her wrists, eager. "Where did you go just now? What did you see when you shook hands with Paul?"

"A light," she said, coming back to the room, feeling claustrophobia seize her. This room was so *small*, out there was so vast. "It's tiny, but it's so damn *bright...*"

"Where*?* Here?"

"Like... in the middle of the country."

"Okay, okay," Paul said, rolling up his sweater sleeves. "Let's not get too excited; this might be good news for *us* directly, but as it stands, we don't have anything yet that might do much against whatever's going on in bloody Coventry. Let's try it again. Doc, can you dose me up with a little of the muscle relaxant? If this is going to be anything like last time, I don't want to take her hand off."

Holbrooks nodded and walked over to a cabinet on the wall.

"Yes, they'll take about thirty minutes to kick in though," Holbrooks said. "Edgwick, can you go to the relay to try to get hold of Straub," he said, "and tell her what we've found?"

"Do you want a chopper prepped for evac?" Edgwick asked.

"Yes, immediately," Holbrooks said, rooting through the cupboard. He glanced at Maria. "I don't know how long this will take, but we'll want the chopper ready to go at a moment's notice. *Dispensatori* will be coming as well, of course." Paul nodded in agreement, even though Maria thought he had no authority there.

"Room 19 is empty," Paul said. "Let's do this in there; we don't need to..." He gestured around himself to the body-bag occupied beds. Holbrooks nodded, and Edgwick opened the door to lead the group across and down the hallway. Maria glanced back at Holbrooks who remained inside Room 14, flipping through trays of meds and checking the settings on a small camera he'd pulled out of a drawer. Maria suddenly stopped in the middle of the hallway.

"Evac to where? Where are we going? And *wait,* it's your *fucking turn!*" she snapped, putting the brakes on her own sense of wonder and yanking herself into the present moment. "I'm not going to have this—I give you what you want and then you show me something super important, and there's *no time to explain...* This isn't a bloody episode of *Lost!* What are you trying to do here—"

"No, no, fair is fair, and for what it's worth, I think you're doing incredibly well," Paul said as Edgwick key-carded the door to Room 19 and held it open. It was identical to Room 14, albeit without dead bodies, and the *atmosphere* of the room was as crisp and fresh as winter air by comparison. Maria reluctantly followed them inside and sat on a bed as Edgwick departed to deal with transport. Maria noticed they'd been left alone—now, they knew she wouldn't try to run? Had people before her sensed what she'd sensed and just been hooked in the same way? Paul sat down on the adjacent bed about two feet away from her.

"Don't patronize me," she said, folding her arms. "Just tell me what's going on."

"Certainly," Paul said. "What do you want to know? Anything."

She had a million questions and didn't know where to start.

"The *Sleepers,*" Maria said contemptuously... then suddenly recoiled, a revelation striking her. She saw that he knew it too, understood the conclusion she'd come to. His expression was unreadable.

"Oh my God," she said. "You boosted all of them, didn't you?"

He nodded.

"It's more complicated than that," he said, but he wouldn't meet her gaze now. "And you, you must already know—"

Something else struck her.

"The Empty Men killed *all* of them," she said. "I've seen them kill—they're selective." *Oh my God*—"You said the Sleepers were all 'top level'—"

A fire alarm began to sound, its volume deafening in the room. Holbrooks burst into the room.

"The helicopter pad, let's go!" he screeched, disappearing.

"*Holbrooks!*" Paul shouted, but Holbrooks was already gone. He jumped to his feet, frantically gesturing to Maria. She could barely hear his shouts over the blaring alarm, and for a moment, she froze, seated on the bed. "Trust me!" he bellowed. "I've only ever heard that alarm once and that was this morning! We don't want to be—*Shit,* come *on!* We need to get to the landing pad—"

Maria leaped to her feet, more confused than ever, but realisation struck them both at the same time.

"*Linda*—" Paul said.

They rushed into the equally deafening hallway to see the Hulk hustling Linda out of her room and down the corridor away from them. Linda spotted the two of them rushing towards her, yelled, "*Come on!*" then turned and ran full pelt.

"What's happening?" Maria yelled as she ran. Ahead of them, the Hulk had opened the double doors, holding them for the runners behind him.

"Is the chopper ready?" Paul yelled to the Hulk, ignoring Maria. The Hulk nodded, his face deathly white. They burst out through the exit doors and into the beautiful natural basin in which Project Ouroboros was nestled, surroundings ruined not only by the ugly military buildings but by the alarm that continued to blare over unseen speakers. Maria, even as her heart beat in her ears, expected to see something similar to what Linda had described during her final day: people running everywhere, chaos. She saw maybe five plain-clothes soldiers running. The place only had a skeleton crew left, that was certain. Everything must have changed after the Stone Man went home.

Ahead, at the far end of the facility, she spotted a huge grey helicopter set against the high, green, sloping hills of the Ladybower Reservoir, its rotary blades beginning to turn. About twenty feet further back, another chopper was already taking off, and another one further away than that sitting stationary while two or three people climbed aboard. The Hulk led the group of runners, glancing over his shoulder to make sure his physically unfit charges were still coming.

Linda, surprisingly, was just about keeping pace with him, Holbrooks a little way behind her, while Paul and Maria ran side by side, several feet behind.

*"Where are we going?"* she yelled. *"I only just got here! Isn't this where—"*

Paul was too breathless and red-faced to answer, wheezing already, but he pointed upwards to the top of the hills. They were going up there? Why would they have to—

Then she saw them.

To her great credit, she never missed a step and charged faster towards the helicopter. She turned her head left and right as she ran, craning her neck; they encircled the top of the hills above, completing their noose by standing in that line around the top of the basin. They looked like giant fenceposts, a silent and terrible white crown for the Ladybower Reservoir.

The Empty Men had come to Project Ouroboros. There were hundreds of them.

They began to descend the hillsides, the noose tightening.

The helicopter was still a long way away. They might make it.

*No, you'll make it, of course you'll make it,* she thought wildly. *You wondered if it was true, and these guys have all but told you that you were right, right?*

She looked back to the hillsides; the Empty Men were already halfway down, moving more quickly than they had before. Why were they—

Then she felt it. This was different. She... she'd still make it...

Before it had been a scouting party, a line sweeping the countryside searching for whatever they were looking for. This was a group with one purpose and one purpose only. Just as she'd been bathed in that *thickness* in the room of the Sleepers, she felt it coming off the Empty Men in waves.

She'd drawn them there.

*They only came here after you shook his hand,* she thought. *You became a beacon. They're all only here* for you *this time.*

She looked at their sheer numbers. This time she wouldn't escape. She knew it to be true like she knew her name. This was several hundred all tightening around *her,* here only *for* her. Even at this range, she felt the focused searches of the creatures brushing up against her, patting the ground around her. They *knew* where she was.

She glanced at Paul, terrified, and knew that *he* knew they would never get to the helicopter before the Empty Men reached them. She tried to focus, clenching her fists and trying to remind herself that she'd touched Paul, she'd been *boosted* now, whatever the hell that meant—

*Leave us alone,* she thought. *Leave us alone—*

She looked up at the Empty Men through a veil of terror, hoping desperately to see them pause, to move away like before, but there was no break in their connection, no disguising it. All she felt was that reaching, grasping search getting even closer. Why wasn't it working? Then the obvious answer came, deniable no more: *there were just too many of them looking specifically for her. She couldn't hide.*

"LEAVE US ALONE!" *she screamed.* "LEAVE US ALONE—"

It was frantic and futile.

*No, you idiot,* her chimp-brain yammered. *It wasn't leave them alone or leave us alone, you tried it with the woman in the line of cars, and it didn't work. It's leave me alone, remember? It's you that hides and the people* around *you get to—*

She looked at the Empty Men, tall and devoid of any humanity and two thirds of the way down the hillside and remembered the *pop* she'd felt as the woman ran away from her between the cars.

Out of her range of influence—

She watched Linda and the Hulk pulling away as they ran. Saw Edgwick standing by the helicopter now, frantically urging them on. Saw, to her surprise, Private Binley sitting at the controls, beckoning desperately. Another man—the Crying Man from earlier, she realized—was running headlong towards Paul, waving and yelling, and Paul frantically beckoning him on as well. All of them physically out of her reach before the Empty Men would pass through them; the Empty Men would be upon them before they reached the helicopter.

She stopped running. She might be able to save *them*—

Paul blundered a few feet further forwards after seeing her halt, then yelled to her.

"*What are you doing?*" he screamed.

"*All of you!*" she screamed back. "*Linda!*" Linda turned back but the Hulk continued to drag her onwards. She was helpless against his strength and momentum. "*Come to me! We won't make it!*" She ran forwards a few steps, wanting to get closer, but knowing she needed to stop, to *breathe.* There were so many of them. *Too* many.

She stood still, beckoning to the others while trying to calm a heart rate that was making her chest pitch like a piston engine. She closed her eyes for a second.

*Breathe* down, she begged herself. *You have to this time,* please *calm down...*

She opened her eyes; Paul and a terrified-looking Holbrooks were already jogging back to her, and Linda was hitting the arm of a confused Hulk to let her go. Maria looked over to the chopper: Edgwick was going bananas, Private Binley was frozen in the pilot's seat. Hulk had stopped dragging an apoplectic Linda and stood looking confused, waiting for instructions from Edgwick. Even the unknown Running-and-Previously-Crying Man looked and started charging in their direction too.

Paul understood.

*"Take off and hover, we won't make it to you!"* Paul yelled. Edgwick nodded rapidly and said something to Binley who looked shocked but turned to the control panel in front of him. The chopper's blades began to speed up. In the helicopter's open doorway, Edgwick barked something into his radio that the Hulk rogered before dragging Linda towards Maria, this time making her protest about being unable to keep up.

Maria began to run towards them, deciding she had time to get a little closer before she dug in, but then she looked back to the hills; many of the Empty Men were now out of sight behind the top of the outbuildings. If they weren't at the base of the hills now, they would be in moments.

Maria stopped and closed her eyes.

*"Can you do it?"* Paul yelled, reaching her and understanding what she was about to try.

*"Maybe I can now! You changed something!"* she yelled over the still deafening alarm, wishing desperately that someone would

please turn the thing off. *"We won't make it to the helicopter anyway!"*

*"There's too many!"* Paul yelled.

*"Maybe not!"* Even in her terror, she was marvelling at her own ability, feeling *something* begin to activate, an eagle spreading its wings for the first time. The sense of instantly becoming part of a wider, unimagined world was indescribable even as it fell away beneath her like an abyss. Paul reached out his hand to her, and she understood but shook her head. *"I can't, I need to concentrate for this, the pain—"* She watched as the others continued to race towards her. She clenched her fists, closed her eyes.

*Leave me alone. Leave me alone.*

She could feel the Empty Men more clearly than ever before, not just because of their proximity, but because Paul was right. He *had* boosted her. There was a cold clarity in them, an awareness, and it was looking—

*FOCUS,* she commanded herself. She screwed her eyes as tightly as she could, her fingernails digging into her palms as she became aware of her circle of influence as if it were a physical thing. There was a ripple in her mind as the others drew closer to its edge, under her protection. *But was it a protection?*

*Leave me alone,* she thought. *Leave me alone.*

She opened her eyes and saw, in the near distance, that the wall of Empty Men was beginning to pass through the outbuildings.

*Pop. Pop. Pop.*

That was the Hulk, Linda and Holbrooks, maybe thirty feet away. They were back inside the circle.

*But it isn't working,* Maria thought desperately. *Leave me alone, leave me THE FUCK ALONE!*

She saw it; some of the Empty Men paused. Stopped. Some of them started to flicker... then vanished. Gaps appeared in the white wall as it thinned by maybe twenty per cent. *Yes!* How many had just left? Fifty?

She had a moment to wonder where they were going to when the gaps in the white wall were immediately filled as the rest kept coming. The Crying Man was still beyond her range but coming on fast. *Maria* was beyond her own range, and then that horrible, creeping *searching* found her, dragging her back into herself. The sensation went through her like a poisonous X-ray, and then she felt the full force of their focus.

There *were* too many.

"I'm sorry," she said to Paul, just before the Empty Men stopped, flickered and vanished.

*What—*

There was no time to think about it.

*Pop.* The Crying Man was inside her circle now too, pulling up. Holbrooks, Linda and the Hulk all did the same, turning about themselves in surprise, chests heaving, seeing the complete disappearance of the Empty Men and not believing their luck. They were all perhaps around ten feet away from Maria and Paul, their gasps and wheezes inaudible over the sound of the chopper's blades spinning as it rose into the air and moved towards them.

There was an awful, silent flash of white, and the Empty Men re-emerged in a dense, impenetrable circle, inches away from Maria and Paul's faces.

# Chapter Nineteen:

# Eric and Maria

### \*\*\*

### <u>Eric</u>

Eric wrapped his arms around Harry on instinct, trying to pull him free, but a terrible nausea washed through him with such force that he fell sideways, helpless, landing hard on the concrete as his untrained stump failed to break his fall. All he saw around him was an advancing wave of white, and Harry's struggling, Empty-Man-coated limbs falling still.

*Harry!* he thought, desperately trying to regain control of his limbs. *Oh God, Harry—*

Harry's whiteness-encased body twitched a few more times—

Then something was *there* inside Eric's head. He felt it as clearly as if it had snatched him up in an embrace.

*Who is that?* he thought crazily. *Who is that? What's happening—*

The world flashed over black for a second, and then he could see the Empty Men all around him once more, one of them wrapped around Harry like a spider coating its prey. Eric crawled towards his friend, moving as if *he* were the drunk one and landing pathetically flat on his face. That presence was still there in his head, as if considering him and trying to find out what he was, and as Eric felt its power, he asked it a question in his desperation.

*Can you help us?* Eric begged, as helpless as an injured child. *Help Harry, help Harry—*

He cringed as a scream rattled through his head in response. The presence died away.

*Whatever that was,* Eric thought deliriously, *they can't help you.* As Harry began to gag and choke, Eric looked up to see three Empty Men standing over him, moving in.

*\*\*\**

# **Maria**

All Maria could see was white. She had a second before the Empty Men were upon her, she could already feel their terrible inner gaze, and even before they latched onto her, she knew she didn't have enough to hide her group—even hide herself—from them, no matter how much she screwed up her eyes or tried to imagine herself invisible.

*Oh my God,* she thought in horror, *it's going to happen to me like it did to Ruth—*

Then Paul grabbed her shoulder and spun her round. Her hand came up, seeking his, a Hail Mary move, knowing that her mind would be sent anywhere but where it needed to be, and their fingers intertwined. They gripped hands, hard.

Her eyes were suddenly full of light.

The Ladybower Reservoir vanished. She was aware of her pulse racing, of the Empty Men being upon her, but the knowledge was distant, detached; a view of the country spread out before her mind's eye again in nanoseconds, and the vision was so much *clearer* now, as if the steam had been wiped from a window. Near to the bright point of light—how did she not see it before?—was a huge black shape, like an uneven but enormous building. It was the thing from the news, that big black structure at Ground Zero, that's what it was—

She was aware of the intense pain in her hand as a pressure started to build in her head. Still, she looked more closely. Both the light—so bright it hurt to look directly at it—and the black shape were *inside* something powerful but transparent. That had to be that bubble thing above Coventry—

There was something else in between the black shape and the light too, so close to both that she could *see* them—two shapes, people perhaps?—their outlines emerging from the noise of the landscape around them like the image in a Magic Eye picture. No, like *sonar,* their shape only visible thanks to whatever was coming off that horrible building nearby, casting into faint visibility by its aura.

*Those* are *people,* she realized. *Two of them, standing by that big thing in Coventry,* special *people and one is in trouble—*

*BUT THE EMPTY MEN ARE HERE,* she thought, *THEY'RE* UPON *YOU—*

Still, drawn helplessly to the people in Coventry, she reached out to them with her mind as the pain in her head and hand became so great that she couldn't ignore it.

"*—arry! Oh God, Harr—*"

What was that? She could hear someone's voice, a man's voice, and they were in great pain. Oh *shit,* her *fingers,* the growing pressure in her head was bad, but her *fingers...* Paul was crushing her bones together, bearing down like a man having an epileptic fit. She held on.

Nausea flooded into her consciousness, and the image in her mind wavered as she knew that they were standing completely within the whiteness of the Empty Men. They were trying to begin the process of purging.

*Who is that?* It was a man's voice—very faint—and he was screaming. No, he was *talking to her. Who is that? What's happening?*

*Hello?!* Maria sent back, but she knew it hadn't gone through. She tried to pull her hand free because, *Oh God,* she couldn't *take* any more. There was a sensation of something rushing from her brain, down her spine, her arms, her legs. The pain in her hand was blinding, and she felt like two people: one a woman suspended in this void that was above everything and another whose hand was being crushed in a field in Sheffield.

*Can you help us? Help Harry, help Harry—*

There was a *crunch* as three of Maria's fingers broke. Paul's enormous, crushing hand had ground Maria's fingers to a literal breaking point.

She crashed back to reality just as the boost completed.

Maria let out a scream of agony, unaware of the Empty Men wrapping themselves around her, unaware of Paul's fitting body, foam flying from his lips as his eyes rolled over white.

He released her hand.

*** *** ***

## **<u>Eric</u>**

*Theresa,* Eric thought. *Jenny. I'm so sorry. I never kept any of my promises.*

Then the presence was suddenly back in his head, stronger and twice as loud as before.

*YES,* it said.

***

## <u>Maria</u>

*They're mist to you,* Maria thought. *That's all they are.*

She breathed out and it was almost a sensation of joy as the completed boost sunk into her mind. She felt herself wrap around every human in her presence like a protective blanket. They'd all frozen like rabbits, and she watched in amazement as she tried to remember why. Didn't they know? These things couldn't harm them. She now saw that they were only phantoms. If she didn't want to be under their influence—if *none* of the people with her wanted to be under their influence—then they didn't have to be. It almost seemed silly to worry about it. The Empty Men that had wrapped around her—several had done so at once, it turned out— were already reassembling as if she had vanished. Several of them were beginning to drift away, seeming lost. She looked at her hands. Looked at Paul on the floor, rolling on his back, gasping in air.

Holbrooks was slowly backing away, looking in horror at the cluster of suddenly aimless Empty Men around Maria. The Hulk held a hysterical Linda back as the Crying Man moved closer to Maria, pointlessly trying to help.

"*Freeze!*" Maria barked, holding out a hand. The Crying Man stopped. It was bizarre; she was aware of her tension, her panic, but it was as if her body had simply turned on a red light to politely note *Unpleasant Feelings.* She didn't *have* to engage with them, not in this state. She felt like she'd connected to the Fourth Rail, and while she was doing so, the disappearance of tension was... what was the word for it?

*Bliss.*

Then the pain in her fingers broke through—that constant that philosophers refer to as *the problem with pain*—threatening to break her concentration and make her lose whatever she'd tapped into within herself.

*"Everybody... stand still!"* she commanded, straining to be heard over the chopper's blades, her trembling voice sounding like it belonged to someone else. Everything was blind terror, yet everything was complete peace. The pain was still there, but she discovered she could compartmentalize it in her mind. If she could stay in the moment... but how could she, immediately torn between two places as she was—

*Coventry,* she realized, *the Empty Men that left here, they went there to head to that black building, and they'd found—*

Without meaning to, her mind went to whoever had spoken to her from far away, found him—

Then she was *seeing* both places at the same time, seeing the Empty Men in Coventry, the ones at Ladybower. The ones around her seemed lost, but the ones in Coventry—

Then she had it. She found the other man's mind.

*YES,* she said, and sent herself there. She could help the people in Coventry, but she would have to shrink her influence a little at Ladybower to do so. That seemed okay; the Empty Men at Ladybower had halted now and begun to flicker, the ability to sense their Quarry lost. They slowly began to drift wider and wider apart, the white wall separating; first they were apart like fence posts, then road signs. She looked at the two men in Coventry, as close to her now as Paul was at her feet. One was younger and white, the other older and black, both of them cast grey somehow under the dark influence of the... *Prism,* that's what they called it, the name hung in the air between them as a connected understanding. It was one of only a few things they shared. *Connections,* she thought, and the word resonated. *That's what this is about. Making them and—*

Ending them. Of course.

*How the fuck do you know how to do this?* regular, control-needing Maria asked.

*It is what it is,* outer Maria answered. *Don't ask me— I'm going with it.*

In Coventry she made a scissor motion with the fingers of her left hand and snipped the white man and the black man out of their connection with the Empty Men as easily as turning off a light switch. The pain in her fingers broke through her awareness again, briefly flashing her back to the Ladybower, and as it did she suddenly realized something about the Empty Men's connections there too, her hyper-sensitive mind like a radio picking up all frequencies at once. She could feel them searching around, trying to pick up the scents they'd just lost; while they could no longer sense the people under her protection, they were only trying to find... three? Four? But how many humans were on that patch of grass, inside her circle? Six?

Thoughts of Paul fitting burst through the chaos in her head. Interrupting her thoughts.

*"Somebody... walk through the space between the Empty Men and check on Paul... please!"* Maria yelled, her eyes closing, *"Someone put him in the recovery position!"*

*"What the fuck is 'appenin'?!"* she heard someone bellow in a Scouse accent and realized it had to be the Hulk, speaking for the first time as he scurried over to Paul.

The Empty Men flickered some more, then faded.

They vanished.

Maria felt the higher level she'd reached begin to fade as well.

*NO—*

She reached out in desperation to cling onto it, but of course, the moment she did so, she stepped back into the real world, the world in which she feared scarcity and needed control, and the power crumbled away. With great sadness, her awareness began to rapidly descend back into only conscious thoughts and feelings rather than pure, delightful intuition. As it did so, she heard the distant voice of one of the men in... Coventry? Had she been right about that? Already she was unsure. A great sense of loss settled into her heart.

*Where are you?* she thought she heard the man's voice say. *How are you doing th— Wait, how do we find you? Who are you?*

*I'm Maria Constance,* she thought to him. She wanted to tell him where they were going, but she didn't know—

The helicopter had landed again, closer than before, and Edgwick was leaping out.

*"Where's the helicopter going?"* she yelled to him, her voice heavy, her eyes closed. She felt like crying. *"Where is the Chisel?"*

"Isle... the Isle of Skye," Holbrooks' voice stammered nearby, sounding amazed that he was alive. Linda and the Crying Man had run over to Paul's fallen body to assist the Hulk.

*What... Who was that?* the Coventry man's voice asked. *I couldn't hear it. Did you say the fucking Isle—*

The connection faded into silence. Maria staggered suddenly, the departure of the very last of it rocking her on her heels. She opened her blurry eyes to see Linda standing in front of her, jaw hanging wide open.

"Maria... how did you...? Are you alright, love—your nose, oh God, let me..."

Maria looked up at the basin around her, her body coursing with endorphins that made the pain in her broken fingers feel far away. She absent-mindedly put her good hand to her nose. It came away streaked with red. She didn't mind. She held her wet hand up to the air and felt the breeze chill it. She looked at the grass at her feet, watching it move in the same wind and decided that she was *done for the day.*

"Small steps, my backside," she heard herself say, and giggled deliriously before the world went black, and she collapsed onto the grass.

***

# Eric

The Empty Man that had been smothering Harry began to pour *upwards,* freeing Harry as it reformed itself. Eyes wide, Eric could barely believe it. He looked at the army of white that had been advancing in his direction. It had halted. The silence was eerie. The streets around them were as dead as ever, the Empty Men as noiseless as the grave. They stood still, some as close to Eric as a foot away. There were several that had stopped in between himself and Harry. Eric didn't dare move, sensing escape but too terrified to believe such a thing could be. Harry hadn't moved either. A fresh fear sliced through Eric's veins—Was it too late? Was Harry dead? He didn't look like he was breathing.

As one, the Empty Men began to move forwards. Eric froze like a rabbit, terror commanding his limbs to stay still as there was nowhere to run, and suddenly, his world was full of white as they moved *through* him.

Eric felt nothing. They were as intangible to Eric as the air around him. Still, he held his breath, not wanting even the air that the Empty Men had touched entering his lungs. He stood there, his fear first rising to a peak as a seemingly endless procession of Empty Men passed though him, and then beginning to drop as he realized that whoever the woman was that he'd heard, she—

*Wait, the woman,* he thought. *What the fuck was* that?

He glanced at Harry, wanting to run to him but scared to move in case that somehow put him inside the Empty Men's influence.

*Is she still there?*

She was, her presence still tangible... but fading. He reached out with his mind, the feeling suddenly as natural as breathing even as he marvelled at what he was doing.

*Where are you?* he asked. *How are you doing th—*

No, that wasn't important. This woman was special, she had to have answers—

*Wait, how do we find you? Who are you?*

The answer came back, the voice less clear than before.

*I'm Maria Constance.*

Then she said something else, but it was inaudible, as if she were suddenly talking in another room. Eric thought he heard something else—a man's voice to his surprise—sounding as if he was saying *ira sky.*

*Ira sky,* he thought. *What the hell?*

That couldn't be right.

*What? Who was that? I couldn't hear it,* Eric thought back quickly, feeling the woman fade further and further away. *Ira sky,* he thought frantically then realized it was an answer to his question. *Isle of Skye! Did you say the fucking Isle—*

Then she was gone. The Empty Men continued to pass him by, looking like a funeral procession of restless ghosts, and Eric realized that they were rapidly heading into the Prism as he looked at Harry's still body.

*He isn't breathing—*

There was still more Empty Men to pass, at least five feet deep.

*HE ISN'T BREATHING—*

Eric jumped up in the air and grabbed a breath of 'uncontaminated' oxygen above the Empty Men. Held it as he landed, crouched, and moved the four feet over to Harry. Harry still wasn't moving as Eric squatted down *into* the bottom halves of the Empty Men as the last of them continued to pass by. He shook Harry, wanting to call his friend's name but not wanting to open his mouth. The back of the wall of Empty Men finally moved beyond him as he dropped his ear to Harry's mouth to listen for breath. From his vantage point, it looked as if the front line of the Empty Men would be reaching the Prism. He couldn't say for sure, but then the Prism flashed white.

*What?*

Eric had half expected them to straighten up or throw their horrible elongated heads back on their necks, mimicking the actions of the Shufflers, but they didn't. He saw what the flash had been. As the front line of them touched the Prism, they just kept going. Their bodies flattened quickly against the surface but *spread* like liquid, lightning fast. They kept on spreading, widening like an expanding puddle until their bodies had stretched so far that they covered the entire surface of the Prism before fading into it. The whole process maybe took a half second, the sudden rapid contrast of the spreading white against the dark surface of the Prism making it look almost like a *pulse.* It flashed across the enormous edifice and vanished. As the others followed suit, carrying out the same strange process, there were suddenly so many impacting upon it—and so quickly—that the Prism seemed to be strobing in front of his eyes.

*Harry—*

*Mouth to mouth,* Eric thought frantically. *How the hell do you do mouth to mouth—*

He'd never been trained, but he'd seen it in films. It was ten, right? He went to put one hand on top of the other, realized he only had one, and pressed Harry's chest with that one hand—feeling the thin flesh and bony chest underneath—and he pushed against the back of his good hand with his stump. He pumped up and down as hard as he could, worrying that he would crack Harry's fragile-feeling sternum. He anxiously counted ten compressions, one eye on the Prism all the while. The Empty Men continued to pour silently into it, making the whole thing seem so much more unreal. Eric had been told by movies and books, all the way back to the Bible, that miraculous and magical things were accompanied by sound and trumpets; the Horns certainly fit into that category. The long wave of Empty Men still didn't make a single sound as they bled into the Prism, the only noise in that place coming from Eric's grunts as he pumped Harry's chest and then roughly pulled the older man's jaw open. Harry's fetid breath wafted out like hot air from a rancid oven. Eric pinched Harry's nose like he'd seen on TV and dived in anyway, desperate to save a man he barely knew. He huffed two long breaths of air into Harry's lungs and began pumping his chest again.

*Come on, Harry! Come on!*

The last of the Empty Men disappeared—*merged?*—with the Prism. The Barrier-tinted, unnaturally grey sky began to clear. The clouds and sky were slowly revealed in their true colour; the scene looked like an old Polaroid photograph self-developing as the Barrier returned to 'normal'.

Then the ground began to rumble, so suddenly and sharply that Eric fell sideways, breaking off his rhythm, hearing himself shout *no* in desperation. He leaped back up as the rumbling began to increase, redoubling the force of his efforts. As he did so, he heard a faint sound of cracking concrete and remembered the rest of the boxes inside Ground Zero.

The evidence. The *truth*—

The ground continued to shake as Eric continued to pump, reaching ten again; he dived towards Harry's mouth once more, his frantic gaze still on the Ground Zero building. If it collapsed, he didn't know if he would ever be able to get those boxes out—

He straightened up. Harry's eyes were still closed. Was he already dead? The rumbling became worse, deeper. Eric continued the urgent compressions, one eye on the trembling building.

*If he is,* Eric told himself, *then you could be wasting your only chance for nothing*—

He reached ten. He breathed more air into Harry. The man's eyes weren't even flickering. Eric bent his head, listened for breathing. There was none. *There was still time,* he could go now, he really could—

The rumbling echoed off the canyon of buildings around him.

And a little piece of Eric Hatton died while another came back to life as he realized that if he gave up even a slim chance to save his friend then Theresa would have thought him a *total* prick.

"*Come on, Harry!*" he shouted, and pumped Harry's chest harder than ever. The rumbling continued, getting louder still. Was something else arriving? Before Eric had time to wonder if his own death was imminent, Harry suddenly awoke with a choked gasp, holding his chest and coughing.

"*Yes! Yes, Harry!*" Eric cried with delight, tears springing to his eyes. "*I thought you were fucking dead, you bastard! You bastard! YES!*" He rolled Harry onto his side, raising his voice over the rumbling so Harry could hear him. "*Are you okay?*" he yelled. "*Can you breathe?*"

Harry nodded, coughing, but his eyes darted around him as the rumbling continued.

"*Something's happening to the Prism—*" Eric began, but then the cacophony of the walls of Ground Zero finally giving way drowned him out. The roof gave next, buckling inwards with a rumble as heavy as the thick concrete of which it was made. Dust and smoke plumed into the air, and Eric's moan of dismay was drowned out by the noise of the precious boxes—not to mention the incredible creatures in the lab—being buried. A feeble thought came up. *Maybe he could dig them out?*

It was possible, but he doubted it very much; the thickness of the crumbling slabs would require a JCB to get them out of the way. Even over the rumbling, Eric could hear the loud arcing of exposed wiring. Ground Zero was now a live-wire death trap, at least until the power source gave out. He didn't know enough about wiring to guess.

Either way, it didn't look good for the fucking boxes.

Eric dropped onto his backside and watched as the last of the building collapsed into a high pile. The rumbling from the Prism continued, oblivious to the fate of the Ground Zero building. Eric looked at the only box they'd managed to salvage, sitting a few feet away.

Harry sat up in panic. "*Are they—*"

"No," Eric shouted back. "*They're... I think they're leaving, Harry!*"

Then another huge crowd of Empty Men suddenly flickered into life, right in front of the Prism.

"*Jesus!*" Eric yelled, but this new arrival immediately followed the others into the black shape before them. They disappeared almost as quickly as they arrived.

*Not a new Arrival,* he thought. *Those must be the ones who left earlier. Could they be something to do with that woman you heard?*

Harry coughed again, groaning as he bent forwards, trying to breathe. "*What did you do?*" he shouted, shielding his eyes from the small bits of grit and dust that were beginning to blow around them. "*How did you get it off me?*"

"*I didn't do anything,*" Eric whispered. "*This... A woman did! Didn't you hear her?*"

"*No. Christ, my chest hurts!*" Harry moved to stand but Eric stopped him.

"*Give yourself a moment—*"

The rumbling stopped. Both men froze. The only sound was the continuing trickle of concrete. Nothing happened for a few moments.

"Now *I* gotta piss," Harry whispered.

"Do yourself a favour and wait," Eric said quietly. He didn't know whether to laugh or cry. "You don't want to be in the shitter when the end of the world comes."

The Prism began to move.

"It's *leaving,*" Harry whispered.

"Actually... I don't think so," Eric whispered. He was right. The initial movement they'd seen was misleading. "Look. It's shrinking."

The word *shrinking* made it sound like the motion was uniform, each side retracting evenly towards the centre. It *was* condensing but the change was uneven and inefficient; one side would retract inwards, leaving the Prism asymmetrical for a moment, and then the other side would shorten. It kinked and jerked in this way as it shrank, eventually forming a new, chaotic-looking shape, as if someone had carved some crazy-angled sculpture from a bigger, Prism-shaped block. It was now roughly twenty feet lower in height and had lost around the same in width, the tip of it bent to one side like a partially straightened hook. Eric looked up. Above them, the Barrier still held.

"What the fuck are these arseholes doing *now*—" Harry moaned, holding his chest, but his words cut off as a blast of cold—so intense that both of them cried out—suddenly hit them like a slap.

Eric's heart began to beat in time with a rhythm that he heard in his brain like distant war drums in the jungle.

*Of course,* he thought, the blood draining from his face.

# Chapter Twenty:

# Dispensatori

### ***

Paul was conscious again, rubbing at his bloodshot eyes and waving Holbrooks away for the second time in an hour. He sat up on the grass as the world lurched for a moment, and then he quickly turned to where Linda and Edgwick were checking on Maria's prone form, also placed in the recovery position. The officer held up a hand, nodding.

"She's out," he said, "but she's breathing fine. Binley. Fletchamstead. Go get a stretcher, and we can get out of here." Binley and the Hulk—Fletchamstead—walked away, listing slightly from side to side as they did so, their faces blank. "She's *fine*," Edgwick repeated, seeing Paul's doubtful expression. Linda ran to Paul and hugged him, her whole body shaking.

"I'm alright, are you?" Paul asked.

She stepped back and nodded. "It's my fault," she sobbed. "I lied to her. I said I wouldn't—"

"If you hadn't, I think she'd have been killed eventually," Paul said, taking Linda by the shoulders. "She got boosted because of what you did. It's okay." He looked behind her; the previously Crying Man was staring off in the distance, towards the prefab building. "Gimme a second," he said to Linda, and walked towards the man known as *Dispensatori.* He opened his mouth to call to his comrade and stopped; he still felt strange using the bloody codename they insisted on using on the premises. Given the circumstances, he nearly didn't bother, but in the grounds of the project, even the man himself liked to be referred to by that name. Paul assumed that it was because he wanted to forget the past, even though his friend had never actually expressed such feelings.

"*Dispensatori,*" Paul called softly. "You okay, mate?"

"Yeah," the man said, not looking up. "Sorry I was out of it when you were doing the thing with the lady there. I, uh… I was just thinking about…" Paul knew what he meant. *Who* he meant. Someone he'd met here at Ladybower, amongst all the madness.

*You've* both *suffered here,* Paul told himself. *Don't forget that. You've paid your dues.* It was a phrase Paul often told himself, desperately needing it to be true, but they certainly had done a *lot* of work. Here, and to a lesser extent at Project Chisel. The days and weeks and months had blurred together on the Isle of Skye. Even there, the work had been so intense that Paul could remember almost being outraged by the bullshit gold-and-chrome 'sonic weapon' sideshow the Prime Minister wheeled out for the press at Ground Zero; *Project Orobouros, Chisel,* these names meant *sacrifice* to Paul.

He snapped out of his thoughts as his friend waved a hand at the prefab building then shook his head and walked across the grass towards Paul. When Paul saw the wetness in the other man's eyes, he wrapped his friend up in a hug.

"This wasn't your fault, mate," Paul said earnestly, trying to hide his own tears. "None of this is anything to do with you."

"I know, I know," his friend sniffed, backing away and composing himself. "*Jesus…*"

"Come on," Paul said, putting his big hand on the other man's shoulder. "Let's get in the air. We need to go." He paused. "You're allowed to be glad that it wasn't us, you know. That's okay."

"Should've been." If *you've paid your dues* was one of Paul's phrases, this was one of *Dispensatori's.* Paul gave his usual response.

"You don't mean that."

"The Sleepers… They tried that because of me."

"Worked for you the first time. Are you saying that those people would be alive if they *hadn't* tried that?"

"No…"

"Then don't talk bollocks. That very nearly *was* you. Don't ever forget that."

"Mmm."

He turned his friend towards the waiting helicopter. The now brightly shining sun was high in the sky, illuminating the lush and verdant green of the Ladybower Reservoir. The intricately designed aircraft looked blunt and vulgar against such a backdrop. It was time to go; the Isle of Skye—*Project Chisel*—waited. Paul heard a heavy sigh, followed by a sniff-cough-grunt as his friend tried to put on a brave front. Paul knew what the man was about to say next—the *other* phrase he constantly used around the base. Paul was never sure if the other man continually said it because he needed to convince everybody else, or himself.

"I know," said Andy Pointer, clearing his throat. "You're right. And don't forget, I was absolutely, one hundred per cent, *going* to jump out of that fucking window."

# Chapter Twenty-One:
# The Fifth Arrival

***

## Eric

Eric heard the beat start to thud steadily in his brain as he looked at Harry; his friend continued to stare at the Prism, looking confused.

*He doesn't know what that sound means, Eric thought. He didn't waste five years obsessing online like you did.*

He lifted his head, feeling as if it weighed fifty pounds, and turned away from the Prism to look into the near distance, towards the top of the St Joseph building. He thought he could make out the light of Jenny's bubble through one of the windows—

*Yes, that one. That's the flat she's in.*

It was the only one with a broken window. Despite the early morning sun, Eric squinted and could make out the golden tint of the light inside.

Eric felt that coldness and knew that Jenny was doomed.

*But you promised her,* he told himself. *She believed you. Can you at least* try *and keep a fucking promise for once?*

He could—a promise was a promise was a promise, as Theresa would have said if she'd been there to remind him. He groaned wearily as he turned back to face the Prism and got to his feet. He held his remaining hand down to Harry.

"Forget what I just said, Harry," he said wearily. "You probably want to stand up for th—"

A low bass note sounded from Ground Zero, drowning him out. It sounded cleaner, crisper, less chaotic. Both men watched the front edge of the Prism start to bulge outwards. The protrusion was a few feet wide, right at the very bottom, but quickly spread upwards by at least ten or twelve feet. The bulge was considerably lighter than the rest of the structure—the way bubble gum lightens when it starts to give—as if the Prism were growing a slowly elongating pimple to bursting point. Eric felt Harry's hand grab his with surprising strength, and he pulled the older man to his feet. Harry didn't say a word.

*What is that bastard of a thing made of?* Eric thought. *It looks like gouged rock, but it can stretch and move like—*

The pimple continued to push outwards as the bass note got louder. This one was on the air too, not inside their heads like the Horns but almost as painful.

"*What's it doing? Is it growing a door?*" Harry yelled over the din, tugging at Eric's arm.

It looked like it; the dimensions would be right if not for the way the bulge curved at the top. It kept coming until it jutted out of the Prism by a good four or five feet. Then the front of it began to split away from the main body as the protrusion started to retract. It was leaving something behind.

"No, Harry," Eric sighed grimly, his worst suspicions being proved horribly, terribly correct as that crazy umbilical cord disappeared back into the Prism. It had left its progeny standing a clear twelve feet tall right in the middle of Ground Zero.

Five years before, its dark predecessor would have stood in the same spot.

"It's not a door."

The proportions were roughly the same, if perhaps a little taller, a little thicker. The same lipstick-ended hands, the same head that only just seemed to emerge from its shoulders, almost one embedded in what would be its trapezius were it a man.

"Is that..." Harry whispered.

If it *were* made of Stone, then from Eric's viewpoint, its colour was that of nigh-translucent, pale yellow flesh, as if someone had taken chicken breast and bleached it.

"I think so, Harry."

"What's...? It's different..."

"Yeah." He checked which way the new Arrival was facing; of course, it was facing directly towards Jenny's building.

*So,* he asked himself, *what are you going to do about it?*

Eric left Harry for a moment as he crossed to the sledgehammer, lying where Harry had dropped it, and picked it up with his remaining hand. He suddenly felt that they needed both weapons, as useless as they may be. Its weight felt reassuring. Eric was glad it was only a ten pounder. That meant he could swing it too, if he had to. He could use it one-handed, although perhaps with limited force.

*This will all be surely over soon, either way,* he thought. *Just give it everything you've got. That thing is fresh, so fresh it looks like steam should be coming off it. Newborn. It even* looks *different. Maybe that means it's vulnerable?*

Eric didn't think he believed that for one second, but—like an outnumbered, belligerent drunk in a bar fight—they were to fight regardless. He knew he'd rediscovered something about Eric Hatton in that empty and crumbling plaza, some essential piece that had gone away for a long time, and he now knew that he wouldn't roll over *just* yet.

*Gonna give it our best shot, Jenny,* he thought.

He held the sledgehammer out to Harry, whose gaze was locked on the new visitor.

"Harry... here."

Harry took the sledgehammer from Eric and began to *thwack* its heavy head into his free hand, even as his eyes were wide in disbelief. Eric slowly drew the pistol from its holster. He had a gun, a sledgehammer, three fists and an alcoholic sidekick. It would have to do.

Eric suppressed an urge to laugh like a lunatic as he and Harry began to walk towards the new Arrival, jaws set. A crazy thought kept echoing inside his head, reaching a mad crescendo so loud it nearly drowned out that nightmarish bass coming from the Prism.

*No matter what,* it said, repeating endlessly as Eric realized it was mirroring a staccato rhythm that had begun to beat away in his blood. *No matter what... we're going down swinging.*

Before them, the newborn Stone Man waited.

**\*\*\***

# TO BE CONTINUED

*BEFORE WE GET TO THE AUTHOR'S AFTERWORD: IF YOU ENJOYED THIS BOOK, PLEASE LEAVE A STAR RATING ON AMAZON; THEY MAKE ALL THE DIFFERENCE TO WHETHER OR NOT A BOOK SELLS! IF YOU WANT TO HELP A BROTHER OUT, PLEASE LEAVE ONE ON THIS BOOK'S AMAZON PAGE (MAYBE BEFORE YOU FORGET, I MEAN HEY, I'M SURE YOU HAVE A LOT OF THINGS ON YOUR MIND, YOU'RE HUMAN AFTER ALL...) BUT NOT IN THE 'RATE THIS BOOK' SECTION AFTER COMPLETING THIS STORY ON YOUR KINDLE, AS THOSE STAR RATINGS DON'T ACTUALLY SHOW UP ON THE BOOK'S AMAZON PAGE FOR SOME REASON (WHICH ALWAYS SEEMS A LITTLE CRAZY TO ME.) UNIVERSAL AMAZON LINK HERE*

*AND HEY! WOULD YOU LIKE A FREE LUKE SMITHERD STORY, AND ALSO TO FIND OUT WHEN THE NEXT BOOK IN THIS SERIES IS RELEASED? THEN VISIT WWW.LUKESMITHERD.COM AND SIGN UP FOR THE **SPAM-FREE BOOK RELEASE NEWSLETTER**, AFTER WHICH YOU'LL IMMEDIATELY BE SENT A FREE SHORT STORY. SOCIAL MEDIA: TWITTER @LUKESMITHERD, FACEBOOK: LUKE SMITHERD BOOK STUFF, INSTAGRAM: @LUKESMITHERDYALL. THANKS!*

# Author's Afterword

*Current list of Smithereens with Titles—and your name if you left a review of KILL SOMEONE— are all after the afterword!*

As I think I mentioned before, I finished the first draft of THE STONE MAN on a plane to New York. I vividly remember closing the laptop and looking out of the window as the city was just starting to come into view at night. The story was wrapped up... but also thought that there was probably more to tell. I knew Andy would be alive, that much was certain. If not, why else had I deliberately made it so that he was killed 'off-screen'? And if Andy was alive, that meant more things *had* to happen. Over the years, usually while driving or making dinner, my mind would wander back to what the Stone Men would do next, and bits and pieces of the rest of the tale began to come together. Over time, I *knew* there was more to tell. I didn't know if I'd ever get around to writing the sequel though, as at the time, I didn't have an audience. Why write a sequel when only a handful of people had read the first book? I always thought that if I ever *did* wrote a sequel, the first one would be a direct follow-up to THE PHYSICS OF THE DEAD (and A HEAD FULL OF KNIVES doesn't count, that's just an expansion of an idea) but again, while that book has its hardcore fans, it's never set the world alight (but that won't stop me... one day we are going to be hearing some more about our brown-suited friend, if I have my way.)

Then I changed THE STONE MAN'S cover for the third time, reviews hit decent numbers, and after a few years the book began to sell. Thoughts of a sequel became more concrete; people might actually want to *read* about these ideas. I started writing some of them down. But even then, imposter syndrome kicked in: yes, the first book had sold—writing THE STONE MAN had changed my life—but would enough people be interested in a sequel to make the endeavor worth it? I decided to work on other things, saving the Caementum Comeback until such a time that I thought the book would actually reach people. Then the awesome Sophie Plateau from Audible put me in touch with some people there who asked very nicely if I'd ever *thought of doing a follow-up to TSM?* Of course, I said, playing it totally cool and failing, but y'know what, I have this *other* book that I'm finishing called KILL SOMEONE. Would you be interested in taking a punt on that first? *Yes we would,* they said. And, I asked, pawing at the floor with my foot and inspecting my fingernails, if that book, say, didn't sell as well as you hoped, would you *still* be interested in audio-publishing (and more importantly, promoting) TSM2...? *Yes, we would,* they said. My only request was that Matt "For A Price" Addis be brought back to narrate again, because I worry about him not being able to maintain his solid gold backscratcher habit.

We were off to the races.

This was the 'other book' that I mentioned in the afterword of THE MAN WITH ALL THE ANSWERS (available now on Amazon and Audible) and the one that was written in a cabin in the woods during the winter of 2018. But before then, I almost had a nervous breakdown over it. My readers seem to have liked, for the most part, all of my catalogue so far; some more than others, but I'd yet to truly drop the ball, it seemed. Now suddenly I had to write the sequel to my biggest book, and it all became very real. If I was going to bring Andy back (although, in my head, he never went away) then the story *had* to be good. I knew some people would really hate it, and the only way to win them over was to try to write something that they were as unlikely as possible to complain about. The pressure, to me at least, was horrible. Making decisions seemed impossible. The plotting was agony; I already knew how Andy was alive, what the end goal was, key scenes inbetween, what the deal was with the beings behind the Stone Men (and the Empty brethren) and what the government had been up to in the meantime, but I couldn't find a way to put it all together. I would describe it to friends as trying to do a jigsaw puzzle in the dark. Along the way I realized that this would need to be two books to tell the whole story.

My dear friend Richard McGlone kindly let me stay in his apartment in New York while he was away for a few weeks, and being in that city always fires my mind up. That, and a godsend in the form of the highly-recommended plotting software Plottr (it helps you move your story elements around and wrangle them into place) meant I could finally figure out the outline after restarting several times, and got to work.

35,000 words and several painstaking months in I realized that the outline was wrong and the novel I had in progress was to be scrapped. That was a rough day. In the original draft there was no Eric, just Maria, and it was impossible to make it work with Maria needing to see the goings-on in Coventry *and* elsewhere in the country. I even drew out a map of the UK to try and figure out how Maria could move around, but no dice. I realized that we'd need two characters, and so Eric came in... and then suddenly everything clicked. His backstory, his abilities, how he would factor into the bigger narrative, it all seemed to be what was missing. The story seems impossible to think about without him now. As a side note, Eric's original name was Carter, but that was changed when I noticed that the name of the soldier in TSM that found Theresa Pettifer's dead baby was, by a bizarre coincidence, Carter. My

partner jokingly suggested naming a character after her—Erika—
and so Eric was named.

So I took myself off to a cabin near, yes, the Lincolnshire coast
and Louth, and stayed for three months while I got this bastard
written. I sent it to my agent. She said that she didn't think that
Maria *would* keep an audio diary (because in the original draft she
was keeping one as part of her therapy, and Eric was of course
documenting The Work, meaning the book kept the same first-
person format as Andy's diary from THE STONE MAN). I thought
she might be right, but if Maria's story was going to be in the Third
Person, then Eric's shouldn't be either.

So I rewrote the whole thing again, putting it into the Third
Person. It's better as a result. The wonderful Sam Boyce had the
unenviable task of editing this book and getting me to kill my
darlings, and to make the book better for it (although losing a scene
on one of the doomed planes flying out of Birmingham
International was a hard one to accept needed to be cut. I'll send it
out on the Spam-Free Book Release Newsletter one day, which of
course you can sign up for at lukesmitherd.com). Reads from my
good friends Keith Lawrence, Mike Hands and Peter Robinson
helped me know what needed clarifying, and the excellent Barnett
Brettler was with me pretty much every step of the way. He's
helped me in more ways than one and I'd like to publicly thank him
for that. I also have to thank Dominic McGourty as he was reading
it too, but I stopped him midway as I realized it needed a rewrite.
Sorry Dom. Sincere thanks to Emma Carter for being so generous
with her time and all her help with my research notes. She
probably won't be able to spot anything of our conversation in here
if she ever read it but trust me, those talks helped shape this plot.
Thanks to my old friend and partner in musical crime Tom Martin
for pointing out that, of course, bus doors are on the bloody left.

Thanks also to Henna Silvennoinen, Laurence Howell, Alice Morgan, Victoria Haslam and Sophie Plateau at Audible, and also to Tom Guest and Andrew Rosenheim for their patience (Audible have been *extremely* patient with me throughout this process.) Thanks of course to my agent Kristin Nelson and my manager Ryan Lewis for all of their help. Also a thank you to one Bash Badawi.

The St. Joseph building in Coventry doesn't exist, by the way. Speaking of Coventry: I said something in the afterword of HOW TO BE A VIGILANTE: A DIARY about finding myself feeling sad when I visited the city, like visiting your childhood home and finding another family living there. I didn't know at the time that I would go on to spend most of the next two years there, and that my feelings were due to simply not being there very much and not feeling connected to it. I can honestly say that Coventry, despite not being where I grew up, is absolutely home to me; I feel a genuine pride when I see how the city is continuing to rebuild itself and improve (hey: *UK City of Culture 2021*, don't you know.) A lot of people slag the place off. They can get fucked.

And so here we are: Eric and Harry are heading out to meet the Fifth Arrival, and Maria, Linda, Paul and Andy of all people appear to be heading to the Isle of Skye for some reason. Speaking of Andy, for all of you Annie Wilkes out there possibly doing the *he didn't get out of the cockadoodie car!* routine right now: you're right, how *could* Andy have been put into a coma? I mean, didn't Straub tell Paul, and thus the reader, that Andy jumped out of a hotel window?

Hmm. Yeah, she did, didn't she? But... why would she do that? Don't worry. You'll find out. ☺

Just like you'll find out what Paul and Andy have been up to for the last five years, what the hell the deal was with the Kindness Protocol, what's been going on over at the Chisel Project on the Isle of Skye, what's going to happen to Jenny and her bubble, and what the heckins is going on with, as my agent put it, the chicken-broth yellow Stone Man? All to come. There some more stuff to say about the story (including the origin of the Empty Men's physical appearance) but not only will some of that be better to discuss after Book Three (in progress as I write this) and this afterword is already long enough as it is. I'll leave it here for now. For some these afterwords are pointless, but I know there are a lot of you that enjoy hearing about how these stories come to life.

As always... if you enjoyed this story, please leave a star rating for Amazon and/or Audible. You may think this book won't need it, but it bloody well will, and this book is by *far* the most important release of my career. What's that? *Pride,* you say? Uh... no, doesn't ring a bell. Plus, I can't hear you very well from down here on my knees. While I'm here, do you want the usual, or...?

For the first time ever, though, I have a request about what I'd like you to *not* say in your reviews: **no spoilers about Andy, please. No hints, no references to it, please don't spoil the surprise for other readers!** Thanks ☺

**\*\*\***

And *this* part of the afterword was written after the COVID-19 lockdown novella release THE MAN WITH ALL THE ANSWERS. Holy shit, 2020! God*damn.* I'm in the UK but not in Cov as, until only recently, you weren't allowed to go anywhere so, needing to get my own place, I'd just holed up in the first joint I could find that seemed nice. As it stands, I ended up in a lovely little bungalow in Nottingham on a street of nothing but more bungalows. All of my current neighbours are very old and regard me with great suspicion. They're nice, but I think they think I'm going to start having sex and drugs parties, or at least sex and drugs parties with guests other than myself. I'm spending my time writing, working out, learning the drums, and reading. YOU SEE THE MONSTER (mentioned in the TMWATA afterword) is with my editor as we speak (I like to work on two books at once at the moment). YSTM may be out before Book Three, but we'll see how quickly Book Three gets finished. Speaking of which: want to be alerted when Book Three is coming out? Then visit lukesmitherd.com and sign up for my Spam Free Book Release Newsletter! The Germany book deal I mentioned in TMWATA was, incidentally, for THE STONE MAN trilogy... thanks very much to Piper publishing. I can't wait to see it on a German book shelf; if we're ever allowed to fly anywhere ever again, I'll make a trip specially. Note for the Kindle version of this book: While I'm here, the list of Smithereen titles has kept growing. If you want one and want it to appear in the Kindle edition of the next book (like the one at the very back of *this* book) then drop me an email and tell me what you want your title to be and what/where you want to be in charge of, and if I get it before the next novel comes out, then it goes in. But keep it small-scale... no cities and no countries or states. Honourable mention to Steven Stewart who tried to circumvent the grandiosity rules by asking to be name The Stone Man of Smithereen (technically it isn't breaking them... but I just couldn't let that one slide. Felt too much like a power grab.) For more bullshit from me, check out my podcast Are You Sure? with Smitherd and Shaw, available wherever you get your podcasts. It's very silly. If you're reading this at a time when Book Three isn't out yet and you maybe haven't tried any of my work other than THE STONE MAN, why not try THE MAN WITH ALL THE ANSWERS in the meantime?

See you soon for the still-as-yet-untitled Book Three (that title for that one is really driving me crazy. I have a few ideas but I just can't decide)

Stay Hungry folks.

Luke Smitherd

Nottingham (for now)

August 31st 2020

----

*Insta: @lukesmitherdyall*

*Twitter @lukesmitherd*

*Facebook: Luke Smitherd Book Stuff*

*Also by Luke Smitherd:*
# WEIRD. DARK.

### PRAISE FOR WEIRD. DARK.:

"WEIRD and DARK, yes, but more importantly ... exciting and imaginative. Whether you've read his novels and are already a fan or these short stories are your first introduction to Smitherd's work, you'll be blown away by the abundance of ideas that can be expressed in a small number of pages." - Ain't It Cool News.com

Luke Smitherd is bringing his unique brand of strange storytelling once again, delivered here in an omnibus edition that collects four of his weirdest and darkest tales:

MY NAME IS MISTER GRIEF: what if you could get rid of your pain immediately? What price would you be prepared to pay?

HOLD ON UNTIL YOUR FINGERS BREAK: a hangover, a forgotten night out, old men screaming in the street, and a mystery with a terrible, terrible answer ...

THE MAN ON TABLE TEN: he has a story to tell you. One that he has kept secret for decades. But now, the man on table ten can take no more, and the knowledge - as well as the burden - is now yours.

EXCLUSIVE story, THE CRASH: if you put a dent in someone's car, the consequences can be far greater - and more strange - than you expect.

**Available in both paperback and Kindle formats on Amazon and as an audiobook on Audible.**

*Also by Luke Smitherd:*

# IN THE DARKNESS, THAT'S WHERE I'LL KNOW YOU
*What Is The Black Room?*

There are hangovers, there are bad hangovers, and then there's waking up someone else's head. Thirty-something bartender Charlie Wilkes is faced with this exact dilemma when he wakes to find finds himself trapped inside The Black Room; a space consisting of impenetrable darkness and a huge, ethereal screen floating in its centre. Through this screen he is shown the world of his female host, Minnie.

How did he get there? What has happened to his life? And how can he exist inside the mind of a troubled, fragile, but beautiful woman with secrets of her own? Uncertain whether he's even real or if he is just a figment of his host's imagination, Charlie must enlist Minnie's help if he is to find a way out of The Black Room, a place where even the light of the screen goes out every time Minnie closes her eyes...

Previously released in four parts as, "The Black Room" series, all four parts are combined in this edition. In The Darkness, That's Where I'll Know You starts with a bang and doesn't let go. Each answer only leads to another mystery in a story guaranteed to keep the reader on the edge of their seat.

*THE BLACK ROOM* SERIES, FOUR SERIAL NOVELLAS THAT UNRAVEL THE PUZZLE PIECE BY PIECE, NOW AVAILABLE IN ONE COLLECTED EDITION:

**Available in both paperback and Kindle formats on Amazon and as an audiobook on Audible.**

*Also By Luke Smitherd:*
# How to be a Vigilante:  A Diary

*In the late 1990s, a laptop was found in a service station just outside of Manchester. It contained a digital journal entitled 'TO THE FINDER: OPEN NOW TO CHANGE YOUR LIFE!' Now, for the first time, that infamous diary is being published in its entirety.*

-------------------------------------------------------------------------------

It's 1998. The internet age is still in its infancy. Google has just been founded.
Eighteen-year-old supermarket shelf-stacker Nigel Carmelite has decided that he's going to become a vigilante.

There are a few problems: how is he going to even find crime to fight on the streets of Derbyshire? How will he create a superhero costume - and an arsenal of crime-fighting weaponry - on a shoestring budget? And will his history of blackouts and crippling social inadequacy affect his chances?

This is Nigel's account of his journey; part diary, part deluded self-help manual, tragically comic and slowly descending into what is arguably Luke Smitherd's darkest and most violent novel.

What do you believe in? And more importantly ...should you?

**Available in both paperback and Kindle formats on Amazon and as an audiobook on Audible.**

# Current list of Smithereens with Titles

Emil: King of the Macedonian Smithereens; Neil Novita: Chief Smithereen of Brooklyn; Jay McTyier: Derby City Smithereen; Ashfaq Jilani: Nawab of the South East London Smithereens; Jason Jones: Archduke of lower Alabama; Betty Morgan: President of Massachusetts Smithereens; Malinda Quartel Qoupe: Queen of the Sandbox (Saudi Arabia); Marty Brastow: Grand Poobah of the LA Smithereens; John Osmond: Captain Toronto; Nita Jester Franz: Goddess of the Olympian Smithereens; Angie Hackett: Keeper of Du; Colleen Cassidy: The Tax Queen Smithereen; Jo Cranford: The Cajun Queen Smithereen; Gary Johnayak: Captain of the Yellow Smithereen; Matt Bryant: the High Lord Dominator of South Southeast San Jose; Rich Gill: Chief Executive Smithereen - Plymouth Branch; Sheryl: Shish the Completely Sane Cat Lady of Silver Lake; Charlie Gold: Smithereen In Chief Of Barnet; Gord Parlee: Prime Transcendent Smithereen, Vancouver Island Division; Erik Hundstad: King Smithereen of Norway(a greedy title but I've allowed it this once); Sarah Hirst: Official Smithereen Knitter of Nottingham; Christine Jones: Molehunter Smithereen Extraordinaire, Marcie Carole Spencer: Princess Smithereen of Elmet, Angela Wallis: Chief Smithereen of Strathblanefield, Melissa Weinberger: Cali Girl Smithereen, Maria Batista: Honorable One and Only Marchioness Smithereen of Her House, Bash Badawi: Lead Smithereen of Tampa, Fl, Bully: Chief Smithereen of Special Stone Masonry Projects, Mani: Colonel Smithereen of London, Drewboy of the Millwall Smithereens, Empress Smithereen of Ushaw Moor, Cate1965: Queen Smithereen of her kitchen, Amy Harrison: High Priestess Smithereen of Providence County (RI), and Neil Stephens: Head of the Woolwellian Sheep Herding Smithereens, Chief Retired British Smithereen Living in Canada, L and M Smith - Lord Smithereen of Gray Court, SC, Jude, Lady Smithereen of Wellesbourne, Joan, the Completely Inappropriate Grandma of Spring Hill, Vaughan Harris - Archbishop of Badass, Rebekah Jones Viceroy Smithereen of Weedon Bec, Avon Perry - Duchess of Heartbreak and Woe, Dawnie, Lady cock knocker of whangarei land, Renee - Caffeinated Queen of the Texas Desert, Carly - Desk Speaker Fake Plant Monitor AirPods Glass of Vimto, John Bate - Infringeur Smithereen of Blackpool, Stephen Stewart - Smithereen of Outer Space

Printed in Great Britain
by Amazon

78961966R00235